True LOVE Story

WILLOW ASTER

Printed in the United States of America

True Love Story

Copyright © 2013 by Willow Aster
"Saffo o dell'Amore" by Elena Cermaria
Cover Design by Sarah Hansen
Formatting: JT Formatting

ISBN-10: 1482319055
ISBN-13: 978-1482319057

To my real life Ian.
No crossed out love here. I love you. Always.

- 1 -

Layover in hell

It has been a year, two months, and seventeen days since I last saw him. Two years, ten months, and five days since he broke my heart—well, since I *knew* that he had broken my heart. Technically, he began breaking my heart the moment I met him, five years, eleven months, and one day ago. I've traveled across the country to get away from him, changed my phone number so he couldn't keep calling, had one botched relationship after another, all in an effort to forget.

And now I'm 1,600 miles from home, waiting on another flight to head 500 miles further south, and he's walking toward me in DFW airport.

Ian Sterling is oblivious to the fact that our lives are going to crash in… five, four, three, two…

I can't move as he walks up to my gate and begins talking to the agent. I've seen the puddle-jumper we're about to get on together. There is no escaping him.

Caving to the inevitable, I take him in. He is perfection, and I'm not the only one who thinks so. The ticket agent looks all aflutter as she gazes up at him and stutters. His thick hair is sticking up in every direction, just the way I like it. He looks sleepy and obscene; I want to slap him and wrap my arms and legs around him and breathe his air—me and every other woman who lays eyes on him.

1

The guitar by his feet is like another appendage; I've rarely seen him without it.

Before I even know what I'm doing, I am on my feet and sprinting through carry-on bags and travelers' feet. I have to get out of here. If he sees me, I can't guarantee what will happen. I just don't think I can risk it. My heart can't take any more.

I avoid his general direction and am making progress when I get snagged on a zebra print suitcase with purple trim. The hem of my mini catches on the handle of the bag and one yank doesn't do the trick. My skirt *will not* budge. Panic begins to overtake me; my hands are a shaky mess. I am just about to rip a hole in the material so I can keep moving when I hear him.

His raspy voice cuts through the chatter around us. I've missed that voice. "Sparrow?"

My whole body goes still. Except for the tremors in my hands and knees and guts. I grab my skirt again, and this time it miraculously comes loose. *Traitor!*

Ian is clutching the counter in front of him and for a moment, I think he's going down.

"Sparrow?" He says again and gives his hair a nervous tug. His eyes swallow me up, and I know I have to sit before I'm the one that goes down.

I put on my calmest face and give a polite, but cold smile.

"Don't get any ideas," I say.

He nods and reaches out to touch my face.

I back up. If he touches me, it's over. I pretend to not see the hurt in his eyes.

"Sit with me?" he asks.

I collapse in the first open seat. So much for getting

away.

Ian sets his guitar in front of me and sits on the higher end: elbows on his knees, knees against mine, his eyes trying to read me. Those eyes have been the death of me many a time. I sink into them far too easily. He has the eyelashes that all women envy and I study them instead, remembering all the times I've teased him about being so pretty. He leans in even closer. I cannot burrow any further into my seat than I already have.

All of a sudden, he backs up and looks around. "Is your mom with you? I knew I should have shaved," he mutters.

A surprised laugh pops out. "No, Charlie isn't here. Settle."

"Whew." He rubs the stubble along his jaw and grins. "I can't believe you're here in front of me. You look good, Sparrow. So beautiful."

He reaches over and gently pulls one of my curls, watching it boing back into place. He places a hand on each cheek, his eyes studying me until they stop on my lips. He always had a thing for my mouth. And my hair. He used to list what he loved about each of my body parts, going into such detail that my neck would get splotchy. And then he'd tease me about all the splotches, while kissing each one.

I have to stop my brain.

"I see this face every night when I close my eyes. All day long, I think I see you, everywhere I go…" His eyes cloud, and he drops his hands. "I've dreamed this so many times, I'm not even sure you're real right now. *Are* you really here?"

A thick lump burns in my throat, making it harder and

harder to swallow. I know all about seeing his face everywhere. And not sleeping. And how long it took me to even eat again after he tore my heart out and stomped on it with the black combat boots I bought him that hellish Christmas. Shoving the ache down, I take a deep breath and fix my face as a blank slate, void of all feeling. Except the hate I wish I could have for him.

In our stupor, I think we've missed a few of the boarding calls because the ticket agent looks pointedly in our direction as she loudly makes the FINAL CALL TO BOARD. All the other passengers are sitting and waiting on us when we get on the plane. I sense some hostility. I don't want to make a Texan mad at me.

"Well, what do you know, our seats are next to each other," he smirks.

"I'm sure it helps that we're the last ones on," I snap out of the side of my mouth. I sit down and yank the neckline of my shirt up higher when I see his eyes wandering.

He sits down and laughs. "Come on, baby, I have you for one hour. Let me look at you." The way he says *have you* makes me feel feverish.

"Don't call me that."

"Let me see your ticket." He grabs it before I can say no. "4B." He holds his up so I can see *4A*. "I couldn't have planned this any better myself..."

I lean my head back on the seat and close my eyes. It's not even two minutes before we're rolling and taking off. Now I know why there is a general glare in our direction from the other passengers—we held up the flight.

The air is thick with sorrow and desire. I have always known the minute he is in a room. It didn't matter if it was a room of a hundred people or across thousands, I could spot his inky black hair and swagger from a mile away. Being in such close proximity after so long apart is threatening to make me sick. Ian is watching me, his head leaning on the seat and his whole body shifted toward mine.

A flash of color catches my eye—no, surely those things aren't still in circulation.

"Tell me you're not still wearing the elephant socks."

His grin takes over his entire face, stopping my heart in the process.

"They're a little holey now."

I snort. It's a good thing my mom isn't here, she'd be mortified. "Yeah, I bet."

"I've never stopped loving you, Sparrow Fisher."

I focus on breathing and not losing my coffee and muffin all over him. That would serve him right.

"I've never loved *anyone* but *you*." He goes on, seemingly unfazed by my silence.

I turn my head and the look on my face seems to scare him. His eyes widen.

"It doesn't matter, Ian. Love … it means *nothing*, at this point. And I'm the only one in this non-relationship who can truly say that I've never loved anyone but YOU. So don't even give me that nonsense about only loving *me*. That's a load of crack." I huff and look out the tiny window, trying to forget he's there.

He chuckles and I whip my face around to see what could possibly make him laugh.

"You still love me," Ian whispers, stroking my cheek. "And you said, *crack*." He smiles sadly at me; his eyes searching mine, pulling me in … deep.

"We don't say *Crap*; we say *Crack*." I recite.

"We don't say *Shi*—" I clamp his mouth shut before he can say the rest. "We say *Shoot*," he finishes, muffled. He kisses my hand and I am sinking, sinking fast. My stomach is back on the ground, and my heart is in my throat. I'm not sure how long his mouth mesmerizes me. His tongue flicks around my middle finger, and I'm jarred awake. I rip my hand away.

"Oh, Spar..." he begins.

"You know what? We're stuck on this flight together. I don't want to talk this way anymore. We can talk about other things. Like—what's new with you? Or, what's happening with your career? How is your mom? Things like that ... the rest, I just do not even want to hear come out of your mouth. Got it? And if you can't keep your end of the bargain, I can ignore you the rest of the flight. Deal?"

His eyes are dancing, and I want to smother him with the airsickness bag. Yeah, I can't say *barf bag* either, okay? I have this thing about words. Sometimes it feels like a disease; other times, it feels close to a gift when I'm writing and come up with meaningful words instead of slang drivel. Disease or not, my editor appreciates it.

"Deal," he says and he reaches out to shake on it. His rough hands feel like home, laying claim on me all over again.

I gradually thaw just enough to carry on a conversation. I figure for all the times I've wanted to know where he was, what he was doing ... this is my chance. I can pick up the hurt again later. The rest of the flight breezes by in fast-forward. We talk about the details of his career, although I'd kept track of a lot of it online. Ian's a professional musician and has spent time in both L.A. and New York playing on any and everyone's projects. He's considered the best guitar player out there; guitar companies vie for him because Ian Sterling playing their guitar *one* time will increase their sales by insane percentages. But even more than that, his songs … he can write a song like no other. And then there's his voice; it's raspy and intimate, unique. He tells me about his new friendship with J. Elliot, his lifelong idol.

"Working with Elliot has been a dream. He's really pushed me to do a solo project with the songs I've written over the last few years." He does his anxious hair tug thing and looks at me, watching for a reaction.

I know what this means, but don't acknowledge it. I've known it would come to this. The songs he wrote for me a couple years ago will be playing every time I go to the mall, every time I turn on the car radio and probably in a cute romantic comedy that I need to avoid. Ian Sterling has been successful for years, but with Elliot behind this project, he will explode. And I'll be the roped up ball of sadness. That's what my future holds right there. Little prickly threads of devastation hanging out of my gnarly, ransacked heart.

"You deserve all the royalties. Every single song is about you." He leans over and rests his forehead on mine. "God, I want to kiss you."

My eyes close and for a moment, I just inhale him. How many times have I dreamed of being this close to him? I feel the pull he's always had on me and am tempted to give in one more time. Sanity fortunately returns. I shove him off, and he holds up his hands as I stare him down. "Fine, fine! I'll behave!"

Relentless. I'm torn between throwing up and making out with him in this tiny airplane.

"What are you doing in New Orleans? Besides being by my side day and night?" He smiles as my eyes narrow. "What?" he asks with a shrug. "It's a reasonable question."

"Tessa's getting married on Saturday. I'm the maid of honor. There's a lot to do in the next five days."

"Ah, Tess. I've missed her."

"Me too."

I lean my head back on the seat again. Ian is staring me down and I'm exhausted.

"Sparrow, we don't have much time left on this flight." He presses his eyes with his fingers and takes a deep breath. "Give me your number. Please. I promise I won't … well, I can't really promise that. Just say you'll see me again while you're here."

"It's not a good idea." I shake my head, as much to myself as to him.

"Well, my number is the same. I will never change it. You know, hoping one day you'll call and say you're taking me back," he says earnestly.

"You're impossible."

"You're delectable."

"You're incorrigible."

"You're edible."

I sigh, frustrated and turned on.

"You know it's true." He inches closer.

"No, I can't really say that I do."

"Well, I can."

"Ian!"

His eyes are distraught when he looks at me.

"Sparrow, I know you've already heard me say I'm sorry, about a thousand times … but if you can't hear anything else, hear this … you changed me. Please let me…"

I hold my hand up and look straight ahead. It helps to not see his face. "Don't. Just … don't."

His face crumbles and I think I see his hand tremble as he runs his fingers through his hair. His eyes fill and for a moment, he doesn't look nineteen. He doesn't look thirty. I see what he will look like at sixty and it torments me.

The plane is already beginning its descent. I look out and see the lights of the city and think about how I'd give anything to get lost in Ian's words. It's a powerful feeling, to know this magnetic, dangerous, quirky, beautiful, sexy … man wants *me*. Agony is almost worth it if I could just be with him.

It's as if no time has passed at all. I see with sickened clarity that I will never be over Ian Sterling. Never.

He's watching me, waiting for me to say something. Just one word to give him hope and we will be back in our own little world of love and lust and banter.

I turn to face him and he looks at me with expectancy, willing me to let him back in. Willing me to say yes…

I shake my head and the cobwebs clear. I remember. I remember it all. I want him to hurt.

"How's Laila?"

- 2 -

5⁺ years ago

The Meeting

It's hard being a pastor's kid. My dad pastors the largest non-denominational church in San Jose, CA, and even though I've always been proud of my parents, the pressure can be overwhelming at times. If you want to know the job of a pastor's kid, it's this: be perfect.

My parents are wonderful, loving people … just a little on the strict side with their only daughter. They adore me though, and unfortunately, they love to show me off. Charlie, my mother, is a force to be reckoned with—I think my dad is the only one who has ever been able to tell her what to do—and rarely at that. Otherwise, she rules with a pearl fist: smooth and white on the outside, but if you bite it, you just might wind up with a broken tooth. She knows how to get things done.

I'm pretty sure if Charlie has her way, there will be a wedding before I'm twenty.

I'm not blind; I know I'm not bad looking. I've had a few boyfriends in my short time of dating, but to my *parents*, I am absolutely gorgeous, unbelievably smart, the most talented girl EVER, and they want me to marry another equally gorgeous, smart, talented PREACHER.

I do not see preacher's wife in my future.

People have been telling me I look older than I really am for the last four years. I'd like to think it's because I act so mature, but something tells me that's not it. At thirteen, I reached 5' 9" and have hovered around there, add an inch or two, ever since. Dressing like an old woman might have also had something to do with it. All right, old woman might be a stretch—let's just say, I dress about a decade older than most girls my age.

In just a few weeks, I will be moving across the country to start school at New York University. Taking my entire loose-fitting, conservative, and very proper wardrobe to Goodwill is at the top of my To-Do List. I'll go shopping for a new, younger life once I get there.

I'm going through my massive collection of books when my mom knocks on my door and opens it.

"You almost ready for our lunch date?" My mom is always a little overly dressed, and one of her huge earrings threatens to blind my left eye as the light catches it just right.

"Yes, I just keep trying to weed through the books. I'm down to two boxes of books now," I cringe. "I can't stand to think of not having all the ones I want with me. A little bit of home…"

"Don't get me crying, honey." Charlie leans over and hugs me. "I'm just now making my peace with leaving. You can't take all your books too, your room will feel like you're gone forever."

"I'll be back. I guess I should leave my favorite books here, so I'll have a reason to come home," I tease.

"Hey now…" She tweaks my nose. "Good thing your boyfriend's staying behind … that should help entice you home."

I think about that for a moment. Michael is quiet about the approaching separation lately, and it makes me wonder for the millionth time how the distance will affect us.

"Get ready, so we're not all waiting on you. I'm excited for you to see Jeff and Laila. It's been so long. And I know how much Michael is looking forward to meeting them. He's supposed to be here soon to pick you up, isn't he?"

"Yep … I'll hurry."

I've been dating Michael for the last four months. He's twenty-two and beyond hot. Our four-year age difference would be a problem for some parents, but this is where my "maturity" comes in. Oh, and Michael is my dad's right hand man and the youth pastor at our church. Problem solved.

I have a date with Michael later tonight, too. He's been talking about a restaurant he wants to try in San Francisco. He's also been talking a lot about meeting Jeff Roberts, now that I think about it. Jeff is an international speaker and has written at least three bestsellers. He and his wife have been friends of our family for years, but I can't even remember the last time I saw him. I barely remember his wife at all.

I catch sight of the clock and jump up. After the world's fastest shower, I look for something that doesn't need ironing. I hate ironing. I put on a new fitted, short t-shirt dress that I bought last week on a whim. This is the exception to my All Things New in New York expedition. I just couldn't help myself with this dress. It's too cute and I'm so ready for a change.

I quickly diffuse my long hair and have the usual internal argument with my mother that I always have regarding my hair, only it's typically not internal. She prefers my hair up because I look older, or calmed down with hot rollers. My naturally curly hair makes her nervous. It's too wild, too "wanton." Her word, not mine. But secretly, I think it really might be my only sexy feature, at least of the ones that show. Or maybe my mom put that in my head by using the word *wanton*.

Michael has been exploring more of my "sexy" features lately when we make out. With all the layers and such, I'm not sure how he will ever find anything at this rate. He has amazing patience; I'll give him that.

I take one last look in the mirror, giving my hair a final fluff. Michael will most definitely approve of this dress.

I bounce down the stairs, suddenly feeling a bit excited about the lunch. I read Jeff's last book and was impressed. Maybe I can get inside his head about how the writing process is for him. Do writers ever truly think they're great? If so, I'd like to roam inside their brain and let all that self-confidence ooze over my guts and pores and cells. It would make writing a lot simpler.

Michael is just coming in the door. It bothers me slightly that he comes in without knocking. My parents keep the door unlocked most of the time, which is crazy, even in our nice neighborhood. However, my dad gave Michael a key before we even started dating, when he house-sat for us. My parents think nothing of it; in fact, they encourage him coming and going as he pleases. They see Michael as the son they never had. This concerns me, but only because I don't want anyone to be disappointed if we don't work out. I have a feeling if we did break up, they'd choose Michael.

He really is gorgeous. Michael is the first blonde guy I've ever been attracted to—I'm usually all about the tall, dark and mysterious. Michael is tall, blonde and there is nothing mysterious about him. He is so fun … so funny. Every girl sits up taller and giggles louder when he comes into the room. Even my mom. His eyes crinkle up when he laughs. I haven't even started on his body. Oh my, the arms, the lower abdominals. I now know the term *V-cut muscle,* thanks to Michael. I didn't even know I cared about all that until I saw him without a shirt and all of a sudden I did care. I cared a *lot*.

He asked me out a half dozen times before I said yes. If he'd just shown me his chest, we could have settled the matter much sooner. The fact that I'd be leaving for school troubled me, but there was also the little complication of getting involved with someone who worked for my dad … and the whole preacher thing itself.

Can I just clear the air right now by saying that I love Jesus? I do. I believe he's way better than we give him credit for. I love Christians. Okay, I love SOME Christians and the rest only because I HAVE to. I love my parents, period. I just don't want to be a preacher's wife. Now that that's settled, hopefully we can move on.

Michael has a thing for my feet. When I said we

"make out," it's not that we do a ton of that, but a couple nights ago, he did this thing where he washed my feet—I know, it's a little weird when I think about it, but I went with it and have no regrets. After he finished washing them, he slowly licked and sucked every single one of my toes. He took his sweet time, and I thought I was going to come unhinged. Never in a million years did I think I would want that done to me EVER, but land sakes, it did things to me. Things that I can't even fully explain just yet.

Is sucking someone's toes off even considered making out?

Michael's eyes pop when he gets a look at me. Uh, yeah, he's not going to have trouble finding anything now. Shoot. I didn't think this dress through.

"You look amazing!" He kisses me and hugs me tight. I think I just heard him groan.

I hear my dad before I see him. "Hey kids, you ready?"

Michael jumps back like a scalded dog. I laugh and he shakes his head at me, knowing he's caught.

I kiss his cheek and call out to my dad. "We're ready."

"Come on, let's ride together," he yells from the back door.

Michael leans into my ear and says, "I don't know whether to ask you to wear this dress every day or to never ever wear it again."

"Wow, who knew something that actually fits could cause such torment?" I grin mischievously.

"You're going to get me into so much trouble."

"I'm pretty sure you have my parents wrapped."

We round the corner, and my dad is holding the back

door open for us.

"Michael, looking good. Hey, Rosie, you're looking good too."

I could wear a tow sack and my dad would think I look good.

"Thanks, Dad," I kiss his cheek.

"Anthony, how are ya?" Michael shakes my dad's hand.

When we get to the restaurant, I go inside with my mom. Michael and my dad are finishing up a discussion and are taking too long to get inside. I am HUNGRY, and you don't get in my way when I'm hungry. I am about to ask my mom if she sees the Roberts when I see *him*.

"MOM, Ian Sterling is here. That's Ian *Sterling*. Look!" I am clutching her arm and about to pass out.

She takes a look at the hunk in front of us and shakes her head, "I don't think so, dear. That *is* Jeff and Laila he's talking to, though."

"It's him. I know it's him."

Just then Jeff and Laila turn around and spot my mom. "Charlie, hello!" They walk forward and take turns hugging her and then see me. "Sparrow, oh my word, you're all grown up! I can't believe it!" Jeff looks thoroughly pleased to see me.

Laila is one of the most beautiful women I've ever seen. I shyly hug her, and she comments on how pretty I am. "Thank you. You're so beautiful," I nervously say and then I feel silly.

Jeff turns around and says, "And we brought a dear friend of ours, Ian Sterling? Ian, come meet Charlie and Sparrow. Where is Anthony?"

Ian steps forward and takes my hand. I immediately feel my skin blaze; the flames start in my hair, down my face, neck, guts, all the way down my entire body … at least that's how it feels. He is staring down into my eyes. The way he looks at me, I feel exposed, raw, awake…

I've been looking for you, his eyes are saying.

You've found me now, I'm certain my eyes are responding.

Actually, what he really says is, "Sparrow Fisher. There's a story there, I'm sure. I'm Ian." He grins and squeezes my hand. I melt. "Nice to meet you."

"I've been looking for you," I say. NO! Did I just say that out loud? Ohgodohgodohgodohgod. Please tell me I did not just say that out loud.

He smirks. Oh, he's so hot. Pretty, even. However, there is nothing but raw masculinity bouncing off him. "Have you? Well, now you've found me. I wasn't aware we knew each other? I would have remembered this face." He runs his eyes from my head down to my toes and back up again, painfully slow. "I would have remembered you for sure," he leans down and whispers.

I'm dying. I wish a hole would swallow me up now. I've got to find a way out of this. I can't tell him…

"Jeff!" My dad's boisterous voice fills the air and I breathe a sigh of relief. They hug and I feel an arm go around my waist. I assume it's my mom until Michael says, "And you are?"

I'd completely forgotten Michael. Oops.

Ian lets go of my hand to shake Michael's and my hand has never felt so bereft. I hear Michael say, "Sparrow's boyfriend," but it sounds very far away. My eyes have never left Ian's face. Ian looks back at me, and he seems amused.

"She's stunning; you're a lucky man," I hear him say.

"I know. I'm so glad she's *mine*."

This pulls me out of my stupor and my temper flares. I glare at Michael, but he is oblivious. He's too busy strutting his peacock feathers to notice I want to take his head off.

When I look back at Ian, his eyes are laughing, and have a light in them that makes me feel faint. His lips curve up and I stare at that mouth, wishing it was on mine.

What in the world is happening to me.

I try to snap out of it as we find our seats. Unsure of how it even happens, I find myself with Michael on my left and Ian on my right.

"There you are, Brady," Laila pats the seat next to her and across from me. "Brady, this is Sparrow and Michael. And you remember Anthony and Charlie from their visit last fall?" Brady nods and shakes everyone's hand. He looks about twelve and seems very shy.

I try to concentrate on the menu, but Ian's leg is flush against mine. We're on the booth side of the table. The other side has chairs. I should have sat in a chair, so I could breathe and so I could look at him. No, this is better. I don't need to breathe anyway.

After we've ordered, Ian turns his whole body toward mine, places his elbow on the table, rests his head on his hand and stares at me. He slowly begins to ask question after question. It's at this point that I tell God I'll do whatever He wants, I'll even BEHAVE—and that's saying a LOT for me—if He'll just please not let me get hives and if He'll also please let all my words come out intelligibly.

"So what are you into, Sparrow Fisher?" he asks.

"Besides Michael, that is…"

I roll my eyes at him.

He grins. "Unless, you'd like to talk about that. I'm sure Michael would be pleased."

I look at Michael and for the moment, he's mesmerized by something Jeff is saying.

"How long have you been dating?" he asks.

I don't want to talk about Michael with him. "Four months," I answer.

"Ah, a new romance," he teases. "So he shouldn't take it too hard…" his voice trails off.

Something in his tone makes me defensive. My mother has drilled being "hard to get" as far back as I can remember. "We're doing just fine, thank you very much."

He raises his eyebrows and continues studying my face.

In middle school they used to say, "*Take a picture, it'll last longer.*" But I'm studying him just as thoroughly and don't want him to call ME out, so I resist the sass.

"What about you? Do you have a girlfriend?"

"Why? Do you want to fill the spot?" The mischief is back. He's something else.

"You're quite the tease, aren't you," I laugh and want to say, *Yes, I'll fill the spot. Pick me, pick me.* I'm startled when Michael takes my hand, and I feel the first twinge of guilt. *Took you long enough*, I berate my conscience.

"You seem able to take it," Ian replies.

The waitress comes with our food, and I promise, she practically lays her entire chest on Ian as she sets my food down. He looks at her and smiles. "Well, hello," he says. She stands up and brazenly tucks her number in his pocket … the pocket in his jeans, no less. "Okay … thanks?" He looks back at me and raises his eyebrows.

"That happen often?" I ask.

"It happens," he shrugs.

"Ah, so pretty much old hat, then." I feel indescribably angry and sad that I have no right to this emotion when it comes to Ian Sterling.

He pulls the number out of his pocket and hands it to me. "If you'd put your number on this paper, it would be worth something," he says quietly.

"Are you really hitting on me with my boyfriend sitting right here?" I am both proud and appalled by his audacity. Scratch that, I am *loving* his audacity.

I'm a horrible person. Let's not even try to sugarcoat it.

He looks over at Michael, who has my hand, but is laughing at something Jeff has said. "Jeff's keeping him occupied. He's good that way." He leans in closer and gets right in my face. "Your boyfriend doesn't seem very attentive," he whispers.

"Oh, he's attentive," I whisper back.

"Well, I guess if you like them like that."

"Don't you worry about what I like."

"Can't promise you that."

"Why not?"

"Well, look at you. I already want to steal you." With these last two words, his nose bumps mine and for a moment, I think he is actually going to kiss me. My stomach takes a nosedive into my feet. I'm pretty sure I turn magenta.

Wanton Waitress—now that's a better description for this tart than my hair, right?—has to ruin the moment by checking to see if everyone is *okay*. I haven't eaten a single bite. I stare her down as she returns for more of Ian. She doesn't notice me. She does, however, make sure to put on a show as she walks to another table. If there was a pole in the vicinity, she would be *Worrr-king It* right now.

"So you changed the subject before … what do you like to do, Sparrow?"

"Uh, well, lots of things," my voice sounds shaky and I want to raise my fist to the heavens and force God to honor our agreement, however one-sided it might have been.

Ian smiles. "Lots … of *what*?"

"Books," I say firmly. "I'm crazy about books."

He laughs. "Okay. That's cool."

"I like to read them and write them," I say shyly.

Hello, my name is Sparrow and I am a nerd.

He lifts his eyebrows, and his eyes land on my mouth. "God, everything you say is hot." He runs his hands through his hair, making it go another equally fabulous direction. I wish I could do that. "So let me get this straight … you look like *this*" —he waves his hand up and down in my direction— "and you're a book-smart, writer goddess too?" He inches closer to my face again, and I am positive he can hear my heart pounding. "Do you have glasses and wear your hair up with a pencil, too? That would be too…" He closes his eyes for a second and when he opens them, his pupils are huge swimming pools. "I don't know if I could even take it." He shakes his head.

I laugh hard then, coming far too close to snorting for my comfort. *Keep it together, Fisher.* I clear my throat and look down at my food, momentarily thinking it can save me. It does nothing to help, but does stare back up at me, looking tasty. I try to dig in, but seem to have lost my appetite. Ian doesn't seem to be eating either.

"How do you know Jeff and Laila?" I ask, trying to lighten the air.

"Jeff is actually my third cousin. We just got back in touch a few years ago and have gotten a little closer. I stay with them when I come through San Francisco. They also have a house in L.A. I'm there a lot, too."

"Do you come through here a lot?"

"Not San Jose, really," he says. "I'll be back in San Francisco next week, though. Laila mentioned you're all coming out next weekend?" He nods his head toward me.

"All?"

"Yeah, this whole clan," his eyes twinkle. "You gonna bring Michael?" he whispers.

"You're impossible."

"You're delicious."

I ignore him. It's the only way I won't kiss him. "Where are you off to this week?"

"Dallas. I'm playing at the House of Blues a couple nights this week. Have a few rehearsals to show up to … I'm a musician," he explains.

"I know."

"Oh, okay."

"I heard you play … four years ago," I confess.

"Really! Where was this?"

"It was at a huge concert in Central Park."

"Central Park? You saw me in Central Park four years ago and you're just now telling me?"

"We just met."

"Yeah, an hour ago. We've covered a lot of ground in that time, wouldn't you say?"

I get flustered yet again. Shoot, just when I think I'm

getting past the nerves a little. "Yes, I would tend to agree."

He grins that smirky grin and I swear he's thinking of me dressed as a librarian again … which doesn't help me calm down at all. I raise one eyebrow and he runs his hand over his mouth, attempting to look serious.

"So Central Park … tell me about it."

"I saw you before you played. I had no idea who you were. I was there with my parents. My dad was there for a crusade. Did Jeff tell you my dad is a preacher?"

Ian nods.

"We really only had one free day and spent it at the park, listening to the music. At one point, I spotted you by the stage, and the next thing I knew, you were going up there. Your set blew everyone completely away. I've never heard anything like it."

It's his turn to be flustered. I'm touched that he seems a bit embarrassed by my flattery. I'm sure it's something he hears all the time. He is truly amazing.

His phone beeps and he looks down, frustrated that our conversation is interrupted. "Oh, wow. I have to go. Honestly, I thought I'd be thrilled to have an excuse to leave, but I'd give anything to stay now that I've met you." His eyes are so genuine, I actually believe him. "I have a meeting in a half hour."

"Oh. Well … it was really nice to meet you," I stutter. I am surprised by the emotion in my voice.

His voice sounds thick too. "Sparrow, the pleasure is all mine, I can assure you. You've made a forgettable day memorable. Hell, you've made it positively newsworthy." He's smiling, but there's a sadness behind his eyes. He grabs my hand and kisses it.

In that gesture, I feel my childhood slip off of me like an old, worn-out cloak that has been barely hanging by a single thread. I know that something has shifted in me. It's primal. I want this man.

I smile at him. He continues to grip my hand and leans around to see Michael. "Michael, I'm heading out. Take good care of this girl here."

And with that, he stands up and leaves. I watch him walk past the window. He looks like he just lost his best friend.

What I didn't tell Ian about seeing him the first time was that I cried the whole time he played. I had never heard anything so beautiful. I found his name on a program and thought it fit him perfectly. When I got home, I took out my journal titled *Important Things that Happened in my 14th Year* and wrote: I Saw Ian Sterling.

I've been looking for him ever since.

- 3 -

What?

The hazy stupor of meeting Ian Sterling hovers over me all day. Playing and replaying every touch, every inflection and every word spoken, I come up with various theories on what it could really mean. My crazy mind plays a serious contradiction game with itself that goes a little something like this:

I think Ian Sterling fell for me today.

There is no way that Ian Sterling feels anything real for me.

I fell for him at first sight four years ago.

Of course, I don't believe in love at first sight.

Okay, if not love at first sight, then I fell in love with him today, when we spoke … when he took my hand in his.

That was pure lust, not to be confused with love.

I've never felt like this.

I'm young and don't know what I'm feeling.

I'm not an idiot; I know my own mind better than anyone.

He is a master flirt and it was meaningless.

I think I rocked his world.

I hate it when I do the girl thing. I'm sure Ian left lunch this afternoon and didn't give me another thought. Why can't I be like that?

Serious time with Tessa is what I need. She's been my best friend since we were nine and knows me better than anyone. I texted her after we left the restaurant that I'd met Ian Sterling and she flipped, but I haven't had a chance to talk to her yet. As far as I know, she's the only one who isn't completely gung-ho on Michael. I can't get a straight answer on anything she doesn't like about him, only that she doesn't think he's the one for me.

And Michael ... I have a half hour before he picks me up for our date, and all I can think about is Ian. I have to pull myself together. Michael is perfect. Really, he is. My parents say it all the time. The guy is stinkin' hilarious. He can pull out a random line from any movie and do all the voices. He kills me every time with that bit. And I know this is not everything, but he *was* the best looking guy I'd ever seen ... until I saw Ian up close and personal.

I think I might be in trouble. Everything about Ian does it for me. Sexiness oozes around him like vapors, tugging me into his aura and making me want to do all sorts of naughty things. He is in a whole other bracket as far as his looks. I feel bad for even thinking it, but in *every* area ... well ... he makes Michael look somewhat homely in comparison.

I am a hideous, hideous human being.

The things that came out of his mouth; he's so irreverent. I'm not used to people saying exactly what they think. Filtered talk is as popular as filtered water these days. More than all this, though, that hour with him made me feel more alive—more awake—than I have ever felt. I realize heart poundage does not a relationship make, but land sakes, feeling alive sure is worthy.

"Spaaaaarrrow! Miiiichael's here!" My mom calls.

"I'll be right down," I yell back.

I slip on my shoes and grab a light jacket. The City always cools down at night.

Michael looks swoon worthy in his suit. I take it back about him being anything near homely. He's not at all.

My gut twinges guiltily as I think about how *Ian* would look in that suit.

The drive goes by quickly as we speed and sing along with the radio. The lighthearted mood changes a bit once we get to the restaurant. I've done fairly well not obsessing about Ian, but it is taking considerable effort. Michael seems more serious than usual as we're seated at a beautiful, candlelit table, overlooking the ocean. There are roses at the table and when I look at them closer, I see a little card with my name on it.

"Michael! You did this?"

He grins and for a moment, I think I've misjudged his seriousness. He kisses my cheek and tells me I'm pretty.

"The flowers are gorgeous! Thank you!"

I open the card and it says,

For an unforgettable night with an unforgettable girl.

Yours forever, Michael

I hug him. I don't deserve any of this sweetness from Michael after practically ripping all Ian's clothes off—I know it was only in my mind, but they say it's what's in the heart that matters.

27

Who said that anyway? Oh yeah, the Bible.

"That's so sweet. I can't believe you."

"Well, I have big plans for tonight, so get ready," he smiles at me.

"What plans? Flowers? A swanky restaurant? What are you up to?" I smile back at him.

He laughs and locks his lips, throwing away the key.

Maybe I don't need to be all awakened anyway, when I have such a thoughtful guy in front of me.

To be honest, I've been really nervous about what leaving will mean for Michael and me. We've barely talked about it, but for the last couple of weeks, I feel the cloud hanging over both of us. I will really miss him. Skype, texting, and talking on the phone all the time—not my idea of a fun relationship. He's promised to come see me and I will try to fly home for the longer breaks.

I look out the window and get lost in the water. Give me the ocean and it's the equivalent of a yoga class or meditating in India … not that I've ever done either of those things. Wherever people go to find peace—that's what I find in the ocean. Hopefully, I'll find a favorite beach out east.

Michael clears his throat and startles me. I turn and watch him fiddle with his tie.

"So today was interesting," he says.

"Yes, it was. Did you like Jeff? He's nice, isn't he?"

"Yeah, he really is. I liked him a lot."

I pick up my menu and slowly read through it. A minute or five ticks by and when I look up, Michael is still watching me.

"What is it?"

"Ian Sterling sure was into you."

My face goes hot. "He was just being friendly."

"Yes, *very* friendly," he mutters.

I look at my menu again and am torn between being ecstatic about Ian, while also feeling bad that Michael was there to witness it. I thought he was too engrossed in conversation with Jeff to notice. I wonder how much he heard. How would I feel if he talked to another girl like that with me sitting right there? And even if he didn't hear anything, he *must* have noticed how we looked at each other.

The more I think about it, the more awful I feel. I know now that I didn't imagine the *entire* thing with Ian. Who knows? It might be the way he talks to every female, but I should have shut him down. It was just such an unexpected thrill. *Ian Sterling*, for crying out loud.

Michael takes my hand and his eyes are intense. "You're so beautiful. Any man would be crazy not to want you."

I seize the napkin in my lap and suddenly fold it into square after square until it's too tight to fold another. My own shame is threatening to swallow me up. Michael looks pensive. I'm afraid to know what he's thinking.

The waitress comes and we order. The sunset gradually takes over our conversation; it's spectacular. There is nothing like watching the sun disappear into the water. Michael relaxes more and more. Soon I find myself doing the same. The anxiousness melts away, and I'm happy to be here with him. I'm happy he doesn't bring up Ian again.

The sea lions are making a racket on the wharf below. Sea gulls swoop around the sea lions, teasing them with their catch of the day. Our food arrives and the steak and scallops are delicious. I eat every bite.

We're sharing a chocolate soufflé when Michael goes serious on me again. It's hard for me to concentrate on anything but the chocolate. I am passionate about good food and this is perfection: warm cake with a gooey chocolate center and two chocolate sauces on the side. I pour another dollop of the dark chocolate sauce over my last bite and moan—it's that good. I wish I hadn't agreed to share. Why did I do that? Maybe we can order another...

As soon as I set my spoon down, Michael takes both of my hands. "I want to talk to you about something."

I take a deep breath, and Ian flashes through my brain. Chocolate and Ian. And Ian with chocolate. Ian and me and chocolate...

"Sparrow?"

I blink and Michael swims into focus. Dang, I'm hopeless. I *will* get Ian out of my mind and focus on my boyfriend.

"You know I'm in love with you, right, Ro? I have been since I first laid eyes on you a year ago. Being with you the last several months has been the best time of my life." He reaches down and kisses my hand. He looks up at me with those crinkly, smiling eyes, and I can't help but smile back at him. He's so sweet. "I thought we would wait—I know we're young—but I can't wait. I *know* that I want to be with you for the rest of my life."

My inner brakes screech and my eyes bug out. What did he just say?

Michael continues, completely unaware that I'm beginning to panic. He is as somber as the guy on the commercials about erectile dysfunction.

"I've already spoken to your parents, and they've

given me their full approval." Michael reaches into his pocket and pulls out a box and sets it on the table.

I begin to choke. No, really, I lose all breath and cannot get it back. Michael's loving expression turns into fear as he realizes that my gagging is not stopping. He stands up and pounds on my back. I've heard that pounding on the back is not really what you're supposed to do when someone is choking, but it seems to knock some sense into me and I heave a breath that finally works.

"Are you all right?" Michael stands beside me and grabs my water glass. He looks so concerned; I want to cry.

I take a sip of water and concentrate on breathing.

Michael returns to his seat and tentatively takes my hands again.

"We'll have quite a story to tell our children," he attempts to joke, but it hangs in the air, flat.

"What do you say, Sparrow? Will you marry me?"

He has guts; I'll give him that. Apparently, I was wrong about the patience.

He opens the ring box, and I stare at the gorgeous solitaire. I open my mouth to speak, but nothing comes out. I'm in shock.

A scene flashes through my head of me at eighty, mouth still hanging open and the nurse at the nursing home talking about me like I'm not there— "She hasn't spoken for over sixty years!"

Going silent would certainly help keep me out of trouble. I wonder if my brain would keep functioning fully, though, if I went that long without speaking ... that would be really hard.

After we sit there, looking at each other for an

eternity, Michael finally says, "I've freaked you out, haven't I."

Uh yeah, I think. But the words still don't come out. I also think, *What the hell?* But my mama taught me to *not* think things like that. So I'm conflicted, you see.

"Say something, Ro. Anything," Michael urges.

I take another drink of water and finally put my head in my hands. Michael is saying something, but I'm not even hearing him. I just want to go home. This day needs to be done. It's too much.

He clutches my arms and I lift my eyes to meet his.

"Michael…" I croak.

"Sparrow, just think about it…"

"Michael, what? I'm *eighteen*!" I shake my head at him.

"You'll be nineteen before too long. Both our parents were married at nineteen. Look how they've made it. My parents only dated for six weeks and they just knew. I feel that way about you … we just fit." His voice fades at the end.

He looks at me and wills me to say something.

"I did not see this coming, Michael. I don't even know what to say. I'm going to NYU in a few weeks. I want to be able to concentrate on school and…"

"You can still do all of that. We'd just be *engaged* while you do that. Maybe get married in the summer? You'll be going on twenty by then. And you could transfer to Stanford or Berkeley next year…" He gives his most charming smile, the one that usually wins me over.

"Michael," I say sadly. "If I wanted to go to Stanford or Berkeley, I would have. I don't want to go to New York thinking about how soon I can get out of there." I cannot *believe* he is doing this right now. "Four months. We've dated *four months*. That's not enough time to know. Besides, you knew about New York *before* we started dating."

"It is for me."

I try to keep from glaring at him. "*What* is for you?"

"Four months is enough time for me to know."

"I like how we are now. We have fun. It's good. Simple. Let's just keep it like this," I plead.

"Why won't you tell me you love me?" He asks.

"You know how I feel about that."

It's not something I can say lightly, not with boyfriends anyway. I don't plan to tell a guy I love him until I'm sure.

"Do you love me?"

"Michael, please. You know I love you. You're wonderful, and I care about you so much."

"That's not what I mean and you know it. Do you love me?"

I take a deep breath and can't look at him. "I love you, but … I'm not sure I'm *in* love with you."

That stuns him.

"I know you haven't said it back, but I thought you were feeling it," he whispers.

He puts the box back in his pocket, loosens his tie and looks out the window for a long time. When the waitress comes around, Michael pays the bill and tosses me a peppermint.

I feel terrible for hurting him. I try to think of a way to make the mood lighter, but it's just not happening.

Finally, he looks at me and tries to give me a reassuring smile. "I can wait. We're going to be all right, aren't we? You don't want to marry me … yet. But some-day?"

"I … don't know." I answer.

But inside I'm afraid I really do know. And even though I'm mortified with the direction my thoughts have taken me, I am almost fully certain that I would have said the exact same thing even if I *hadn't* met Ian Sterling. But since I *did* meet him, it is suddenly as clear as that massive sign down the street from LAX airport that used to say, "LIVE LIVE NUDE NUDES!" There was no questioning what was inside; you knew exactly what you were getting if you went in the building by the sign with those humongous letters.

I stare at Michael and see the life he has planned for us. We would marry young, work in my dad's church together, be financially stable, have two kids by the time I'm twenty-four and be our parents made over. I know it's what my parents want for me too, and I wish like every-thing that I could want it. I just … don't. And as much as I wish I could change my mind, the writing is on the sign.

I cannot marry Michael.

The next few days are rough. My parents seem disappointed that I turned Michael down, but they don't push it much. Still, I'm frustrated with them for even considering it as an option right now. They don't under-stand why I can't be sure about Michael. He's "perfect for me" and it's obvious to them that we're supposed to be together. They feel it's only a matter of time before I see it and that if I can't say yes to him now, I shouldn't make any decisions at all. In other words, leave him hanging.

They ultimately just want me to be happy, so they back off, but just knowing how they really feel is confusing. Isn't it supposed to be the other way around? Shouldn't they be pushing me to wait and to be sure? I think I must be living in an alternate universe and surely I'll wake up soon.

Michael comes over four days in a row and for the first time in our relationship, we fight. Thankfully, my parents completely stay out of these discussions. I think I'd bang my head against a wall if the three of them ganged up on me at once.

I sort of thought we had broken up when I turned down his proposal, but apparently that was just phase one of wearing me down to a nub. The first day he's mopey and pitiful. The second day he's edgy and ticked. The third day he's sad and all hands. (I know he thinks the handsy approach will work because he knows I have a slight weakness toward the slutty. Okay, not just slight.) The fourth day he's a half mope/half edgy mix, and I am worn out from the whiplash. The fifth day he calls and says he's going to see his family in Seattle for a week. He needs to think. A month ago, I would have been sad for him to go, especially this close to leaving for school, but I am so relieved.

Tessa calls after I get off the phone with Michael. "Is Loverboy over there?"

"No, he's going home for the week. To mull over his heartbreak." I snap.

"You're heartless," she laughs.

"I *feel* heartless after all this drama! It's been pure craziness. It's like I'm the only adult around here!"

"Well, I wouldn't go that far … but well … yeah, it does sound like you're the only one thinking clearly."

"Thanks for not jumping on the marriage bandwagon. You could have been a kickin' maid of honor."

She sighs. "Yeah, I thought of that. Believe me. I could stand some excitement. A wedding would have been fun … besides that one little complication of you being *married* afterwards. That would completely suck. You know, that would wreck our entire New York plan."

"It's sad that my life is your highest form of entertainment. You definitely need more exciting friends," I sigh. "And you know I could never wreck our New York plan. We've worked too hard for this!

"You're right. I would have a REALLY hard time forgiving you if you bailed."

"Well, now everyone *else* won't forgive me, so I'm going to need you as a best friend a little longer … wanna do something later?"

"Yes! It's about time you pay me some attention. Come spend the night. Let's have a movie marathon."

"Sounds perfect. I'll be over in an hour."

Tessa is exactly what I've needed. I find myself relaxing for the first time since the Child Bride Project. We make a massive pile of nachos, get our Cokes propped beside us and put a movie in the DVD player. We've been doing this since we met in fifth grade. I don't think we've ever gone more than two weeks without seeing each other.

Tessa was the first person I met when I started a new school in the middle of fifth grade. She was a blonde little nymph that practically sailed in the air as she ran up to meet me, all bubbly personality. I saw warmth in her eyes and clung to her like she was the safety harness on an upside-down roller coaster.

We've wanted to go to New York for as long as we've been friends. Honestly, I began looking at NYU only minimally because of their writing program. I really just wanted to be able to say I lived in New York once in my life. It was a pleasant surprise to learn that the school has an excellent reputation within the literary world. Same with Tessa—she will be going to Parsons, even though there's a perfectly good Fashion Institute in San Fran. That's us, though, never ones to do things the easy way.

We haven't made it through a single movie yet. It's still paused, and Tessa's asking question after question about Ian. Michael's proposal barely made a blip in her radar; she's onto the more pressing topics…

"So tell me again what he said when you told him you like to read books AND write them?"

For some reason, this cracks her up more and more each time. I tell her the whole story at least three times before she is fully satisfied. Yes, she confirms. He's way into me.

"But you didn't give him your number, did you?" She wrinkles her nose.

"No! Michael was *right there*!"

"Pssssshhh," she scoffs. "That didn't stop you from practically kissing each other! You may as well have given him your number while he was asking for it."

I cringe. Ugh. This is bad. This is really bad.

"Can you imagine if I did end up with Ian Sterling some day? It's really farfetched, but let's say I did. When people ask how we met, what would I say? 'Well, uh, I was at lunch with family friends and had my boyfriend on one side and Ian on the other. It was love at first sight.' Ahhh!" I put my head in my hands. "I would never live that down. Or what about if I did marry Michael and everyone wanted to know about how he proposed? 'Well, let's see … he proposed right after I met the man of my dreams.' There is no tidy outcome to this situation."

Tessa's voice startles me in the middle of my downward spiral. "Oh, since when do you care what anybody thinks?"

"Since always?"

She's crinkling her forehead at me now, looking like I've grown a horn in the middle of my nose. "Noooo, you're nice and respectful, but you've still always done your own thing. This might be a little 'inconvenient', but everyone who knows you sees that you follow the beat of a different drummer boy. People would be disappointed if you did the expected."

Now I'm looking at her like she has a third ear. I'm used to her giving her own twist to expressions, it's not that. This is news to me: *I* know that I'm a bit of a weirdo, but I didn't realize I wasn't doing a better job of hiding it.

"That might be the sweetest thing you've ever said to me," I say. "And it's beat of a different drummer, no boy…"

She continues, not fazed in the slightest by my mush and my correction not registering either. "I'm surprised he hasn't called you anyway. He sounds like he isn't afraid of being persistent. He could have gotten your number from Jeff."

"I think he was going to have a busy week. I wonder if this weekend is still happening … I think I'm supposed to see him day after tomorrow! We're all supposed to go to Jeff and Laila's on Saturday."

"You didn't tell me that part! How could you forget

to tell me THAT? Here, ask your mom ... text her really quick and see," she excitedly throws my phone.

Within minutes my mom texts back that the plan is still on for the weekend and Tessa squeals. "Okay, what ELSE did you leave out? Start from the beginning AGAIN."

- 4 -

Being oblivious has its perks. And when it comes to my appearance, that has always been my motto. This time a week ago, when I was getting ready to meet the Roberts, I don't think I even bothered to shave my legs. Now, it's like I'm possessed. I have gone through every beauty ritual possible within the confines of my limited budget. I have exfoliated and buffed and polished. My hair follicles are completely hair-free in the places where that is desirous, and the hairs on my head have never looked so good, let me tell you. The curls, they are practically aglow with all the attention they've been given. Loose waves fall down my back, with nary a frizz in sight. My mother will be proud.

Tessa is so sweet ... or maybe she just couldn't bear the thought of me wearing my norm and knew I was too stubborn to break my New York/Clothes mission again, but she showed up this morning with my outfit. The poor girl has been dying to dress me for years and I haven't let her waste her time—she's been too busy doing alterations at her job to sew for me. Whatever her motivation, I am so appreciative. The girl is beyond talented. She made a long, plum slip dress that fits to perfection. It's comfortable and looks effortless, which is really what I want, even though I have contradicted myself with my actions. Sigh.

It's not a date, I realize that. Truly, I do. I just can't seem to stop the primping. This concept is foreign to me and I'm afraid it will lead to a disastrous character downfall if it continues. Besides loathing shallowness, I really don't want to lose my, shall we say, *edge*—over a *guy*. Aloof has been my middle name for years, and after just one lunch with Ian Sterling, that seems severely threatened.

I'm buckling my sandals when Charlie comes in my room. Her mouth gapes when she gets a look at me. "Wow, honey. You look gorgeous!" And then, with a slight frown, "Are you sure you don't need a tank under that?"

I look down and see that I'm pretty pleased with where things are and aren't. "No, I don't think so."

"I'm not sure I've ever seen the—" she points left and right, back and forth toward my chest, "—so prominently displayed."

I snicker.

"Your dad's not gonna like it…" She continues to study me. "Have you lost weight?"

"Nope."

"Well, you sure look like it," she says, half-concerned and half-impressed. "Have you heard from Michael?"

"No. But it's only been two days. Have you?"

She's still frowning over my dress, so it takes her a moment to answer. "Dad did yesterday. He said he sounded so sad."

"Hmm." I'm not sure what to say to that. "I'll just grab my jacket and I'm ready."

"All right."

We pull up to the Roberts' beautiful Victorian. Their house sits tall and proud on a hill, overlooking the entire bay, like Mother Superior. My parents visit every time Jeff and Laila are in town, but I only remember coming two or three times as a kid. The house is memorable. I have this recurring dream about the front doors—two wooden doors with intricate engravings that stand out against the white house. The dream is never exactly the same; in fact, the only recurring part is the doors. I stop and stare at the doors every time, but they never open to the same room. I've been every age in the dreams. I must have looked at those doors long and hard as a child.

When Laila opens the door, I realize I'm holding my breath—in anticipation of which room I will see this time, but also of who will be in it.

"Hello!" Laila hugs all of us and Jeff follows suit. Over their shoulders, I do a quick inventory of the room.

He's not here. Check.

They've updated the living room. Check.

It's lovely. Check.

My dad and Jeff move to the deck to check the meat on the grill, while Laila ushers my mom into the kitchen. I'm lagging behind, trying not to be too obvious, but I peer through a door or two. Very subtly, of course.

"Sparrow, I was hoping you'd bring Michael," Laila says loudly.

I round the corner and enter the kitchen.

He's not here either. Check.

"Michael went to see his family in Seattle this week," I answer.

"He is *so* good-looking," Laila laughs, fanning her face.

I laugh. "Yes, he is."

"He asked Ro to marry him last Saturday," my mom, the traitor, tells Laila.

"You're kidding!" Laila looks at me. "How exciting. You're so *young*, though. Jeff and I got married too young—I was eighteen! I wish I'd waited. You need to live a little!"

I resist the urge to gloat at Charlie. We begin carrying the rest of the food outside.

"He would be extremely hard to turn down. I don't blame you! When's the wedding?" Laila laughs.

"Who's getting married?"

The flames take root again, lapping around my feet, up my legs and chest, sizzling red-hot out my pores ... just at the sound of his voice. I nearly drop the huge salad bowl I'm carrying. Fortunately, only the tongs go flying, landing on the deck with a loud *thwack*.

I am pathetic. My girl-ness is betraying me, dangit.

Ian is behind us and I'm not sure how long he's been there. His hair is wet and standing every which way. He crosses over to the tongs and gives me a blinding smile just before he bends down to pick them up.

"Hi," he says.

"Hi," I whisper back.

"Our lovely Sparrow here..." Laila answers.

I look at her in horror. Ian sees my expression and looks confused.

"Our lovely Sparrow here what?" he asks, grinning at me again.

"Michael asked her to marry him," Laila announces. "Later, I'll pull out the champagne!"

Ian's smile falters and he looks down at the tongs as

if he's forgotten why he has them. A full minute or two ticks by. I'm not sure if everyone goes on talking or if they're all watching us. I only see him.

"Lucky bastard ... congratulations," he says softly.

I let out an exasperated sigh. "I didn't say *yes*."

He takes a deep breath and blows it out slowly, shoulders sagging for a moment as he stares me down. He steps in closer, standing in what would normally be my personal space. My throat catches as I wait to see what he's about to do.

"Why, you *little* ... heartbreaker." He's serious for a moment and then his eyes crinkle and he's beaming again. In fact, his whole face looks like the Cheshire cat on Christmas morning. "So you came to your senses about Mike, huh?"

"I don't know about *that*. I'm just not ready to *marry* Mich*ael*."

He waits for me to say more.

When I don't, he nods his head and steps back. I get the impression that I've just disappointed him and I want to fix it, say more, have a re-do ... but the moment passes and he's taking my arm and leading me to the table.

"Here, Ian, hand me the tongs," Laila scoffs. "If we left it up to you, we'd find dirt in our steak." She goes to the kitchen and returns with a clean set.

It's harder to talk to him in the smaller setting. We mostly listen to my parents and Jeff and Laila. I focus on getting bites of steak in my mouth and not on my lap. And taking a drink without having all the ice rush forward. I hate it when that happens. It's never pretty or conducive to good timing. Ice just knows when you're trying to impress someone and always picks that moment to go flying up your nose.

A shift occurs in the conversation and my parents want to know all about Ian. They didn't really get to talk with him the last time. He answers them respectfully and when they ask about his music, he seems honest, but humble in his response, which is impressive to me. I know he could be arrogant about being so talented.

"I've been playing as long as I can remember and it's about the only thing I'm really good at." His smile is self-deprecating, but when he looks up at me, I see mischief. I'm absolutely certain he's good at many, many other things. "I'm fortunate to be making a living doing what I love to do. And as long as people keep listening, I'll keep playing. Actually, even beyond that—I would have to play music even if no one ever listened. It's just … like breathing."

He seems shy when he's done talking. I didn't notice him ever being shy the other day. His cheeks are even a little flushed. I'm smitten all the more. My parents also seem intrigued by him and continue grilling him about who he's worked with, the back story on some of their favorite songs of his and his upcoming schedule. I want them to stop the interrogation, but it's also affording me plenty of time to study him. He completely weaves them into his spell. He's good; he's really good.

After lunch, we carry everything inside and Laila shoos us out of the kitchen, saying she'll get it later. I'm following everyone into the living room when my arm is tugged another direction. Ian pulls me into what looks to be an office.

"Let's get out of here." His eyes pierce into mine.

45

"What about Jeff and Laila?

"Don't worry about them. You up for it?"

"Sure," I say, not exactly sure what I'm agreeing to.

"Your dress might be a problem," he frowns.

"What?"

He laughs at my tone and runs his hand lightly over my arm, sending a shiver in its wake. "You look *electrifying*. That dress could wake a dead man." He takes my hand and turns me around slowly, making me very uncomfortable with his sounds of approval. "Did you bring a change of clothes?"

"*No!*" I glare at him.

"Okay, not a problem. We'll work it out. Come on, let's go while it's still so nice out."

Everything happens so quickly. I let Ian do the talking and before I know it, my parents, Jeff and Laila are saying they'll meet up with us later tonight. We walk out to the garage and Ian stops in front of a Harley. I'm not into motorcycles, but even I can see that it's a beauty. Ian pats it lovingly. He looks like a character out of a romance novel—and not the cheesy Fabio kind either—or he could be a movie star, only taller. Or a soap opera star, only one who can pull off his lines. Or maybe a model, only straighter than straight.

I pride myself on my writing skills, but when I consider writing about him, I realize he brings out the cheese puff in me. The coal hair, the ever-changing eyes … are they really just hazel? Such an ordinary word for eyes that are sometimes green, sometimes khaki, with flecks of blue and gold, and then his cushiony red lips. This man is combustible. Add the bike and I feel that if I look at him too long, I'll electrocute myself.

46

"Ever been on a bike?" His voice is all husky seduction.

Oh, good grief. And then there's the voice. All of a sudden, I can't look at him. He's too much for me.

"Sparrow?"

"No." I answer, a couple notches too high.

"Well, how about it?" He's already raising the garage door as he asks the question, never doubting that I will ride with him.

He hands me a helmet and inwardly, I groan. This is why I should never spend so much time getting ready. What a waste. I take a long look at him. *Get a grip, Fisher!* I am not about to be all googly-eyed over a boy. I never have and I never will.

"Your face is going to stick like that if you don't relax the grin," I throw out as I secure the helmet.

He throws his head back and laughs, climbs onto the motorcycle and reaches an arm out to help me on. I hike my dress up past my knees and climb on.

"I was wrong. This is the *ideal* outfit for the bike," Ian says as he traces a finger up one of my bare thighs.

I feel the sudden need to think about baseball and granny panties. I've heard that helps.

But then he leans back, his face an inch from mine as he says, "Hold on for your life." And all thoughts of huge knickers are out the window.

I've never been on the back of a motorcycle. I've never had any desire to be. But when Ian and I ride through the steep, winding streets, I understand the appeal. Having an excuse to hold onto Ian is liberating; at first, I uncomfortably wrap my arms around his waist, but when we go flying around the corners and up and down hill after hill, I lean into him and hold on with all I've got. I *love* it.

We pull up to a stop sign, and Ian looks down at my legs and sees chill bumps. He rubs his hands together and then over my legs to try to warm me up. It just makes my chill bumps hot, but doesn't actually make them go away.

"Let's get you warm," he says before taking off again.

We drive to Fillmore Street and park in front of Peet's, home of my favorite coffee. He gets off first, still holding the bike up and watches as I hurriedly yank my dress down, grinning mischievously all the while. Either this man is seriously happy or there is something about me that cracks him up. I have a feeling it's the latter and if I didn't feel so happy myself, I'd want to put him in his place a bit more.

"Let's check out this..." He's stops mid-sentence, mouth slightly ajar, as I take the helmet off and shake my hair out.

"What? Is it bad?" I try to finger through my hair, smoothing out the tangles.

He clears his throat. "Uh, *no*. Not bad. At all."

He looks unsure of what to do. For a minute, I think he's going to take my hand, but he pauses and puts his hand on my back. The thought that he is withholding affection leaves me divided. I'm relieved because I know now more than ever that I have to settle things with Michael for good. There can't be any question whether we're together or not. Time won't make me care more for him than I do now.

However ... the ache that takes over my body from Ian's caution becomes a weight the longer I'm around him.

My hands *crave* him.

Instead of going to Peet's, Ian leads me down the street to a cute boutique.

"Let me buy you something."

"No!" I shake my head and look at him to make sure he's listening. "You don't need to buy me anything."

"You were freezing on the bike. And I just … want to get you something," he says, ducking his head onto my shoulder for the briefest second. He holds up a pair of wicked jeans. "Will you think of me every time you wear these?"

The jeans are fabulous. I'm swayed for a moment. "They're great. But no! You don't need to spend money on me."

"I'm going to keep you warm. You may as well get the right sizes because we *are* leaving here with an outfit." He rubs his hands up and down my arms. "See? You're still chilly. And I don't want to take you back to the house. Please. Unless you want to go back?"

"No … I don't. But…"

"Okay, it's settled. Will these fit?" He hands me the jeans and when I try to look at the price tag, he rips it off.

My mouth drops open. He laughs and lifts my jaw with the back of his hand. He picks up a fitted long sleeve shirt and holds it up to me.

"Yep, you are dangerous in red."

"It's really low."

"I know."

"You're a sneaky one." I accuse him.

"You're a smart one."

So far, he always has the last word. I kinda like it.

"Do you see something else you'd like to try?" He

49

asks politely, attempting to look innocent and failing.

I'm not much of a shopper—I think we may have already established this, but when I have a day with Ian Sterling, I *really* don't want to waste time shopping.

I shake my head and go into the fitting room. The jeans fit like a dream. I didn't even know I had this booty. My legs look miles long. And well … the top … I'm speechless. This shirt makes me look like a sexpot. I have NEVER … I don't know if I can do this.

I make one more attempt to adjust my cleavage and glance back in the mirror. My hair almost reaches the waist of my jeans and it's holding up fairly well, considering the windy ride. I don't quite recognize myself, but it's a GOOD THING. Folding my dress, I take a deep breath and step out.

I hear him before I see him. He curses under his breath.

I turn around and raise an eyebrow. *Do you like?* My eyes ask.

"Hell, *YES*," he says out loud.

He won't even let me properly thank him, much less pay for any of it. I thank him anyway and he says, "No, thank *you*."

We walk outside and I'm warm from the inside out now. Ian is quiet, but doesn't take his eyes off of me. It's disconcerting. He points to Peet's when we get back to the bike. I nod and think this is the best day I've ever had.

As we drink our warm drinks, we sit and watch each other. Once I realize he's not expecting me to say anything, I relax and stare back at him. So much is being said without a single word. I'm not sure how much time passes; at least long enough for both of us to finish our coffee/mocha.

Finally Ian breaks the silence. "What are you doing to me, Sparrow Fisher?" He says it completely serious.

I don't know what to say. How do you answer that?

I'm not sure why or how the mood shifted, but it's less playful and a dozen notches more intense when I climb onto the back of the bike this time. When I wrap my arms around his chest, he puts his hands on top of mine and holds them there.

He turns his head and says, "You up for a little adventure?"

"I'm up for anything."

When we're going up, up, up, I lay my head on Ian's back and close my eyes. The bike finally levels out and when I open my eyes, we are at the top of Lombard Street, the crooked, brick street with eight hairpin turns in one block. I gulp.

"Do you trust me?" he asks over his shoulder.

"I think?"

He shakes his head. "Wise woman."

"Let's do it," I say.

I'm a bit terrified as we pull around and get behind a couple of cars to go down the steep street. The view at the top is one that would be easy to take for granted when you're used to seeing it all the time. There are almost too many scenic views to soak them all in, but we both fill our lungs with air and do our best. The billowy clouds are close enough to touch. Coit Tower is in the distance and the Golden Gate Bridge is way past that. I think I might even see Alcatraz.

When it's our turn to make the gradual decline, I'm

not scared, even though the bike feels like it could tip forward if we aren't careful. We lean with each turn, laughing all the way down. At the bottom, Ian pulls over and we look back up the street.

"Let's do it again!" I yell.

And so we do.

We're headed back across town, closer to the water. It takes a while. We go the long way, taking detours to see the prettiest spots. We both know the city pretty well and keep thinking of one more place to drive past. Dusk is settling in and the lights are beginning to twinkle like thousands of lightning bugs. It's becoming more and more enchanting with each further dip into twilight.

A twinge of remorse about Michael squeezes my gut as we near the wharf, but I try to shrug it off. We drive past the touristy areas and cross the highway into the land of the houseboats. I've always been intrigued by the thought of living on the water. I think I could do it.

Ian comes to a stop outside a quaint sushi place. "Do you like sushi? This place is great."

"I love it."

"Are you hungry yet?"

"I can pretty much always eat."

His lips lift in his adorable grin. He turns off the bike and just sits there a moment with my arms around him. I realize I have to let go if he's going to get off and so I reluctantly move my arms to my sides. He looks back at me, and I wish I knew what he was thinking. He's gone all contemplative on me since the boutique.

We order like we haven't eaten in a week, even though we both did damage to the steak at the Roberts' house.

"So tell me something no one knows about you," Ian says.

"Hmm. Well, very few people know that I have a selective smeller. My nose has never worked properly. I've never even smelled a skunk. No one ever believes me when I tell them that, so I've given up talking about it. They will be holding their noses and gagging and I will do a heavy SNIFF and nada. Not even a faint whiff. But then, I can smell some things. Just here and there and enough to make me think it does work … until I go to describe the smell and realize I don't have a clue—I can't even begin to make a sensory comparison. So it's usually a dumb reference. Like, that smells … good?"

He stares at me for a moment before letting out a huge laugh. "I never know what's going to come out of your mouth. You've seriously NEVER smelled a skunk?"

"Never."

"Crazy!"

"I know!"

Ian clears his throat. "Can I ask about your writing?"

"Sure."

"What do you enjoy writing?"

"Well … I enjoy writing about simple things, really, but in a funny, honest way. I'm not too flowery or even deep. I mean … I can go there, but it's most fun to put a twist on an every day subject. Or to write a love story that has *real*, flawed characters. I don't like things to be wrapped up with a bright red bow. Life isn't that way."

He nods his head. "I know what you mean. Is it hard to write that way? Not everyone likes to hear the truth."

"Yes," I'm surprised that he gets right to the root of

things. "This is a topic I think about often, especially with all the conservative people in my life. I don't want to upset anyone, but I can only seem to spew out honesty."

He lets out a choked laugh, mid-sushi bite. "How can that be wrong?"

"Oh, there are many, many ways," I sigh. "I'm not published yet ... but I'm trying to prepare my family that they might not like it when I am."

"Never hesitate to tell the truth. It's the only way it will be any good."

After a brief pause, I think about how easy it is to open up to him. My writing is a topic I'm not comfortable delving into with just anyone. There's something about him; he seems to pull all the vulnerabilities right out of me. It's actually freeing to be this exposed.

"What about you? What is your writing process like?"

He sighs. "I have to fight to write an honest song. There's a lot of fluff out there and the public seems to eat that up. I think my mission is to challenge listeners—I'll never be satisfied to whip out a tune just for the sake of creating a hit. A good song has to be something that evolves, something that is birthed from an emotion, an idea ... an emptiness that needs filling. And it's not enough to just write it all at once and be done with it. I work and rework lyrics the way you probably do when you're writing a story."

"You're so *intense*," I tease.

"Ha. You ... you're ... you're one to talk." He points at me and shakes his head. "You're making me stutter like a schoolboy."

"I don't think you've ever stuttered in your life. And you're like an overgrown schoolboy ... so ... I don't think it's me…" I laugh.

By the time we've finished every bite of food—seriously, how did we put all of that away?—I feel like I can tell him anything. While we wait for the check, Ian leans his chin on his hand and watches me.

"What?"

"I've never met anyone like you," he says.

"I've never met anyone like you either," I reply.

"Yeah, but I suck and you're wonderful," he says without an ounce of irony.

I snort. "Nooo."

"It's true."

"You barely know me," I say.

"I know enough. You are … carefree, smart, *really* funny … honest."

My new low-cut blouse is not helping cover the splotches that are taking over my neck. It's my curse. I can't handle all this praise. We thank the waitress as she takes our plates and leaves the bill.

He leans in even further. "And you're the most beautiful woman I've ever seen."

Okay, now my entire body is one enormous blotch. Color me red.

He points at my neck. "Keep that up, and I will have my way with every single one of those little blushes. I can't be trusted."

I'm not sure how long we're there; both of us are so deeply in this conversation. I vaguely recall hearing Ian's phone go off several times, but since he's ignoring it, I do too. Finally, it lets off a continuous buzz. I guess someone *really* wants to get in touch with him.

He takes a look at it. "Sorry, I should take this, I

guess. This is one aspect of cell phones I don't like," he whispers as he answers the phone.

"Hey ... yeah. What? (Pause) (Sigh) Ask when they're ready to go and I'll have her back by then, how about that? (He smiles at me, eyebrows raised. I smile back in agreement) (Long pause) (Another sigh) God, Laila, relax. I'll get her there. (Silence) I said I'll get her there!"

He hangs up and frowns. "I think your parents are fine. I don't know why Laila's in such a snit. We'll meet them at Caffé Greco and get dessert, if you'd like."

"Sure. If I can fit in another bite of anything by then. Aren't you full? This was *so* good."

"Yes, it was. I think I would be saying that even if the food tasted like shit, though."

I giggle.

"Your company, Miss Fisher ... it is exceptional."

I don't even have to think about what to say to that because he stands up, holds out his hand and I take it. I would go wherever he wanted me to go.

The Roberts and my parents are sitting at a cute table outside with their lattes and cheesecakes when we pull up. My mom gets a look at my outfit and her eyes widen, but she doesn't say anything. I'll hear about it for the next couple months, I'm sure.

Ian and I are going inside to order when Laila grabs Ian's arm and pulls him aside. They stay outside and I go in to order tiramisu. Who am I kidding? I can always eat. I glance out the window and watch Laila and Ian for a moment. She is doing the talking, and he is running his hands through his hair. They both look angry to me, but maybe I'm imagining it.

I step outside with coffee in one hand and my dessert in the other. Trying not to look Laila and Ian's way, I sit down at the table closest to my parents. Mmm, tiramisu...

Ian walks away from Laila and walks inside. The waitress lights up when she sees him. My eyes narrow when she laughs at something he says. He turns and sees me watching him, and he turns back around and tugs his hair again.

Ian comes back out with coffee and stands while drinking it, looking down the street. He doesn't look at me and if I didn't know better, I'd think I had done something to make him mad.

"Would you like to try some of this? It's delicious..." I hold my plate up and he glances over for a second before turning away.

"No ... thanks." His voice is flat.

Ian takes a couple more slugs of coffee and sets it down on my table. He bends down and looks at every inch of my face, almost as if he is memorizing it.

"Thank you for a spectacular day, Sparrow Fisher."

"Thank *you*, Ian Sterling."

He stands up, says his good-byes to everyone, hops on his motorcycle and rides off into the night.

What happened? My heart starts pounding, and I am horrified when my eyes threaten to well up. I don't DO the crying thing.

I will not cry. I will not cry. I will not cry.

I guess every perfect day has to come to an end.

- 5 -

It's Over

Michael's call wakes me up early the next morning. I barely slept. Scenes from the day ran around all night in my head, making sleep impossible. I lean up on my elbows and croak out a hello.

Michael is all sweetness and charm ... until he asks what I've been doing, and I tell him I was in San Francisco yesterday with the Roberts ... and Ian. He gets really quiet and then says he has to go.

I fall back to sleep and dream about opening that wooden door. Ian is standing on the other side. It doesn't open into the Roberts' living room, but into the entryway of my house. The rest of the dream blurs into mush.

My mom comes in a couple hours later. She sits on the side of the bed and wants to know all about my time with Ian. I tell her the details—how much fun we had and how easy it was to be with him. It helps ease the despair I can't shake, for at least a full minute, and then I'm back to thinking about how he left. Why did he suddenly go glacial on me?

I'm grateful that Charlie doesn't try to convince me of all Michael's wonderful attributes, but listens and seems excited in all the right places when I tell her about Ian.

Perhaps the fact that he is famous gives me a free pass to have a date when I'm not fully broken up with my boyfriend/wannabe fiancé. Or maybe she took a genuine liking to him. I don't mention how weird the end of the night was, and she doesn't say anything about it either. I'm not sure she even noticed, since she didn't see firsthand how we were with each other the rest of the day.

The sky is as grey as my funk. I have a hard time focusing on anything. I go through my desk drawers, organize what's left of my closet, try to read a little, watch a movie … anything to distract me from thinking of any males whatsoever. I need a break from all of them.

My attempts don't really work. My brain is on the menu setting of a DVD where it plays an endless circle of clips. My parents have always said I have a one-track mind. It's another curse. Sparrow One-Track Splotchalot.

The sun barely sets and I'm already wishing for my bed. The stress of the week and the topsy-turvy day with Ian has left me exhausted. I shower and am just putting on my favorite sweats and t-shirt when I hear the doorbell ring. I don't give it much thought until I hear Michael's voice.

"Sparrow?" My mom knocks on my door and walks in. "Michael's here," she whispers.

I sit down on the bed and pull my wet hair on top of my head, securing it with a ponytail holder. "Send him up," I sigh.

"He's a wreck. Be gentle with him."

"I'll do my best," I mutter.

Michael comes in a few minutes later, looking rough. His eyes have shadows around them. His hair is haphazard, and he doesn't usually do the messy look. He

59

sits beside me on the bed.

I put my arm around him. A sideways hug. The hug of friends … cautious friends.

He lets out a ragged sigh.

"How did you make it here so quickly?"

"I was in Portland when I called this morning. Stayed with Aunt Patricia the last couple of days. Hopped in the car as soon as I got off the phone and drove straight through."

He still hasn't looked at me. He's wiped out and staring dejectedly into space.

"I'm losing you. That's what's happening here, right?" With that, he turns and looks at me, his eyes bleak.

"Michael…"

"I need to know. I want to spend my life with you. I thought I could wait as long as it took and you'd come around. I thought I'd get back tonight and you'd be so happy to see me, you'd run down the stairs when you heard my voice…" He shakes his head. "It's not happening, is it? You're never going to…"

My eyes fill. All the aggravation I've had with him over the past week is gone.

"I wish I could love you like I should, Michael. You deserve so much more than what I've given you," I finally admit.

"What am I missing here?"

"Nothing. You are … exceptional. Truly. I just don't feel *it*. I care about you so much."

"There has never been any doubt in my mind about my love for you."

"I'm so sorry," I whisper.

"I don't want you to be sorry!" He says loudly,

causing me to jump. "Don't look at me like that, Sparrow," his voice is quiet again. "I know you're not trying to hurt me … but don't *feel sorry* for me."

"I don't pity you … I *am* sorry, though." A tear falls off the tip of my nose and tickles. I wipe my face and lay my head on his shoulder.

He stands abruptly and runs his fingers through his hair. "I've gotta get out of here."

"Please—don't go like this. I have to know you're okay. Michael, look at me."

He walks out of the room and out of my life.

***

The next few weeks are filled with all the hustle and bustle of leaving. I split my time between family and friends, going to favorite restaurants and beaches that I will miss when I'm far from home. Michael doesn't call or come by, but I do see him at church … from a distance. I try to catch his eye and smile, but he seems to have an eye meter that tells him the *exact* distance to look *just* close enough, but never *really* land on me. It's unsettling. I'm used to him always finding my eye across the room and sharing a smile over something that strikes us funny. I am going to miss him more than I can even comprehend.

I'm trying to catch a minute with Michael the day before I leave. Various giggling girls surround him. Word traveled quickly that we'd broken up. I'm sure the new girlfriend position will be filled in no time. An elderly lady walks up and gives me a good-bye hug.

"I will be praying for your journey," she says.

"Thank you so much, Beverly," I smile.

"Be blessed out there. And hurry home to Michael. God has big plans for the two of you."

I bite my lip and resist telling her we've broken up before I walk away. I know I can't compete with what she thinks God has in store for us.

I see an opening with Michael and move toward him. He sees me coming and for a moment, I think he's going to bolt, but he doesn't. He smiles faintly and I want to kick myself for breaking his heart. Just before I reach him, Josie Sanders glides in front of him. He looks over her shoulder at me and I stop. Josie doesn't miss a beat. I wait a few minutes longer and then give him a shy wave before leaving. He smiles and waves back and my heart lifts just a little. I think we might be all right. In time.

New York is exactly what I hoped it would be. It's hectic and energetic. Fun things to do are available at all hours of the day or night—not that Tessa and I have fully taken advantage of that yet, but still—we absolutely love it.

We've finally gotten settled into our apartment. It's small, but cozy, and we've put our hearts into making it as cute as possible. I'm crazy about my room: a pink tufted headboard that Tessa and I made, with white, pink and red linens. There are Tiffany blue touches added throughout the room. Tessa's room is the complete opposite: bold with a black tufted headboard and colorful fabrics swathed from ceiling to the floor around her bed.

Our cozy living room just fits a couch, bookshelf and TV. The red leather couch was our first big purchase. We're going to have a serious arm wrestling contest when we move out to see who inherits it. Our kitchen is the smallest kitchen I've ever seen. It's nearly impossible for us to be in there at the same time. I may or may not occasionally crawl on the counter to get past Tessa when she's not moving as quickly as I'd like. Okay, I totally do, but I'm going to have to stop. I've hit my head one too many times on the cabinet above the counter.

I love that we're living on our own, completely across the country from everything familiar, except each other. It's a bit surreal to have moments of feeling like actual adults. The fact that we keep telling each other we're grown-ups might mean we're not quite there, but it sure is feeling that way more and more. This time would be perfect if it weren't for all the drama before I left.

I really miss Michael—his friendship most of all. I guess maybe we should have only ever been friends. I know this *now*, but that's the kind of thing you can only know after it's too late. School has been the best distraction. I'm knee-deep in homework at all times. It would have been difficult to have a solid relationship with him when I'm so focused on my studies.

Well, that's not entirely true. It would be hard to have room for him in my brain when the space is so filled with Ian. Since Ian looked through me and took off on his motorcycle, he has preoccupied almost every single waking and sleeping moment. I'm actually really disappointed with myself and profoundly guilty, too, when I think of how I've hurt Michael.

Still, I can't get Ian out of my mind.

I've played and replayed every single part of that day and cannot figure out what happened. Why did he go so cold on me? How could we seemingly have such an intense spark and then … nothing? I have not heard a single word from him.

It hit me in mid-replay one night—I don't think mention was ever made about me coming to New York. My insides clench and churn with this realization. I can't see how that wouldn't have come up, except that when I was in the thick of my rosy haze around him, I didn't think of anything or anyone except him and that very moment we were living in.

It's for the best. Things ended on such a weird note anyway. It's not like he's been calling my parents' house night and day looking for me or anything. What I thought was special was probably just what he does with every girl he goes out with. I saw how every female ... and male, for that matter, checks him out. He has probably not given me a second thought.

I try to bury myself in my books and writing projects. A really cute guy in my Sociology class asks me out, and I turn him down. I haven't done a very good job making friends. I have Tessa and am otherwise on autopilot. After all, I hurt Michael bad enough. There's not much room in my head or heart right now to involve another single person.

So, when my parents call the week after Thanksgiving to tell me we're taking an impromptu ski trip over Christmas break and that the Roberts and Ian will be part of the group going, I choke and snap out of cruise control. I invite Tessa, but she has plans with her family.

By that evening, I have an email with my flight details. We're all meeting in Colorado and scheduled to ski in Breckenridge for an entire week. I think I might be in shock. I'm elated that I'll see Ian again and yet ticked that I haven't heard anything from him in all these months.

Poor Tessa gets an ear full of my rantings on the whole subject. God bless her, she lets me go on and on. Until she realizes I don't have cute ski clothes.

"What are you going to wear on the slopes?"

"I don't know." I huff. "I haven't ever even skied. How would I know what I'm wearing?"

"Well, we need to figure it out." She grins wickedly. "You have to show Ian what he's missing!"

"Can you help me?" I moan. "I don't even have a coat that will work. Aaaaagggh. Why did my parents agree to this?"

"Well, they probably don't know that you've obsessed over Ian since the day you met him. Otherwise, I'm sure they wouldn't be going. Have they given up their hopes for Michael?"

"I'm not sure they'll ever give up on the thought of me and Michael. Every time I talk to them, they tell me how awful he looks. He goes over there and talks about how much he misses me."

Tessa lifts both hands and shakes them at me. "You haven't *died*! He could still be your friend, for crying out loud."

I snort. "I love it when you get all passionate. And I *wish* we could be friends … maybe eventually."

"This trip will be fun. Don't even think about Ian for now. Think about how great you're going to be on the slopes."

"Pft, yeah. You know I'm a monumental klutz. How am I going to survive on skis?"

"You're a good skater. Maybe you'll be a good skier too," Tessa says.

"Since when did you become Miss Pep Talk of the

Century?" I grumble.

"Since you needed a good shaking." She leans over and gives my shoulders a soft nudge. "Seriously, Ro. You've barely left this apartment except to go to school. I hope this trip will shake you out of the funk you've been in."

"I haven't been in a funk! I love it here. It's been so great to be on our own…"

"You haven't gone on a single date. Maybe this is just what you need. You'll see Ian and either know why you're not meant to be with him, OR you'll make sure you keep him this time."

I glare at her. "I didn't know you were thinking all this. Why would I go on a date when I'm thinking about someone else … and I've already broken one heart? I don't like to hurt people!"

"I know you don't, but we're in college, far from home … you're supposed to be living dangerously. *I'm* supposed to be living dangerously."

I roll my eyes. "Okay, 'Little Miss Dangerous'. I'm not stopping you. Just help me find something to wear, okay? And then you can go *live it up* with all your wild and crazy dangerousness!"

"Gladly," Tessa smirks. She starts tapping away on her laptop and pulls up several ski outfit choices. My ire softens somewhat because I'm impressed that she found something so quickly. She's a whiz on the googling. Tessa Googlelot might have to be her new nickname. She clears her throat and I snap out of my Googleshedaisy train of thought. One outfit is electric blue and the other is a vibrant pink. She turns toward me and gets an inch from my face. If she weren't so close, I'd be able to clearly see that her eyebrows are working overtime, but as it is, they're a big blur with all their wiggling.

I can't help but laugh. "These are both great, but so, '*Hello, I'm a snow bunny.*' And they're really … colorful. And show … surprisingly much for covering every inch of skin."

"He needs to be able to see you coming," she emphasizes.

"Well, he certainly wouldn't be able to miss me in that one." I point to the blue outfit. It definitely would stand out in the snow. Or anywhere, for that matter. It's actually pretty fabulous. I might need to do a thousand sit-ups and squats every night before trying to go out in the Cat Woman-esque get-up.

"They have the whole outfit in that store on 43rd," Tessa says. "We could run over there right now for you to try it on. You know, get out of the house for a while, and see what it's like out there in that big old city we came ALL THIS WAY TO LIVE IN."

"No need to get huffy," I grin and jump up. "Come on, let's go."

As much as I hate to admit it, Tessa is right. Getting out in the brisk air feels great. I can't believe how I've been hunkered down in my room and books the last few months. I'm all about being a good student, but maybe I've taken it a little too far. I feel the rank cloud shedding off of me, like an oily layer floating to the top of the surface.

The city is beautiful as we walk along the crowded streets. The trees are already lit with Christmas lights. I can't believe I haven't even noticed until now. Maybe the breakup and move across the country affected me more than I realized.

"Earth to Sparrow." Tessa is snapping her fingers in front of my face. "Ro? You with me? I've asked you the same question three times."

"Oh, sorry … what?" I turn and see the concern in her eyes.

"Are you okay?" she asks softly.

"Yeah," I bump her shoulder with mine. "I'm sorry I've been such a downer the last couple of months. I can't believe how patient you've been with me."

"I know you were crazy about Michael. Not as a boyfriend, necessarily, but he was one of your best friends. And Ian…" she shakes her head. "He really did a number on you. I'm kinda mad at him right now."

"Ugh. I know. I am, too. But I can't be, he didn't do anything wrong. I'm more mad at myself for how much I felt so soon … and … how excited I am to see him again in a few weeks." My whole face crinkles into one big crease. "I'm ashamed to even admit that out loud. I need to just be cold with him and not give him the time of day."

"But really, why would you? Like you said, he didn't really do anything wrong and maybe he just hasn't been able to find you," she finishes hopefully.

I stare her down. "We both know he could have found me if he wanted.

She sighs. "Just wait and hear what he has to say."

"Yeah, if he bothers to talk to me at all. We didn't leave on the finest note."

"Here we are!" Tessa sings and pulls my arm into the store.

Oh, so many choices. So little time. Tessa's also right about the blue get-up. There will be no denying I'm in the vicinity when I put it on. Ian Sterling won't know what hit him.

- 6 -

A couple weeks later, I'm packing all my cute new clothes into a suitcase, along with a few books I've added, just in case I'm a disaster on the slopes. Oh wait, I've packed a half dozen books. That's going to be heavy. What can I say? I'm a fast reader. It would be so sad to get there and run out of reading material. This is a vacation after all.

After my shopping trip with Tessa, I confess something might have been birthed in me. I finally get what all the fuss is about with shopping. Tessa could not be happier about this new transition. I can't get too addicted to it, until I have more money under my belt, but it's really fun to finally spend the money I've been saving forever on clothes that I actually really like. I would never say this out loud, but it's possible that I will be completely fine with just looking *good* on this trip. And reading. If I have it my way, I will look good *while* reading. You didn't hear it here. But really, who needs skiing when I have all these fabulous clothing choices to cover?

Oh gross. I don't even recognize myself anymore.

But back to the fashion...

My cable knit sweater Uggs are the most comfortable shoes I've ever worn in my entire life. I didn't get the hype about Uggs either, until I tried on a pair. I don't ever want to take them off, so naturally, I'm wearing them, along with a short cream sweater dress, when I get on the airplane and nervously fly to Denver.

Okay. I should be completely honest. I've looked for any kind of diversion, including fashion, to get my mind off of the fact that I'm terrified of breaking a leg. Specifically, I'm terrified of breaking a leg in front of Ian. I have never even had a desire to ski. It's not come close to crossing my mind since I can trip falling UP the stairs. I can trip over nothing. My own two feet are fully capable of betraying me without any warning. They're vicious, really.

These thoughts are warring in my brain as I look out the window and gaze into the cotton puff clouds. I guess it's better than obsessing over seeing Ian again. I won't deny that I've battled pushing him out of my brain, deciding to not overthink anything with him. I will just see what he has to say, if anything, when I see him. Consequently, all I've thought about for days are all the ways I can stay OFF the slopes. I have an arsenal of reasons/excuses to pull out, should anyone corner me about why I'm avoiding my skis.

These theories are all shot to dust during the car ride with my parents to the resort. After many hugs and kisses are passed around, they start right in.

"We're scheduled to have a skiing lesson at 8 A.M.," Charlie informs me.

"About that…" I start.

"Your mom and I will join you. You'll do fine, Rosie."

"You know how to ski, you don't need to wait up for me. Take advantage of all this," I wave my hand, wildly pointing at the snow-covered mountains. It doesn't work.

"No, I could use a refresher course," my dad says.

"Me too. How long has it been since we've done this?" Charlie pipes in.

This leads to a ten-minute trip down memory lane. The last time they skied was when they spent their anniversary in Lake Tahoe. I tune out for a minute, admiring the beautiful sunset, when I hear Laila's name. My ears perk up and I rejoin the conversation.

"Have you seen Jeff and Laila yet? Is everyone already here?"

"We saw them briefly as we were leaving to get you. There's quite a group here."

"Really? How many?" I want details.

"Oh, I'd say at least fifteen, maybe twenty..." My mom looks back at me and smiles. "Ian asked about you. He wondered if you were coming ... seemed surprised you weren't already with us."

"Hmmm." I say with all the nonchalance I can muster. Meanwhile, my insides are doing trampoline circus tricks.

***

It's dark by the time we get to Crystal Peak Lodge. The glistening lights of the resort against the backdrop of the mountains and starry sky is a sight to see. Every stressful thought from the last couple of months dims, and anticipation takes its place. This will be wonderful. I am determined to make it so.

I thought I wasn't ready to see Ian yet, but my eyes scan the lobby, searching every corner for him. All of a sudden, it's very real that I WILL BE SEEING IAN SOON. I can't wait. Even if it doesn't go the way I might hope, I just want to look at him.

"There you are!"

I turn around and am immediately swallowed in a hug from Jeff. Laila stands next to him and smiles, her warmth a few notches cooler than the last time I saw her. It bewilders me momentarily, and then her smile widens and I push my thoughts aside.

"Sparrow, hello! You look so pretty. Did you have a nice flight?" Laila looks me over from head to toe and back up again. I want to ask if I passed inspection.

"Thank you. Yes, it was fine," I smile.

I'm glad when my parents pick up the conversation. My dad goes to our condo to put my luggage away while my mom and I follow the Roberts to the lodge's restaurant. Our group is already there and introductions are made all around. Still no Ian. Everyone seems pretty nice. My parents go for the older group—the parental side—congregating to the left side of the huge table and I venture to the younger side. I sit by Wendy, who appears to be around my age. Across from Wendy is Carl, and I think they're a couple. On the other side of Wendy is a gorgeous blonde, Jade. She's a bit icy, but I guess you can get away with that when you're so beautiful. Next to Carl are two handsome brothers, Jake and Jared. I realize belatedly that they're also brothers to Jade. The J siblings. They could all be models.

I realize I'm the baby when everyone around me orders fancy cocktails and beer. No one says anything about my choice of Coke with a squeeze of lime. Small talk resumes and it turns out, they're spread all over:

California, Indiana, Texas and even New York. Jared perks up when I say I'm at NYU. He's finishing up his last year at Columbia. The food arrives and my tenderloin is delicious. I can never resist a good steak. I'm really enjoying getting to know everyone, especially Wendy and Jared, when I feel him in the room. I turn around and sure enough, Ian is walking into the restaurant.

Carl sees him next. He waves, and Ian lifts his hand to Carl, but his eyes are on me. He walks straight for me and stops just behind my chair. I look up at him and can't help it. I'm fairly certain I light up like a tacky lawn at Christmas, complete with a flamingo.

"Sparrow…" His lips curve up. "You made it. How are you?"

"I'm well. How about you?"

"Same. I see you brought the beauty to Colorado."

"I think it was doing fine on its own."

Ian's smile widens. "No … no, I don't think you know what you do…"

We stare each other down … until Jade clears her throat. "I saved you a seat, Ian," she calls out. "You're just in time for dessert."

Ian doesn't look at her right away, but when he does, the spell breaks. He pats my back in a friendly gesture and goes to sit by her.

I can't help it. I'm stung. I don't know what I expected, but it was something a little … *more*. I want to kick myself for having any expectations at all. I pass on dessert and mostly listen to the conversations around me. I can't hear what Jade and Ian are saying, but it sounds like they're not having any lull in topics.

"Sparrow?" Wendy is looking at me, waiting for my

response.

"I'm sorry, did you ask me something?"

"I was wondering if you want to head to our condo," she points to the others, "we're just gonna hang in the condo tonight and get up early to ski in the morning. Come with us."

"Aw, thanks. I better … go back to my own tonight. I haven't seen my parents in a couple of months. And I have a skiing lesson first thing in the morning." I try not to grimace as I say that.

Jake pipes up, "You haven't skied before?"

"No, never."

The table goes silent when I say that. Jared waves his hand nonchalantly. "Oh, you'll be fine. I think I had my first lesson here…"

I smile at him and then turn to the others, making eye contact with everyone but Ian and Jade. "It's so nice to meet all of you. I'm beat tonight, but I'd love to catch up with you tomorrow night."

They all agree to look for me the next day, and I stand up to head back to my room. My parents are still in deep discussion with their new friends and the Roberts. It could be a while before they're ready to go. All of a sudden, I realize I'm not just making it up—I really am exhausted.

I head to the other side of the table to kiss my parents and am turning to leave when I nearly run into Ian. "Let me walk you to your room," he says.

I don't trust myself to speak, so I don't. We walk out of the restaurant and into the hallway of the lobby. He looks at the packet holding my room key to see which direction to go. He puts his hand between my shoulder blades and leans his head over to mine, giving me a sideways hug of sorts.

When he pulls back, his eyes are luminous. "Hi," he says again.

Mercy sakes. He just … does it for me. Whatever *it* is, he does it.

"Hi," I whisper.

He leaves his hand on my back, leading the way toward my condo, even though I couldn't begin to tell you where we're going. He keeps watching me, smiling and assessing me with those eyes. I can't think of a thing to say, and I don't want to spoil the moment with trivial thoughts or accusing questions.

All too soon, we're at my door. He takes both my hands and clutches them firmly in his. "When you're done with your lesson in the morning, will you ski with me?"

"Oh—" a nervous laugh escapes, "I'm not sure that's such a good idea. In fact, I'm sure it's NOT. I don't really expect to take to it." I scrunch my face up and shake my head.

He laughs back at me, his even, white teeth shining like a perfect toothpaste commercial. "You'll be great. And if you're not, I can help you."

"Right. Because you're an excellent skier, aren't you?"

"How did you know?" He teases, as his thumb softly outlines my thumb and the palm of my hand. I shiver. "Are you chilly?" he asks.

"No," I sigh, feeling more than a little foolish. "You should really go ahead and do your thing—I don't want to hold you back and I'm sure I won't have it down after one lesson."

"Stop that. It'll be fun. What time are you done?"

Noon? Later?

"I think just before noon."

"Great. How about we meet around one. Come warm up for a while after your lesson, rest, eat, and then be ready to do the real thing."

I reluctantly agree.

"You must be tired. It's, what—two hours later to you?"

I nod and unlock the door, smiling shyly at Ian.

"Sparrow…"

I go completely still and wait for him to speak.

"You're a vision," he almost sounds bashful as he says it.

I start to say something, but draw a blank. My face warms up and my cheeks hurt from smiling. I open the door and go inside. The last thing I see before I shut the door are his light bulb eyes shining at me, as his hand briefly touches his cushiony lips. I know who I will be dreaming of tonight.

The time change works to my benefit the next morning, when I'm awake bright and early. The view is so spectacular in the morning light, I actually gasp when I step outside. The mountain peaks don't even look real.

I have a serious case of the jelly stomach as we pick up our skis and shuffle across the snow in the awkward snow boots. I haven't been this nervous in … I don't remember when. Our small class gathers at the bottom of the bunny hill. There are only seven of us, including Lars, the instructor. He looks like a surfer dude who is slightly out of place, but he surprises me. In no time at all, he has us doing things I never thought possible. I master the wedge; let me tell you, I have worked out how to stop. As a last case scenario, Lars shows us the best way to fall if we can't stop.

We do wide laps across the bottom of the hill for a long time and before I know it, I'm ready for more. Can you believe I don't even fall once? In fact, the scariest part of the entire lesson is when we graduate to the ski lift. Now, *that* could wreck the entire experience for me right there. I nearly panic when I come *this* close to missing the seat, but it carries me off just in time. I catch my breath as I try not to think about how high it's going … with nothing holding me in.

My dad yells out in the seat behind me, "You all right, Rosie?"

I don't dare turn around, but yell back, "Yes!" my voice approximately two octaves higher than normal.

Lars is in front of me, and I study closely how he gets off the lift. When it's my turn, I copy his moves to a T. Whew. That was intense. And then I turn around and see what I have to go down. What was I thinking? I do a few huge gulps, ignore that quivering that has returned in my guts and then take off down the mountain.

A huge grin is waiting for me when I get to the bottom. Lars is so proud. I'm pretty sure my grin matches his. I've never felt such an exhilarated rush. We spend the next hour fine-tuning what we've learned. The last few runs, Lars shares the lift with me. He's charming and makes me laugh, so the time passes quickly. After he's finished up his last tip and told everyone to enjoy the rest of their stay, he skis up to me.

"Looking great out there, Sparrow," he says, still beaming.

His voice reminds me of Owen Wilson. In fact, that's

who it is—I've been racking my brain the whole morning to figure out who it is he favors. He's much younger and cuter than Owen, but the messy blond hair, nose that's been broken a time or two and the constant smile lurking on his lips has him looking like he just stepped out of a romantic comedy.

"Sparrow?"

"I'm so sorry. What did you say?" I mentally kick myself for getting distracted for who knows how long.

"I was just wondering if you want to meet up later? I know where the prime snow is ... and some kickin' places around town."

I see he has the surfer lingo down pat. Maybe that's how skiers talk too.

"Well ... that sounds fun. You've been really ... fun. I'm actually supposed to meet up with a friend later. But there are a bunch of us here—all better at this than me. You're welcome to join us anytime." If I say "fun" one more time, I'm going to choke myself. Give me too much attention, and I find a way to humiliate myself.

"I'd love that," he says. He reaches into his jacket and pulls out a card. "I'll be watching for you, but here's my number. I'm free most afternoons and evenings this week."

"Thanks," I take the card and awkwardly tuck it inside my pocket.

He pushes off with his poles and turns back over his shoulder. "There's something about you, Sparrow. You're gorgeous, but ... it's more than that. There aren't many people coming through here that I want to get to know better ... you're an exception." He lifts his pole up and does a little bow before taking off.

I've just decided I love winter gear. I can splotch to kingdom come and no one will be the wiser.

I feel loads lighter as I get ready to meet Ian. Knowing that I'm not going to fall every other step has put my mind at ease. Beyond that, finding something that I'm halfway good at in the athletic department makes me downright giddy. I never dreamed I could pull that off. I pig out, brush my teeth and sigh when I realize I still have about twenty minutes before we've agreed to meet.

I'm absentmindedly putting my gloves on as I step outside. The brisk air feels so good after the heat in the Lodge. A high-pitched giggle grabs my attention and I look up to see Ian and Jade standing by the coffee bar. She leans over and pulls Ian's face closer to hers to whisper something in his ear. He smirks and shakes his head, while Jade looks like the cat that ate the canary. She swishes her blond hair back and places her hand on his chest as she says something that requires feeling him up.

I feel my eyes narrowing as my blood nearly boils out of my skin. I never thought I was a jealous person, but I just might be.

They don't see me, so occupied with their own little tête-à-tête; they are oblivious to anyone around them. I study them both and wonder what she is to him. Jade looks stunning. Her long hair is perfectly in place, the straight edge of her blond ends are in a perfect line across her pink coat. Her skin is rosy and flawless. Even from this distance, her eyes stand out. It isn't her looks that make my green-eyed monster go on the prowl though, it's the complete ease she has with him and the way he hasn't even looked around for me once.

I'll give him five minutes and if he hasn't walked away from Jade, I'll conveniently forget about meeting him.

Approximately 4 minutes and 30 seconds later, and with 10 minutes left before he's supposed to meet me, I see Ian glance at the gigantic clock on the outside of the ski rental shop. He puts a hand on Jade's shoulder, she grabs him into a hug and he walks away. I nearly try to hide so it doesn't look like I've just been waiting and spying, but figure I'd trip or something equally embarrassing.

When Ian sees me leaning against the building, he flashes his brilliance my way. His eyes take me in, and for a moment, I forget all about Jade and ride high on his attention.

"Sparrow. You are lighting up the whole damn mountain," he grins.

I smile because I was thinking the same about him. "Have you had a good day?"

"It's been great. We all went out early. I'm seeing a nap in my future."

"Oh, did you want to meet up later?"

"Nooo, are you kidding me? You woke me right up."

"You looked plenty awake before you ever saw me," I smirk.

Ian's grin doesn't fade, but his eyes narrow just a little, as he tries to measure what I'm really saying.

"How was your lesson?"

"It went surprisingly well!" I can't even tone down the excitement in my voice and what shocks me more, is that I actually want to get back out there.

"I'm not surprised. Well, come on. Show me what

you've got."

Ian leads me to one of the longer, more difficult runs, one that I haven't gone near yet. Once we're on the lift, it sinks in that I'm in such close proximity to Ian. I wasn't sure if I'd ever even see him again.

"So, Sparrow…"

I look over at him. If we never have another moment together, I know I will still always remember this moment here, right now, with his phenomenal face perfectly surrounded by the snowy peaks.

"Your name … tell me about that."

"It's from that verse in the Bible about how the Father sees when every sparrow falls. And my parents are half-hippie, so my name had to be unique. My middle name is Kate after my grandmother, and I used to write that on everything because I was embarrassed of Sparrow, but now I kinda like it. I'm just glad they didn't name me something like Zipporah. Not that there's anything *wrong* with that," I grin.

"It fits you. But then again, you could probably even make Zipporah work," his laugh echoes over the mountain.

We get off one lift and get on another to go higher up. I'm starting to get nervous about how high we are.

"So what is your middle name?"

"Oh no. No. I don't think you're ready for that one just yet."

"Ohhhh," I snicker, "it's like that, is it? Okay, at least give me an initial."

"O."

"Oh what?"

"No, O. That's my middle initial."

"Hmm. It's probably something hideous like Orville, that would be so funny…" I laugh my head off. "Or…" I look over at him because he's not laughing. He's facing forward and while he still has a huge smile on his face, it almost looks like he's blushing. Oh no. I sober up fast. "Oh … it's not really … Orville. Is it?"

He nods.

"Nooooo!"

He nods again.

"You're kidding."

He shakes his head and then the loudest rumble comes out of him and he's laughing so hard, the lift is shaking. I feel so bad.

"I'm so sorry. I can't believe that. It's not *hideous* … but really? Why would your mama do that to you? I mean—" I give up because now he's wiping his eyes and it really is too funny.

He can barely breathe, but in between gasps and laughing, he's saying, "I can't believe you guessed it…"

"Well, O didn't give me a lot to work with…"

He straightens up and I look forward. We're almost to the top.

"There's Oliver or Oscar … Omar…" he starts laughing again. "I'm named after my grandfather."

"Well, now I really feel bad."

"Don't. That's the funniest thing that's happened to me in a long time."

- 7 -

Child's Play

My stomach is growling to beat the band by the time we take off our skis and walk to the condo. My feet feel like they're still gliding on snow. We run into Wendy and Jade outside the lodge and they invite us to eat with the group. I feel Jade's eyes on me, taking in every look Ian gives me. So far, he seems nice to both Wendy and Jade and not as flirty as it seemed earlier. She doesn't quite give me daggers, but I can tell she's evaluating the situation and sizing up how much of a threat I am.

Lars is walking out of the building just as we're going inside. "Sparrow!" his voice booms. "How did the rest of your day go?"

Everyone turns to look at me, waiting expectantly for me to speak. They act like it's a foreign concept that I would have already made a friend.

"Hey, Lars! It was so great! I LOVED it!"

His smile stretches wide. "Well, you're a natural."

Jade lays her hand on Ian's arm. Ian looks back and forth from me to Lars.

"Aren't you going to introduce us to your friend?" Jade speaks up.

"Oh! Yes, this is Lars. He was my instructor this morning."

Ian nods and reaches out to shake his hand. "Ian."

"Jade and Wendy." I do a sweeping arm in their direction.

"You should join us," Jade announces. "We're going to that pizza place on the corner. Come with us."

Lars looks at me and raises his eyebrows. "Well, sure. I don't want to intrude, but pizza sounds good, actually."

Jade links her arm through Ian's, and he looks at me with a mixture of confusion and apology.

"Sparrow?" Lars asks. "You're going, right?"

"Uh, yeah … I'm going. I'm starving."

Lars chats all the way to the tram. Jade and Ian walk in front of us, and she's hanging all over him. Jared and Jake meet us on the tram. Lars sits in the seat next to me and I feel Ian's eyes on us the whole ride. I avoid looking at him. If he wants Jade attached to his hip tonight, he can have her.

At the restaurant, I find myself between Lars and Ian. It feels like the day I met Ian all over again. Except Lars is a lot more attentive than Michael was. By the time the night is over, I'm exhausted with trying to block the levels of testosterone that seem to be bouncing off the walls by the minute. Ian keeps his arm on the back of my chair, his hand lightly resting on my back, but Lars seems oblivious and keeps interrogating me with first date questions.

Jade is getting more and more agitated because now she not only doesn't have Ian's attention, but she doesn't have the new guy's either. It's obvious she's used to being the center of the hurricane. I'm dying from all the attention and wish I could just go back to the condo and cover my head.

When I've answered where I'm from, where I'm

going to school, what my major is, my favorite color, if I have pets, do I want any pets and have I ever thought of spending summers in Colorado, Ian finally speaks up.

"Hey, little bird … do you have plans for tomorrow night?"

That shuts Lars up.

It shuts me up too and I wasn't even talking. *Little Bird*, I kinda like that. Makes me feel delicate and not so … tall and gangly.

"Ohhh…" Lars says. He smiles weakly at me.

I feel bad for Lars and shoot dagger eyes to Ian. He laughs and shrugs, then he leans over and whispers, "I'll let you get back to this little … whatever this —," he subtly points to Lars, "—is … for tonight. As long as I can please have you tomorrow night?"

I want to murder him and thank him at the same time. Lars's Twenty Questions were about to send me running for the hills.

"Shut. It." My whisper comes out with a bite.

He rears his head back and laughs and then comes back in for my ear. I want to bop the mischief right off his face. "Just trying to get a word in," he whispers. "I meant it, though…"

He looks at my mouth and all reasonable thought leaves my brain. Fortunately, Jade comes to my rescue and pulls the focus back on herself.

"Ian! I talked to Milly the other day."

There's a turn in the air as Ian acknowledges Jade's statement. It feels a bit thicker in here, like a huge fog just rolled into the restaurant.

"Cool," he says. "How's she doing?"

"Great! She's loving life. I think she'll be getting

pregnant before we know it." Jade looks at me and then says, "You know … you kind of look like Milly." Her lip curls just a touch when she says it.

I don't want to give her the satisfaction, but I *am* curious. "Who's Milly?"

I can tell by Jade's smirk that I've done exactly what she hoped I would—taken her bait. She's very pleased to be the one to tell me that Milly is Ian's ex-girlfriend.

"They dated forever," she says. "I love that girl. She's so funny … and gorgeous."

"You don't look alike," he assures me. "And we obviously didn't date forever."

Somehow that doesn't make me feel better. I don't like the feeling in the room. The shift in Ian's mood is enough to dispel any lighthearted vibes I had picked up from him all night. I'm ready to go and I don't care if I ever see Jade again. She's trouble, that one.

"You think you'll ever be married to anything other than your music, Ian?" Apparently, Jade is just getting started.

I turn to Ian and I don't like how sad his eyes have turned. "Well, it *is* the only thing I'm good at," he says quietly.

"Lars, I'm ready to go. How about you?"

Lars brightens up and there is a momentary twinge of guilt when I realize I might be getting his hopes up. I determine to straighten that out on the way to the Lodge.

Ian stands up as I put on my coat. "Sparrow, wait, I can—"

"I'm sure I'll see you tomorrow, Ian … thanks for the fun day. Good-night, everyone."

Jared watches the whole exchange. He hasn't said

much all night. I wonder what he's thinking.

The next morning, my parents and I head out to ski together. When we open the door to our condo, Ian is just walking up with 4 steaming coffees.

"Oh, Ian, how nice!" my mom gushes. She doesn't tell him that we just finished 2 cups of coffee with our breakfast.

"I'm probably too late, but I hoped I'd catch you before you went out. You up for having one more with you today?" He looks at all of us as he asks, but his eyes land on me last.

I don't answer his question, but take the coffee and thank him for it. I look at my dad and he answers for all of us.

"Sure! The more, the merrier!" My dad chuckles. He is the nicest guy, he really is.

"Great," Ian lets out a breath and for a minute there, I think he's nervous. Ian Sterling is actually nervous.

"You're looking *sweet* this morning, Little Bird," he says low and sexy. And there it went. All nervousness out the door for him and back on me in heaps.

My mom's eyes light up at his endearment, while I shake my head at it. "Little Bird? Do I look little to you?"

"You do have a point there," he whispers and I swear his eyes do a sweep over my chest. Oh my word.

That's it. I tell my parents we'll meet them in five minutes and as soon as they walk off, I light into him.

"Look. I can't handle the little innuendos in front of my parents today. I'm not sure I can when it's just the two of us, but my 'Little Bird' heart REALLY can't take it in front of them. If you want to be with us today, *behave*!"

He laughs so hard, he has to bend over to catch his breath.

"Oh, Sparrow … you are … perfection."

He is wiping tears from the corners of his eyes, his now standard reaction to me, I note as I glare at him.

"Don't you think that was just a *tiny* bit funny?" He holds up his thumb and forefinger close together and quirks his eyebrow.

"You … are … trouble." I huff.

He nods and pulls a solemn face. "You're right about that."

Ian is on his best behavior the rest of the day. My parents love him. We have a blast on the slopes, and the worn-out feeling we have when we're done feels good. As we're walking back to the condo, he brings up our date.

"Are you still up for going out with me tonight?"

"I don't remember ever agreeing to that."

He stops and puts his hand on my arm. "You're right. You didn't." There isn't any teasing in his voice now. He's completely serious. "Tonight."

"Well, my parents were hoping we'd join them tonight. I think they're wanting to do an early birthday surprise for Jeff while everyone's together."

"Oh, Laila did mention something about that. I didn't realize it was tonight. All right. Tomorrow night?"

"Tomorrow night is the Pictionary competition at Wendy's!"

"Well, we certainly can't miss that!" he says, matching my tone. "That leaves our last night. Do you think you can carve time out of your busy schedule to go out with me Friday?"

"I guess I can squeeze you in."

He looks me up and down and I don't even want to know what his dirty little mind is cooking up. I'm too afraid to know.

Jeff's party is in the swankier restaurant of the Lodge. The fun seems to be in full swing when my parents and I get there. I immediately find Ian. He's surrounded by beautiful women and seems completely at ease. I'm not sure how he can see past the blond in front of him, she leads with her breasts, but somehow he manages to spot me immediately. I watch as he excuses himself and hightails it my way.

He's eying me like I'm a dessert he wants to inhale. It seems my red cocktail dress was the right choice, after all.

"Damn, Sparrow. Fu—" he clears his throat and gives his hair a tug. I love it when he does that. It makes his already messy hair look even more disheveled. It levels me. Like a bulldozer that completely flattens the ground and doesn't leave a single grain of dirt in the wrong place. I don't even want to think straight when he looks this good.

"Ian."

"You…" He's quiet for what feels like minutes, but probably isn't.

"Yes?"

He does the hair thing again and I try to hold my ground without a) going down, or b) blushing. So far, I'm still standing. Pretty sure my neck and face are the shade of my dress.

"You look nice tonight," I tell him.

"You…" he shakes his head. "God, girl, you've

90

rendered me speechless."

"Well, that's a first." I smile.

"Come sit with me?"

He takes my arm and puts it through his, laying my hand on his arm and holding it there. We sit at a smaller table next to the large birthday table and I realize that Ian still sort of got his way—it feels like we're on a mini date here in front of everyone.

After we order, Laila makes her way over to our table and comments on how pretty I look tonight. She's standing over Ian with her hands on his shoulders as she says it. I compliment her too—she really is so pretty. Ian doesn't say much, he just watches me. The whole night, he watches me. He's quieter than usual, but the restaurant is so loud that we both give up trying to have much of a conversation.

It's the same the next night; there isn't much chance to have a conversation. I'm happy for the time on the ski lifts during the day where we can learn all about each other.

"So what do you enjoy besides books?" he asks. "You can't have your nose in a book all the time … can you? I mean, you know I'm all about your sexy librarian vibe, but…"

I roll my eyes at him and say, "Well, every now and then I do something else just as nerdy."

"No, you have a way of making everything look enticing. You're like this … Renaissance woman … an odd, but lovely rarity."

"Do these lines just pour out of you or do you have a running repertoire that you recycle? You're far too quick for them to be—"

He puts his fingers on my lips and holds them there as his forehead touches mine. "You pull the truth out of me, Sparrow."

I don't know what to say to that, especially while his finger is tracing my upper lip that way.

"Tell me something, anything, about you," he says, moving his finger along the middle of my bottom lip.

"Uh … flute." Shoot. Why did I let that out?

He leans back, surprised. "Flute? You play the flute? What else do you play?" His eyes narrow as a big grin takes over his face.

"Piano." I sigh.

"Oh, this is too good. Little Bird is musical. Oh, we're going to have fun with this," he vows.

I groan. "No. I'm not playing for you. Ever."

He gives me a playful hurt look and gets back in my face. "Oh, you will. And I can't wait…"

I'm still inwardly groaning about that when we go to Wendy's condo. The thought that I would ever play for Ian Sterling is ridiculous.

Ian and I are on a team together for Pictionary. Jade has gradually gotten the point that Ian isn't going to be interested in her this trip. She scowls at us as we win. I'm not an artist, but he is, so we are racking up the points. Each time we score, Ian squeezes my hand and looks like he wants to come in for a kiss. He doesn't. But I wish he would.

Our last day of skiing is bittersweet. I never dreamed I'd come on this trip and actually love it. I'm disappointed at the thought of not being able to ski again for a while. If I'm honest with myself, I'm also slightly heartsick that I will be saying good-bye to Ian tomorrow and I have no idea when or if I'll see him again. That hasn't come up in any conversations—the When Will I See You Again? topic. And I'm not going to be the one to broach it.

We run into Lars on our way back to the Lodge. We've seen him a few times throughout the week, and it's been congenial every time. He even skied with all of us one afternoon. He is genuinely a nice guy.

"Sparrow!" he calls. "You headin' out tomorrow?"

"Yes, I am," I yell back. "Thanks for showing me how it's done!" I grin at him.

"Gladly." He walks closer and does a fist bump with Ian. "Take it easy, man. Hope to see you both out here again."

I give him a big hug and we go on our way. I'm glad he doesn't hold any hard feelings. That would have been more awkward than it already was.

The long awaited "date night" arrives. I've been fairly relaxed around Ian all week, but being alone with him is a different story. I know how the air is charged enough when we're around a group of people. He has this way of looking at my mouth that leaves me unhinged. I've had the protection of Wendy and even Jade, to keep anything from happening, but land sakes, the way he looks at me … I'm not sure I'll maintain my virtue.

And the fact is … I'm completely ready to be defiled.

Of course, I dress to kill. My outfits have floored my mom. She just *thought* she was shocked back home when I finally wore something fitted. Each time she sees me in

93

something else, I think she might have a conniption, but she's managed to keep her barbs to a minimum—a huge feat on her part. I'm relieved. At least everything I've worn is tasteful … but they're also extremely flattering and ahem, alluring.

I will never wear gunnysacks another day in my life. Never. Ever.

I was right—it does feel different. The air around us is positively popping. From the minute Ian takes a look at me, I know I'm in for something. I'm not quite sure what yet, but something…

As soon as we shut the door, he holds out his hand and laces his fingers through mine. We haven't done that yet, so I have a little giddy moment inside my chest. We end up at the gondola lift. I've been wanting to ride one since we got here, but haven't had the chance. We climb in and Ian sits on the same side as me. His arm goes around me and I think my heart is going to pound out of my chest. The lights are beautiful, shining down on the snow. The Victorian town of Breckenridge is so quaint and beautiful.

We're both unusually quiet. All week, we've been gabbing each other's ears off at every opportunity.

"You okay?" I ask.

He raises his hand to my face and cups my jaw. "Look at this face," he looks like he's memorizing every feature.

He stares at me and I stare back, until the gondola makes a slight lurch. Our noses bump—why won't he just kiss me? I can almost feel it, we're that close.

He looks away and says, "Oh, look, time to get off." I hear a little bit of relief in his voice and it makes my stomach hurt. Maybe he's just all talk and isn't quite feeling what I am for him.

Our lift goes about ten feet further and then stops. We climb out and Ian doesn't let go of my hand.

Not many hands fit my hands. My fingers are long and slender. Guys with fat hands and short fingers just don't work with mine. I file this away in my little Perfect Guy for Me Notebook.

Before I know it, we're going inside a fancy steakhouse. "I hope this is okay. I've heard good things about it," Ian says.

"It sure is pretty."

"YOU sure are pretty," he speaks up. "*More* than pretty…"

He seems nervous again. He pulls out words like 'sweet' and 'pretty' when he's nervous. I'm ready to get to the bottom of it.

We're barely seated and before I can stop the words, I say, "What do you like about me besides my looks?"

"The fact that you would ask me something like that is a clear indication of the kind of person you are, Sparrow Fisher. You have this grounding quality about you. I don't know a better way to put it. It levels me. I've never been at home anywhere, but I am with you."

I look at him and know exactly what he means. All my life I've said what everyone wanted me to say, worn what everyone wanted me to wear, acted just so—never realizing until this very moment that I've been waiting for someone to look past it all and actually see *me*.

"You make me feel like I can completely be myself, Ian. That's a rare thing for me."

"I wouldn't want you to be anyone but yourself," Ian

says with a smile. "Sparrow?" He clears his throat. "I need to ask you something. Or … tell you something…"

Our waitress walks up and I can tell Ian is flustered and wishing she would go away. We hurry and order our drinks.

I wish he'd hold my hand again because he's making *me* nervous.

"I've been wondering … do you know how old I am?"

I don't know what I was expecting, but this wasn't it.

"Well, I guess I assumed you were 22, maybe 23." I look at his boyish face. I'd actually think he was younger if I didn't know he'd established quite a music career by now. His face is flawless, no lines whatsoever. If I were to guess without knowing a thing about him, I'd say more like 19 or 20.

He pulls a face and takes his hand away from mine to do that hair tug thing he does. He's starting to really make me anxious.

"Why? How old *are* you?" I ask.

"Well, I thought *you* were around 22 or 23 when we went out that day in San Francisco." He puts his head in his hand and peers up at me slowly. "You're tall, I think that makes you look so much older. I had *no idea* you were 18…" He gulps.

"I *have* had a birthday since then…" I smile.

"Oh thank God," he says. He looks a little green. He still hasn't taken my hand. "Sparrow, I'm going to be 29 this year … well, next year."

"Nooooooo." I can't help it. I am shocked.

He sighs. "Yes. Not for another 9 months or so, but still." He looks down and I study the way his eyelashes curve up at the ends. Way better than any eyelash curler could ever do.

"So you're 28." I state the obvious.

He nods.

"And I'm 19."

He nods again.

"Wow."

"Yeah. Wow."

"Well…" I start tugging *my* hair now. "Wow." I guess you could say I'm struck speechless. "Well, okay," I finally say.

"Is it weird for you?" he asks.

"Um, yeah, a little bit. And I already know it weirds you out. But … you really don't act like you're 28! And you certainly don't look it."

He grins. "Thanks?" He clears his throat. "I just had to get it out … Laila brought it to my attention in San Francisco and made me feel like a creeper. I'm old. And I would normally never in a million years go out with anyone who wasn't at least in their mid-twenties. I just haven't done very well at staying away from you. I've tried. I really have tried."

I laugh at his earnest expression. "Well, it's not like you're ancient or anything. Although, you're getting there." I give him a sly grin. "But, it doesn't have to matter. I would have never known your age and you would have never known mine if it hadn't been for someone else. The way we are around each other—it doesn't seem like we struggle with relating to one another."

"No…"

Surprisingly, this revelation doesn't keep us from moving on and chatting about a million other things throughout the night. I barely even think about the age thing once we've changed the subject. When we're done eating, we go to the piano bar across the street. It's so dark in there, I wonder what they would do if they knew Ian Sterling was in the place.

All too soon, it's late and we're back on the gondola, riding back to the Lodge. Ian has one arm around me and the other is playing with my hand, touching each finger and giving me chills with each stroke. I shiver and he holds me tighter.

"Cold?" he asks.

"A little bit," I whisper.

He wraps me up in his coat and lifts my chin up with one hand. "You have the best lips, I can't keep my eyes off them," he whispers. His finger traces my mouth again and this time, I know he's going to kiss me. My eyelids feel heavy. So soft that I almost think I'm imagining it, his lips are on mine. Then, there is no doubt. He kisses me, sweetly at first, and then when our tongues touch, greedily, like he can't stand another moment until he has thoroughly laid claim on every part of my mouth. His hands are on my face and mine are finally tugging his hair, exactly where my hands have wanted to be since the day I first saw him. I pull him in deeper and deeper; I can't get enough.

All kisses before this have been mere child's play. I drink him in and know my fate is sealed: I am his.

- 8 -

Floating AND Falling

Even after we get off the lift, he has his arm wound around me, holding me tight against his side. He leans his head down and keeps kissing my hair, my forehead, my cheek. I smile up at him and his eyes are shining brighter than they have yet. He takes my breath away.

We end up in front of my door. He leans down, runs his tongue lightly over my bottom lip and groans. "I don't want to let you go," he whispers.

I can't even speak. My heart feels like an old-fashioned alarm clock with the bells ringing so hard that it falls right off the table.

He presses me against the door, coming in for more, when we hear a loud click. The door opens and we nearly fall inside. Charlie is standing there, and she has the decency to not act too shocked at our disheveled state.

"I thought I heard knocking," she says. When we just stare at her, she closes the door.

Awkward.

Ian and I look at each other and if I didn't feel so good, I'd want to crawl in a hole right about now.

"Thank you for a wonderful night," Ian says, kissing my hand. He leans in and whispers, "You taste even better than I imagined."

I know I'm so flushed, I'm purple, but I can't help it. This is too much sensory overload for one night.

"Little Bird? You okay?"

I nod and he smiles.

"Goodnight. Are we still good for breakfast in the morning before your flight?"

I nod again.

Ian gives a loud knock on the door and when my mom opens the door this time, he tells my parents goodnight and gives me one last wink before he goes out the door.

My mother glances at my lips and I know that *she* knows.

I start laughing and can't stop. "How can you tell?" I manage to spit out.

"Well, your eyes were both lit up like Christmas when you fell inside the door," she huffs.

"We went to a great restaurant and had the best time." I sigh.

My dad hasn't said a word. I eye him warily and he gives me a weak grin.

"Just be careful with that boy, Sparrow," my mom warns. "He's far more experienced than you … and he's used to getting whatever girl he wants."

"I know … and he's not a boy. I found out how old he is, Mama … 28! Can you believe that?"

"Noooooo." Her slightly put-out face is now replaced with a worried crease in the middle of her eyebrows.

Uh-oh. Not good.

"I know, that's what I said too," I say softly.

My dad speaks up then. "Jeff told me how old he was

that day in San Francisco…" He goes back to reading his book.

My mom and I look at each other and then pounce on my dad. "What do you mean? Why didn't you say anything?"

"I've never thought age mattered much. I married me an older woman myself," he grins. It's true. Charlie is five years older than my dad.

"Hmm," I say. "I guess not. Still seems like something you would BRING UP." He laughs at my emphasis. "It hasn't really mattered at all before now, since I had no clue. I guess if it doesn't bother him, either—"

Charlie shakes her head. "Just be careful, Sparrow."

"Yeah, Mama, I know … I need to…"

When I walk into the restaurant the next morning, I immediately see Ian. He is sitting in front of massive windows with the white mountains behind him. He could be on a movie set, only he's better looking than any actor I've seen.

His smile doesn't quite reach his eyes this morning, and my heart drops in my stomach. I think maybe I've imagined it. Maybe he's just tired.

"Mornin'," I say softly.

"Mornin', Sparrow." He rubs his face with both hands, and I have the thought that if we were actually together, he'd look like he was going to break up with me.

"Everything okay?" I ask.

"Yeah…" He smiles, but I'm not buying it.

I pick up the menu and try to figure out what I could possibly eat when my stomach hasn't quite returned to its proper place yet. The waiter walks up and asks if we'd like coffee. We both gratefully say yes.

He doesn't say anything for a while, and I just look out the window and try to rein my thoughts in—what did I miss here?

Finally, he says: "So … do you have a full semester coming up?"

Small talk, really?

"Yes, pretty full."

He nods.

This is painful.

"What about you—do you have a busy winter touring?"

"Yeah, I'll be all over the place for the next few months."

We place our order with the waiter, and I sit awkwardly while we wait for the food. I can't believe how this feels. Why does it end like this every time I'm with him? I wish I had the nerve to ask him, but I'm afraid if I do, I'll end up crying. I'm not used to my emotions being such a mess. I don't like this up and down business.

I can only manage a few bites of bagel before I give up. He slowly eats his omelet and doesn't finish it either.

He takes a long drink of coffee and then a swig of water. "Sparrow—"

I look up from my plate and wait.

"I've really enjoyed being with you this week. Watching you ski and just being near you, getting to know you … it's … been one of the best weeks I can even remember." He looks shy as he's saying this. "You are … the most beautiful woman I've ever seen…"

My mouth must drop open because he says, "You are!" And then he reaches over and lifts my chin up gently with his hand.

"You're kind and smart and … kissing you—" he shakes his head and closes his eyes. "I'll be thinking about that for a long time to come." He opens his eyes and puts his chin in his propped up hand. He stares me down until I'm uncomfortable. Just when I think he's waiting for *me* to respond, he says, "You know I'm trouble. Right?"

And then before I can say anything, he runs his fingers through his hair, making it go every which way. His eyes look green with the bright sunlight behind him. They look haunted.

He reaches over and grabs my hand and laces our fingers together. "You're going to break my heart, Sparrow Fisher."

And I think, Not before you break mine.

He says some other things about all the other hearts I will break along the way and really, I tune him out because I don't even know what to think. I was expecting a little romantic extension of last night. I don't know why I wasn't thinking about what next week would look like or the next month or the next, because I was too busy assuming he'd be in the picture.

When it's time to go, we stand up and he gives me a long, sweet hug. His kiss is soft and brief.

I have to get out of here and fast.

"Well … if I don't see you again, I guess I'll see you in heaven … if you make it." I do my best to grin lightheartedly and he does too. I walk away before I lose it, but I make the mistake of turning back one more time before I round the corner.

Ian Sterling has his head in his hands and the whole world on his shoulders.

Guess who is on my return flight?

Jared.

I want to hide when I see him—not because I don't like him, I do. He seems so different than his sister, and even nicer than Jake. But I'm exhausted and have been holding off on having a good cry all morning. I'm afraid if someone shows me the least amount of rudeness OR kindness, I'm going to start leaking big, fat, sloppy tears. I am so out of my element.

He flashes his sweet smile at me and lifts his hand in a wave. "Sparrow! I'm glad to see you! I was wishing for a chance to say good-bye. This is even better."

His brown eyes are so sincere; I'm immediately at ease. "Hi, Jared. Yeah, it's good to see you. You ready to get back to school?"

He laughs. "Well, I don't know about that … I'd rather ski another week."

"Me too."

"From what I could tell, you sure picked it up quickly."

"I'm still in shock over that, let me tell you. Athletic is NOT my middle name."

"Well, you could have fooled me." He grins. "Hey, where are you sitting?"

I pull out my ticket and find the row. He's peering over my shoulder. "12 D," he says. "Would you want to see if we can change our seats? Sit together?"

I'd rather sleep the sleep of the dead, but nod instead. "Sure."

He goes up to the ticket agent and wouldn't you know it, they manage to find two empty seats together.

When we have been flying for approximately twenty-eight minutes, Jared gets right to it. "So what's the story on you and Sterling?" He doesn't even look at me when he says it, but busies himself with the tray table in front of him. He puts it down. Pushes it up. Puts it back down.

"Story?"

"Yeah. It seemed like you two had some history already?" He says it as a question and I look at him, waiting for him to say more before I try to decide what to say back. "Are you guys, you know ... going out?"

I've always thought "going out" was such a weird way of saying you're in a relationship. There really is no great way to say it. *Is he your boyfriend?* sounds so retro. *Going out* makes me think of getting some fresh air. *Dating* just feels ... dated.

"Well, the times I've been around him ... I do like him *a lot*." I turn to him as I say it. I'm trying to be as honest as I can, given that I really have no clue what Ian Sterling is to me, or better yet, what I am to him. But I do know that much: I like him a lot.

It's enough. Jared gets it. He nods his head and looks ... disappointed. I don't know if it's disappointment in me or about me. I know I really don't want to think of anyone else's feelings just now. Mine are all I can barely handle.

"Just be careful, Sparrow," Jared says, still looking straight ahead.

I nod my head and feel my stomach sink about Ian, while also feeling relief that maybe Jared and I can really just be friends.

I lean my head back on the seat and change the subject. "Was it hard saying good-bye to your family this morning? Or are you used to it?"

"I can only take them in small doses, so it was just right."

I smile at him. It's hard to imagine that he's Jade's brother. They're so completely different. Everything about Jade screams spoiled, rich, obnoxious snob. Jared seems like a kind teddy bear hidden under toned arms.

"What about you?"

"I'll miss my family. It was great to see them … but yeah, I'm glad to be getting back. I've been a little distracted. I'm ready to get focused now. I hope, anyway…" I trail off.

"Hey, what are you doing tomorrow night?"

"Tomorrow night?"

"Yeah, New Year's Eve?"

"Oh, I hadn't even thought about it! I don't know—I need to see what Tessa has planned."

"Well, you should both come to the party Asher Caldwell is giving—come with me."

"Asher Caldwell—that sounds so familiar."

"Music producer? He's a family friend. Nice guy. His career has taken off in the last three years."

"Really?" I can't help but chuckle. "How many famous people do you know?"

He laughs and shrugs. "A few, I guess."

I'm so relaxed that the next thing I know, my head is bouncing off Jared's shoulder as we're skidding across the runway, landing with speed. I smile apologetically at him and his eyes crinkle up.

"Feel better?"

"Yes, thanks for providing the shoulder. I didn't realize I was quite so tired."

"Not a problem."

At baggage claim, we exchange phone numbers. He promises to call about the party, and I promise to think seriously about going. At the moment, though, all I feel like doing is visiting my bed. My vacation is finally catching up with me.

It is SO good to see Tessa. She wakes me right up, wanting to hear all about my trip. As soon as we get in the door, she's making hot chocolate and then pulling me over to the couch, asking question after question.

I'm not quite as forthcoming as she'd like, and finally, she scowls at me and says, "What's the deal? Was it great or not? What *happened* with *Ian*?"

And I cannot ignore the lump that's been in my throat all day long … well, since breakfast with Ian. I'm on the verge of tears and start blubbering.

"It was perfect. Every day was perfect and then last night … we went out and it was so wonderful and we kissed. And oh my word, he's the best. WAY better than Bobby, who you know I always thought was the very best kisser. Always. And then this morning, he'd asked me to breakfast, but when I got there, he was so distant and said I'd break his heart, but also said *he* was trouble so it was *so* confusing and it was like we were starting all over or like we were strangers and…" I run out of breath and sit there, wishing I had a paper bag. Instead of breathing in it, I'd cover my head and go ahead and put myself out of my misery.

Tessa's brow is creased into a deep V. She does NOT look happy.

"Wait. Start over. *What?*"

It doesn't go much better than my first attempt, but by two in the morning, I have sufficiently explained every word, every look, every touch, and every assumption I made about what he was thinking and what I thought about every single thing. You know, we do the girl thing and DISCUSS.

Turns out, Tessa doesn't have a big plan for New Year's Eve. She wanted to keep her options open. So, when I told her about Jared's invite to Asher Caldwell's party, she was all about it. In the morning, Jared calls and asks if we'll please come. I say yes.

As we're getting ready that night, Tessa is far more excited than I am. I've just had the best week of my life and the letdown is thick. When I think about Ian and how things were left between us, I have to fight hard not to fall into a sinking pit of … all that is disgusting. Mostly, I just feel really stupid for letting myself get so caught up in the romance of the trip. I don't exactly feel played because he certainly didn't take advantage of me, but it's almost worse because he acted like he really had strong feelings for me. Like he meant every word and every touch.

I'm so confused.

I choose a short black dress and my hair is falling in loose waves down my back. I haven't gotten a haircut since I came to New York and it's grown like crazy. I slap on some makeup, but my heart isn't into any of this. Tessa's wearing a green dress that brings out the green in her eyes. Her hair is that perfect shade that every woman with blonde hair wants. She looks stunning.

The party is already going strong when Tessa and I get there. It's in Asher's swanky penthouse. I've never seen anything like it. The only word I can think of is:

opulence. Everywhere. Everything is so over the top, it's almost gaudy. I have on some killer heels so I can see over most of the crowd and spot Jared right away. I grab Tessa's arm and we make our way to him.

The music is pumping and there are couples already sweating as they dance. Some of them are making me uncomfortable as they take the meaning of grinding to a jaw-dropping, shudder-inducing, I-need-to-go-scrub-my-corneas level. Ew.

Jared turns just as we are within a foot of him, and he yells over the music, "Sparrow! Hey!" He starts moving toward us, and I can hear Tessa murmuring under her breath. She likes what she sees. Oh yes. This is good. Why did I not think of this before now? It isn't often that I meet a man worthy of Tessa. Jared just might be.

He gives me a hug and kisses my cheek. "You look amazing tonight, Sparrow," he says.

"You look really great, too, Jared. Hey, this is Tessa!"

He has already turned to her, and I can tell he likes what he sees, too. She is beaming up at him, while he takes her hand and holds it up to his lips. Oh this is good. This is really good.

We talk for a few minutes and before long, Tessa just can't stand still anymore. "Do you wanna dance?" Jared asks.

She clutches his arm and they go out on the dance floor and start doing their thing. I stand and try to wipe the huge smile off my face. It's far too soon to be excited. It's just a dance.

I decide to grab a drink and on my way to the bar, I see Asher Caldwell talking up a blonde Playboy type. He's taller than I expected and even better looking. The girl is holding onto his arm and edging closer to him by the second. I've googled the projects Asher has worked on and I'm impressed. He's turned several floundering bands completely around with his production. *I wonder what Ian would think of me being at Asher Caldwell's house* runs through my mind. Who cares? I'm tired of wondering what Ian Sterling thinks.

As I step up to the bar, I'm so close to Asher, I can hear his husky voice. I've always had a thing for hoarse voices. In my opinion, it's the only worthwhile part of having a cold. Or I guess in his case, he's just lucky. That would be even better.

Ian is taller and his voice is even sexier, but who's comparing?

I am sipping my raspberry flirtini when I turn around to find Tessa and Jared, and I nearly run over Asher. He has suddenly appeared on my heels. I lift the drink to keep it from spilling all over him and it douses my hand.

He seems amused.

"I'm so sorry. I nearly ruined your jacket." I gush before I have time to think.

Asher seems to only have eyes for my chest. I clear my throat. He lifts his eyes slowly, taking his time. Until he realizes I am staring at him, and he curses under his breath and holds his hand out to me.

"Sorry. You caught me gawking. Who *are* you?" He takes the drink out of my hand and leans over the bar for a napkin. "Here, this will help." He motions to the bartender and the guy gets to work making me another.

I dry my hand as best as I can with a cocktail napkin.

"Come on, we'll get you cleaned up." He ignores my sticky hand and tucks it in his arm.

I still haven't said a word. I suppose I should feel nervous when he leads me down a hallway away from everyone, but he is being so polite, I don't feel worried.

He opens his bedroom door and I open my mouth to protest when he says, "My room has the nicest bathroom. I'll guard the door so no one bothers you."

"Thank you." I follow where he's pointing, and he keeps his word and stands at the door. The noise of the party is nonexistent back here. It's definitely the nicest room in the house, much more understated. Maybe his wealthy great-great aunt decorated the rest of the place.

I quickly wash my hands and ignore my temptation to snoop. When I open the door to the bathroom, Asher is leaning against the closed bedroom door and studying me.

"You are gorgeous," he says.

"Thank you," I say, quietly.

"What's your name?"

"Sparrow."

"Beautiful." He seems fixated on my legs now, and it's getting uncomfortable. I get to the door and am reaching out to grab the handle when he puts his hand on my arm. "Dance with me?"

I open the door now and walk out. He is right behind me.

"Hey, I'm not as lecherous as I seem, I promise," he laughs.

"Yeah, you need to alert your eyeballs. Stick them back in your head, buddy." I roll my eyes at him. Childish, I know, but really.

His laugh echoes in the hallway. "Oh, she's got a mouth on her, too. I like that." His eyes are laughing at me.

Just as I'm about to reach the end of the hallway, he reaches out his hand again. "Sparrow. One dance?"

I sigh. "Sure." I give in. I really do think he's harmless. Not to mention, really good-looking. He's like the polar opposite of Ian. Bleached blonde hair, blue eyes, tattoos peeking out of his shirt. I've seen pictures in People with his shirt off and he's covered with ink. He makes it look hot, that's all I know.

Playboy girl is one of the first people I see when we come out, and Asher puts his arm around me as we walk past her. It makes me cringe. I don't want him to get the wrong idea, and I also feel bad for her.

I turn to say something and his face is so close to mine, my nose touches his chin. "Maybe this isn't a good idea," I say.

"What?" The music is really loud, but I know he heard me.

"I don't think—"

He grabs my waist and pulls me in, as close as he can possibly get. What is one dance gonna hurt? I begin to move and let the rhythm take over. Asher is matching me move for move. The longer we dance, the more I put Ian out of my mind and enjoy the night. One song goes into another and another and another. It feels good to let go.

Asher doesn't leave my side the rest of the night. As it turns out, the guy is really funny. I forget all about him being Mr. Richie Rich, even when we go by his gold-plated fireplace to catch our breath and have a drink. Tessa and Jared walk over and Jared introduces Tessa to Asher before I get a chance. Jared and Tessa are clearly into each other.

Tessa leans in, "Are you okay, Ro? Having fun?" I

nod and she slits her eyes to the side, looking at Asher out of the corner of her eye, appraising him. She leans in closer and gets in my ear. "Well, you know what I always say, '*The best way to get over one music hotshot is to find another.*' I might have just made that up." She winks at me while I hug her and laugh. "It's a good one, though, right?"

"I think you might be onto something." I whisper in her ear. "I didn't think I'd have fun tonight."

"I'm so glad you are," she says and kisses both my cheeks.

"Sparrow, you ready to get back out there?" Asher points over his shoulder. I've never been with a guy who likes to dance like he does. The man can move. *Really* move.

We finally stop dancing when the countdown to midnight begins. I look around for Tessa and she and Jared are still joined at the hip. We're all yelling, "5, 4, 3, 2, 1— Happy New Year!" Streamers and confetti go flying and while I'm still looking up at all the flying colors, Asher Caldwell pulls me in and kisses me.

- 9 -

The MORNING After

The next morning, I wake up and stretch my tired muscles. I'm grateful I didn't have too much to drink last night because I'd really be miserable this morning. My body aches like I'm dying. I didn't realize I was so out of shape.

I crawl out of bed and head to the coffeepot. I had such a fun night, but I can't shake the troubled feelings I'm having about Ian. It feels like I betrayed him somehow. The kiss with Asher. I didn't see that coming. It was a good kiss. But ... it doesn't seem right. I remind myself that Ian and I have made no promises to each other. In fact, I think I got the brush off when we parted ways. I shouldn't feel guilty for acting like any college girl would. And Asher Caldwell. I still haven't wrapped my mind around that. First Ian Sterling and then Asher Caldwell. I wonder if they know each other.

I'm trying to make sense of it when a wave of nausea stops me mid-step. The next second, I'm running to the bathroom and coffee is a distant memory.

The day fades in and out like this. I can't stop throwing up. Every part of me hurts. I have a fever and dream crazy dreams. Tessa comes to check on me and I shoo her out of the room, so she doesn't catch whatever I have. My phone rings off the hook, and I turn it off and sleep the day away.

The next day, Tessa comes in with toast and hot tea and tries to get me to eat. I'm still feeling awful. She's looking at me like she's got a huge secret and I lean up and croak, "Spill. What's going on with you?"

"Well. We can talk when you're feeling better." She can't stop grinning. "For now you need to rest.

"I'm tired of resting. What is it?" And then it hits me. "Jared." I grin back.

Her whole face lights up. "He is amazing! Sweet Judas's mother … did you see his arms? And we kissed at midnight." Her eyes close and her lips are practically touching her eyeballs, they're up so high. "I'm going out with him tonight."

"You are? Oh, Tess. I like him so much!"

"Speaking of kisses…" Tessa's eyes are glittering. "Um, hello. You kissed Asher Caldwell the other night."

I hide under the blankets. "I can't believe I did that. I don't know what I was thinking." I groan and cover my head with the pillow, too.

"You guys looked HOT dancing together. I saw that kiss coming a mile away."

I groan again.

"I'm gonna give you a break since you've been so sick, but when you get out of this bed, we WILL talk about it."

I stay under the pillow until she leaves.

My fever breaks sometime in the night and I wake up the next morning feeling better. It's a good thing because I have to get to class this afternoon. When I get to the kitchen, a newspaper sits on the table—we never get the paper. It's opened to the Entertainment section, and I do a double-take when I see a picture of Asher and me taking over half the front page. We're in a provocative pose, dancing, and looking into each other's eyes like there is no one else in the room. So maybe I did have a little too much to drink. I'm already feeling weak from being sick, but this doesn't help. I take another look.

I rush to my computer and google Asher Caldwell and a dozen pictures of us come up from the party. I look at all of them and when I see the last one, I drop my head in my hands. It's us, kissing. No innocent kiss. His hands are on either side of my face and my hands are in his hair. And if I remember correctly, our tongues were down each other's throats. You can kinda tell in the picture, too.

My face is on fire, and it's not the fever.

I pick up my phone and see that I've missed 27 calls.

4 from my parents, wishing me a Happy New Year and then wondering why I'm not returning their calls…

3 from Tessa, checking on me, asking if she should pick up some chicken noodle soup and then saying never mind, she's picking up some chicken noodle soup.

17 are from various gossip magazines and news channels. I erase them all.

2 are from Asher. Very sweet. Saying he loved dancing with me and that meeting me was the best thing that happened to him last year. Cute. Oh, and when could we see each other again?

And then the last one. Ian.

My heart speeds up when I hear his voice.

"Uh, Sparrow? Hey, it's Ian. Look, I'd like to talk to you. Wanted to make sure you made it home fine … and to say Happy New Year. So…Happy New Year."

He sounds more awkward than I have ever heard him.

"Also, I'm gonna be playing out there in a few weeks. I'll text the exact date, but … I'd love to see you when I'm in town."

Pause.

"Well, sorry for the long message. I'm sure you've got better things to do than listen to me ramble." He laughs softly. "Bye, Little Bird. And … tell Asher hi for me."

And there it is. I should have known he'd come out of the woodwork when he saw me with another guy. Asher, no less. On a whim, I google their names and find several pictures of them together at various benefits and music award shows.

Seeing all the pictures of Ian makes me wonder why there was never any paparazzi on us. Never. The only thing I can figure is that Asher seems to LOVE the camera, and Ian always seems to be hiding from it. Interesting.

I'm mortified and here's why:

*Kissed someone within hours of meeting them
*48 hours from kissing the one I want
*Enjoyed both

God. What would Charlie say?

The next week, I get flowers from Asher. He calls every day. Sometimes I answer. Mostly, I don't.

Finally on day 7 of this, he says, "Why are you playing so hard to get?"

"I'm not playing anything," I say.

"I know you were into me. That kiss … the way we

move together."

"I really enjoyed the party. And I love to dance." I know I'm sounding mean, but I'm not trying to be. I really don't want to lead him on, and at the same time, I do genuinely like the guy. "And sometimes I enjoy the occasional kiss," I add, trying to soften my tone, but also trying to let him know that I don't want more with him.

"Are you seeing someone?"

I pause before answering. "There *is* someone I'm interested in." I mentally chew Ian out for making this complicated. How did he get me so wrapped up?

"Oh. Well, are you exclusive with this guy?"

"No." A sigh escapes before I can stop it.

"Then go out with me. Come on, Sparrow. It'll be fun. I can't stop thinking about you."

"I'm not looking for a relationship, Asher."

"Okay, perfect," he replies.

"I don't really want to be all over the gossip mags, either." My voice is sounding agitated, but I don't care.

"Why not? You look like a model!" He laughs. He lowers his seductive, husky voice. "Have you ever considered modeling for Victoria's Secret?"

I don't know what to say to that. I squeeze the phone so hard; I accidentally push the mute button with my cheek. I hurriedly fix it.

He laughs harder. "Hello? You there? You know you've got a body that needs to be seen."

"No!" I moan. "Forget it. Why are you tormenting me?"

"Relax, girl. Tonight? Pick you up at 7?"

"As friends." I brighten up. Yes, why can't we just be friends?

"Yeah," he draws out slowly, "whatever."

We hang up and I try to get homework done until I absolutely have to start getting ready. I keep going back to the kiss—it was nice. Really nice. Not like kissing Ian … but Ian isn't here.

My date with Asher is way mellower than I expected it to be, which is a relief. He was so intense the other night, screaming sexy with every move … I was a little afraid of what it might be like to be alone with him. I like to think I have boundaries, but well, he is a hot musician and apparently, I have a thing for those.

We go to a small hole in the wall restaurant. If there are cameras around, I am not seeing them. Asher is full of hilarious stories and has a hard time being serious about anything. It's been a long time since I've laughed so hard. I'm having such a great time and don't feel uncomfortable at all. I can't think about it too much; it's all a little too Twilight Zone. Maybe God is testing me to see if I can avoid temptation. I eye Asher's bulging arms while he's talking, tuning him out to study his tattoos. I never even liked tatts until this very moment. The way his muscles are straining against his shirt. Yes, the heavens are definitely messing with me, and I'm pretty sure I'm gonna fail.

Talk about a change—I briefly wonder about Michael and miss him a little bit. Something about Asher reminds me of Michael—I think it's the level of comfort I feel with both of them.

Before I can get further distracted, Asher is standing up and holding his hand out for me. "You still with me? Your eyes are glazed over."

I bug them out for him and he leans over and kisses

me. So much for just being friends.

The next few weeks sweep by with school and dates and lots and lots of conversations with me saying: *Friends*. And Asher saying: *Yeah, whatever*.

He seems fine knowing that I will still be seeing other people, but I haven't really had time to test that. He could be seeing a slew of other girls on the side, I haven't really thought about it. I know it wouldn't bother me if he is.

I've heard from Ian once since that voicemail and it was a text giving me the date and time of his show. I'm tempted to not go, but … who am I kidding? I can't *not* go. And who knows, maybe seeing him will give me closure somehow.

Tessa is determined to meet Ian. I haven't talked about him since that night I got back from the ski trip, and she's known better than to broach the subject. But when I told her he was coming to the Village, she immediately made plans with Jared for them to join me. Jared and Tessa are going strong; I love them together. He is completely smitten. She acts like she's nonchalant about the whole thing, but I can see the way she looks at him when she thinks no one is watching. Since she's dated a lot of frogs, it's probably best that she's being cautious, but I'm secretly hoping that Jared is the real deal.

When the night of Ian's show finally arrives and Tessa and I are getting ready together in our tiny bathroom, Tessa goes serious on me. "Ro." She says it so severely that I stop messing with my hair and look at her in the mirror.

"I know you've got it bad for Ian."

I don't bother denying it.

"Just be careful. Jared says he's a player—he has a different girl everywhere he goes. I just don't want you to get hurt."

My heart is thudding. I'm listening. I haven't wanted to think about this, but I know she's probably right.

"He obviously feels something for you, or he wouldn't keep coming back for more. But you can get any guy … don't waste your time on someone who doesn't appreciate what he's getting."

I nod my head and feel strangely close to tears. Ian seems to have that effect on me.

"On the other hand, if you think you've got him wrapped," she grins mischievously now, "then you lay it on him. Don't mess around. Put it ALL out there and get his balls in a vice once and for all." With that last statement, she adjusts my shirt so cleavage shows. I hike it back up so it won't. She pulls it back down and we continue our shirt battle a half dozen times until she huffs and says, "Trust me!" I leave it alone.

She's scary when she means business.

I'm a skittering tangle of nerves. When we get to the underground blues club, I give our names to the bouncer and he doesn't even ask for ID. I'm ushered right inside to a suede-covered booth close to the front. I'm happy for the dark. The atmosphere is romantic and I tell Tessa and Jared to go get a drink and take their time. The kid glove treatment is just making me more anxious.

An older redhead comes onto the stage, along with a guitar player and a guy with an upright bass. The woman looks like she's seen some miles. The club is packed and noisy. When she sits down at the piano and begins singing, the noise softens a touch, but doesn't die down. She's good, but doesn't seem to garner attention.

Forty-five minutes later, Ian comes out. The place goes mad with cheers and catcalls. Ian once said that he loves these small venues and would be content with this for the rest of his career. I wonder if he means it or if he secretly wants to be more famous.

When he hits the first note on his electric guitar, the crowd is deafening. I tear my eyes off of him long enough to stare at the people who have jumped out of their seats and are now standing as close to the stage as they can get. His voice rings out, a sultry gravel that cuts through the room. Everyone is fully immersed in Ian Sterling. He commands the room.

Later, when he's switched to acoustic guitar and is singing a soulful ballad, the room is silent as they take him in. I can't stop watching him. He has bewitched me.

All too soon, he's done. I can't even be happy that this means I will be with him; I'm too sad to hear him stop the music.

Ian exits the stage and for the first time in a couple hours, I look over at Tessa and Jared. They're staring, transfixed at the stage. I tap Tessa. "You okay, Tess?"

"Holy shit," she says. "Sorry, Ro."

"I know," I confirm.

"I get it now." She looks at me and nods. "I get it. And God, he's gorgeous." She clears her throat. "Sorry, Jared."

Jared shrugs. "I'm not blind."

"It's not just the music thing, though." I feel the need to explain what it is about him that has me spellbound.

"Really, it's not. He's so much more…" I give up. It's impossible to describe something that I don't even understand.

An enormous man with bulging biceps comes to the table. "Mr. Sterling asked me to escort your party back-stage." He holds out an arm and I stand up and take it.

"You remind me of the guy from that one movie … what is it? It's older. Stephen King. The Green Mile!" I say, stretching my neck up to look at him.

"I hear that a lot." He smiles down at me. He nods and pats my arm. A softie giant.

Tessa and Jared are behind me and when Softie reaches a red door, he stops and knocks.

Ian opens the door and is hugging me before I have a chance to think. After a long embrace, which renders me limp and useless, he pulls back and cups my face in his hands.

"Little Bird," he says. He looks almost relieved when he says it.

I love him.

- 10 -

PROSPECTS

We're all piled into a Lincoln Town Car, with Ian behind the wheel. He seems completely unfazed by the New York traffic. He pulls up to a quaint little restaurant in the Village. We've all been talking nonstop the entire drive. Excitement shares the space with us. I'm happy to see Ian and that Tessa seems to really like him. Tessa's happy to meet Ian and seems surprised by that. Jared is happy that Tessa's happy. And Ian just seems happy to see me. My heart is full.

Our conversation never falters once. Tessa grills Ian about where he's been the last month. I know she's wanting to get even more personal and ask "why the hell" he hasn't called me, but she restrains herself. Thank God for small miracles.

There's only one awkward moment when Tessa brings up Asher. I think she catches herself off guard, but tries to cover quickly. Ian is answering her question about playing with Jagged, the alternative band that has gone platinum in the past six months.

"Asher produced them, didn't he, Ro?" It feels like every eye turns on me all at once.

"Um, yeah. I think he did," I stutter.

Ian looks at me then, his gaze different than what it's been throughout the evening. I hate the word *smolder,* but I can't think of another word for what his eyes are doing in

124

this moment. It's like they've gone black and are swimming with feeling. Ugh. What has he done to me? I'm talking in romance novel terms.

I can't read what the look is saying, though. Then, he smiles and my heart lifts. The moment loses its awkwardness.

It's some time later when we drop Tessa and Jared off at the apartment. I look at Ian. "Would you like to come in?" I ask.

"I was thinking we could go for a drive … if you're up for it."

"I don't have class tomorrow. I'm up for it," I awkwardly reply.

"Perfect."

We drive through the traffic and end up at Prospect Park. It's beautiful, even in the dark.

"This is one of my favorite places in New York," Ian says. "It's gorgeous in the daytime. We'll have to come back."

My breath quickens at the thought of a future date, even though I'm trying to play it cool.

The weather is brisk but feels good on my flushed skin. Around Ian, I am in a constant state of heat. Take that however you want, it will fit.

We stop by the water and look at the small bridge across the way. The water is still and serene. I can't remember the earlier nerves that threatened to overtake me. I'm calm and content. Ian has my hand in his and he looks down at my mouth. His fingers brush over my lips. Light as a feather, his fingertips tease me.

"I could be so bad with you." He groans and pulls

away, holding his hands in the air. He gives his hair a haphazard tug. "God, girl. You're driving me crazy."

The feeling is mutual. He makes me want to forget my own name.

We walk a little ways, the moonlight bouncing off the water and making everything shimmer.

"This reminds me of a lake we used to have by our house," Ian says softly, pointing at ducks getting out of the water. "I like to visit this park every time I'm in town. And remember when things were simpler."

He leans back against a tree and pulls me back against him. We look out at the water and I feel his lips against my neck, kissing so softly it makes me shiver. My body is zinging with hopped up nerve endings.

"I miss the ocean, but this is peaceful, too," I whisper.

"Sparrow," he says against my neck. His breath feels hot against my goosebumps.

I can't think when he does that.

He turns me around to face him and holds my face in his hands. When he leans down to kiss me, my body feels heavy. My knees do that obnoxious weak trick. His lips tease me, just as his fingers did before. And then his tongue flicks in softly and I think I'm going down. I can't hold back any longer. I grab his hair and kiss him as hard as I've been wanting to all this time. He groans and his hands start roaming as he has his way with my mouth— and abruptly, he stops. He leans back so he can look in my eyes. "Baby. We should go." He wraps his arms around me and hugs me while we catch our breath.

He holds out his hand and we walk back to the car. I sigh and get back in my seat, buckling up. That rebuffed feeling returns, and I try to ignore it. I should be glad that he's being so considerate of me. I'm not, though. It stings.

We're both quiet. Before I know it, we're in front of my apartment and Ian is giving me a chaste kiss goodnight. "Can I see you tomorrow?" he asks.

"Of course."

"I'll let you sleep. How about I pick you up at 11?"

I nod. "That sounds perfect."

He puts his hand on my cheek and leans his forehead against mine. "Sparrow. You are perfect."

"No, I'm not."

"To me, you are."

I shake my head and he puts his finger on my lips.

"You are," he whispers.

I try to get out of the car without collapsing in a heap. That man. He does things to my insides, making me the equivalent of mush.

The next day, I dress in the jeans Ian bought me that day in San Francisco and a new sage green blouse that Tessa says looks insane with my eyes. I hope I will be irresistible to Ian. He shows up right at 11 and I'm slightly shy as I show him our teensy place.

"I like it," he says as soon as he walks in the door.

I laugh. "You've barely even seen it."

"I can tell. It's homey. It feels good in here."

"Come see my room," I grab his hand bashfully and lead him to my bedroom.

He shuts the door behind him and pulls me in. "Mmmhmm. Feels good in here, too." He kisses my nose and then lightly touches my lips with his.

I smile against his mouth. "Have you even looked?"

He pulls back and twirls me around in a circle.

"Um. Yes? It's lovely," he answers and his hands close around my waist. "We have a city to go explore," he says, playing with one of my curls. "You ready?"

We head downstairs to the car.

"You hungry?"

I nod. "I am. I haven't eaten yet."

"Okay, how does breakfast sound then? I know a place you'll love…" He leans down and kisses my cheek before opening the door.

"Let's do it." I smile up at him.

We go into a diner that looks straight out of the movie *Grease*. Instead of sitting across from me, Ian slides in next to me. He stares at me and his finger runs along my cheek, down my neck and stops just short of where my blouse dips into a V.

His eyes are seductively hooded and I couldn't look away if I tried.

"You're an angel."

"You're trouble," I laugh.

"I can't keep my hands off you," he says.

"I don't want you to."

"Is this how you talk to Asher?"

My hand had been playing with the veins in his arm and it goes completely still. "No."

He laces his fingers in mine. "Good." He closes his eyes for a moment. "I mean, you're free, Sparrow. I know I don't have any claim on you, I hope you know that. I just … I like to think we have … something here…" His voice trails off. "There's something about you that makes me feel I could do this…" He waves his hand back and forth between us and then puts his head in his hands and goes silent for what feels like an hour.

The waitress brings our food in the meantime and neither of us make a move to touch it.

"I don't know what I'm saying, Sparrow. I *am* trouble. You should run now. Run while you can. Before I screw you up. Asher is a nice guy."

"Ian. I was joking. Why? Why do you do this? Every time we're together, it feels like we..." I stop when he places his fingertips on my lips.

"Sparrow—forget I said anything, okay? Let's ... let's just enjoy this day."

I shake my head.

"Please?" he asks.

Against my better judgment, I agree to it and the mood lightens considerably. It's like nothing ever happened. Just like that, Ian is his usual carefree self. I swallow the fear that this really is *it* this time and make the conscious decision to do what he said: Enjoy the day.

We fill the day with incredible memories. Clam chowder in a bread bowl. Feeding the ducks in Central Park. Staring at the Statue of Liberty across the water. Buying little trinkets in Chinatown.

And his eyes all day long, as if they're memorizing every trace of me.

All too soon, it's late. I hate to admit it, but I'm exhausted. We've pulled up to my apartment, and I don't want to let him go.

"Come up?" I ask.

"I better not."

I chew my lip nervously and he leans over and puts his forehead against mine.

"I think I love you," he says.

I scoff at him. "Don't say that unless you mean it."

He shrugs. "I meant it." His eyes look luminous, even in the dark.

And just like that, I have hope. All the warnings, fears and apprehension about Ian Sterling melt away and peace takes its place. I have no idea what he will do next, but in the rented Lincoln Town Car outside my apartment, it doesn't matter. It will be all right.

He walks me to the door and for the first time, our departing words don't leave me in despair.

I float inside and Tessa is there waiting for me. She sees the look on my face and grins from ear to ear.

"Ahhh, you look like a satisfied woman. Did you ... did ... you guys?" She tries to read my expression and crinkles her eyebrows together.

"Nooooo, we didn't," I answer. "But ... it was a good day. I feel like we made progress. Finally. And he said he thinks he loves me," I say, trying to tone down my excitement.

"What?" She yells. "Well, isn't that—well, he's just full of surprises, isn't he. That's a little ... sudden."

"I know. I basically ridiculed him when he said it, but ... I don't know. I didn't say it back. I'm not ready for that, but—what if he really does? Love me?"

"He'd be crazy not to!" Tessa says. "This is bonk. He's all over the place. All about you and then aloof and then back again and then in love. I can't keep up with him. So, when do you see him again?"

I cover my face. "I don't know. I don't know! This really *is* crazy. All I know is he makes me feel things I've never felt and I don't care—he might be all wrong for me, but I don't care!"

"I hope he's worth it, then," Tessa says as she wraps me in a huge hug. "If he hurts you, I will hunt him down and cut his fingers and toes to the knuckle."

I lean back and look at her. "*What?*"

"Never mind. YAY!" She smiles again and I can't help it, I laugh until I get the hiccups.

The next morning, my phone wakes me up. I smile as I groggily answer it, sure that it's Ian, calling before he leaves town. I look at the clock. 9 A.M. Whoa. He left hours ago.

"Hello?" I try a sexy voice on for size.

"Hey," Asher says. "Been missing you. Wanna get some breakfast with me today?"

I feel a pang in my chest. I need to talk to Asher and better that I do it in person than over the phone.

"Sure, I can meet you in 40 minutes."

I walk to the pastry shop that Asher and I have frequented since we became friends and he's already there, waiting on me. His face lights up when he sees me and that guilt is more than a sharp pang this time.

He stands up and hugs me as I near his table. "Hey, gorgeous. How are you?"

"I'm really well. How about you?"

He hears the standoffish lilt in my voice and studies me. "You sure?"

"Yes. Asher, we need to talk."

"Uh-oh. Come on, sit down. Do you want your usual?"

"Yes, please."

When he comes back with my coffee and a croissant, I thank him and get right after it. "Asher, remember how I told you I'm interested in someone?"

"Of course, I do," he says. "But it seems like you've been spending an awful lot of time with me."

"Yes. And I've loved it. You're wonderful. I'm so glad we've become friends." I reach over and take his hand.

He grimaces. "Ouch. I hoped I could help you forget."

"You've helped, but you haven't helped me forget."

"Who is this guy, Sparrow? And does he know what he has? Because I'm not willing to give you up if he doesn't."

"Well, the funny thing is, you know him…" I look at him and wish I didn't have to tell him who it is.

"Who?" he demands.

"Ian Sterling."

A sharp laugh comes out of him, making me jump. "You've gotta be kidding me. Ian Sterling? That's who you're throwing me to the wolves for?"

"Come on, Asher, don't put it like that. I've told you all along that I just want to be friends."

"Your kisses didn't feel like friendship."

"I'm sorry for that. Turns out I'm a bit of a kiss whore," I say with a half-grimace smile. "I really am sorry."

He laughs in spite of himself. "Sparrow … you're … I can't be mad at you! You did tell me all along the way. I should have listened. It's like I'm the girl here." He shakes his head, but his eyes are still smiling. "Have you really thought this through? Ian Sterling is a vagabond. Not to mention, he likes the women. Hell, I know what it's like to have women at my disposal. I'm not sure Ian can give that up, though. I know you're not ready to settle down yet, but when you are, I already have everything in place. I'm not sure Ian will *ever* settle down."

"I can't help who I fall for," I answer.

He looks sad as he nods. "I will be here if you change your mind."

I wonder when Asher decided he was capable of settling down. From all the things I've read about him, he appeared to be just as much of a player as Ian. It's confusing.

"Asher…"

"Can we still hang out?" he asks.

"Yes!" I'm relieved, but still cautious as I take both of his hands. "Yes, please. If we can, you know … not do the kissing thing and really just be friends now?"

"I'll try," he promises. He removes his hand from mine and holds it out again for me to shake. Hopefully, we have finally come to an understanding.

I'm a little disappointed when Ian doesn't call all day. I really thought he would. By the time night falls, I've talked myself into being okay about it. He's not a phone person. Why would he start to be now? I'll probably hear from him tomorrow. Or maybe the next day, when he's settled somewhere.

Two months go by.

The wondering is agony.

*Where is he?
*Why hasn't he called?
*Did he mean anything he said?
*Has he met someone?
*Why won't he just call?

And then the pseudo answers.

*He's out playing all over the freakin' country.
*He must really hate the phone. Or it's his schedule.
*He meant it; he just doesn't know what to do about it.
*He's meeting a different *someone* every night.
*The time difference screws everything up.
Then there's the self-ridicule.
*I was crazy to think he would ever be a permanent part of my life.
*He wouldn't waste his time talking to *me* on the phone.
*Of course, he didn't mean a word of it. Who do I

think I am?

*There are a thousand prettier, smarter, more talented, funnier, bigger boobs, longer haired, better legs that are NEVER hairy, way sexier, more experienced girls out there.

*He will never call me.

And then he does! He calls. It's late one Friday night and I've been up studying. And I'm so happy to hear his voice, I can't even stay mad. At first, I'm distant, but he just keeps asking question after question. We cover school, family, New York, Tessa, Jared and more school. It's been over an hour and he doesn't seem ready to let me go. He's been all over the country, just as I thought. But that doesn't seem to be ending anytime soon, so I'm not sure why he's calling now.

"Little Bird … are you happy?"

"Well … I don't know. I'm okay. Are you happy?"

"I miss you," he says softly.

"I miss you, too."

"You should come see me. Do you have any time off soon? I'm gonna be in Texas for a while. I'll fly you out."

"I do have a long weekend in a couple weeks."

"That would be great."

He asks the exact dates and I mark it on the calendar by my desk: GO SEE IAN!!!

"You must be tired. It's late here and even later for you. What are you doing tomorrow?"

And then another hour has passed. By now, I'm in my bed, phone clutched to my ear and we're both talking in sleepy whispers. Neither of us wants it to end. But eventually, he can tell I'm about to fall asleep.

"Night, Sparrow Kate Fisher. Dream of me tonight. I'm already dreaming of you."

"I will," I say and I know that it's true.

My dreams are all over the place, but Ian is in every scene.

The next night he calls again. And we repeat our gloriously wonderful dance of sweet talk and every day chatter. I'm so happy, I can't even stand it. He must be past whatever was holding him up. I make the decision before I fall asleep to not over-analyze it any more. He's calling me! We're on the right track.

When he doesn't call the next night or the next or the next, I'm still riding high from those two conversations. He'd said he was flying out to California, so I know he's busy and now there's an even larger time difference.

When he still hasn't called the next week and the dates to "GO SEE IAN!!!" are looming over my head like a raging gorilla in heat, I begin my downward spiral.

The dates come and go.

Nothing. Not a word from him.

I'm angry. No, you know what? I'm *pissed*. Yeah, that's right I said it.

Pissed, pissed, pissed, pissed, pissed. Flippin' *pissed*.

Another month goes by and it's the last week of

school. I have studied until I feel like I could unscrew my head and all that would be left is string cheese. After it's been left out of the refrigerator. When it's all floppy.

I'm exhausted, but manage to get through finals. I have no idea how I'm doing and at this point, I don't care. I've written paper after paper after paper and couldn't tell you what any of it is about. It will be a shock if any of it makes sense.

Ian Sterling has invaded my head space, my body, my guts, if you will. Even now, he's in there waving his arms around, shaking up all my organs and muscles and nerves and blood and leaving me all gutted out.

Asher is a steady presence. He knows I'm sad about Ian, but I haven't told him much about it. Half of the time, I'm glad for his company and the distraction. The other half of the time, I'm mad at him, too. He keeps trying to show me how wonderful he is, how doting, how sweet. At every turn, I throw in some remark or gesture to remind him that we're friends and that's all it will ever be. I get the sinking feeling that he thinks if he just keeps doing all the right things long enough, he'll convince me otherwise. It's exhausting. I can't handle the guilt of hurting some-one. He keeps pushing, and I keep putting more distance between us.

I do agree to go to a charity function with him. He asked me months ago and it had sounded fun at the time. He calls to see if I'm still going with him.

"Sure, I'll go. I just … yes, yes, I'll do it."

"I might have bought you a little something."

"You did? You shouldn't have."

"Wait until you see it to decide."

Later that evening, I open the box that Tessa has

placed on my bed. She's waiting to watch me open it. "Asher dropped it off this morning. He seems excited about whatever's inside."

I heave a huge sigh. I've been doing a lot of sighing these days.

Inside the box are champagne-colored shoes with tiny jeweled flowers stitched along one side. They're exquisite. The prettiest pair of shoes I've ever seen.

A little note card says:

These reminded me of you.
Asher

I put my head in my hands.

"He's got it bad," Tessa says.

"What am I going to do about him?"

"Why do you have to do anything? He likes you. He knows how you feel or *don't* feel…" She sits beside me on the bed and pulls my head onto her shoulder. "Look, I know you're a mess over Ian. But, you've got a great guy here who is willing to let you be a mess. Go, have fun for a while." She squeezes me tighter. "And don't feel bad about it! I mean it!"

We go shopping later and I find the perfect dress. It's a short vintage dress, sleeveless, with a fitted bodice and flowy skirt in the same shade as the shoes. It's like the two were meant to go together.

Asher's mouth drops when he sees me. My hair is

pulled back. I do feel elegant. Maybe Tessa's right and I need this time out. I've been sad long enough.

"You are stunning," Asher says.

"Thank you. And thank you so much for the shoes, Asher. They're beautiful."

"Beautiful shoes for a beautiful girl." He smiles at me and then his look gets mischievous. "Your legs look a thousand miles long, mm, mm, mm," he shakes his head and does a quiet whistle.

I roll my eyes. "C'mon, you, let's go."

After my little fit with the New Year's Eve pictures, Asher has done his best to keep our appearances in the gossip magazines to a minimum. Every now and then, a photographer finds us and I'll see a picture in Tessa's stack of magazines, which is just surreal, but for the most part, we've maintained some distance.

However, all the big dogs are out tonight. When Asher and I pull up in his limo and step out, the cameras' clicks are a dull roar. He takes my hand and leads me through the chaos. Just before we step inside, Asher turns around and gives the paparazzi a wave. I look back too and am blinded by all the flashes.

The dinner is delicious. The entertainment entertaining. Asher is a perfect date. He has our table charmed and keeps the conversation going whenever there's a lull. I'm trying really hard to be fun, but my mood is still dark. I can't seem to snap all the way out of it.

Asher bids on a gold antique mirror that used to belong to John Hughes' first wife, Ella Rice. It's beautiful, but I always preferred silver myself. *It's for a good cause.* However, it will fit right in with Asher's gaudy apartment.

A vast amount of money is raised to keep the arts in

public schools. And everyone goes home with a warm, satisfied feeling. After all the champagne, I'm even feeling fairly warm and satisfied, until Asher takes me to *his* house instead of mine. I didn't even notice where we were until we get out.

"What are we doing here? I thought you were taking me home." My tone is edgy. I'm tired and while it's been a fun evening, I just want to go to bed.

"I thought it would be nice if we have a drink here before I take you home," Asher says, rubbing my shoulder. He leans down and nuzzles my neck.

I brush him off. "Asher," I say with warning. "It would have been "nice" if you had asked me first." I stare him down.

Asher nods. "You're right. But come on, you would have said no. You've been on edge for weeks. I just want you to have a good time. I'm ready to see you happy again."

My hands are on my hips. I want to glare at him, but I can't really be aggravated with him. He has done everything he can to make me feel better, and I can't even spend another hour with him?

"Okay. But just for a little while. I'm really tired."

An indistinguishable time later … I have had countless raspberry flirtinis and am feeling lighter than I have in months. I twirl around the expansive living room and watch how the skirt of my dress flies out perfectly. I know something is nagging me just under the surface, but I can't even think of him tonight. Thinking of him is killing me. It's wearing me down. I don't want to be worn down. I want to dance. I want to laugh. I want to take off this dress now. It's hot in here, and I'm so tired. I just need to twirl more.

Asher is feeling happy too. He laughs when my dress falls to the ground. He reaches out and touches my skin and I jump, flirtini splashing across my chest. I can't ever keep a whole cocktail in the glass when I'm in this house. He pulls me close and leans down, and so softly that I can barely feel it, he licks the liquid off, his tongue flicking just under the top of my lacy bra. It gives me chill bumps. I close my eyes. It's nice.

I really do want to forget. Maybe this will help me forget.

I vaguely remember Asher laying me on his bed. I can picture him over me, but then—nothing. The rest is a blur. When I wake up the next morning, my head is pounding, and at first, I don't know where I am. The sheets feel so soft against my skin. I sit up. Panic. I am completely naked.

God. What have I done?

I look over and Asher is still sleeping. He's faintly snoring. I get out of bed and look down where I'd slept. My stomach turns. I run to the bathroom and get sick. I grab a towel and wrap it around myself, willing the nausea to stop. It doesn't. I'm sick again, until nothing is left.

I've lost my virginity. I didn't even know it went missing, but now it is long gone. The blood on the sheets was my first clue. The soreness between my legs, a confirmation.

It might be minutes or it could be hours, I'm not sure,

but all the pain of the last few months hits, and I weep on Asher's cold bathroom floor. I've never felt so desolate, so alone, so angry. And even though I got myself into this mess, I still feel violated. I don't even know what happened. Did I come onto Asher? Were we so drunk we couldn't help ourselves? Why can't I remember anything?

Then it comes back to me. I remember taking off my dress. I caused this to happen. I don't remember anything else, but I know that I can't blame Asher for my stupidity. I force myself to get up and creep to the door, making sure Asher is still sleeping before I sneak out of the bathroom. He is. I grab my underwear, make my way to the living room and pick up my dress. My hands are shaking so hard, I can barely put it on. I see the shoes from Asher and I want to be sick all over again. Only because I don't want a cab driver to ignore the crazy barefoot girl, I put the shoes on and close the door behind me.

A fleet of cab drivers wait outside Asher's building, and I'm home in no time. I quietly let myself in and get in the shower. The tears pour out of me as scalding water pounds onto my skin.

I had saved myself this long—nineteen years, to be exact. I wanted my first time to be special. My parents taught me to wait for marriage and I always thought I would … until I met Ian. Then all I could think about was how I wanted him. For a blink of an eye, it seemed like I might have him and then I lost him again. No, I didn't lose him. I never *really* had him. Just the almost promise of him.

At the very least, I believed that I'd be present for the

experience. Now, I wasn't even given that. Just a drunken encounter with a guy I thought was my friend. Was he so drunk that he couldn't be bothered to wait until we were coherent?

Rage settles in my chest.

When I get out of the shower, the steam is thick. My skin is beet red and has stripes on it from the water. I put on my sweats and go to my room. My phone is on the bed with a text from Tessa saying she's at Jared's and a dozen missed calls from Asher. I don't even listen to his messages; I just delete every single one.

I've taken something for my head and am crawling into my bed, when there's pounding on the door. It goes on and on. I ignore it. I hear him yelling, "Sparrow, please! I need to talk to you. Open the door!" I cover my head and put a pillow over the covers. He stops for a couple minutes and then starts knocking again. "Sparrow, I'm sorry!" Finally it's quiet.

I fall asleep under the pile.

It's been a couple of weeks since that night, and I still feel numb. Asher calls once a day. I still haven't talked to him. I've started a compulsive habit of showering multiple times a day since it happened. I know I'm not right in the head about it all, but I don't know what to do to get better. Part of me wishes I knew what happened, but mostly, I'm glad that I don't. I wonder if any of it will come back to me.

Tessa and I have three more days in the city before we fly home. She's going to spend most of that time with Jared and even though she keeps trying to talk me into coming along with them everywhere, I turn her down. I haven't told her what's wrong with me. She knows it's bad, but she's not pushing me. I forcefully told her once that I can't talk about it and she backed off then. She knows I will when I'm ready.

I've found a new coffee shop, one where I'm sure I won't run into Asher, and I'm about to head there when the phone rings. I grab it out of my pocket and am trying to see who it is, but am all clumsy. I accidentally push *talk*.

Oh, crack.

I hold it up to my ear.

"Hello?" he's saying. "Little Bird? You there?"

"Hello?" I answer and then kick myself for saying anything. I should have just hung up.

"How are you?" he asks.

"Oh, I'm just fine, Ian. Just *fine*." My voice is one big razory bite. "And how are you?"

I don't want to know how he is. Even in my hostility, the never-ending manners I was raised with force their way out.

"I'm good. It's so great to hear your voice, Sparrow. So great. I'm in Atlanta right now, on my way…"

"What do you want, Ian?" I interrupt.

"What do you mean?"

"I mean, what do you want? Why are you calling?"

"I just had to hear your voice," he says.

"Well, now you've heard it. Anything else?"

"Sparrow … I …"

"What? *Sparrow,* what?" I mock his confused tone. "Spit it out, Ian."

"I'm at the airport right now, I'll be in New York this afternoon. I want to see you." He does spit it out. I didn't know he could talk that quickly.

Complete silence.

"Sparrow?"

"I don't think so, Ian."

"What do you mean?"

"I *mean*, I don't *think* so, Ian." I pull the phone away from my ear and am about to hang up when I hear him.

"Sparrow, wait! Please. Please just once?"

I hang up the phone and walk out the door to get my coffee.

- 12 -

Set STRAIGHT

I pull the shoes out of my purse and give them to the guy accepting donations at Goodwill.

Bye, prettiest shoes I have ever seen. I wish I'd never laid eyes on you.

Next, I walk by a farmers' market and even though we're leaving in a few days, I decide to bring some flowers home. I love the purple and green flower lettuces. I have them under my arm and am trying to see if I can smell even a hint of anything. Nope. I sigh. I can't seem to give up hope of smelling something someday.

I nearly get sucked into the bookstore, but resist the urge. I already have about two dozen books that I want to take home. I've missed reading for pleasure. It's so nice to put the textbooks aside for the summer.

Just as I near the corner by my apartment, the wind picks up and the air suddenly feels charged, electric. I turn, and there, on the stairs going up to my place, sits Ian. I want to run the other way, but he sees me and stands up.

He's smiling and holding a huge white flag. He waves it like crazy as I walk toward him. His smile falters when I don't say a word, but walk right past him, up the stairs and into my building. The door is closing behind me when he catches it.

"Sparrow," his voice is a caress.

That voice will be my undoing.

I get to the stairs and stop to look at him. He lifts his eyebrows, worried this time, and waves the flag again.

"I surrender." It resonates in the stairwell and pings from his mouth to the wall to the mailboxes to the stairs, and straight to my heart. Ping! It bounces back off again.

I turn around and walk up the stairs. All three flights. He tails me and when we reach my apartment and I go to open the door and walk inside, he pauses and speaks again. "Can I please come in?"

I open the door wider and he meekly walks in. I walk straight to the kitchen and put the flowers in water, arranging them in our only vase. There, that looks so pretty.

"Sparrow, please look at me."

I place the vase on the table by the couch and sit down, looking up at him. He sits down, hastily.

"You're mad at me."

I snort. I can't help it, it just rushes out.

"I deserve it," he says. He stares at me, trying to weigh how he should handle me, I'm sure. He's lost all his swagger and seems completely vulnerable. He looks like a little kid who's waiting for his punishment.

"You do," I finally respond.

His breath rushes out in a burst, and he reaches out to take my hand and drops it just as quickly when he sees the ice in my eyes.

"What can I do?" he asks.

"I don't know, Ian. I don't know what you expect."

"I'm so sorry. I just couldn't come into town and not see you."

"And you thought we'd jump right back where we left off, like we always do?"

He looks sheepish. That's exactly what he thought.

I jump up off the couch. I have to keep some distance between us. I pace in front of him.

"You invited me to come see you, Ian. We even talked specific dates and then *nothing*. Months go by. And not just this time, but *every* time, we say good-bye and I never know if I'm even going to hear from you again!" My voice is getting louder and louder with every sentence. "Just when I think '*it really is over this time*', you pop back up and everything's just hunky-dory? I don't get it!" I'm so mad, I want to cry. I take a deep breath instead. "You told me you thought you loved me. Not that I really believed it, but ... how messed up is that? You say that and then leave *again* and I don't hear from you for months *again*?"

I sit back down, but as far from him as I can get.

"I can't keep doing this," I say, feeling wrung out. "I'm sick of being out of sight, out of mind."

The loud hum of my refrigerator is ominous in the otherwise silent room. Out of the corner of my eye, I see Ian tugging his hair until it's a mess. It's a wonder the guy has so much hair left on his head, what with all the yanking.

Finally, he speaks. "I'm so sorry, Sparrow. I ... I haven't been fair to you. I've wanted you to have the full college experience. You're young; you need to do exactly what you want and not have any regrets later. That's what I want for you. When I'm with you, though, I can't see *past* you. I just want you and no one else, and I don't want anyone else to have you either. That's not fair."

148

"That's not your call," I tell him. "I've only wanted you, and you keep leaving me on the roller coaster by myself."

He inches closer to me, and I hold up my hand. He stops where he is and doesn't go any further.

"I'm no good with relationships, Sparrow. I'm not."

I laugh a dark, hollow laugh. "Yeah, that much I do know."

"Not a single man in my family has managed to keep a relationship. Not one. They've all destroyed the women in their lives. My dad, worst of all. My mom was a strong woman whose only wrongdoing was loving him. He crushed her. Every day. At first she didn't fight back, but when she did, the yelling and abuse would go for days on end. He wore her down until she was in the hospital, sick and incapable of surviving with him another day. As soon as she was away from him for any length of time, she got well again. She lost herself for a while, I didn't know if I'd ever get her back. Now, you'd never know she was ever sick. But she wouldn't be alive if she'd stayed with him. The Sterling men are cursed."

I reach for his hand then, and he lifts his eyes to mine, grateful. "I don't believe you're cursed," I tell him.

He runs his fingers over my hand and his expression is pained. "I'm not a good person, Sparrow. I … I'm not. I look at you and I see all the good and I know that I could never deserve someone like you."

My eyes well up. "That's not your call, either. I'm not perfect, Ian. And you *are* a good person. I don't know everything there is to know about you, but I do know that much."

His eyes go dark and he stands up, looking out my

window. His shoulders are slumped, defeated. I can't help but feel like I'm missing something. When he turns around, his features are soft again and he looks calmer.

"I think about you all the time. I just … I'm not good at this, and I don't want to keep you all tied up in me when I'm such a mess…"

I wait for him to say more. It's not quite enough.

He turns to face me then and takes my other hand in his. "You make me want to try. I almost feel like I could do it when I'm with you."

"Could do what?" I'm a little confused.

"Be in a relationship. With you. I don't really do the relationship thing, Sparrow."

"What does that mean? You just sleep around with whoever appeals to you at the right place, right time?"

"Well, not exactly, although, I went through a phase of that … back when I was around your age." He looks at me meaningfully then, making sure I'm listening. "I hope I'm a little smarter than that now, I don't want my dick to fall off, after all … with all the…" He waves his arms around and stops when he sees the look on my face. "What?"

"Eww."

"Which part?

"All of it."

"I'm sorry, I'm just trying to be honest with you. Should I have just said, 'No, I don't sleep around with random strangers'?"

I'm still trying to wipe the disgusted look off my face. "Yeah, maybe."

He shakes his head and the corners of his mouth lift up, but he tries to hide it.

"What about when you're not with me? What happens when you leave me?" I ask, finally throwing it all out there. "Do you have someone in every city? *Friends* who aren't *random strangers*?"

"Well, I'm single. Of course, I have *friends*, but none of them have ever come close to making me feel what you did in just one conversation…"

I take that in and process it for a few minutes. I make the mistake of looking at him while I think. He's intoxicating. And he's staring at me like he will move heaven and earth to do whatever I ask. I pinch the inside of my elbow to see if this is really happening. "Yep!" I yelp.

His forehead creases and he comes back over to sit by me. "What just happened?"

"*This* is happening. I just had to pinch myself to be sure."

He laughs then and the relief on his face is what gets to me most. He really does like me. I think he really does.

"What do you need from me? I'd like to try. To do this. Just—tell me what to do." He looks so earnest I believe he means it.

"Well, for starters, you can't assume that if we go months without talking, that we'll pick right back up to acting like a couple when we do see each other again."

He nods, his expression grave. "Agreed."

"And you don't have to call me all the time, but the nothing in between is definitely not working for me."

"I can call. How much would you like me to call? What's too much? What's too little?"

"Well, how often do you want to talk to me?"

"Every minute of every day." He lets out a small grin then.

I allow myself a small grin back, but then I dig right back in. "And if you invite me to come see you and even set a date for me to do so, don't you EVER back out of that without letting me know. And you better have a good reason for it if you do back out. There was no reason for you to just not even call and let me know if it wasn't working or you changed your mind ... or *whatever* happened."

"I'm an ass."

"Yes. That's still no excuse."

"You're right. I'm so sorry. Will you forgive me?"

"We'll see," I answer.

"Can I hug you?" he asks.

"Yes," I whisper.

His arms wrap around me and I love how I feel almost petite in his huge arms. My long gangly arms are tiny in comparison. His heart is pounding through our shirts and it endears him to me more. He seems so fragile right now, so vulnerable. I close my eyes and even though I'm afraid to hope, I want to believe him. I want him more than I want to be safe. I want him more than I want to stay sane. I want him more than I want anything.

"It's probably not going to work for you to call every minute of every day."

"Damn, I've already blown it."

The smile is bigger this time—I can't stop it. He leans over and kisses me lightly. It makes me dizzy.

He pulls back. "I'm not going to ask you to only belong to me, Little Bird. As much as I want you all to myself, I still think you need to enjoy your next couple years at school and not be too hung up on me."

I put my hands on his lips. "I'm already hung up on

you."

He puts a hand on each side of my face and kisses me again. "Still. I'm serious. You should date other people. But only when I'm not around. When we're in the same city, you're mine."

I wonder if the same is true for him. I'm his when he's not around. Is he mine? I don't ask this, though. My head is swimming with the way things have turned right side up again. And truth be told, I'm afraid I might not really want to know the answer to that question. What does this mean for all of his *friends*? I decide to take a risk and not try to figure it all out today.

Before I can panic with where my thoughts are already leading me, his lips are on mine again, silencing anything but the lust that is rousing from its sleep. I can't think straight when he does that with his tongue. My knees really do go weak, and I hang onto him for dear life. I want to feel his skin on mine.

Thoughts of Asher rush in my mind and nearly knock me over. I really am a slut. It's only been a couple of weeks since I ended up naked in Asher's bed with no memory of what happened the night before and now I'm going all weak from wanting to rip off Ian's clothes.

The guilt is an all-consuming cloud, threatening to open up and soak me with rain. My brief minutes of genuine happiness are now drenched. I back away from Ian and clear my throat. He looks concerned.

"Are you okay, Little Bird? What's wrong?"

"I'm no better than you," I say. "Trust me."

His seductive grin is back. "No, I'm way worse than you, I promise."

"No, really."

"No, *you* really."

I playfully push against his chest. His hard, muscled chest. He doesn't even budge. I close my eyes and lean my head against him.

Almost as if he's heard my thoughts, he says softly, "I'm yours, Sparrow. If you'll have me, I'm yours."

I don't say anything. I'm not sure what to think just yet.

"I'd like to take you somewhere. I think you'll like it." He runs his hands up and down my arms.

I look up at him. "Where?"

He holds out his hand. "Come on, let's go."

We grab a cab and pull up to Cupcake Heaven. I've heard of this place, but I've never been. The display case is magical. The flowers on the cupcakes are dreamy, so elegant.

"They're so beautiful. How can we eat them? They're too pretty to eat."

"Oh, but they taste so good." He kisses my hand. "Almost as good as you."

My skin goes hot. I wonder if this does last between us, if I will ever be cured of the splotches around him.

The girl behind the counter gets flustered when she sees Ian. Clearly she recognizes him. "Hi, Ian, how are you?

"Hey, Daisy. I am *great.*" His eyes crinkle as he smiles over at me.

She nods and smiles, glancing at me briefly before her eyes are drawn back to Ian. I understand. I can't stop looking at him either.

"One second, I have your order in the back."

I raise my eyebrow at him. Order?

She goes through the door and when she returns she has a large white box with a cute sticker that says *Sparrow*.

Now I'm raising both eyebrows at him. And he looks a little embarrassed.

He leans down and whispers in my ear, "So I may have called in this order BEFORE you and I spoke this morning." He stands up tall and waits for my reaction.

"Kinda presumptuous of you to assume I'd even be speaking to you after all the…" I wave my arms back and forth between the two of us.

"You're completely right. I won't make that mistake again," he vows. "But you *are* here, aren't you?"

I glare at him until I see his shoulders shake. He's teasing me again. I bite the insides of my cheek to keep from smiling.

I shove him, this time hard enough to make him step back. He's laughing, and he looks absolutely beautiful. The sun shines through the windows and highlights him just so…

He grabs me and holds me close. "I'm sorry, baby. I wasn't even thinking. You might have to set me straight on the protocol of keeping you … happy."

"I'm not hard to please."

Poor Daisy. I finally realize she's been standing there the whole time, her head following us back and forth. Her mouth is hanging slightly open and she looks envious.

"I'm sorry," I tell Daisy as I take the box, "don't mind us. Since it has my name on it, does that mean I can open it?"

"It sure does, Little Bird." Ian smiles sweetly.

I open up the box and gasp. Nestled inside are 6 cupcakes. The frosting is Tiffany blue and on every cupcake is a beautiful white sparrow, each one unique.

"They're perfect! I love them. Thank you!" I look at Ian and lay my head on his shoulder and then look at Daisy. "Did you make these?"

She nods shyly.

"They're spectacular. Each one."

"Thank you," she murmurs.

"Which one are you going to eat first?" Ian asks.

"Oh, I can't eat them. No. I won't be able to do that."

Ian lets go of me. "Nuh-uh. I will buy you more, baby. You're eating these." He looks up at the menu. "Need a coffee to go with it?"

He might be relationship-delayed, but he sure knows how to do *some* things right.

We take our cupcakes—Ian bought a few for himself, so he wouldn't be eating all of mine—and we walk over to Bryant Park. We sit close enough to hear the piano player but away from all the people. Our own little cupcake picnic.

Ian takes a cupcake out of my box and gently removes the paper. He leans over and puts it in front of my lips, waiting for me to take a bite. I look at him nervously. It's gigantic; I don't know how I'll ever get it in my mouth. The frosting makes it a MASSIVE cupcake. I realize there is no way to look sexy and get the thing eaten, so I just go for it. I open all the way and...

"Ohhhh. Myyyy. GOD. It's sooooo gooooooood. Mmmm," I moan and close my eyes.

"Hell, baby, you're causing problems for me," he

says against my lips. "Moan like that again and I can't be responsible for what I do." He licks the frosting off my mouth and then with his finger, he adds more frosting and repeats the process. When his tongue has certainly gotten all the frosting, he lifts the cupcake back up for me to take another bite. His pupils are taking over, like glistening black onyx.

I take another huge bite. "Mmmmmmmm." I'm not even putting on. It's seriously the best thing I've ever eaten.

He doesn't just lightly lick the frosting this time. He grips my face tight and plunges his tongue down my mouth. He's not messing around. I think he wants some of my cupcake for himself. I'm happy to give it to him.

By the time we've completely violated one cupcake, we're both sticky and incredibly turned on.

- 13 -

CRACK

"So I haven't even asked yet, what are you doing in town?"

We're back on my side of town. After getting all hot and bothered with the cupcakes, we decided to drop the rest off at my place and try to behave in the daylight. At least, I think that's what we've decided. I might be tempted to misbehave more if the situation presents itself. For now, we're walking around the Village.

"I'm playing with Jagged this weekend. They're coming in tomorrow and have sold-out shows tomorrow night and Saturday night. I came a day early to see you."

"Good thing I was in town." I can't resist throwing that out there.

He nods and looks at me with that hangdog expression that just seems to melt me more. "Yes, it is."

"I'm going home on Monday, so I really am glad I didn't miss you."

He leans over and kisses my cheek. "Me too. I'm sorry I was such a 'presumptuous' bastard."

Forgiven. "Just don't let it happen again," I say firmly.

"Agreed. I will do my best to never assume," he promises. "The bastard part, I can't guarantee. Speaking of presumptuous … I sorta surprised you today by just showing up. If you need to be doing something else, I completely understand."

I stop in front of a used bookstore and rifle through their sale cart. "No, I had a couple errands and laundry on the agenda. Nothing exciting. Just been getting ready to be gone for a few weeks and Tessa's spending every minute with Jared." I grin thinking about how cute they are together.

"I do have tickets for you, if you'd like to come. Both nights, if you want. Tessa and Jared too…"

"That sounds fun." I look up at him and can't believe we're here, doing everyday things and feeling more like a real couple than we ever have.

He's staring at me so intently that I get flustered and pretend to get engrossed in a book. I have no idea what it says. I feel his eyes singeing wherever they touch.

"Wh-where are you staying?" I stutter, determined to get my bearings back.

His voice is a silky rasp, like he's covering me with velvet in every syllable. "I'm in a swanky place—the Chatwal, ever heard of it? I'm in a suite large enough for, oh … at least 6 people? You should come visit."

"I'd like to see it," I admit. I have a thing for hotels. I love them.

I'm so out of sorts with his steady gaze on me not going anywhere, that I move over to the next cart to gain some distance. And trip over seemingly nothing but my own feet. I stump my big toe, since I'm only wearing flip-flops and it hurts. "Dagnabbit!"

Ian is at my side in no time. "Are you okay?"

My toe is bloody and gross. "I'm fine," I sigh. "I'm such a klutz."

"Let's go get that cleaned up. Doesn't look good."

"Oh, I do this sort of thing all the time, no big deal."

"I think we're close to my hotel—wanna catch a cab over there now? Watch a movie in my room or something?"

"That actually sounds really good."

We're in the cab and Ian says, "Um, Sparrow ... did I really hear you say *dagnabbit*?"

I whip my head around to face him, my face red, eyes wide. My dorkiness has finally come out.

"Because it sounded like you did ... say dagnabbit ... and well, I don't know if I've ever heard anyone under 70 actually say that word." His shoulders are shaking now and his eyes are starting to get watery from him trying to hold his laughter in.

I flick his hand and look back out the window, trying to hide my smile.

"I have an issue with cussing."

"Oh really? What is your issue?"

"Well, other than the fact that I can't do it, I just can't *do* it. It doesn't sound right coming out of my mouth."

"Try something. Say something naughty."

"No!"

"Come on, Little Bird, let me hear you say something *bad*." Now he *is* wiping his eyes. The jerk.

We pull up to the hotel just then and I breathe a sigh of relief. We get out and walk through the beautiful lobby and when we get inside the elevator, he says, "You're not off the hook."

"We have a strict clean word policy at my house," I say primly.

"Okay, fair enough. But you're not at your house right now." His smile covers his face, mischief spilling out. "What would you say right now if you could?"

"That's the thing. It's like my mouth will physically not let me. I don't mind it when other people do, it's just I can't. I have this weird thing about words. Even normal ones. For example, you will never hear me say M-O-I-S-T."

We're getting off the elevator now and Ian stops at his door. "MOIST?" he practically shouts. "What's wrong with MOIST?"

I cringe with every M-word.

"PLEASE, *don't*," I beg. "You can say the F-word even, just please not the M-word."

He is howling now. Oh please.

"I'm happy I can amuse you," I snap.

"So you're really okay if I say *fuck* but not *moist*?"

"ENOUGH WITH THE MOIST!" I gasp and cover my mouth.

His mouth drops and he points at me. "You said it!" he shouts, and then he laughs so hard, I think he's going to burst a blood vessel. It's catching, especially when he winds his arm around me and hugs me tight. "You are too cute," he says, catching his breath. "So ... what do you say when you're really ... *angry*?" He laughs at himself again, and I know he had another word on the tip of his tongue.

I smirk at him. "You think you're so funny," I say, jabbing him in the stomach. "Welllll, I will tell you how it goes. We don't say, *Crap*, we say *Crack*. We don't say, *S-H-I-T*, we say Shoot. We don't say *Effff*, we say *Fudge*. And on and on."

Ian tries desperately to get serious and nods. When I

get to the *Effff,* he loses it again.

"What?"

"You can't even SPELL *fuck*, can you?"

"Now you're getting it," I admit.

"Aw, baby. That might be the best thing I've ever heard."

"It's stupid is what it is."

"No, it's you. It *is* hilarious and I'm not sure I understand why you can say *fudge* when you really MEAN *fuck,* but I can't question that brain of yours." He smiles that ornery smile again and I know he's trying to not lose it again.

"That's the thing, I really do mean *fudge.* My brain doesn't go to the other."

"Wow. See? You are perfect."

"More like conditioned..."

And then I notice our surroundings. He's had me so distracted, I didn't even appreciate the grandeur we're standing in. "This room is amazing! Or apartment, I should say! I didn't know they had such large hotel rooms in New York!"

"Apparently Jagged likes to live large." He smiles. "Let's clean up your foot and then I'll show you my favorite part."

After the blood is washed off my toe and it looks much better, Ian takes my hand and we step out onto the terrace. We're up on the roof. The private deck is massive, larger than my entire apartment. We can see over 44th Street. There are plush chairs to enjoy the sunshine and view.

"I love it!"

"This is the "Producer Suite." Ian winks. "I guess

Serge, the bass player, will be staying in the other bedroom tomorrow night, but for tonight it's all mine. I think he could be here now and we'd never know it."

"So this is what it feels like to be a famous musician," I tease. "I can see the allure."

He shrugs. "I've also lived in a van before. Not that I don't appreciate all this, I do. It's much better than a van, that's for sure. I just know it can all go away in an instant."

The mood just shifted and he sounds serious.

I study his eyes that change colors in every setting and wonder where he goes when his eyes cloud like they are right now. I determine to find out. Maybe not now, but soon. I want to know everything about him.

He shifts suddenly and places his hand on my cheek. "Sparrow? I know I've really messed up with you. I saw you … that very first day when you were with … Dave." He pauses and waits to see if I'll react.

"Michael."

"Oh yeah. Mike."

"Michael."

"Michael, Mike … Dave, whatever." He gives me an ornery grin, but quickly turns serious again. "I—felt something that day that I haven't felt, I don't know, maybe ever. Maybe when I was a little boy and when things were good with my parents. Too long to remember, anyway. But seeing you, being near you, talking to you, hearing your laugh, watching your lips move, all of it. I felt awake. Alive. Crazed, almost. And I haven't known what to do with it. Seeing you each time, it just intensifies, which never happens for me. With you, I just want more— instead of wanting to run, I want *more*. But you're here, and I'm all over the place. You're just getting started, really, and I'm already worn and … old."

I have been hanging on his every word. His expression is so sincere. It seems too much, too soon still, for all our stops and starts, but when I look at him, I could almost swear I see the love. To diffuse the seriousness of the moment, I make a scoffing sound. *Pfft.*

"You're not old."

"That's all you heard of what I just said?" His eyes crinkle and his lips quirk up as he leans down for a kiss.

Kissing him is like the sun breaking through a deep fog. I know *exactly* what he meant.

He leans away and smooths down my hair, tugging on the end of a curl. "I'm a pessimist," he says.

"I'm an optimist." I shrug nonchalantly.

He looks at me with a sweet expression. "You're a complete idealist, is what you are."

"What's wrong with that?"

"Not a thing." He kisses my hair and my hand and my eyelids.

"I'm not sure you're right about that. I think I see things how they really are."

"I want to be who you think I am."

"I want you to be who you *are*." I grab his face and look at him, studying his eyes and trying to get inside his brain. I wish I could pop into his head and swirl around in there for days and days. There's so much behind the surface, I know he's trying to let me in, but it still feels as if layers and layers flap over a mound of thoughts and feelings. Ian Sterling is one deep puppy.

"This is me, baby. This is the most me I ever get." He grins and comes in for another kiss. This one knocks me off my feet, truly, because the next thing I know, he's picked me up and is carrying me back inside. I've had my first threshold moment.

He lays me back on the bed and kisses me slowly, taking his time as his fingers roam down my shoulder, along the sides of my arm, onto my stomach, up the middle of my chest, where they rest for a moment. My shirt is just low enough that his fingers touch exactly where the swell of my breasts begin and I'm afraid to breathe for fear he will move away. His fingers lightly tickle down my cleavage, but go no further. His lips trail down my neck and follow his fingers. He looks up at me then, looking like a mischievous angel. Keeping his eyes on mine, his tongue follows where his lips have been. Every touch is slow and deliberate and it's making me crazy. He moves the material down my shoulder then, bringing my bra strap down with it and stops just at the top of my bra. He kisses all along the top of my chest, but it just feels like teases.

A sudden image of Asher pops in my head and I can see him throwing my bra across the room. I try to shake it off, but something must flit across my face because Ian sees it and stops.

"Little Bird?" His head comes up to mine and he leans over me, his nose touching mine as he looks at me. "I'm sorry. I wouldn't have done more than kiss you. Is this too much?"

I make a decision then. "Please don't stop." I want to do way more than kiss.

He kisses my cheeks and all over my face, stopping on my lips. His touch is sweet and light.

"You know what? How about we order some food?

Watch that movie. You look distracted. Are you hungry?"
He tweaks my nose and leans back.

I want to tell him I'm hungry for him because that's
the truth, even if it is cheesy. But he's right. I really am
distracted. I'm so mad at Asher for wrecking this moment
for me. What happened that night? What did I do? What
made him think I wanted him? I can tell Ian thinks I'm
weighing over the option of making out with him for more
virtuous reasons, but I really just want to call Asher and
yell at him.

"I'm the one who's sorry," I tell him. "You know
what? Food does sound good. Will you just pick out
something? We've eaten together enough times, you know
what I like." I try to grin reassuringly as I pick up my
purse and feel for my phone, but pull out my lip gloss
instead. "I'll be outside, catching my breath." I rush out of
the room, to the balcony and up to the roof. Ian's going to
think I'm a loon. I dial Asher's number and fume as it
rings.

"Sparrow! I'm so gla—"

"Just answer me something, Ash. What happened that
night?"

"You don't *remember*?"

"Tell me the truth. What made you think I wanted to
have sex with you? Why did you do that?"

He lets all his breath out. "Sparrow. I had no idea
you—."

"That doesn't matter right now. Why? Why did you
do that?"

"I thought you wanted to … at first. You kept saying
you were so hot. And you took off your dress … I
thought…"

"I *was* so hot!" I snap. "I was drunk, and I should have never taken my dress off, but you *knew* I was drunk. And I passed *out*. I can't believe you thought that was an open invitation—" my voice catches on the last word and I blink quickly. *I will not cry. I will not cry. I will not cry.*

"Sparrow, I am *so* sorry. So sorry. I didn't mean to. You just looked so beautiful and I was drunk too ... really drunk..." he trails off. "Sparrow, please..." He sounds like he's crying now. "There isn't a second that I haven't regretted what I did. I've wanted you for so long."

Now I'm crying. "And so that gave you the right to just take me when I was at my most vulnerable? I thought you were my friend, Asher."

"I am your friend, Sparrow. I made a mistake. I knew it when I woke up and saw..."

"Don't you dare! Don't you dare talk about that. You're not ... you don't..." A sob comes out just as I hear footsteps. Ian wraps his arms around me, brushes my hair back and looks at me, concerned.

I hang up the phone with Asher still talking, and bury my head in Ian's neck. The tears pour out of me and he just holds me as tight as he can. When I finally start to calm down, he pulls my head back and wipes my face. I try to wipe it too, knowing I look terrifying. I have never been able to cry in front of people. Ever. I'm horrified.

"Baby? Can you tell me what's going on? I came out to tell you what I ordered, in case you wanted to change something, but ... you were in the middle of it."

"What did you hear?" I ask with dread.

"I heard you say Asher's name," he says quietly. "I wasn't trying to eavesdrop, I really wasn't. Are you—uh, are you seeing Asher still? Do you wanna talk about it?"

I walk over to the lounger and plop down, head in hands. "No, I'm not. I thought he was my friend. He wanted more, but I ... I've been too hung up on you."

Ian sighs and sits down beside me. "I've been an idiot. But what has you so upset?"

And I don't know how he does it, but I tell him everything. At least what I remember.

Ian has paced for twenty minutes and is still pacing when the food comes. He's ordered a feast and can't stop pacing long enough to enjoy it. Anger is boiling out of him, pouring over the pan and running down the stove. His gray, green, blue eyes are practically glowing yellow at this point, and I've had to keep him from crashing his fist into a wall. I would die of shame if I caused him to damage his hand. I'm in somewhat of a stupor from sharing. I've always been able to keep things in, even from Tessa sometimes, when I don't want to upset her or it's just too much, but Ian kept probing and asking the key questions that pulled it all out. We've moved all over and I've ended up on the couch inside with my arms hugging my knees. Just watching him pace, wishing I could help him now. I, surprisingly enough, feel better. I don't feel the need to shower once. I think not remembering made me downplay it, but I guess I still needed to talk about it. Knowing how angry Ian is with Asher makes me feel justified in my feelings. Maybe I can stop second-guessing myself now.

- 14 -

Purple LACE

Ian and I stay up all night talking. For hours it's all heaviness, about Asher, about the anger I feel toward him, even the sadness that my virginity is gone and I didn't even get to enjoy it. I talk Ian down from wanting to go beat Asher to a pulp. To be honest, I still don't trust that he won't. The thought makes me nervous, although, I wouldn't mind Asher getting a little pop on the jaw. I just would rather be the one to do it.

Later, we talk about some of Ian's anger issues because it's obvious now that he has some. I find out more about his dad and what happened to his mom as a result. Ian had to be shuttled between an aunt who didn't want him and elderly grandparents that couldn't really take care of him, while his mom recovered in a mental facility for a year.

Ian says it all as if he's talking about a stranger. "Right before she was sent away, he beat her so badly, I had to call an ambulance. I walked in from school and he was using her as a punching bag. I went after him … hitting, kicking, biting. Every shred of hatred I'd carried toward him, I put right here." He holds up his fists and his eyes look so sad.

"He hit me back—"

The words hang in the air...

"When we finally stopped fighting, I realized the shape my mom was in. She was in the hospital for a couple of weeks with a broken nose and ribs and internal bleeding that wouldn't stop. From there they sent her away, and that was the last time I talked to my father. I was eleven."

"Is that when you went to your aunt's house?" I ask, unable to stop touching him. We haven't let go of each other the entire time we've talked. He built a fire and turned up the air conditioning, so we wouldn't be too hot. We're sitting cross-legged in the middle of the bed, facing each other. It's about two in the morning.

"Yeah, I was there for four months, but my aunt had two kids and didn't need an eleven-year-old with a temper. My grandparents took me and gave me free rein. When my mom came back, I pretty much had free rein too. She stayed isolated for a long time. I got into a lot of trouble during that time. Not all of it was bad, though." His eyes sparkle in the firelight and I groan.

"Girls?"

"Yep."

"You started out young, didn't you."

"Thirteen."

"No!" I can't help it, I'm appalled.

He laughs. "My girlfriend was four years older … I was tall for my age," he says by way of explanation.

"That's just … gross." I crinkle my nose. "That's way too young. And if it were the other way around and you were the one deflowering *her*," I say with obnoxious air quotes, "there would have been hell to pay."

He nods and uncrosses his legs and stretches out, elbows up and his head resting on his hand. "Not

170

something I'm necessarily proud of … now. Back then, it was sort of a—wait a minute, did you just say 'hell'?" He grabs me by the arm and waist and pulls me down to him, tickling me everywhere he can reach with no signs of letting up. I'm snorting and wheezing and sputtering, and yelling when I can catch a breath. I am SO ticklish. This just encourages him. "You said, 'hell', you said, 'hell!'" He's relentless. Pretty soon, though, he's laughing so hard at me that he loses his grip for a second and I slip out of his arms. I jump off the bed and he chases me, but I'm just one beat faster. I run around the suite and end up in the other bedroom. I grab a pillow and hold it up for protection when I realize it wasn't the smartest idea to come into this smaller room.

He leans against the doorframe and watches me smugly. He can't wipe the mischief off his face and every now and then he'll act like he's coming toward me, only to make me jump higher. It sends me into a fit of laughter every time he makes a start for me. I'm like a little kid who screams just at the threat of being tickled, without even being touched.

I lean over and put my hands on my knees while I try to put a serious face on and catch my breath.

"Uncle," I finally say when I lean back up.

"What's that?"

"Uncle, you know … like, I give?"

"Oh, I just didn't hear you. You were saying you give up?" He laughs as he stretches his arms on either side of the door, reminding me there's no way out but past him.

I cross my arms and attempt a glare. "Yes, I've had enough tickling."

He crosses his arms then, copying me. "Oh, you

have? Are you sure?"

Something about the way he says that makes my blood go hot. "Yes?" I whisper.

His smile fills his face and you'd never know we'd been talking about traumatic things all night. My heart feels lighter than it's ever felt.

"Come here, baby," he says softly.

I inch closer to him, still not trusting him to be done tickling. I get close enough and he swoops me up in his arms and carries me back to his bedroom.

He lays me on the bed and holds up his finger for me to wait a second. He opens his suitcase and pulls out a large t-shirt. "Want to wear this?" he asks.

I nod.

"Can I put it on you?"

I nod again.

He grabs my hand and pulls me up until we're both on our knees. He slowly lifts my shirt up over my head, looking in my eyes the whole time. When it's off, he leans back and runs the tips of his fingers right above where the fabric of my bra starts. I'm so glad I'm wearing a pretty lacy one. He places light kisses down my neck—down, down, down—but comes right back up to look at me again. I'm breathless and don't want him to stop.

"God, you are something else, Sparrow. You are … I could kiss every inch, all night long…"

Okay.

He undoes the buttons on my jeans and slowly pulls them off. I do a quick check to make sure my panties are matching, happy when I see they are. His hands cup my bum and for a moment, his eyes close and he catches his breath.

When he opens his eyes, he bites his lower lip and I wish I could do that myself. "Purple," he says, patting my bra strap and grinning. "I've never loved purple so much." He's taking his time, his eyes roving up and down my body, making my nipples perk up and take notice. I don't move. I let him look, surprised that I'm not trying to cover up. I want him to see me and enjoy it.

"I hate to do this. I hate it so much, but we should … get some sleep." His eyes are betraying what he's saying, even as he puts his t-shirt over my head and slowly tugs it down. It stops just below my underwear. He yanks off his shirt and jeans, leaving on black boxer briefs. I try not to stare but just can't help myself.

Wow.

Ian groans as he hugs me close and pulls me down on the bed, turning me away from him and cradling my body from behind. We each hold the other's hands, all four hands in a warm clump by my face, and eventually, I drift off, thinking this is the best night I've ever had.

The next morning, we're still in the same position, only I'm sweating like a cow. I've always gotten so hot when I sleep. Ian has his arms wrapped tight around me, his body outlining mine. He feels divine.

I take a deep breath and he grips me even tighter. I struggle to not giggle like a schoolgirl about the way his body is pressing against mine. He unconsciously grinds into my bum cheeks and a little laugh sneaks out. He makes a groggy moan and says, "Let's just forget I did that, okay? I was having such a great dream." I laugh outright then and his body responds, but he doesn't let go. "If we just ignore it, it will go away," he whispers. I laugh harder. "Aw, hell, who am I kidding," he mutters and starts to untangle from me.

"You don't have to go anywhere, " I say softly.

He nestles back in. "Mmm, okay." He runs his hand down my arm and my nerve endings feel like bacon, sizzling and popping all over the place. "You're hot!"

"Why, thank you," I say like the cheeseball that I am.

He snickers. "You're welcome. But seriously, you're like a heater." He leans over me and props himself up on his hands. His shirt is baggy on me and a V-neck, so it's hanging low. With one finger, he wipes in between my boobs. "You're sweating."

"Uh. Yeah?"

"That's hot."

I laugh at him. "You're crazy."

He leans his head down and licks where his finger has just been. "You taste good, too." He runs his tongue just under the lace and then he lays his head on my chest and gives a big sigh. He's still for a minute and then his finger lightly touches the lace of my bra, like he just can't help himself from sneaking a feel.

I think I stopped breathing back when I woke up, so when my stomach drops in on itself with that touch, I get lightheaded.

The next thing I know, Ian is on his feet, off the bed and hightailing it to the bathroom. He leaves me staring longingly at the back of him, propped up on both elbows and wishing I could have caught a better look.

I hear the shower running and five minutes later, Ian is out and walking through the bedroom in a hotel robe. His black hair is dripping wet, but still standing up everywhere. He looks like he didn't even dry off, just put on the robe. He's brushing his teeth and I hop up and skitter past him to the bathroom. I brush my teeth first and look at myself in Ian's shirt. In the morning light, I'm a little embarrassed by how I look. My cheeks are flushed. My hair is massive and a little frizzy from the sweat. Tessa would say I have sex hair, but sadly it's always without the sex. I decide to not over-think anything today and hop in the shower. I take the fastest shower ever, only pausing long enough to see if I can smell the shampoo. I *think* it smells good. Hopefully.

When I get out, I put on the other robe and walk out, wondering what I'm going to wear for the day. It wasn't exactly planned for me to stay here overnight. The bedroom is empty; in fact, the whole penthouse is empty. My phone is next to the bed and there's a text from Ian.

I'll be back in 15, Your Hotness.

I smile and get to work on my wet hair. I have 15 minutes—wait, no, 7 minutes!—to get this mop looking fabulous. I quickly give up the thought of even trying when I realize I don't have a single product in my purse. It will just have to be a frizzy day. I hurriedly put on a touch of makeup from my purse and am getting to the mascara when Ian walks in and stands beside me, watching.

He's quiet. I look at him through the mirror and continue with the mascara wand. He reaches out and touches my hair reverently, following the trail of one curl from the crown of my head all the way down to my waist.

"I love your hair." His voice sounds raspy and sweet,

like hard whiskey sauce poured over bread pudding. Sweet, but with a kick.

"I love your voice," I whisper back.

He hops on the bathroom vanity and faces me, carefully running his finger across my lips. "You have the kind of face artists want to paint."

I stop what I'm doing and just look at him. "You should think about— oh, I don't know—writing songs for a living." I grin at him.

"It's the truth." He holds up his hand when I start sputtering back a retort. "I can say it if I mean it," he yells over me. He's laughing and tugging on me, leading me out to the bedroom. "You don't need to do anything else. If you look any better, I'm gonna maul you on this bed right here and now." His face falls when he thinks about what he said. "I mean ... shi-oot, Sparrow. I'm sorry. I didn't mean that."

Asher hangs over us, unspoken.

"Did you just say, 'shi-oot'?" I don't want the air to feel heavy. I wrap my arms around his waist, trying to find a ticklish spot. He's laughing at me calling him out, but he's not even flinching. "What? Are you not ticklish?"

"Nope," he says proudly.

"You have to be ticklish. Everybody is."

"I've learned how to not be."

"That's impossible." I'm tickling every spot I can think of, but he doesn't budge. "Well, you're no fun."

He leans over and kisses me on the tip of my nose. "Take that back," he says.

"Okay, I take it back."

"I got some coffee and these chocolate pastry things that looked really good, want some?"

"Yeah! Are you kidding?" I race to the bag and pull out an enormous chocolate croissant. "Oh, how did you know? I LOVE THESE THINGS."

"You are so fun to feed." Ian laughs.

We sit down and begin to eat. The coffee is hitting me just right and the croissant is so good, I can't think straight. Ian watches me with an amused expression. His look of adoration is something I could certainly get used to. It fills me up with more boldness than I'm used to feeling. I like it; I like what he does to me.

"Little Bird?" he says softly. "I'm not the best at talking things out, but I think we should talk about Asher more and about what happened to you."

"I don't know what else to say about it. I don't even know how to make sense of it. Not knowing all that happened, I can't even process how to feel about it. I've remembered a couple of things. One was yesterday, when we were…" my voice awkwardly trails off.

"Is that why you ran out of here so fast? You remembered something? I just thought you needed to confront him."

"Well, that too." Suddenly, the room feels like it's closing in on me and I don't want him to look at me anymore. "I remember him throwing my bra across the room," I say, embarrassed. "And then, nothing. I must have passed out right after that. So, maybe I totally made the moves on him."

Ian's gaze cuts through me as he listens. When I don't say anything else, he says, "No, Sparrow. If you passed out, you weren't making the moves on him. How much did you drink, anyway? Do you think he put something in your drink?"

I hadn't even thought of that. I don't even *want* to think of that. Despite everything, I still need to think Asher isn't that coldblooded. I don't tell Ian how sore I was for days after it happened. That's probably normal. I wouldn't know.

"He kept giving me flirtinis and I don't drink very often. I've never even gotten drunk before," I moan. "I can't believe I did that. But I ... trusted him."

Ian jumps up and grabs his phone. "I'll be right outside, I need to make a phone call. Are you okay for a minute?"

"Of course."

He's outside for closer to ten minutes, and he seems more relaxed when he comes inside. He kisses my forehead before he sits back down. "I hope you don't mind—I called Jared. Tessa was with him and she offered to bring by some of your things. Is that okay? I told them about the tickets and they'd like to go. You still don't have to come to the show if you don't want, you can lounge around here, if that sounds better." He looks at me, trying to read what I'm thinking.

"I want to come to the show! If you want me there, I'll be there."

"I want you wherever I am," he leans across the table and kisses me gently. When we can't seem to stop, he stands up, never breaking contact and pulls me out of my chair. I lose myself in him. When his mouth touches me—anywhere—I feel it throughout my body. His hands are just grazing the edges of my robe and he's beginning to move us toward the bed, when someone knocks on the door.

He leans back and smiles. "That's probably Tessa."

"How did she get here so fast?"

"Well, we've been kissing for about … oh, twenty minutes?"

"No!"

He laughs. "Time stand still when you're with me, baby?" I roll my eyes and take his hand while we walk to the door. My lips do feel a little bit raw. "It stood still for me," he whispers, "I just saw that clock right there when I first stood up to kiss you." He points at the huge clock on the wall.

Tessa is wide-eyed when we open the door. Me in my fluffy white robe and Ian in his clothes. Her face is speaking volumes, but she maintains her composure. She has a load—a little rolling suitcase and a couple plastic garment bags draped over her arm. She beams at me and hugs me after Ian relieves her of the luggage.

"You did it!" she whispers.

I pinch her arm. "Shush."

She leans back and assesses my face. She scowls when she sees my expression.

"Sparrow? I need to go run a quick errand. Do you mind if I head out while you're getting ready?" Ian asks. He's distracting me by running his hand through my hair.

"Of course, go ahead."

"Tessa, make yourself at home," he says, grinning.

As soon as he goes out the door, Tessa sets in. "What? Still no? Whyyyy—" If she were typing, it would be in shouty caps. "Ro, you are the last one on earth still holding onto your V-card. This guy that you have mooned over for years is looking at you like you're the last goddess standing."

I laugh at her and she waits for me to answer her

nonsense. "What did you bring?" Distraction is always the best way to avoid confrontation.

She opens up the suitcase and proudly shows me all my toiletries, curling iron, my prettiest underwear and hidden underneath that, she holds up a sexy nightie. "To push you on over," she smirks.

"Tess," I groan. However, I pick it up and see if it's the right size. It is.

"This is a *nice* hotel." She knows a thing or two about distraction.

"Isn't it something?" I open the garment bag and see a gorgeous green dress that is so short it looks like a long blouse. It looks tiny, but the material gives, so it should fit. It's something the girlfriend of a rockstar would wear and I gulp when I think of going out in it. I will have to avoid leaning over even the slightest bit. So help me, if I drop something, I am NOT picking it up.

"Open that zipper, I put the shoes in there." Tessa motions toward the outside pocket of my suitcase. An amazing pair of shoes are in there.

"How did you pick this stuff out? He barely called you, not even an hour ago!"

"Well … I might have heard from him yesterday. And he might have asked me to pick up something for tonight then," Tessa grins mischievously.

"Really. Well, thank you, Tess." I hang up the garment bag. "But you could have picked up something that would at least cover my …"

"Oh, I had specific requirements to follow. This man LOVES your legs, let me tell you. Under no circumstances was I allowed to buy something to cover them up." She laughs. "Now these two outfits were just supposed to be comfortable, but of course, I had to find cute AND comfortable."

"Wow, I can't believe you both did all this. I can't believe you didn't tell me he was coming!"

She looks at me sheepishly and shrugs. "Surprise?" she says.

I think about all the trouble Ian has gone to this weekend—when I had no idea he was even coming—and I smile at Tessa.

"I think I might give him a chance," I tell her.

And by *might*, I mean I am *definitely* going to forget about all my fears regarding this man and go with my heart.

- 15 -

Bewitched

Watching Ian on electric guitar is a full sensory experience. I've seen him play both electric and acoustic guitar, and he says he prefers the acoustic, but there is something about him strapping on the electric that makes me want to take him down on the stage and have my way with him. He looks feral; his light eyes taking on different colors with the spotlights and his hair with all its haphazardness. He has on a fitted blue t-shirt that outlines his toned arms and torso. I just want to take it off…

Ian does background vocals here and there, but mostly just plays the guitar like a maniac. It's obvious the band is thrilled that he's with them. They feature him on guitar solos practically every song, grinning and closing in on him as he plays these crazy, screaming runs. I can't take my eyes off of Ian. Every now and then, he'll make a hilarious face, and it pulls me out of my lustful state just long enough to laugh at him.

Girls scream like banshees whenever Ian takes a solo. They yell his name, and the ones closest to the stage hold their arms out to him, as if just touching the bottom of his shoe will make them complete.

When the show is over, we go backstage where Ian has told us to meet him. I've already gotten a text from him, saying: **Where are you?**

It takes us a while to get through the crowd, even though we're in the front. We wind our way through and get to the guard who stands blocking the door. He asks for my name and when I tell him, we get through. Various people from the show are either chatting or busily getting gear out to the bus. I'm trying not to be paranoid, but it feels like the room goes quiet and all eyes are on me. I lower my head to avoid making any eye contact with the gawkers. I just want to get to Ian.

He's standing just outside the room where he told us to come. He's sandwiched between two tall models who have their hands all over him. He doesn't look bothered, which annoys me. He looks amused and a little distracted. It might be the only time I've ever been happy with my height. I'm just as tall as they are. However, they're gorgeous. One is leaning over and whispering something in his ear, and he laughs and shakes his head. I'm ready to turn around and keep walking when he spots me.

"Baby!" he says, loosening himself from the leeches. My insides warm that he just called me 'baby' in front of these two. "Holy fuck!" he says and then lifts both hands high in the air. He's trying to drag his eyes back up to my face but having a really hard time. He pulls me to him and grabs each side of my face. "Sorry. That just popped out."

"You don't need to apologize. I know you have a mouth on you."

"I'm gonna have this mouth on *you* … all night long…"

My body takes on a few dozen degrees of warmth with that statement.

"You look—so—*effff!*" he laughs. "God. Whoever picked that dress out for you deserves a medal." He grins at Tessa as he says it and winds his arm around my shoulder, kissing my hair. Tessa beams back. Whatever the two of them worked out in their phone conversation to set up this whole surprise visit has completely won over Tessa.

"Hey, man." Jared is wrapped around Tessa, but Ian and Jared do the whole fist bump thing with their spare hands.

Ian has showered and is wearing different clothes. He looks even better than he did on stage. He has cologne on that I can actually smell and it's like a direct pheromone to my nostrils. I want to ditch the after party and go straight to the hotel.

Ian looks as if he can read my mind. He gives me a searing grin that makes my stomach drop to the ground and settles back up in my lower regions. The *nether regions*, as my mom would say, although for the life of me now, I can't remember why she would ever say that to me at all. I don't want to think about it right now. It's spoiling my sexy moment.

The models are skulking against the wall as we walk by, looking me over from head to foot and seeming none too pleased. I try to ignore the smug feeling that settles in my gut and just focus on walking by without tripping.

The whole night is like endless foreplay. Not that I've ever had much of that before now, so maybe actual foreplay is a lot better, but this is the next best thing. I'll take it. For now. Ian and I dance all night. I'm decent on the dance floor, but with him, every move I make is the right one. I was made to dance with him. He anticipates my every move and is in tune with my body, an extension of it.

My favorite is when he flips me around and runs his hands down the front of me as he's pressed against my back. I'm a puddle just thinking about it. On the way home, after our cab drops Tessa and Jared off, Ian doesn't take his eyes off of me. He runs his fingers along my skin, and he looks like he wants to pounce. When it seems like he can't take it anymore, his mouth is an inch away from mine … and the cab stops.

He asked me at the club if I would stay the night with him again, and I didn't tell him, but I had assumed that was the point since Tessa brought over my suitcase.

When we reach the hotel and get in the elevator, he kisses along my cheekbone. His restraint is driving me mad. His eyes are roving everywhere his lips want to be. His fingers follow, tantalizing and promising more. The elevator dings and we fall into our room.

He backs me up against the wall and does things with his tongue that leave me breathless. Down, down my neck his mouth goes, his hands all over me. He loves my breasts and my bum and my legs. I know because he says so as he runs his hands along the edges of every part, never quite touching all the way, but just enough. His eyes are fiery and my legs feel like they're falling out from under me.

I pull on his shirt and then yank it off. "I've wanted to do that all night," I whisper.

"I've wanted to do a lot more than that all night," he whispers back. He leans back and looks at me. He groans and gives my hair a slight tug as our mouths collide again. When I think I can't take anymore without ripping all his clothes off, he pulls back and kisses my shoulders and his hands reach for the back zipper of my dress. He lifts his eyebrow, as if asking permission. I smile at him, giving it.

"I just want to look at you," he says, as he slowly unzips and pulls my dress down, little by little. He kisses my body with each inch of skin he exposes. He skims over my breasts, kissing my bare stomach, skims over my panties and down my thigh. When my dress is on the ground, he stands back and stares. "Baby..." he says in a husky voice. "I've never wanted anyone so much, Sparrow. I want to do things right with you, though, okay? So we're not—we're just gonna—"

"You talk too much," I whisper, taking him by surprise and wrapping myself around him. I then get the giggles at my aggression. Dang, I always laugh at the wrong time.

Like when we had to pick out band uniforms and Laura cried because they were so ugly and I laughed in her face, until I realized she was serious.

Or when my dad fell really hard on the ski slopes and had actually broken his wrist.

Or the time during Casey's funeral, on stage, when the choir was getting ready to sing. Laughed so hard I couldn't stop.

"You think too much," he says, coming in for another kiss, but before he can, I reach up and undo my bra, letting it drop to the floor with my dress. His eyes go wide. He wasn't expecting that. He looks stunned speechless. Take that. I have to bite the inside of my cheek. I will not wreck this moment with nervous laughter.

Fortunately, he's too mesmerized by my chest to notice. It just might be the only part of my body that I'm completely happy with—I wonder what he thinks. I know he's seen more than enough women.

"Sparrow…" his grin takes over his face, but he still hasn't looked up. When he does, his pupils are dilated and he looks drunk even though he isn't. "You're perfect." He reaches out then and lightly touches the tips of my nipples with his middle fingers. And then his huge hands cup my breasts. "Mmm, you were made for me. Look." I look down to see how my breasts fill his hands. He leans down and glides his tongue where his hands have been, flicking around my nipples and then pulling one in to suck it. My eyes close of their own will and a whimper escapes. I can't believe this is really happening.

His hands are everywhere, leaving traces of electricity wherever he makes contact.

Suddenly he flips me around, like he did when we were dancing and pulls my back into him as his hands run the whole length of my body. I can feel how much he wants me. He slowly leads me to the bedroom, kissing my neck the whole way. When my knees bump the bed, he turns me around and presses me to him, skin to skin.

After he hugs me tight against him, he pulls back and brushes my hair off my face. He takes a deep breath and something in the air shifts. His expression is confusing me. I look up at him, feeling vulnerable with my nakedness for the first time. He leans his forehead on mine. "Listen … I'm flying out tomorrow. So are you. Sparrow, I—I'm not gonna make love to you and then leave you. As much as I want to, I just don't want our first time to be rushed in any way. Or you to be left to deal with whatever you might feel afterward, alone. You've been through a lot the last month. I don't think it has all fully registered yet."

I wrap my arms against my chest, embarrassed that I stripped off my bra. I look down and nod.

He lifts my chin up, so I'll look him in the eye. "I want you more than anything." He puts my hand on his chest where his heart is still beating so fast. He points down to the tent in his pants and grins. I flush and he laughs, tugging me into another hug. "When we do this, I want to have days and days where I do nothing but show you what you mean to me," he whispers in my ear. Every single hair on my body stands up and takes notice.

Even though every nerve in my body is singing, I hear what he's saying and I'm relieved. I would rather have sex with him right this minute, but I know the torment of being away from him. He's right, it would be harder if I give that part of myself to him tonight and then have to say good-bye. I still have to see what will happen when he leaves—if this time will really be different.

I step away and grab my nightie out of the suitcase, putting it on quickly. It's red and doesn't leave much to the imagination.

"You're killing me, you know that, right?"

I shrug and smile. "Too bad."

We don't get much sleep. We talk until the early hours of the morning and when we do try to sleep, Ian's arms wind around me and his hands keep finding my breasts. Now that he's touched them, he can't seem to help himself. I don't mind. It's leaving an ache, though; I want more and my body is practically humming with need. We kiss. A lot. But it just keeps getting to a certain point and then he pulls back, reminding himself of the restraint he promised. I can tell it would be amazing: sex with Ian would be explosive.

The next morning, we drag ourselves out of bed. Sadness hangs over us. Ian even has a hangdog look about him.

"You look sad," I state the obvious.

"I don't want to leave you," he says. "And I'm not used to feeling that way."

I just leave that hanging in the air and don't say anything back. My emotions are too close to the surface. I don't want to say too much or even worse, cry. I can't help but be afraid that all the progress we've made over the last couple of days will be over once we say good-bye.

"I'll be in Detroit and Chicago the next couple days and then heading out to Seattle. I don't want to interrupt your time at home, but..." He looks at me expectantly.

I don't fill in the blanks for him.

There's an awkward pause, and he clears his throat. "Would it be okay? If I come and see you while you're home?"

I try to contain my smile just a touch, but I'm pretty sure my whole face lights up. "I'd love it."

"I have a gig in San Francisco in two weeks. You'll be there for three?"

I nod.

"I could come that last week before the 4th. I don't have to play until Sunday night ... the rest of the time, I'll be free."

I nod again, biting my lip because my stomach is doing the whole drop-to-the-floor thing. But I just say, "Sure..."

"Okay." He lets a big breath out and looks relieved.

He grabs my hand and pulls me in for a kiss. His fingers softly caress my cheeks and if I didn't know any better, I'd think Ian Sterling adored me.

Hours later, when I'm on the flight with Tessa and telling her the highlights, she says, "I gave him a hard time, you know, on the phone."

"You did?" I laugh. "What did you say?"

"Well, after he told me about some of his plans for you this weekend, I could tell he *really* likes you. I haven't been sure of how deeply he felt. So, I told him if he really cares about you, to quit flaking on you. You could have any guy, but he seems to be the one you want. He said, 'She's the one I want.' And I believed him." She looks at me to see how I'm taking it. She crinkles her nose and then sheepishly says, "And then I said, 'You better not hurt her or I'll hunt you down and squeeze the life right out of you where it counts. It won't be pretty.'" She lifts her shoulders and holds her head down, as if waiting for me to box her ears or something. "I *had* to nip it in the butt," she says.

"Bud."

"What?"

"The bud. Nip it in the bud."

"I like the other way better."

I can't stop laughing. She finally starts laughing too, once she knows I'm not gonna kill her.

When we land, I turn my phone on, and there are two texts from Ian.

The first: **I miss you already, Little Bird.**

The second: **Have you landed yet?**

I grin. Already this is different than all the other times. Maybe this is really going to happen.

I text back: **I miss you too. Just landed.**

My phone starts ringing and it's him.
"Hello?"
"What have you done to me, baby?"
I laugh. "I don't know. What?"
"You've bewitched me."
"Hmm. Well, I can't say I'm sorry."
"Do you miss me?"
"I do," I say.
"Okay, good. Have fun with your family. Tell Dave hi for me, if you have to see that toad."
A snort sneaks out. Shoot. "I don't know a Dave, but I will tell Michael you said hello, if I see him."
He sighs. "All right. I'll let you go for now. Bye, baby."
"Bye."

- 16 -

Thumpity-THUMP-Thunk

The next couple of weeks are restful and fun. It's good to be home. My parents are their doting selves, and we spend every minute together. They break it to me the first night that Michael has resigned his position at the church and is moving back to Seattle. I'm not sure if I'll see him, and I have to think maybe that's all for the best. I'm sorry for my parents' sake that it didn't work out for him to stay. I know they're going to have a hard time replacing him and are grieving the loss of him in their lives already. I wish I hadn't wrecked that for them, all of them.

Ian calls almost every night, and we talk until we're about to fall asleep. He texts throughout the day, too, and sends funny pictures of random objects, or gross looking food after it's been sitting out too long in the green room, or fliers with funny typos. I also get a picture of a bookstore from every city and at least one a day of coffee in various settings. If I get a picture of him, it's not an attractive one. It's a funny face or a shot that's way too close-up.

He asks for a picture of my boobs at least once a day. I ignore him.

He also asks regularly about Asher—if I've seen him or heard from him. But Asher has disappeared from my life, and I'm not doing anything to try to find him.

I'm wearing my new red short shorts and high wedges when I pick him up from the airport. My navy and white striped tank has a scooped neckline that Ian will enjoy. I skip on out of the house before my parents can get a good look at me. They're not used to seeing me showing any skin. I've spent some time by the pool since being home, and I'm glad my skin doesn't look as pasty white as it did after the winter in New York.

I pull around to baggage claim and have to do an extra loop before I see him. He's standing by his suitcase, with two guitars sitting close by. He sees me and holds both arms up high in the air, grinning from ear to ear. My heart does its usual thumpity-thump that I can only associate with Ian Sterling.

I hop out and he rushes toward me, hugging me so hard, I can't breathe. He holds me back and looks me over, whistling softly. "Mmm, damn those legs. You look so good." He leans over and kisses me, tasting like peppermint. I smile at the thought of him brushing his teeth right before he saw me.

I give him the keys and we drive to Bertolucci's, an old Italian restaurant not far from the airport. He's going to drive to San Jose with me and stay a few days at my house and then we'll come back to San Francisco for his weekend gig. It took some convincing with my parents. They don't necessarily want to share me but know how excited I am about his visit. They also want to get to know him better, so I think they might even be somewhat excited themselves. Then they've also agreed for me to leave them a few days earlier than planned and spend the rest of the time in San Francisco. We're supposed to stay at Jeff & Laila's.

Ian keeps glancing over at me. His eyes are twinkling and he hasn't stopped smiling once. His eyes keep dropping to my legs. "You've gotten some sun." His brows kind of crinkle into a semi-frown.

I've never known a guy to not prefer me with a tan. I've gotten tan my whole life; I guess it was just easier in California. I didn't have to work for it. Until I moved to New York, I thought my skin was naturally olive-toned. Turns out, I am as pale as can be.

"I was happy to not be so ghostly," I mumble.

"I like you white as the day you were born," he says with a grin. "But the color looks nice on you too." He leans over and rubs my legs. "Can't stand the thought of you burning these." He gives me another mischievous grin. "Damn, you're fine. I am so glad to see you."

We get to the restaurant and when he turns off the car, I lean over and kiss him. "I'm so glad to see you, too," I whisper.

My parents fall for Ian during his time at my house. He is his thoroughly charming self, and they can't help it, he gets to them. I see them fighting it somewhat at first, even though they've talked to him before and liked him. Knowing his age and his experience troubles them. But he completely wins them over. He takes time to answer every question, is interested in everything they have to say, and dotes on me like I hung the moon. He is respectful and stays in his bedroom at night, although we have mad make-out sessions in the car and before we go to our own rooms at night. It's obvious this is all new to him, being in a relationship, taking things slowly, and he's enjoying the process.

I, however, am about to go crazy with wanting him.

On the 4th of July, we drive to Monterey and Carmel-by-the-Sea and spend the day looking in the shops and going on the 17-mile drive. At sunset, we get our blanket and find a spot on the beach, where we wait for the fireworks to start. I sit between his legs, laying my head against his chest. My heart is content, full, overwhelmed with happiness. Being with Ian like this is beyond anything I ever even knew I wanted. He makes me laugh. He makes my heart pound. One look from him makes my insides glow. And what makes it even better is, I think he feels the same way.

We get to my house really late that night and stumble into my bedroom, intoxicated by the day we've had together. He kisses me and lays me back on my bed. "Pajamas?" He points at my dresser and I point to the right drawer. He pulls out a tank top and shorts and lifts his eyebrows. I nod. He gets a wicked smile when he looks down at my body. He pulls my white sundress up over my head and nods his approval when he sees my lacy underwear. "Here, you're probably ready to get this off," he teases as he unhooks my bra and lifts it off. He buries his head in my chest. His tongue leads the trail from my breasts, down my belly button to the thin fabric of my underwear and he blows his hot breath *there*. I feel it through the lace and moan.

He looks up at me and I wait, daring him to do more. He sees it in my eyes and he takes my panties off and puts his mouth on me. His tongue, his fingers, his lips. I try to be still, but I can't. He starts a rhythm with his tongue and fingers and goes in deeper and deeper. I pull his hair, and the chaos he is creating in my body feels so good, I lose it. He doesn't stop; he just keeps going until I feel like I'm going to scream. I cover my face with the pillow and yell while my body is wracked with wave after wave … after wave. He raises his head to look at me, and I can barely focus on him. He smiles and goes back down for more. I didn't think it was possible to feel *any* better, but … it is. This time I bite my pillow.

Ian kisses slowly up my body then and when he reaches my head, he lifts the pillow. He kisses all over my face and checks my eyes. "You okay?" he asks sweetly.

"Ta—Ps—sheah," I stutter.

He laughs softly and then goes completely still. "I love you, baby."

"I love you, too." My insides feel like jelly, and he just told me he loved me. I don't think it could get any better than this.

He runs his finger over my eyebrows and across my nose and cheeks. "It's probably not fair that I said that right then. You don't have to say it back."

I *am* still a little speechless. "I meant it. But yeah. You're really … *good* at that. You could probably talk me into … anything…" I admit with a grin.

"I'm gonna get out of your room before I lose what little is left of my restraint. But this was just a small sample of what I plan to do to you. You looked too enticing laying there, looking at me like that." He kisses me and sits up quickly. "As soon as we leave tomorrow, if you're up for it, I have a plan." His eyes never leave my mouth as he talks.

I lean up on my elbows. "Oh, I'm up for it."

He runs his hand down my breasts again and his eyes have that hooded look he gets that oozes sex. "I have to get out of here. If your dad catches me in here like this, it won't bode well for me." He puts my shorts on first, leaving my tank top for last. "I hate to cover them up," he whispers, leaning down to give each side one more kiss.

"When you sleep with me every night, I want you nekkid." He laughs before he walks out of my room.

I go to sleep thinking about sleeping with him every night. Nekkid.

My parents make a huge breakfast before we leave the next morning. We've had a really nice visit. Charlie pulls me aside in the kitchen when we're cleaning up.

"So Ian …" She looks at me and waits for me to say something, and I look at her and wait for her to say more. Finally, she says, "He is crazy over you. That man is in love with you."

"You think so?" I ask, unable to stop beaming.

"I do," she answers. "Are you ready for that, Sparrow Kate?"

"I'm in love with him too," I tell her.

"Well, just please proceed carefully, baby girl. We really don't want to see you get hurt. He's the first one I've seen you date that I know has the potential to really hurt you. But it's also because I see how much you care about him. Just, please…" She hugs me and leans her forehead on mine.

"I'll try, Mama," I say. I know I'm already in too deep. If I lose him now, I may as well curl up in a hole and let worms overtake my body.

She pats my cheek and looks at me with concerned eyes. I want to take her worries away, but I know that I have the same uncertainties. It's a big risk I'm taking, I know this. I can't stop now.

"Okay, make sure..." She shakes her head and stops herself from saying anything else. "Let Jeff and Laila know we'll be by to pick up the car on Tuesday afternoon. I hate that we couldn't come to the show. We just couldn't miss this weekend with Michael gone." She kisses my cheek. "I really wish you could have seen him while you were here. Maybe give him some closure."

"I don't know how much more closure I could give him," I tell her. "I do wish we could have stayed friends, but I get it."

"Yeah, maybe eventually, he'll come around to that."

"Love you, Charlie."

"Love you, too."

Ian and I climb into the car, all packed up and with snacks from Charlie even though we're just going the 45 minutes south to San Francisco. We look at each other with unspoken promise. My belly tickles like I've just gone down a huge dip in the road. I have to look out the window and catch my breath. Ian grabs my hand and we drive the whole way to San Francisco with our hands laced together. We don't talk much. It's a gorgeous day and we're comfortable in our silence. Ian lets a deep breath whoosh out of his mouth, and I look over and realize he's nervous.

"What are you up to?" I ask.

"What makes you think I'm up to something?" He

holds his shoulders up with fake innocence.

I poke him in the gut.

He goes over the Golden Gate Bridge, which means we aren't going to Jeff and Laila's. The houseboats in Sausalito look so pretty, floating happily on the water. It reminds me of the night we came and ate over here, watching the houseboats. I think Ian loves them as much as I do.

"Oh, look at that one!" I point to a huge white one with windows all the way around each side.

We take a turn toward the houseboats and admire several large ones. Some of them have full gardens on their decks. One is painted every color imaginable. A few look too big to move.

"These huge ones are really nice, but I thought we might prefer one more like this…" Ian says, stopping in front of the cutest little houseboat I've ever seen. It has a gorgeous garden on one end of the deck. The roof goes into a point, and the houseboat looks like a cottage treehouse on the water. "Think you would enjoy staying here for a few days? Or would you be more comfortable at Jeff and Laila's?"

"It's just right!"

I'm so excited. I hop out of the car before we've even stopped all the way. It's absolutely perfect. The thought of being in this quaint little getaway with Ian for three days is enough to make me hyperventilate.

Ian shuts the car door and comes up behind me, wrapping his arms around my waist. "Okay, Goldilocks, why don't we step inside and see if it really is?"

We step inside and I gush over every feature. I can't help it. It does feel like I've stepped into a storybook. It's cozy with plush, comfortable fabrics, a wood floor and an old-fashioned wood-burning fireplace in the corner. The kitchen has glass-door cabinets and a bistro table overlooking the water. Two curtains hang on either side from the ceiling and behind the curtain is a huge bed covered with soft pillows. The loft has the slanted ceilings and an all-white bed. Outside the loft is a deck that winds around the whole upper level. The view from the deck is extraordinary.

"I love it, Ian. I can't believe you found this place."

"It's how I've managed to distract myself from sneaking back into your bedroom the last couple of nights," he says, tucking my hair behind my ear and kissing me. Softly. Gently. We're still in the loft and I feel the boat floating more up here than the other two levels. Kissing Ian and floating, that sounds about right. "Someone else was scheduled to be in here, but I presented my case. Rather desperately," he adds.

"Is this our first vacation together?" I raise both eyebrows.

"Yes, yes, I think it is." He tickles my side as he says it and I jump out of reach. He's on my tail, and I run down the narrow stairs to the living room. I give him a warning look as he gets close, and he holds up a hand, letting me know he's done tickling. For now.

I take a better look in the kitchen and see it's fully loaded with food: bottles of wine, loaves of French bread, and a huge basket of fresh vegetables and fruit. Inside the refrigerator, there's specialty cheeses, eggs and bacon. Sliced ham and a rotisserie chicken. Flowers sit on the countertop and two boxes of Ghirardelli chocolates.

"I had some help. Turns out Judi, the owner, is a

romantic at heart."

"Oh my goodness, look, we even have two kinds of ice cream in the freezer. Chocolate Peanut Butter and Maple Nut, my favorites. How did you know?" I stare at Ian, stunned.

"Tessa." He grins.

"Tessa!" That girl. I can't believe how well she's doing at keeping secrets from me. I'm gonna have to have a talk with that girl. Enough is enough. She better start spilling.

"Well, if you're not hungry, should we go explore the town? Go kayaking? Um … fishing?" He holds up a little book and recites all the things that are available to do within a 10-20 mile radius. "Hot air balloon ride? Look at the redwoods?"

"I'm happy just staying in. We have all we need right here. It's gonna take us a while to eat all this food. And look at all the movies they have. Plus, cable." I hold up the long list of channels. "Unless you wanted to go do some daredevil things this afternoon." I shrug. "I'm game for anything."

"I'm game for anything, too, but all I really want to do is look at you," he says.

It's the way he looks at me that says so much more.

Thunk. There went my self-restraint dropping to the bottom of the ocean and anchoring us to this very spot.

"I'll be right back." I leave before I maul him and go to the bathroom to splash cold water on my face. I take my toothbrush out of my purse; it's always handy to carry a toothbrush wherever you go. You never know when you're gonna have sex for the first time … that you can remember.

When I come out, Ian has brought in our suitcases. He looks like he might have splashed cold water on his face too. I know he yanked on his hair because it's got an extra lilt to it that wasn't there earlier.

He stands between the curtains of the bedroom and I walk to him, staring him down. His eyes rove over my body and land on my lips. He gives his hair another tug and I realize he's trying not to swear. It just hits me that he's showing restraint in more areas than one. I can't stop the smile that widens with each step toward him. When I reach him, he picks me up and wraps my legs around his waist, holding me up as if it's nothing. He kisses me like he's starving.

He turns around and tosses me on the bed and leans over me, kissing me just as hard. I pull off his shirt, anxious to get to his skin. He pulls off my dress and curses when he sees my red push-up bra and panties. A laugh escapes my lips and he looks flushed. I unbutton his pants then, initiating a step further than I have yet. He pulls them the rest of the way down and I'm in for a ginormous surprise. It's been dark or he's hidden it well under pants or the covers, but there is no hiding how much he now wants out of his pants and into me. He grins sheepishly at me. "What can I say?" he says softly.

"Say you won't stop this time."

"If this is what you want, I won't."

I reach out and carefully pull off his boxer briefs, not quite sure where to focus my eyes. What's the right thing to do here? Is this a time when it really is okay to ogle? Or try to focus on his eyes in a loving way? I can't help it, I have to peek.

And *that's* what a real man looks like.

I had no idea it would be that … impressive.

He's kissing me and I can't think anymore. I lose myself for a while in his tongue and arms and all the places his fingers explore. He has me yelling his name before he even lays gently on top of me and slowly—*so* slowly—he inches inside of me. My eyes are wide on his as he takes his sweet time.

"You're in me," I whisper.

"I know," he grins.

"I love it."

He closes his eyes for a second and says, "I can't take it when you say things like that."

He leans down and kisses me and while the sweetness doesn't go away, a whole new level of desire takes over.

We begin to move, slow and steady. He goes deeper and deeper, until I feel like he must be bumping every internal organ and giving it a kiss. It's too good and suddenly I'm gasping, "I can't go slow anymore," in a voice I don't recognize.

"Go, baby, I'm right here with you." His eyes never leave my face as he guides my hips and we find a new rhythm.

I do. I go. And the pleasure escalates to such a frenzy, I'm afraid I'll scare every houseboat neighbor within 1,000 yards.

- 17 -

Smooth SAILIN'

For the next day and a half, we don't leave the bed unless it's to get food, go to the bathroom, take a bath together, or to christen the other two beds in the house-boat. We're in the loft bed now, looking at the water as Ian lightly tickles my skin with his fingertips. My body feels languorous, or as my mama would say, limp as a dishrag. I am completely spent, but still whenever he turns to me, wanting me again, my body heats up for more. I'd say more than a half dozen times would not be stretching the truth … I think I lost count after the fifth time. And I know we did it on the deck and the second bathroom at least once. Oh wait, twice on the deck.

I can't get enough of him. He touches me and makes me feel like a hungry nymph. I'm trying not to look at him right now because we need to get up and get ready for his show, but as long as he keeps doing that across my chest, I won't move. I've never felt more beautiful in my life than I do right now, lying here completely naked in this bed with Ian Sterling. He has been over every single millimeter of my flesh and acts as if he's discovering something new with each glance. I have also studied him very carefully and think there can't be a finer specimen on this planet than him. He is perfection in every way. His body is the kind that you see on billboards but don't really believe can exist in real life. And every underwear ad I've seen, pfft. They don't have anything on Ian, let me just make that clear.

If there were a line-up of a thousand penises, I'd recognize his in a heartbeat.

I start laughing at that thought and can't stop. Ian leans up on his elbow. "What?"

I shake my head and can't get a word out, I'm laughing too hard. When I laugh this hard, I do a long wheeze and it sounds like I'm not breathing. 'Cause I'm not.

He starts laughing, too, because the wheeze is infectious. You can't not laugh at the wheeze. It's impossible.

"I want to know what's so funny."

I wipe the tears from my eyes and try to tell him, but all I can get out is, "Your penis!"

He laughs but not quite as hard as before. "Uh, my penis makes you laugh?"

"Nooo. Yes. No!"

"And I would have thought you'd say, 'parts' or 'willy' or some other cutesy name."

"It's where my dad put his foot down. My mom wanted to call the penis a 'fountain' but my dad said no way."

It's his turn to wheeze. "I'm so glad he didn't let that one slip in." He sits up and pulls me with him. "What *about* my penis?"

"I love it." I snort. "I'm sorry. I am *not* good at talking about these things."

"Well, I'm glad. Although, you have me a little self-conscious at the moment."

WILLOW ASTER

"Noooo, you don't need to be. I think you have the best one I've ever seen. I mean ... I haven't seen many. Or *any*, really. Other than pictures, but..." I throw my head in my hands. "Please don't make me talk about penises."

"You brought it up! Just tell me what had you howling." He gives me a good shake.

I whisper, "I thought if there were a line-up of a thousand penises, I'd be able to pick out yours. Because it's the best. Massive. Those underwear ads are of little puny guys with nothing ... I guess seeing one like yours would send young girls and horny women and little old ladies into *fits* in public."

Ian is just staring at me like I'm a lunatic and then he falls back on the bed and laughs until he cries. I think I'm going to have to give him CPR the way he's carrying on.

"Oh my *GOD*! You are a *nut*! You're crazy! You're crazy and I love you and that is the funniest thing I've ever heard."

"Well, it's just true," I sniff, not sure I like being called a nut, but my heart still going into overdrive that he's telling me he loves me.

He wipes his eyes and continues to laugh, shaking his head and then realizing I'm not laughing anymore. "Hey, come here. Don't you get miffed at me. I think you're adorable."

I roll my eyes.

"Baby, you just told me I'm massive and that underwear ads have little puny guys with nothing. I might not have been thinking right when I called you a nut or crazy. *Clearly*, you are the smartest person with the best eyesight EVER, and I commend you on your excellent vision."

"That's better," I scowl for as long as it will hold and

then crack up again.

Getting ready is fun with Ian. It takes twice as long because we end up having sex in the shower, but I diffuse my hair, leaving it curly, which helps save a lot of time. Ian told me it's his favorite way that I wear my hair after he saw it wet that day in New York. Pale and naturally curly hair. Next he'll be saying he prefers me with no makeup.

I put on a silver tube dress that fits like a glove.

"Speaking of massive," Ian murmurs, pushing down the top of my dress to kiss my breasts before grudgingly covering them up. "They—I mean—YOU look like the one I never want to leave my bed."

My body burns with that thought. "I thought you were a leg guy," I say as we get into the car.

"I'm all about your legs," he agrees. "Until I see your tits and then I can't get enough of them. But really your aaa—bum. Your bum is out of this world."

I can't help but laugh at him.

"Your mouth, though, that's my favorite. Your lips. Your smile. When you smile, everything else fades away."

"Unless I take off my shirt."

"Well, yeah, it *is* distracting when you do that. I do always go back to your mouth, though, don't I?" He runs his fingers over my lips.

Sigh. He melts me.

We load all the equipment into the back of The Great American Music Hall and run into the guys in Ian's band—Charlie, Chris, and Aaron. They're all cute, scruffy, and friendly. Reagan Waters walks by and Ian hollers. "Reagan, come here. Reagan, I'd like you to meet

Sparrow. Sparrow, Reagan."

Reagan gives me the long appraisal that most girls always do with me at first and grins when she sees both of Ian's hands on me. Her catlike eyes reach mine, and she give me a slow smile. "Well. It's about time Ian met his match," she says. She tosses her reddish-blonde hair back and holds out her hand.

"Nice to meet you," I say.

"Oh, it's nice to meet *you*."

"Reagan is opening tonight," Ian explains. "And throughout the summer, she'll be opening the shows."

The thought of that makes me feel a little queasy. She really is beautiful.

"I'd love to hear how the two of you met," she says.

Ian is still wrapped around my back and he leans down to kiss my cheek. "We met at a restaurant with mutual friends. She brought her boyfriend…"

I laugh. "That doesn't sound very good, does it … but yeah … that's about right."

"How long ago was this?" Reagan looks between Ian and me.

I look at him. He creases his brow. "You know I'm horrible with dates—but that was about, what? A year ago?" He looks at me. "Can that be right? Wow. A little over a year ago."

"Well, since we met, yeah."

Reagan just stands there watching us with her mouth hanging open slightly. A little bit of fire shimmers in her eyes that wasn't there a few minutes ago. She catches herself and closes her mouth, nodding. "It looks like you've got it all worked out now," she says with a touch of bite. "I'm happy for you, Ian."

"Thanks, Reagan," Ian says sincerely.

Either he doesn't know she doesn't mean it or he's a really good actor, pretending like he doesn't on my account. It's obvious to me that Reagan is trying to talk herself into being happy that Ian has found someone. Pretty sure they've had something between them.

When Reagan walks away, I watch Ian to see if he watches her walk away or if he gives away anything. He doesn't. He kisses me and says, "Where would you like to be? I need to run over a few things with the guys. We've rehearsed like fiends before now, so it was okay that we haven't practiced this week, but I *do* need to touch base with them before we go on. You can be with me, either in the green room or whatever they have set up for us. Or just wherever you'd like to be..."

"Do you think it's okay if I go ahead and sit in the auditorium? I can read for a while before the show starts."

"I don't see why not. If you're sure..." He looks disappointed that I'm not going with him.

After I have gawked at the beautiful building, I read and catch up on voice mails with my phone. I'm trying to ignore the sick feeling I have about Reagan. And her being on the road with Ian for the next few months. And whatever that vibe was with her. The show is about to start, and I put my phone away and people-watch.

"Sparrow?"

I turn around and see Laila at a table behind me. She's by herself and looks stunning with a low cut red dress that looks a lot like the one I have. The room is casting a warm glow and her shoulder-length brown hair shines in the light. She's sipping a cocktail and I debate walking over to her table, but I don't really want to get caught there as the show is starting. The polite thing to do would be to ask her if she'd like to sit with me, since I'm closer, but something about her demeanor gives me pause.

"How are you, Laila?" I ask from my seat.

"Wonderful. How are you, Sparrow?"

"Really great." I smile. "Where's Jeff?" I look behind her, searching the room for his tall frame.

"He's not here. He's working on his book," she says and takes another long swig of her cocktail until it's empty. "He's always working on a book, you know."

I nod uncomfortably.

I've never been so grateful to feel the lights dim and hear the beginning sounds of chords playing. "Well, enjoy the show," I say awkwardly to Laila and she holds up her glass to me.

Reagan is sitting at the piano and has changed into a black edgy evening gown. It looks glamorous on the top, but the bottom is frayed and all different lengths. She looks like an exotic mermaid. When she begins to play, the room goes quiet and she casts us under her haunting spell for the next 45 minutes or so. I look back at Laila, and she is nursing another drink and looking at me. She raises it again, and I wave and turn around, confused by her behavior.

Ian comes out and the place comes alive, yelling and cheering. His band kicks in and I enjoy seeing Ian front and center with his own band. They sound great together. Having the band behind him gives his songs a whole different feel. A little more edgy, rather than the blues sound he had alone. His voice, even with the rasp and edge, comes out of him effortlessly. When he reaches the rafters, he's still controlled. But you feel the emotion behind every note, every inflection. I believe every line he sings.

Some people are dancing up front. I can't move. I don't want to miss a thing.

All too soon, it's over and Laila comes up to my table and sits down. I guess she's ready to visit now. She has a really good buzz on her.

"You look awfully sexy tonight," she slurs. "I bet Ian likes you in that dress."

"Thank you." I'm not sure if she's complimenting me or not, but I don't want to appear rude and give her anything to report back to Charlie…

We just sit for about fifteen minutes, watching the people around us empty out of the room. An usher comes to the table and says, "Mr. Sterling is asking for you to meet him behind the stage." It reminds me of that night in New York and the gentle giant who led me to Ian. I stand up and so does Laila. I expect her to say good-bye and go on her way, but she doesn't. Apparently, she's going backstage with me.

When we get closer, Laila takes my arm and when we get to the door that says Green Room, she just opens the door without even knocking. Ian has his shirt off and is pulling another one over his head. He looks up, surprised.

"Hey, baby," he says. "Laila? I didn't know you were here."

Laila looks between the two of us, her eyes narrowing, and I feel a déjà vu moment all over again. First Reagan and then Laila. What is everyone's deal with me dating Ian? Is it because I'm so young? Not good enough for him? Too good for him? I wish someone would just spit it out already.

"Great show," I tell him. "I loved it, Ian."

"I'm so glad." He looks pleased. He kisses my forehead and smiles at me. It's a little awkward with Laila in the room.

"You two sure seem cozy," she says.

"Yeah," he says, "this girl is something else, Laila." He grins proudly at me and turns to Laila. "No Jeff tonight?"

"No, you know him. He's not much of a social bug. You sounded amazing, Ian. You're such a rockstar. No one's ever told you that, have they?" She laughs and gives an exaggerated turn, the kind where you give yourself away that you're drunk.

Ian takes her arm. "You okay, Laila? You're getting a cab, right?"

"The two of you were supposed to be coming to the house," she says with a whine to Ian.

I had actually forgotten all about that. I guess in my sex-induced stupor, I had conveniently put that right out of my mind.

"We made other plans. I let you know that, Laila."

"Well, that's too bad. I was hoping to have you stay with me," she puts her hand on Ian's chest and leaves it there while she looks over at me. "Ian and I have been friends for a *long* time. Long before *Jeff* ever entered the picture." She gives a dark laugh.

"I think you should get on home, Laila, it's late. Jeff will be wondering where you are." Ian leads her to the door.

"No, he won't. You know that's not true. Don't patronize me, Ian!" Her voice is grating when she does the whine. She looks at me. "Sparrow. You're too young to get caught up with this one, take it from me." She pats Ian on the chest again and walks out of the room.

Ian looks angry as he talks to the guard outside the door and asks him to make sure she gets safely in a cab.

When she's out of the door, he gives me a huge hug, his anger disappearing. "I've missed you," he says.

"I've missed you, too. It feels like a long time since we were in our own little houseboat world."

"Let's get back to it."

"I'm ready."

That night after we make love and I fall asleep, I dream of the doors. The doors to Laila's house. And when the door opens, it's the Great American Music Hall green room and Reagan is inside with Ian. In my sleep, I try to change my dream, and it works. I try to reopen the door, and when I do, it's Laila inside with Ian.

I wake up to Ian softly shaking me. "Baby, you all right? Are you dreaming?"

I try to focus on him and reach out for him, holding him tight. "Hey."

"Hey—you ok? I thought you were dreaming a good one about us at first," Ian says in my ear, "but then you were making this sad, whimpering sound. NOT the sounds you make with me." He studies my face and kisses my nose. "You okay?"

I nod, still groggy.

"Come on, I want to do something." He takes me by the hand and climbs out of bed.

"It's the middle of the night."

"It's 2 A.M. We just had a little nap."

Ian wraps a blanket around our shoulders and leads me down the stairs and out onto the main deck. It's about as warm as it ever gets in San Francisco at night. The air is calm and the moon is split in two. Our houseboat is barely rocking, just enough to be soothing.

"It's a perfect night for a swim."

"Really, right now?"

He gives the blanket a tug and grabs my hand. We run off the deck and splash into the water. It's COLD. The Pacific Ocean is not for the faint of heart. As soon as I come up, I'm shivering and shaking.

"In the moonlight, your lips look blue," he whispers.

"That's probably because they are! We're gonna catch pneumonia."

"Come here. I know how to warm you up."

He wraps his body around mine and my body feels that sizzling burn. I have it so bad for this man. I can't bear the thought of leaving him tomorrow, so I push it out of my mind and focus on the way his skin feels.

"I thought things weren't supposed to work properly in such frigid temperatures," I say between chills. "Oh, well, there you are. What? Are you just always up for it?"

"You haven't been complaining," he says as he drives himself into me.

"No." Breathless.

"This is what you do to me, Sparrow."

In seconds, I'm moaning and so is he, but quietly so we don't wake the other houseboat residents. Three sea lions swim by and look at us curiously, but keep floating past.

"Next time, we can be as loud as we want and blame

the sea lions," I say, as he's wrapping me back up with the blanket on deck.

He lets out a loud laugh that probably wrecked all our efforts anyway.

I love it when I surprise him.

- 18 -

Take ME Home

Our last day on the boat has a more serious tone. For someone who is typically laidback, Ian even seems a little anxious.

My mind is made up.

I will not ask when I'll see him again.

I will not think about what will happen when I let him go.

I will not let my perpetually moving brain drive me crazy. That will happen soon enough.

If I never saw him again, these days in our own little world have been enchanted enough to last my lifetime. I will never be the same. It's just the way it is. I know it like I know books are meant to be savored and writing is what keeps me sane. It's just true.

Ian is watching me pack. We're in the main bedroom, and his things are already packed.

"You're making me nervous." I zip my suitcase and look at him.

"Why? I'm just looking at you for as long as I can," he says.

"Ohhh-kay."

He puts both hands up to his mouth and holds them there while he watches my every move. "I love how you sing your words. It's like everything that comes out of your mouth is a song. You even make 'okay' sound exotic."

I flush. "Oh please…" I mumble.

He leans up, elbows on knees. "Please what?"

"Please, don't be ridiculous. If we're talking about voices, everything that comes out of your mouth sounds like sex on a stick."

He pounces on me, throwing me back on the bed. "Miss Fisher, you know what it does to me when you talk dirty."

"Pssh. Me, talking dirty. I can only say sex and penis. Everything else is off the books."

"Those are the only two words I need to hear," he teases.

"You said I was the nut," I say as I flip him over and get on top. My hair falls on either side of his face as I lean down to kiss him.

"I really wanted to do that pencil thing with your hair," he says between kisses.

"Pencil thing?"

"Where we put it up and make you look like a librar-ian."

My face hurts from smiling so hard. "Oh, I'm gonna miss you."

He grabs my face and brands my lips with his. We make our last hour count.

I'm on the plane before I see Tessa. Ian and I were both running to separate sides of the airport. We took a little too much time saying good-bye. Tessa is in our row, practically hopping.

"You had me worried there, girl." She helps get my stuff situated and gives me a long look. "Oh. My. God. It's happened. There is no doubt this time. I know you've been gettin' some lovin'." She does a little dance with her arms as she says it.

I lean my head back on the seat and say, "I have so much to tell you. I don't even know where to begin. I'm exhausted." I look at her then and raise an eyebrow. "From all the lovin'." I flash her a smile showing every tooth possible.

"WOOOOO!" She yelps, causing all the passengers to turn toward us, their faces expressing everything from good humor to aggravation. "Good news," she says to anyone whose eyes linger longer than a second, pointing to me. "Good. News."

I cover my face and laugh.

I try to act like I'm too tired to talk and not going to share such intimate details, but by the first half hour, she's gotten a lot out of me.

"Sterling the *Stud*." She grins approvingly. "You can just tell by looking that he knows what to do with what he's been given," she says with a sigh. "But the *endurance*!" She says it so emphatically that we both get choked up laughing. "I'm serious, Ro. No, really. You just don't know how lucky you are to get such a *stallion*." We lose it again. She's not done. "I mean Jared loves the sex, but he didn't even do that in the very beginning! Listen, not every guy can keep it up after that many times." She shakes her head.

"I knew I should have waited to tell you when we

were on the ground." I have to fan myself with the Skymiles magazine. She's killing me.

"There was no holding that news off. It is shining on your face to beat the man."

"Beat the band."

"Yeah, that too."

Getting back to our apartment is bittersweet. I'm happy to be with Tessa and even New York, but my mind is still living on that houseboat. It takes a good week for me to wipe the dreamy look off my face. Tessa is teasing me mercilessly, and I don't blame her. I am reliving every moment with Ian.

The night after I get back, I'm in bed and on the phone with Ian. He's been sweet and it just makes me miss him more.

Before we hang up, he throws out: "You've ruined me." His voice is playful.

"Oh yeah?"

"The guys are calling me Red Raw. Red Raw Bows, to be exact."

"Ha, Red Raw Bows? Why?"

"My elbows are bright red, like carpet burn … *raw*," he says and pauses.

I chuckle, but I don't get it.

"From spending so much time on my elbows the last few days?"

Suddenly, I picture him leaning over me, propped up on his elbows, gazing at me with his fathomless eyes, kissing me all over …

"Oh … ohhhh." I giggle. "Ouch. Um, sorry…"

"Are you kidding? I'm wearing my casualties

proudly. I've never had red raw bows before."

"Hmm. So a first for you?"

"*You* are a first for me, Sparrow."

After a couple days of looking, I get a part-time job at a coffee shop in the Village. It's the perfect job for me. It's busy, not long enough to be overwhelming, and it leaves me enough time to write in the afternoons. Professor Shutes, from one of my creative writing courses, really encouraged me to take an assignment I turned in to her and consider expanding it into a novel. I was floored. I thanked her profusely and promised I'd show her something in the fall. Just knowing I am accountable to her helps spur me on. I've been working on it every day, and I'm feeling really good about it.

So my life is busy, but dull in comparison to my time with Ian. We talk all the time, but it's just not the same as being with him. I work and write and talk on the phone and text and see Tessa and Jared and turn down dates from guys … even though, the way we technically left it, Ian and I are "free" to date other people.

I don't like being in a long-distance relationship. I hate it. But it's a world better than those stretches where I didn't hear from him and didn't know what he was thinking. Anytime I'm really heartsick for him, I think about how much worse that was. At least now I know he's wishing he could be with me. That's what I tell myself, anyway, when I'm staring longingly at all the cute couples that come in the coffee shop together. Seeing all the hand-in-hand people in love … the long kisses in the subway … it's a lonesome feeling.

The days both drag and fly by. Before I know it, it's

the end of August. It's been close to two months since I've seen Ian and things are going well, but it's time to see him. Lately, I've been a bit testy with him on the phone. I'm walking home from work and he calls.

"What are you doing this weekend?"

"Uh, well … I'm off work, so I was just gonna write."

"I thought this was your weekend off," he sounds relieved. "Okay, I wanted to check first before I just bought the tickets, but—can you meet me in L.A.? Thursday to Monday maybe? My gig was canceled Friday night and I'll have the house to myself. Jeff and Laila won't be there right now. Come on, I need to see you, and you can write there, too—" he says in one breath.

I'm excited. I don't have to think too hard to jump on it. "I'll have to switch shifts for Thursday and Monday, but that shouldn't be too hard. Nadine's been wanting extra shifts. It would be the last time I could do it before school starts … okay!"

He lets out a sigh. "Sweet. I'll get the tickets now. I've got a rehearsal in an hour for our show tonight. So, can I just text you the details and we'll talk later?"

"Yes! And thank you, Ian! It'll be *so* good to see you."

"I can't wait, baby."

I'm surprised by how nervous I feel to see him. After our last time together and then talking to him every day, I didn't expect to be so anxious. But when I see him, and he picks me up and kisses me like he's never going to let go, it lifts. Pure adrenaline and lust take its place. We can't stop grinning at each other.

"God, you're hot," he says. "I don't forget when we're apart—at all—but it just sort of shocks me all over again when I see you.

"*You're* the hot one in this relationship."

"I don't have anything on you."

"Hopefully that will change soon."

"Little Bird! What have I *done* to you?"

I laugh and turn purple. Turns out I still can't really do the dirty talk. Every now and then, I try to pull it out, and it just makes us laugh. He pulls my body flat against his and makes my legs give when he kisses me again. So, maybe it does work a little. He slowly lets go and opens the car door. His whole face is shining. I wonder if mine looks the same.

He leans in as I'm buckling up. "I'll take you wherever you want to go. You're hungry, right?"

I nod. I can't really think straight when he's looking at me like he wants to devour me.

"Okay, we better have all our outside fun now because once I get you in bed, I'm not letting you out." He kisses the end of my nose and shuts the door behind him.

When he gets in the car and pulls out of the parking garage, I turn to him and say, "How about we go to the beach and eat out there and there's the Santa Monica Pier, we could ride rides ... and a fun bookstore is not too far from there. And I could stand to go shopping for a while. I need some new ... um, underwear and—" I choke up then, laughing at the way his face is changing the longer I go on, "—and the pharmacy for ... nail polish and ... toilet paper..."

"Do I need to pull this car over and screw you senseless?"

"Yes?"

He groans and yanks on his hair. He looks over at me,

running his eyes up and down my body in that slow way that lets me know he's imagining me with no clothes. He smiles his naughty smile, and my heart does its flip-flop.

"Hey, baby," he says, "you're here."

"I know." I beam back at him.

I don't think I could be any happier than I am right now.

We do take longer to get to the Roberts' house than I'd hoped. I think Ian feels like he owes me some fun since I'm in California, so he takes me to the beach and we eat at a great little hole-in-the-wall seafood place by the water. We walk along the beach for a while and Ian keeps watching me, not bothering to hide his lust, until I realize he's teasing me back. Just waiting to see how long I can take it before I break down and attack him.

I act fine, not letting on that every touch he's giving me is making it harder and harder for me to think straight. When he pulls into the parking lot of a CVS drugstore, I lose it and laugh my head off.

"What?" he asks innocently.

"TAKE ME HOME!"

"Well, I thought you'd never ask." He pulls right back out of the parking lot and speeds away, up into the foothills.

The Roberts' home is nothing like their place in San Francisco. It's large and modern, very Southern California. The inside is stark but beautiful. Windows line every side of the house, overlooking a gorgeous view. Everything is clean, no clutter whatsoever.

"Beautiful place."

"Nice, isn't it."

"Where are we staying?"

He grabs my arm and has me snug against him before I can blink. "You ready to be put to bed?"

"I guess."

"You better BE-have." He slings me across his shoulder and runs down the hall to the bedroom, smacking me the whole way.

"I'm BEING-have!" I'm laughing and reach out to bite his bum since it's right in my face.

He lets out a yelp when I do.

"Is this your room?" I ask when he opens the door.

"Yep."

I try to take a look around, but he is having none of it. Soon, I don't care if we're in a tent or the Taj Mahal, I have to have him.

We don't get much sleep that night. The next morning, my body feels sore in the best possible way. Still on New York time, I wake up before Ian and just lay there a while, enjoying his arms around me. Soon, my stomach gets too growly and I lift Ian's hand off my boob and lay it on the covers while I sneak out of the bed. I put on a camisole and panties and sleepily walk to the kitchen to start some coffee. Ten minutes later, I have bacon going and am working on an egg scramble when Ian comes up from behind and wraps his arms around me.

"I missed you," he whispers as he kisses my neck.

"My stomach got the better of me." I turn around and face him, leaning up to kiss him. He looks divine in the morning light. I still can't believe he's mine.

He leans down and plants a kiss on a nipple that perked up as soon as he came near. "Well, let's get you fed. Looks really good," he looks over my shoulder.

I turn off the stove and he gives me one more hug. His hands are roaming down my chest and stomach, like he just can't let go.

Someone clears their throat and Ian's hands go still. We both turn around and Jeff and Laila are standing there. Jeff is trying not to laugh and Laila's look is indecipherable. I tuck myself behind Ian's body to hide.

Jeff speaks first. "Hey! Sorry to startle you! I take it you didn't know we were coming?" He looks at Laila. "I thought you called day before yesterday to let Ian know…"

"I did call him. Did I not tell you we were coming, Ian?" She frowns and stares at Ian.

"No, you didn't," he says, his voice level but cold. I'm not used to that tone coming from him. "I told you Sparrow was coming this weekend." He looks pointedly at Laila.

"Well, the more the merrier!" Laila says with a cool smile. "Looks like breakfast is ready. You better eat up before it gets cold."

"I'm just gonna go … put some clothes on," I say awkwardly.

"We'll get our things put away. Nice to have you here, Sparrow," Jeff says graciously. I can tell he's almost as embarrassed as I am. He practically pulls Laila out of the room. I don't move until I hear them walking up the stairs.

Ian looks at me, and I flinch at the look in his eyes. He's mad. When I cover my chest with my arms, his eyes soften and he hugs me to him. "I'm sorry, Sparrow. I had no idea they would be here this weekend. I'll fix this."

"It's okay. I mean, I would have worn clothes if I'd known they were coming this *morning*, but…" I try to laugh it off, but it doesn't ring true.

"I'll get the food on the table while you get dressed," he says. "Will you bring a shirt for me when you come back?"

"Sure."

I take more than a few minutes getting dressed. Knowing we have company, I feel the need to do way more than I would have with just Ian. When I come back out, Ian and Laila are out on the deck, and Ian is saying something very emphatic to her. She has her hands on her hips and shakes her head. It doesn't look pleasant. This is feeling really uncomfortable.

Ian looks in the window and sees me watching and starts walking toward the screen door. Before he opens it, he says one more thing to Laila and her face falls.

I toss him a shirt when he gets inside and he tries to calm his features, but the tension in the room isn't going anywhere. We sit down and Laila storms through the door and out of the kitchen.

"I'm so sorry, baby. We'll go stay somewhere else."

My appetite is gone, but I try to eat past the lump in my throat. I don't know why this is so weird. I just want out of here.

We don't really talk, other than Ian complimenting the food and trying to make me feel more at ease. He gives up when I don't really have anything to say back. We clean up the dishes, and I go back to the bedroom to take a shower. I jump when Ian steps in the shower not long after me.

"Ian … this isn't a good idea."

"What? To be near you after you've come all this way?"

"You know what I mean."

"Come on, hand me that shampoo, and we'll get out of here. I have a place in mind." He begins to wash my hair and when he massages my scalp, it does calm me.

We get ready in record time, have the car packed, and are down the road before they even know we're gone.

"I'm just gonna call Jeff and tell him we left." Ian's eying me cautiously, not sure what to do with my quietness. I listen to the one-sided conversation. It sounds like there's no problem between Jeff and Ian.

When Ian's off the phone, he takes my hand in his, and we drive into Santa Monica city limits. He veers into The Viceroy Hotel parking lot.

"I feel bad about all the money you're spending right now," I say softly.

"Don't. This is not hurting me in any way. We've been having steady gigs and royalties are coming in from Jagged recording two of my songs. My accommodations are usually covered. I'm sittin' prettier than I ever have, baby," he reassures me.

Hotel clerk girl can't take her eyes off of Ian. Hotel clerk boy can't take his eyes off of me. For all their attention, you'd think we were celebrities. Clerk girl croons in a low, sexy voice to Ian, "The Monarch suite is available, Mr. Sterling. I'd be happy to upgrade you for no extra charge." She leans over to show off her orb-boob cleavage.

I think a not-so-nice thought about her—something about the fact that my breasts are just as big, but without the bulbous globe factor. And then I inwardly kick myself for being so snotty. Charlie would be appalled. Actually, Charlie would be appalled at much more than that. I wonder if Laila will tell her she found me half-naked in her kitchen this morning. I haven't exactly told my mom I'm sleeping with Ian. It would not go over well. At all.

In a fog, I walk with Ian to the suite. It's gorgeous. Full ocean views. The bed is against a mirrored wall, and a white, tufted couch—it would go perfectly with my bed—sits at the end of the bed. It would actually be amazing if I could shake off the cloud hanging over me. I sit on the couch and Ian crouches in front of me.

"Tell me what's wrong," he says.

"What's Laila's deal with you?"

He looks hard at me for a minute. It feels like forever. "She's a little … protective of me," he finally says.

"Protective? She acted jealous. Why would she be jealous of me? She was fine with me dating Michael … all for it. Why doesn't she want me with you?"

"I've never really had a girlfriend around them. When I'm in town, it's just us and I think she's just … I don't know. I don't know why she acted like that." He leans his forehead on my chest, between my non-orb breasts. Yeah, I can't get past those things Clerk Girl was sporting. "Baby, what are you thinking? Come back to me." He kisses the skin right above my blouse. "We don't have much time. I don't want to think about Laila."

"Well, it was just weird," I huff.

"I know and I'm so sorry to put you in such an awkward position. I told her so, too."

"Yeah, I'm sorry. I need to snap out of it…"

Ian gets on the bed behind me and rubs my shoulders.

I look out at the ocean and feel my whole body relax. Slowly, the worries fade away, except for one persistent thought: I won't let Laila ruin this.

- 19 -

Winter BREAK

Fast forward: 1 year and 2 months later

I finish my last final and hurry home to collapse into my bed for a short nap. I only have twenty minutes, but I can't keep my eyes open any longer. When my alarm goes off, I drag myself out of bed and get ready. My parents and Ian are coming tonight and we're going to spend Christmas here, in New York. Christmas night, my parents will drive to Cape Cod for the rest of the week. Ian and I will fly to Minnesota, where I'll meet his mom for the first time. It feels like a huge step, even though we've been dating for a year and a half. I count the time when Ian showed up on my apartment stoop with the white flag as when we "officially" started dating, even though he's had my heart far longer than that.

I put on a short green dress with a perfect twirly skirt and pile my hair up in large, smooth curls. We're going to Per Se, a fancy restaurant that sounds amazing. Ian went recently when he met with a record label that has been courting him, and while he was there, he made a reservation for us tonight.

Everything is going so well. Ian and I are closer than ever, and we both have exciting things happening with our careers. Professor Shutes has a connection at Penguin and my book has just been picked up. By this time next year, I will have a book in bookstores! I can't even believe it. I realize I'm way too young for this to be happening, so I'm somewhat nervously cautious to believe that it is. Ian has several labels vying for him, and he's just trying to pick the best one. We're making the long distance thing work. It's really hard, but we're doing it.

Our only challenge, besides the distance, is the occasional rumor that sometimes comes with dating a musician who is getting more famous by the minute. Ian stays out of the press for the most part, but he's been linked with Reagan a few times and another musician named Jules. I try not to be jealous or doubt him, but when we've gone four months at a time without seeing each other, during Ian's overseas tours, it does tend to up the jealousy ante.

I've done my part to throw complication into the mix—unintentionally, but disastrous nonetheless. I went out with Zach, a friend from work—on what I thought was a casual lunch—and when he opened the car door for me and I stood up, he stuck his tongue down my throat. I told Ian about it right away, and he took it better than I expected. And then there was a friend I'd gone to high school with who was in New York on vacation. He looked me up and we went out to dinner. I told him I was dating Ian, but at the end of the night, he still kissed me. That kiss didn't go over so well, but Ian still forgave me and we moved on.

Occasionally we argue over Laila. I haven't seen her

since last year in her kitchen, but Ian still sees her once in a while, and it seems there's always drama involved. I know he has to be around Laila with Jeff being his cousin, but sometimes, it really doesn't seem worth it. She's always picking a fight. I want him to stop staying with them.

I turned twenty-one earlier this month. Tessa surprised me with a party. It helped ease my sadness over being apart from Ian. He was on a European tour and couldn't get away, and school was too crazy for me to go be with him. Ian sent me a necklace that he found in an antique shop in Paris. It has a branch with a sparrow sitting on it. So perfect. The eye of the sparrow is a tiny blue topaz, my birthstone. He added the stone. It originally had a clear crystal. It's beautiful and delicate and I wear it all the time.

The door slams, and Tessa and Jared come in, both chattering at once.

"Ro, settle a debate for us," Tessa walks to the doorway, the cold air bouncing off of her. Jared stands back a little, grinning.

"Wow, you look amazing, Ro!" Tessa reaches out to touch my hair and looks me over. "Ian's gonna be beside himself in front of your parents. You know how he feels about your legs. He can't be held accountable. Okay. That song that Nat King Cole sings, you know, the one about Jack Frost…"

"Chestnuts roasting on an open fire…" I sing, throwing in some extra vibrato.

"Yes! That one. Settle this for us. Sing a little more."

"Uh … Jack Frost nipping at your nose … yuletide carols be-"

Jared lets out a huge laugh and Tessa yells, "Noooo!" as he tickles her from behind. Their good mood is infectious.

"Why? What did you think it was, Tess?" I giggle. I already know this will be good.

She mutters something softly.

"What?"

"You, I and Carol…" she says louder.

I have to repeat that before it registers. "Ohhh! Right! You, I and Carol!" And then I can't stop laughing. I'm gonna be singing it that way for the rest of my life now.

Tessa rolls her eyes but laughs too. "I've always thought that line was weird," she admits.

That sends us right back over the edge.

"When is Ian getting in?" Jared asks once we've calmed down.

"His flight lands right before my parents', so he'll have a car waiting for them. They're going to pick me up in … fifteen minutes!"

"Well, I'm so glad we got to see you." Tessa gives me a long hug. "I'm gonna miss you. We just came to get our bags. Our flight leaves in a few hours."

"I'll miss you, too. Two weeks. Don't forget to come back."

"Ha. You're not getting rid of me that easily. You make sure YOU come back!"

"Minnesota will not keep me! This much I know!" I raise my fist in the air.

Tessa snorts. "Better not."

They leave in the same flurry as they came in. I pace with excited energy. It's been three months this time … since I've seen him. Four months since I've seen my parents. I'm so excited to see all three of them, but I'm gonna have a hard time containing myself with Ian.

My parents come in first. We all hug, and I look around for Ian.

"He couldn't make it," my dad jokes.

"Not funny, Dad. Where is he?"

"I think he wanted to make a grand entrance," my mom says, smiling over my shoulder.

I turn around, and he's standing in the doorway. I go flying toward him, and he meets me halfway, picking me up and hugging me until I squeak. We kiss like it's been three months: passionate, yet shy, hungry and tentative, all at once.

My dad clears his throat, and we pull apart and laugh awkwardly.

Ian leans in and whispers in my ear, "You're trying to kill me, right here in front of your parents. What the hell? Why ya have to look so damn gorgeous?"

I giggle and lean in for another kiss.

We stare at each other, intense and bashful. It's always like this when we first see each other. It makes all the missing worth it—this giddy rush of being together again.

"You look beautiful, Rosie," my dad says.

"Thanks, Dad."

Both of Ian's arms are around me, and he suddenly lets go with one and grasps his hair in a violent tug. Then he's back, and he softly places a kiss on the back of my neck. "So beautiful," he groans.

Christmas time in Manhattan is magical. Last year we

spent Christmas in California, and it was lovely. It seems as if it's the sunniest time of the year there. But I love having the snow and brisk air during the holidays. All the white lights on the trees make it feel like an enchanted dreamland, and it's magnified when I'm holding Ian's hand.

Our dining experience is fine dining at its best. I've never had such good food in all my life. We have a wonderful time during dinner. I'm so glad my parents love Ian. They still occasionally bring up Michael, but know I was never in love with him. I think they believe Ian's a better fit for me, too, which is such a relief.

"Little Bird? You with us?" Ian grins over at me. Between the two of us, we're two spacey beings. He can be writing a song in his mind, and I have a hard time shutting my thoughts and stories down. It's amazing we can communicate with one another at all.

"I'm here." I reach over and touch his cheek. He is stunning. Looking at him still makes my heart go all wacky. His black suit still has a rocker vibe to it; he looks good enough to eat. My cheeks splotch at the thought, and I have to rein it in. "I'm just thinking about how happy I am that we're all together. I don't know when I've ever been as content as I am right now, here with the three of you. I've missed you so much." I look at each one of them in the eye and blink back the tears that are threatening to spill.

Ian kisses my hand and my dad pats my other hand. We all have a heartwarming moment and then dessert comes … after a 9-course meal. I can't even explain how spectacular the desserts are. It's a small buffet of mini-desserts that arrives at our table, and I try it all. Heaven.

After our dinner, my parents go back to my apartment, claiming they're worn out from the long travel day. I get the impression they're in on whatever Ian has cooked up for me. We hop in a cab and go to Swing 46.

"Your dress is perfect for this," Ian says as we get inside, "when I twirl you around, I can totally catch a peek," he whispers.

I give him a tiny smirk. "I've been wanting to come here!"

"Let's do this."

We dance the night away, and it's such fun. I can't get enough. Ian was made for me. I'm sure of it. We just fit. His eyes don't leave me the whole night; his gaze is hypnotic, pulling me in deeper with each look. It's not all serious. We have a hard time not laughing when we're together, so there's plenty of that too. The evening feels like a long love letter, with sweet touches and looks speaking volumes of truth.

I think we're the last ones to leave. I lean my head back on Ian's shoulder on the ride back to my place.

"You sleepy, Little Bird?"

"I'm happy." I smile at him. I turn to kiss him as his hand softly touches my neck.

"I love you, Sparrow Kate Fisher."

"I love you, Ian Orville Sterling."

My mom has the couch all made up for Ian when we get inside. He smiles when he sees it. He hugs me tight and gives me a chaste kiss. "Thank you for one of the best nights ever," he says. "Goodnight, baby."

"Night." I look at him longingly as I go to my room. It's really hard leaving him there.

The next few days are excruciating. Being around each other constantly, after such a long time apart and still not having much time alone, is a struggle for me. I can't concentrate on what anyone around me is saying.

I want Ian more than food or water. More than air.

He's acting like it's no big deal. Like he can be around me and not cave. It's been three freaking months. I expected him to sneak in my room at night. I thought he wouldn't be able to stay away from me. But he does. And it drives me CRAZY.

By Christmas Eve, I'm agitated with him. I'm snippy at our sweet family dinner. I practically growl at Ian, and he just looks at me, lovingly and amused. My parents look concerned. Charlie asks if I'm coming down with something.

I can't wait to go to Minnesota.

I try to go to bed earlier than normal because I'm having a really hard time not snapping Ian's head off. He's making me feel even worse by being so sweet.

He gives me a soft kiss by my door. "I love being here like this, with you and your family … feeling part of something more … sorry, I'm just … I love you, baby," he whispers.

"I love you."

"Get to sleep so Santa can come." He winks, and then looks like he wants to say more, but he doesn't.

I kiss his cheek and feel like a heel when I close the door. What's wrong with me? I should just be happy he's here, not a walking horn dog.

I'm sound asleep and dreaming about Ian. It's such a good dream and in it I begin to moan. He's making me feel so good. I'm jarred awake when a hand lightly clamps over my mouth. Ian's head is between my legs, his tongue working wonders, and he's trying to keep me quiet. I pull the pillow over my face and try to restrain myself. It's hopeless. He's too good at what he does.

I grab his face. "Get in me. NOW."

He doesn't hesitate. He slides up my body and sinks into me, deep. I'm ready for him. He kisses me hard and we hold on tight as we both immediately lose control.

He strokes my hair as I fall back into a deep sleep.

Christmas morning, I wake up early and stretch, smiling from ear to ear. I had the best sleep and the best dreams. I brush my teeth and go into the living room to see if Ian is awake. He is. He's got his arms propped up behind his head, and he's looking at the tree. He looks deep in thought.

I walk to the couch and he looks up at me. "There's my girl. Merry Christmas."

"Merry Christmas." I smile at him and he returns it tentatively.

"You like me again?" He looks grave as he says it.

"Of course I do, I never stopped," I groan. "I'm sorry for how I've been acting. I've been rotten."

He pulls me down on top of him and kisses me. "You weren't rotten. I just thought maybe you were having second thoughts about me."

I lean my forehead on his. "I'm sorry. You were just so fine about not being with me. It was … getting to me."

I hide my face in his shoulder. I'm so embarrassed, both for how I've acted and that I told him.

"Baby," he holds my face in his hands and smooths

down my hair, "I've been dying. I've just been trying to be respectful of your parents. Last night, I couldn't take it any longer."

I let out a relieved laugh. "I do feel like a new woman this morning."

"If I'd known you were that hot for me, I would have taken you in the stairwell and fixed you up. You've been so on edge, I thought maybe I was getting on your nerves."

I let out a long sigh. "You never get on my nerves. I'm only sorry that I wasted any time with you. I won't let it happen again. Next time, I'll jump your bones before you can leave me high and dry."

He laughs. "You said, 'jump your bones.'"

"You're corrupting me."

Ian and I sit in front of the tree and give our presents to each other. He has a little pile and I have a little pile. The lights from the tree make his eyes glow more than ever.

"Last Christmas was the first time I'd given presents to a girl," he whispers.

"Really? You didn't tell me that." I'm shocked.

He holds up his foot and he's wearing the elephant socks that I gave him last Christmas. I laugh whenever I see them. They're ugly, but he still loves them.

"I didn't want to scare you off on our first Christmas, but yeah, another first for me." He smiles and when I hand him a present, he looks like a little boy; he's so excited. Between each present, we kiss sweet, playful kisses that make my heart flutter. I give him the softest blanket I've ever touched, for those nights on the bus when he's missing me and needs something to remind him of me. He gives me perfume from Paris that I can actually smell—it smells divine. I give him a photo album of all of our trips together. He gives me a sexy red blouse and whispers that there's something to match it that he'll give me later. I give him a baseball shirt—white with red sleeves that says, "Raw Bows" on it.

I point to the red sleeves and then the words, "Raw Bows." We have a good laugh over that.

We each have one thing left to give the other. I hear my parents rustling in the other room. I know they probably don't want to miss out, but we're enjoying this time, just the two of us. The whole morning feels like we're in a magical bubble, on our own little cloud.

"Here, you go first," I say and hold his last present out.

Ian leans over and gets in my face. "I just want you to know … that if you didn't get me a single present … the way you love me would be more than enough."

He makes my heart squeeze when he talks like that.

He slowly unwraps the box, not tearing a single scrap. He folds it carefully and sets it aside like he's going to save the paper. I love him for these little quirks.

He opens the box to see another box inside—a small wooden box with intricate carvings on the outside. It's a beautiful piece of art in itself, handmade by a guy I saw at an outdoor artisan fair.

"Look inside," I urge.

When he opens the box, his breath hitches. There are 100 guitar picks in every color. Some of them have small pictures of me, some have both of us. Others have a sparrow on them. He runs his fingers through them and studies each one. He doesn't say a word. I thought he'd laugh and maybe toss them out in his playful way, but his face is serious as he looks at all of them.

"This is the best present I've ever been given," he says softly. When he looks at me, his eyes water. I've never seen him get teary. "I love this. Thank you, Sparrow."

"You're welcome. I'm so glad you like them." I feel shy all of a sudden.

He kisses me, his brow crinkled in either concentration or passion. I'm not sure which, but he means it, either way.

"Okay. One more for you. Know that if you don't like this, we can do something else."

I frown at him. "Don't be silly. It's wrapped so pretty. What is it?" I give it a good shake.

"Open it!"

I tear it open, unable to unwrap as carefully as he does. Inside is a sterling silver charm bracelet with hanging charms. It's wonderful. Each charm makes me smile and love him more. There's a cupcake, a book, a tiny replica of the houseboat, a sparrow and the only thing with color are two red bows spaced between the other charms.

"We were on the same wavelength with that," he says as he fingers the red bows, "I just couldn't figure out how to portray 'raw' with a charm."

Hilarious.

"I love it, Ian. So much. It's perfect." I hold it up for him to put it on me. He kisses the inside of my wrist before he latches the clasp. "This is the best present *I've* ever been given."

We're kissing when my parents come out. They're shocked that we opened our presents without them, but when they see how happy we are, they can't stay perturbed.

"This is the best Christmas ever," Ian sings in place of a greeting.

"Oh, just you wait. We're just getting started," my dad sings back.

- 20 -

Minnesota BOUND

Minnesota really is a winter wonderland. I didn't know there could be so much snow in one place. It's breathtaking. As Ian and I drive from the airport to his mother's house, I stay glued to my window. The snow is hanging heavily on the limbs of the trees, outlining each branch. Ian says they've just had a snowfall for the snow to still be attached like that.

Ian pulls off by one of the many lakes and gives me a mischievous grin. "Want to take a mini-detour?" he asks.

"Uh ... sure?" I have no idea what he's up to.

The next thing I know, we're driving out onto a frozen lake. Driving!

"What—are you doing?" I squeal.

Ian does figure eights with the car and turns just sharp enough that we slide on the ice.

"Ian!" I keep my hands gripped on my seat, afraid to move.

"See all the ice houses?" He points behind us. I turn around and see tons of little tiny houses on the ice. "It's safe right now. Give it a few months, and I wouldn't be doing this…"

I breathe much easier when we're back on a normal *road*. I love all the old houses and notice there are hardly any fences anywhere. Everyone in California has a fence, even if their yards are tiny. The sun is setting as Ian drives down a dead-end street and pulls in the driveway of an old farmhouse sitting alone on ten acres.

"Mom moved here when I was just graduating, so I didn't spend much time here, but it's as much home as I've got," Ian says. "It's beautiful in the summer."

Ian seems more vulnerable than usual. It makes me want to wrap him up and protect him from whatever and whoever has hurt him. I lean over and kiss him before getting out of the car.

"Thank you for bringing me here."

He looks at me intently. "I'm glad you're here, Sparrow."

I go to the trunk to get my luggage and Ian has it all.

"Can I carry something?" I offer.

"Just carry your beauty, baby. That's gotta be a heavy weight all its own."

I snort. "You're something else."

"What? I'm just speaking the truth."

I'm still laughing as the door opens and Ian's mom rushes out. She's hugging me and kissing Ian and talking a mile a minute.

"I'm so excited you're here. Oh, you're just gorgeous. I can't believe it. Merry Christmas! I'm Ellen. Ian, you look better than I've ever seen you. Sparrow must be good for you." She takes a breath and laughs nervously, her hands clasped together. "Come in, come in, I've got the turkey and dressing all ready for you.

Ellen is beautiful and so kind. She's tall and graceful, and her eyes remind me of Ian's, full of expression and changing colors. I feel at home right away. We sit down to eat, just the three of us, and she takes us both by the hand to give thanks. Ian favors her so much. It's fun to see the two of them interact. He's so sweet with her.

"It's been a long time since I've seen my boy," she says, patting his cheek.

"Sorry, Mom. It's been a crazy year, and when I'm not playing a gig, I'm trying to figure out how to get to Sparrow."

"I'm glad you've found someone who makes you put in that effort." She looks at me. "I was starting to wonder if it was ever gonna happen."

I smile at her and my chest expands with relief that she actually likes me.

Later, Ian is upstairs taking a shower, and Ellen and I are talking in the living room.

"I don't know if you know what a big deal it is for you to be here," she says.

"Well, everywhere we go, Ian never seems to be suffering from lack of female attention," I tell her. "I just assumed that you would have met a lot of girlfriends over the years."

"He doesn't tell me anything, and he's never brought anyone home, especially for Christmas. That's why I knew when he told me about you last year around this time, that you must be someone special." She leans in closer and says quietly, "He has a lot of hang-ups about commitment and even more about marriage." She shakes her head. "I just hope he can let all of that go with you, sweetheart. He hasn't had any examples of a good marriage in his life. Not one."

I nod my head and want her to keep talking, even though uneasiness has settled in my gut. Because for all the ways Ian shows me he loves me, he really doesn't talk about commitment, and he doesn't demand it of me. He didn't like it when those guys kissed me, but it wasn't a deal breaker for him. I was grateful for it at the time, but now it's troubling me. I've tried so hard not to make him feel any pressure about the future. I'm still young, but also, I think I've been afraid of scaring him off.

In some ways, it's possible that I've given him the perfect set-up. We have these blissful times every couple of months, and then we both go live our lives apart. How long will this be enough for me?

When Ian comes in the room, looking all perfect after his shower, I decide to get another shower myself. It's late and I'm feeling the fatigue of the day catching up with me. I go ahead and say goodnight, thinking Ian will enjoy some time alone with his mom. He gives me a look of concern as he kisses my cheek on my way out of the room. Sometimes I wish he couldn't read my face so well.

Ian's room is a later addition to the old house. It's above the kitchen and has hardwood floors and wainscoting halfway up the wall. It's a big room but still feels cozy. When I'm done in the shower, I crawl into his huge bed and pile the heavy blankets over me. I don't even hear when Ian comes to bed.

The next morning when I open my eyes, Ian is leaning on his hand, looking at me.

"Are you watching me sleep?" I mumble, turning over on my stomach, so I don't breathe morning breath on him.

He lightly traces his fingers down my back ... down, down, down.

"One of my favorite things to do."

"Hmm."

He leans down and kisses the small of my back. "It's nice having you in my bed."

"Does this feel different from all the other times I've been in your bed?"

"Yeah, it kinda does."

"Hmm."

He chuckles. "Hmm," he says back. "You didn't budge when I came to bed last night. I was in here within twenty minutes of you coming upstairs and you were *out*." He lowers my panties and kisses my cheeks.

"You still want me around even if I don't put out?"

He goes still. He comes up by my face and kisses my hair. "What's going on with you, Little Bird? Talk to me."

I just stare at the wall until he turns me over and gently nudges my chin to face him. I look at him but don't say anything.

"Don't go quiet on me, Sparrow. You know it tortures me when you do that. What did I do?"

His eyes are anxious and his brows are scrunched together in one big frown.

I look away, and he moves so I can't look anywhere but at him.

I push him off of me and mutter, "I'm gonna brush my teeth."

He sighs and gets up to brush his teeth alongside me. He tries to get me to laugh by making funny faces in the mirror at me, but I can't do more than crack a smile. My heart feels so heavy.

"What are we doing, Ian?" I cringe. I didn't mean for that to come out exactly.

"What do you mean?"

I get back in the bed. "I don't know. I don't even know what I'm feeling right now. Just ... something your mom said started me thinking..."

"What did she say?" He looks at me with dread.

"That she hopes you can let go of all of your hang-ups with commitment to be with me."

"Shit." He rubs his face roughly with both hands. "I've never kept that from you."

"I know, and I've never pushed you for anything ... except to call on a regular basis." I roll my eyes when I hear how ridiculous that sounds. The more I think about it, the madder I get. "I'm just realizing how I've given you the perfect little situation. You go travel the world, meet people all over place, do who knows what, and I'm at your beck and call whenever you want ... which is really only every month or two ... sometimes three or four."

He looks floored. "I don't understand. What have you been wishing was different? I thought we were only able to see each other that little because of how busy we *both* are ... and that it's actually been a lot, considering we're halfway across the world from each other half the time."

There's a lump in my throat the size of a fist. It's thrashing away in there, pummeling me.

"What would you do if I dated other guys? You're not jealous at all, and that's just weird!"

Ian stands up and starts pacing. "I wouldn't like it, but I can't keep you from it."

"Yes, you *can*!" I slam my hand down on the sheets. "You could."

"How?" Ian stops in mid-pace to stare at me.

"Say, 'Sparrow, I don't want you seeing anyone but me' or 'the thought of you with someone else drives me crazy'—that's typically how it works in other relationships."

"Well, isn't that obvious?" Ian does a double-handed hair tug. "I mean, you know I didn't like you kissing those guys, but you went out with them. I couldn't do anything about that. I figured if you didn't want to be kissed, you wouldn't have put yourself in that situation. I don't like it, but if that's what you need, then I'm not gonna stop you."

"I don't need anyone but you, Ian. You're the only one I want."

"You're the only one I want," he says emphatically and stops in front of me. He pulls me up to him and kisses all over my face—my eyelids, my cheeks, all around my lips without actually kissing them.

"I feel that way when we're together. I just … I don't know. I don't know what I'm feeling." I shake my head and wish I could shake off my mood too.

"I'm not good at this, baby. You knew that from the beginning, but I know that I love you and you're the only one I've ever felt that way about. Tell me what you need, and I will try to give you that. You're young. I want you to be sure. I don't want to push you into something you're not ready for."

"You haven't pushed me into anything. Age is irrelevant when it comes to us. I don't need to go out and date a bunch of guys to prove that I love you. I know what I know."

"So … if I were to … ask you to marry me, what would you say?"

My heart thuds to the floor.

"I'm not gonna answer that until you ask me for real." I look at him and try not to act as flustered as I'm feeling.

"You won't even give me a hypothetical answer? So if I put myself out there and asked, I could have an *idea* of what you might say?"

He's not joking. In fact, Ian looks as serious as I've ever seen him. He's actually waiting for me to answer.

"Um. Well, I'd say, we have some things to figure out before we talk about marriage. Where would we live? When would be the right timing? Wait … you know, just a few minutes ago, you were still okay with me going out with other people. And now, you're talking about marriage?" I'm the one who's shocked now. I can't believe how this conversation has turned.

"I was never okay with it. Let's just be clear on that," Ian corrects me. "I was just trying to let you figure it out. If you say you only want me, I believe you," he says. "And you brought up commitment. I *am* committed to making us work. You're the only one who has ever made me even consider marriage, and we've never really talked about it. I'm glad you brought it up."

"I didn't mean…"

"No, I know. I think about it, though, I do. All the time," he confesses. He's touching me again—the awkward moment passing, and a surge of excitement taking over the room.

"You do?"

"I do." He leans down and kisses me softly. "And our babies."

I gulp. I've only allowed myself to think about that when I'm in my bedroom alone, missing him. Otherwise, I might hope too much; my desperation for him might ooze out too much when I'm around him and he'll run.

"I'd want our little girl to look just like you," he says.

I hug him tight, before he can see the tears that are filling my eyes.

"Your heart is pounding out of your chest. Am I scaring you, baby?"

"No," I whisper, "I'm not scared."

"Would we be one of those couples who has to combine our two names to make her name?" he asks, a slow smile crossing his face.

"You mean something like Sparian? Or Ianow? Oh, I know! Orvillate! Yes, Orvillate, that's the one." I laugh.

"What about Orvate? Or Korville?"

I get tickled and can't stop. "Wonai!"

He looks bewildered for a second. "Ahh…"

"See what I did there?"

He laughs. He dips me back and when he swoops me back up, he turns me around in a twirl. I feel loved and pretty until I stump my toe on the floor. It wrecks my nail polish.

"Dang!"

Ian checks on my toe and then stands up and starts dancing seductively in front of me. He pulls off his t-shirt and starts singing in a high falsetto voice, "Dang girl, dang girl, dang girl, dang girl, dang girl, dang." He turns around and starts slowly pulling off his pajama bottoms, throwing in a pelvic thrust. "Dang girl, dang girl, dang girl, dang girl, dang girl, dang."

At first I'm staring wide-eyed at him and then I lose it. He runs his hands through his hair and then goes for his underwear, ripping them off and my mouth drops before I die.

"You've got me saying, 'Dang girl, you're so fine. The way you let me put it down, girl, just blows my mind.

I guess I gotta put it down to—day. I gotta put it down…" he sings.

He's picked me up and is 'putting me down' on the bed. I'm wiping my eyes and trying to catch my breath. Finally he stops and looks at me, grinning. "Dang girl, dang girl, dang…" he whispers as he kisses down my chest.

"You just put Justin Timberlake to shame," I tell him.

"Thanks, you inspired me with your 'dang'."

"I see that." I jump as he tickles my ribs. "It's actually 'damn' though. DAAAAMMMN," I holler as he tickles harder.

The rest of our stay goes without a hitch. We have so much fun. It feels like we've gone through another shift in our relationship. A huge one—as significant as when I came home to find him on the steps to my apartment.

If I were that kind of girl, I'd go home and start looking for a wedding dress. Good thing I'm not.

- 21 -

Be Mine

2 months later

I'm running from class to the coffee shop to cover an afternoon shift for Nadine. My phone starts ringing with Ian singing, "Dang girl." It makes me laugh every single time it rings.

"Hello?" I snicker.

"Would you get a new ring already? So I can hear your sexy, breathless 'hellooo' when you answer instead of you in mid-cackle."

"I thought you loved my cackle."

"You don't really cackle, I just thought you'd enjoy that word."

"You know me so well. I do."

"Whatcha doin', bayyyby?"

"I'm about to start an afternoon shift. What about you?"

"Well, I'm missing you, and I was thinking I'd try to change my flight to come in earlier…"

"Earlier than tomorrow?" I ask excitedly. "Do it! Come on! I only have to work four hours. Can you be here by then?"

"Well, I can be there in six, if everything goes well

with flying stand-by."

"Ohhhh. This is good. I can sleep with you tonight!" I shout.

Several people on the street turn around and stare at me. One mother walking by with her son gives me a glare.

"Sorry!" I mouth to her and then bite my lip until it hurts.

"Yes! I was hoping you'd allow me in your bed."

"If you behave," I whisper.

"Now, come on, baby, you know I can't do that."

"I do have an early shift tomorrow."

"Okay, maybe I'll drag my ass out of bed so I can watch you work."

"We'll see how you feel after I keep you up all night."

"Mmm, I love your dirty mind."

I laugh. "Hurry, get here! I can't wait!"

"Okay, Little Bird. Done. Tonight, I am gonna screw—"

"Sorry, babe. I'm here. Gotta run!"

I hang up, snickering to myself that I cut him off mid-steam.

I rush home after my shift and take another shower. I pick up around the apartment. Tessa has been spending more and more time at Jared's place. I decide I should call her, but only get her voicemail.

"Hey girl, it's me. Just calling to let you know that Ian is coming TONIGHT! And I thought you should be forewarned in case you happen to come HOME tonight for once and hear me moaning … do NOT come save me, I am JUST FINE. Okay. Love you. Bye."

Baked spaghetti is in the oven, the marinara and alfredo sauces are warming on the stove—Ian likes half with marinara and half with alfredo poured over it—lemon icebox pie is already made and the wine is chilling.

Ian decided long ago that he would always get a cab from the airport. He doesn't like me going to the airport to wait for him by myself. I've run into some crazies that are hard to shake every time I go. I seem to draw the crazies like a moth to a flame. Ian says the bugs come to the light. He earned a kiss for that one. Even though I know I can take care of myself, it really is much easier this way.

I'm wearing a long black nightie that has a slit up to kingdom come, and black heels that are come-hither shoes all on their own. I had everything ready for tomorrow night, but he's coming early! I want to make it worth his while.

He texts when he's close, and I unlock the door. I spray the perfume he gave me and walk into it. I brush my teeth one more time and put on some tasty lip gloss. I can't sit. I'm too giddy.

About four minutes before I expect him to show up, I go to the kitchen and pretend to be busy at the stove. Stir, stir, stir.

The sight of me cooking in sexy lingerie is ALMOST as intoxicating to him as Sparrow the librarian. Not quite, but close. That's why I've put my hair up and secured it with pencils. It took four for my thick hair. I wonder if that's overkill.

He gives a soft knock on the door and then opens it. "Sparrow?"

"In here," I call.

"You HAVE to lock your do—whoa. *What* have you

done?" He's looking me up and down and lands on my hair. *Fuck*, I hear him whisper.

I hide my laugh behind an attempted sexy pose. Honestly, this man is *so* easy.

He rushes across my tiny kitchen in one giant step and crushes me against him. He kisses me hard, not taking his time for any slow or gentle build up. He is all in. Now.

God, I love him.

He bends down to pick me up and starts to stride to the bedroom.

"Wait," I say, shaking my head no. "Dinner first."

"What?" His eyes actually look glazed.

"Put me down."

He obeys, strictly because all the blood has left his brain. Otherwise, he would be giving me grief right now.

"Dinner." I point to the oven and try to do a sexy walk. I make it there without stubbing anything. "Sit." I point to the table where everything looks so pretty.

He pulls his lips out between his thumb and index finger until they're squished tightly together. He draws a deep breath and goes to sit down like he's told. Once he sits down, he seems to regain his sass and begins muttering.

"Just because you look all—" he waves his hand up and down, "—and have your hair all—"

"Yes?" I prompt. This is so entertaining. I should have done this a long time ago.

He growls at me.

The joke is on me once we begin eating. The food is delicious, if I do say so myself. But Ian, two bites in, after saying how good it is, turns white. I think it's a trick of the light at first. He's watching me eat with a faint smile on his lips, eyes wide and still. And then he goes green.

"Excuse me." He goes to the bathroom and is in there for about ten minutes.

Oh, this isn't good.

He comes back and looks a teensy bit better, closer to the white than the green.

"Are you okay?" I ask, so concerned.

"I am," he says emphatically.

He tries a few more bites and again, green. He sets down his fork and puts the bottom of the chilled wine bottle on his cheek.

"You're scaring me," I whisper. "Do you need to go lay down?"

"If you had just let me take you to bed like I was trying to, none of this would be happening."

"Oh yeah?"

"Yeah," he croaks out before rushing to the bathroom.

Well, that didn't quite go as I was hoping. I take another few bites of spaghetti and take everything to the counter to cover up and put away. Looks like there will be lots of leftovers. When Ian walks out, he stands in the kitchen doorway.

"Did you get enough to eat?" he asks.

"Yeah, I did. Are you feeling any better?"

"Yes. I'm … just fine." He grabs my hand. "Can we sit on the couch? I thought I could wait, but I can't. I—"

"Okay, now you're really scaring me. What's going on, Ian?"

I hold onto his hand while he leads me to the couch. I sit down and look up at him, waiting for him to sit beside me.

He gets down on both knees in front of me.

"Sparrow, I—"

Wait a minute. Ohgodohgodohgodohgodohgod.

He smiles at me, and some of the color in his face returns. His blue-grey, green, ever-changing eyes kiss me with each glance. He loves me.

"The day I met you, I went home and told Jeff that I had met the girl I would marry ... not 'would' like I thought it would happen, but would, as in, if I could marry any girl in the world ... *any girl* ... I would choose you. He laughed, and I agreed that it was the most farfetched idea I'd ever had because there's no way I could ever deserve someone like you."

He gulps then and his eyes fill, making them even more beautiful. Tears start rolling down my face and he wipes them one by one.

"But then you loved me. I don't know why, but you did. And something small inside of me grew and I hoped that I could be all that you saw in me. I love you, Sparrow Kate Fisher. I love you so much, it hurts. I love you so much, it's taken over right here—" he puts my hand on his chest "—and swallowed me whole until I can't think of anyone or anything but you. You have completely captivated me. And I only want more."

He stops then and pulls a ring out of his pocket. My breath catches. The sparkle from the ring is zinging around the room, casting prisms everywhere. It's beautiful.

"Will you marry me, Sparrow?" He lifts his eyebrows as he holds up the ring, as if the ring is what will entice me. It really is a gorgeous ring.

I look at him and the ring and grab both sides of his face and kiss him. "I love you, I love you, I love you," I whisper between each kiss. "You woke me up the day we met, Ian. Maybe even before that—when I first saw you— enough for me to write it in my diary." I smile and lean my head against his. "You make me feel like I can be exactly who I am, and you'll just love me all the more, however I turn out." I laugh. "And you turn my insides into mush…" When I pull back to see him better, he still looks worried.

"Yes, I will marry you," I say.

"Aaaahhh," he yells, and he stands up, taking me with him. "Yes? You're saying yes? Are you sure? You don't care that we don't have it all figured out yet?"

"Yes," I laugh, covering him with kisses. "No, we'll figure it out. Is this what had you green during dinner?"

"Yes." He hangs his head and peeks up at me under those long, curly eyelashes. "I was gonna take you out for a fancy dinner tomorrow night when I got in and then I saw you and this ring is burning a freakin' hole in my pocket!" he shouts. "And then you wouldn't let me screw my way out of it," he says sheepishly.

"Oh! Is that what you were trying to do?" I poke him in the chest.

"Well, I didn't know you were gonna play hardball with the pencils and slit up to here." He puts his finger exactly where the top of the slit goes. "And then you went all librarian on me with, "No. Dinner. Put me down," he says, mimicking my voice.

"Put the ring on my finger, and take me to bed." I frown.

His Adam's apple goes down and pops back up as he swallows. "Yes, ma'am."

It's late, but I have to call Tessa and tell her.

"Hello?" She sounds half-asleep.

"Tess, I'm so sorry to wake you up. I just had to tell you something."

"K."

"Are you awake enough to understand what I'm saying?"

"Mmhmm."

I'm not so sure she is.

"Ian asked me to marry him!"

"What? WHAT? He did?" She lets out a screech. And then I hear Jared saying something. "It's okay, it's just Sparrow," she tells him. "IAN ASKED YOU TO MARRY HIM? WHAT DID YOU SAY?"

That's more like it.

"I said yes! YES!" I yell back.

"Oh my god, Ro. I can't even believe it. I'm coming over tomorrow to see if you look any different and to see your ring. Did he get a good one? If you two are going at it, I'm just gonna come in real quick to get a look…" She takes a breath. "I'm not even gonna be able to sleep now. I cannot believe it. I am in SHOCK."

"I'm sorry I've got you all wired. Text me when you're on your way tomorrow, and I'll try to keep Ian off of me for five minutes. Turns out getting engaged is a turn on for him." I sneak a peek at Ian out of the corner of my eyes and give him a guilty half-smile, half-cringe.

"What *isn't* a turn on for that guy? Geez. Aw, Ro. I love you. I can't wait to see you. I'm so happy for you. Put Ian on."

I hand the phone to Ian.

"Hello?" he says and then holds the phone away from his ear as Tessa screams. He looks at me and laughs, shrugging his shoulders.

"Thank you. (Pause) Yeah, I was gonna wait until tomorrow night, but if I hadn't gone ahead and asked, I would have been in the bathroom the rest of the night … yeah, you'll have to ask her about that. Not my finest hour. (Pause) I know. (Pause) I know. I can't believe it either. (Pause) Thanks, Tess. That means a lot. (Pause) (Laughing hard and shaking his head) Point taken. Okay, love you too."

I call my parents too. My mom hears my voice and yells, "Anthony, pick up the phone, it's Sparrow!"

Something tells me they know what I'm about to tell them.

"Hey, Rosie," my dad says.

"Hey, you two. So … got anything you wanna tell me?" I ask.

There's a long pause and then my mom says, "Well … uh, why don't you go ahead and tell us what *you* were calling about…"

It takes me a minute to quit laughing at how awkward they're acting.

"Well, Ian asked me to marry him tonight."

"Honey! That's wonderful! Congratulations!" They both speak at once.

"You guys totally knew!" I holler.

My dad speaks up. "Well, Ian came to pay me a visit last week and … well … he asked for my permission to marry you." He gets choked up midway through.

"Awww." I look at Ian. "You went to see my dad?"

"Yeah," he whispers. I lean over and kiss him.

My dad clears his throat. "So, what did you say?"

"I said yes!" I tell them happily.

They both sound thrilled for me. We talk a few more minutes and when I hang up, my heart is completely full. I want to remember this moment—right now—this happiness that I'm feeling, for the rest of my life. I never want to forget.

We've slept *maybe* two hours when my alarm goes off the next morning. I remove his leg and his arm from me and very carefully try to crawl out of bed.

He groans, "Nooooo," and tries to hold onto me.

I kiss his hand and hop up before he can stop me. I'm in the bathroom when he comes up behind me, kisses the back of my neck and groggily says, "I'm coming with you. I'll be good."

I giggle. "Okay." I turn around and nestle into *his* neck. "But we've gotta be quick."

He starts unbuttoning my pants. "I can be really quick," he promises.

I brush his hands off. "That is *not* what I meant!" I laugh. "You are relentless."

There's something cosmic that happens whenever I feel Ian's eyes on me. I can know he's in a room before ever seeing him. It's more than awareness that is heightened—the whole space surrounding me is popping. If we could see energy, I would be completely shrouded with it. Nothing but a mass of colorful energy.

It makes me stand up taller, laugh brighter, listen harder, and breathe easier. It makes me *know*—know that I am a beautiful, quirky mess of something wonderful.

It must be the love in his eyes. I have no other

explanation for it.

Working my shift with him in the shop is a challenge. I tell Nadine and Chloe and a few of my regular customers that I'm getting married, and Ian smiles and waves as they congratulate him too. He's working on lyrics for a new song, but anytime I come out from behind the counter and go anywhere near him, he gives me a sexy grin and finds a way to throw 'Mrs. Sterling' into a quick sentence.

I'm ready to pounce on him when we leave the coffee shop, but he is taking his time, leisurely walking with my hand in his.

"So when are you thinking you'd like to get married?" he asks.

"I … don't know. Once we get to summer I can plan a wedding. Should we wait until I'm done with school?" I ask.

"That's another year and three months … what about the end of summer? Before you start back to school in the fall."

"That's really soon." I look at him with wide eyes. "What kind of wedding are you wanting?"

"One where you're there. I don't care about anything else."

"Well, that narrows it down," I tease. "I don't need a big shindig either, although, if Charlie gets involved, it's going to grow exponentially. They'll want us to get married at the church," I realize. My visions of a beach wedding just skyrocketed and plummeted within the same minute.

"Whatever you want, baby. Just tell me where to be, and when, and I'll be there."

"How about a December wedding? I'll have three weeks off and we can get married in the church."

"I like that. The label is talking about me being in the studio in January and they already know I'm determined to record it here, so I can be with you. They're cool with it."

I nod. I've already been looking forward to that, even though it's almost a year away.

"I might have mentioned to them that I was going to propose." He turns to me and smiles sweetly.

"Wow. So a December wedding. And then you'll be here. With me." I have to say it out loud to let it sink in.

He kisses my hand as we walk up the steps to my apartment. "Yep. It all just became real, didn't it."

- 22 -

Venom

5 months later

It's been 5 months since Ian and I got engaged. I have my dress picked out. I found it in an upscale vintage shop in Soho and fell in love with it. The only problem is what Charlie will do when she sees it. The back is what makes it fabulous—sheer down to the waist with an appliqué of beads. I already know she will want me to fill that in with some sort of material. She'll probably want me to add sleeves too. It's a pale champagne tone with a deep V at the neck, which will most likely also need to be filled in with something less sheer. It's the perfect *beach* wedding dress is what it is.

The invitations make me smile every time I see them. They're plain on the front but have a little sterling silver sparrow hanging down the center from a thin cord. I finished addressing them all last night.

As soon as school was over a month ago, I began planning this wedding. I'll be going home next month, and Charlie, Tessa, and I will knock the rest of it out before school starts again in the fall. I don't want to have to do much once I'm in school.

Ian was just in town and left yesterday morning. He

was quiet all week, not his usual self. If he'd been stand-offish with me, it would have really concerned me, but he was even more loving, if that's possible. He didn't sleep well. Every time I woke up, he was deep in thought. I kept asking if he was okay, and he kept saying yes. We still had a good time. I think he was just having an off week.

He has left the planning to me. All he has requested is that we keep it simple and not do a huge blowout. He's agreed to all the rest. I had to drastically cut the list that Charlie gave me. I don't want people there that I don't even know. Once we narrowed it down to just our closest friends and family, I've been able to pick out things that are more special for our day ... the invitations being just one example of that.

I'm standing up to stretch when the phone rings.

"Helloooo," I attempt a sexy voice.

"Heyyyy, baby," Ian says.

"What are you up to?"

"Well, I'm heading over to Aaron's. I'm gonna spend the night over there."

"Oh, okay. You're not staying at Jeff and Laila's?"

"No. They're back in town, so I'm just gonna go to Aaron's for a while. Give them some space."

"Is Laila being weird?"

"She's always weird," he answers.

"I thought she was better the last time."

"I let her have it for being rude to you at your parents'."

"You didn't tell me that! What did you say?"

"I told her that I'm marrying you and whatever issue she has with you, she better work it out."

"Ian. Why didn't you tell me? Was she mad?"

"She didn't say anything. And I left."

"Hmm. That's intense. And it will be so awkward when I have to see her again. She's being fine with my mom, although my mom says Laila is still saying I'm way too young to get married."

"She's probably right about that," he says.

My stomach starts a slow churn.

"She's not the one to make that call," I say.

"You're right, baby. It's just … are you? Are you sure?"

"What are you asking, Ian? Are you asking if I think I'm too young? Or if I'm sure about you? Or are you the one who isn't sure?"

He's quiet for a minute. The clock in the living room echoes with every tick-tock-tick.

"I can't answer for you. I know I want to marry you," he says.

"I know I want to marry *you*," I tell him.

"That's all I need to know."

I'm really unsettled after our phone conversation. I decide to take a walk and end up walking further than I intended. I end up in front of a restaurant with a cute sidewalk patio and I stop. I always feel kind of sorry for people who eat alone, but I never actually feel bad for myself as long as I have a book to read. I'm hungry. I'm doing it.

I'm just getting to a good part in my book when I hear my name. I look up and Asher Caldwell is standing in front of me. He looks around nervously and then back at me. His hair is darker than the last time I saw him, but otherwise, he looks the same.

"Sparrow. You here alone?" He does another quick scan around us.

"Asher." It feels like I'm swallowing venom just saying his name.

"Mind if I sit down?" he asks.

"Actually, I do."

"Okay, I deserve that," he says with regret. "I'll just stand right here. I saw you sit down and couldn't leave without saying hello. It's been a really long time."

"Yeah, you could have left without saying hello." I give him a pointed look. "We both know why it's been a long time."

"Do you? Because I've wanted to see you since that night." Asher's face has gone tomato red. "I've wanted to explain my side of things. But your "friend" Ian threatened me within an inch of my life the night he put me in the hospital. He said if I came near you, he'd finish what he started." He stands and waits for my reaction.

"What are you talking about?"

Asher smirks. "I knew you didn't know. Ian paid me a little visit a few weeks after that night and nearly killed me."

"I find that hard to believe." I point toward him. "You're standing here, aren't you?"

He shrugs. "Believe what you want. I didn't rape you, Sparrow."

"I wouldn't know, since I had PASSED OUT." I get up to leave and Asher shoves me in the chair. Now I'm scared.

He sits down across from me and gets within a foot of my face. "You listen to me, I didn't rape you. You were leading me on for months and that night you took your dress off right in front of me. If that's not saying you wanted me, I don't know what is. You knew how I felt about you—if you didn't want me that night, why did you come home with me?"

"That thought never even crossed my mind." I shake my head. "I thought we were friends, Asher. I can see now that I was foolish to believe that. Chalk it up to me finally growing up a little. Was that your plan then? Take me home with you and get me drunk? No, you know what? I don't want to talk about that night. It was a long time ago, thank God I don't remember any of it, except waking up in your bed with blood everywhere and being sore for the next *week*. There's something not quite right about that, Asher. Thankfully, for the most part, I have managed to put it out of my mind. I don't need or want to see you or talk to you again. Ever." I hold up my finger to show him my ring. "And I'm engaged to Ian, so all the more reason to leave me alone."

"We *were* friends, until you stopped having anything to do with me," Asher snaps. "I tried for weeks to talk it out with you. I was in love with you, and I *know* you knew how I felt. I thought you wanted me that night, but I still … I felt bad when I woke up and saw you'd left and all the … blood."

I shake my head at him and hold up my hand. "Don't even go there, Asher."

"God, I can't believe you're marrying him. You don't even care that he broke all my ribs and left me with a concussion?"

I give him a steely glare, and my voice is glacial. "Asher, I wish *I* could have been the one to break every bone in your body myself." I stand up. "Now back off or I will make good on that wish."

Asher shakes his head in disgust. "I talked trash to Ian, but I didn't mean it. He was just so arrogant, coming to my place like he owned you. You know what? You deserve him. You don't know shit. Do you hear me, Sparrow? You don't know shit about Ian Sterling."

I start walking away and he's still yelling.

I round the corner and begin shaking uncontrollably. A cab sits nearby, and I rush in and go home.

When I get home, I run up the stairs two at a time, close the door, and lock it. I run bath water and when it's high, I step inside the tub and lean back, hoping the hot water will calm the shakes. I breathe. I cry and I breathe some more. And cry some more. And rinse and repeat until I'm a shriveled up clump. I put on my most comforting pajamas and get under the covers, pulling my laptop with me so I can google Asher.

I haven't been paying attention to the gossip on Asher, otherwise, I would have known that about a month after the episode with him, he went missing for a couple of months. He lost several significant production jobs and went on an extended Caribbean cruise. There was speculation about plastic surgery. The more I read, the more I know that Ian probably did what Asher said. I wish I could be more upset about it than I am. I obviously don't want to be with someone who is violent, but I have never seen an ounce of that in him. I'm not afraid of Ian. At all. I can't say the same about Asher.

I just wish Ian had told me.

When Ian calls again later that night, for the first time in our entire relationship, I avoid his call. I let it go to voicemail and don't call him back. The things Asher said are going around and around in my head. All of it. I fall asleep around 2 and wake up a few hours later, feeling like I've been run through the dryer—my head has been bumping against the side walls as I twirl around in circles. I'm dizzy and my temples are pounding.

I should have called in sick to work because I botch up a ton of orders. I take something for my headache, and Nadine tries to make up for my lack. When I leave for the day, there are four missed calls from Ian. I go home and without thinking about what I'm going to say, I finally push 'call back'.

Before I can say anything, he's talking.

"Sparrow? Are you okay? I've been worried about you … if this is about our conversation, I'm sorry, I just-"

"I'm okay," my voice falters and it all comes rushing out. "I ran into Asher after we spoke, and it didn't go well."

"What happened? Did he hurt you?" Ian's voice instantly sounds harsh.

"No, but it was pretty awful."

"Tell me everything, what did he do?"

"Well, he told me you put him in the hospital," I say quietly.

Silence.

"Ian?"

"Yeah, I did," he says.

"Why didn't you tell me?"

He doesn't say anything for a long time and when he does, it's slow and resigned. "The night we were in The Chatwal—the only time I left you, remember? When Tessa came? I went to see Asher. I wanted to hear what he had to say. I didn't go over there planning to do what I did." He lets out a ragged breath. "He had this weird smirk on his face the whole time and when I confronted him about you, he bragged about being your first ... baby, are you sure you want to—"

"Tell me what he said, Ian." My words bite.

"I saw red, Sparrow. I asked him if that was the only way he could get laid—to get a virgin to pass out and he laughed ... and said it did make it a lot less complicated..."

My chest hurts. I've given up trying not to cry and tears are falling, dropping on my chest or splatting across the dining room table.

"I started hitting him and I couldn't stop. The only time I've ever gotten in a fight was in middle school. I don't do that, baby. You have to know that. You do, right?"

I don't say anything. So he just keeps talking.

"But Asher just kept that fucking grin across his face the whole time. I told him I'd break every bone in his body if he came near you again and I'd tell his constant little paparazzi caravan the truth about him if he so much as breathed a bad word about either of us." Ian heaves a huge sigh. "And then I called the ambulance and got out of there."

"He said you nearly killed him."

Ian lets out a hollow laugh. "He wasn't dying, Sparrow. Far from it. I hurt him, pretty bad, but he was nowhere near dying. I called the ambulance because I wanted it on record exactly what did happen to him, just in case he pulled something like this."

I mull all of it over. My headache is back. I lay my head down on the table and try to process it all.

"I'm still not convinced that he didn't put something in your drink. But even if he didn't, he knew what he was doing..." he pauses. "Baby? Please say something."

"I need to go, Ian. I'll talk to you later, okay?"

He's talking as I hang up, and I don't even care. I walk into my room in a daze, get in my bed, and fall asleep.

I wake up to Tessa hovering over me. "Ro? Wake up. Ro?"

I try to focus on her face. "What time is it?" I groggily sit up.

"It's morning. Are you working today?" She props up my pillows, and I sleepily lean back on them.

"Not until this afternoon."

"Okay. Well, I was at Jared's and didn't check my phone until this morning and there are, like, a dozen calls from Ian. You probably have more. He's freaking out, Ro. What's going on?"

"Long story," I say, looking in her eyes and then down at my fingers. I pick at my nail polish.

She sits down on the bed. "You know I've got time. Spill. What's going on with you two?"

"Well, it's more about Asher Caldwell." I lean my head back and close my eyes. I'm still so tired. Tessa's body gets tense. "There's something I never told you about him."

I tell her the whole story, start to finish. Afterwards, we're holding onto each other in my bed, both crying and blowing our noses. She's livid with Asher, so sad that I went through that on my own, and trying to convince me that Ian was just protecting me.

273

"I know, but he still went about it all the wrong way. And then he should have told me what he'd done—and not let me hear it from Asher! What was he thinking? He could have gone to jail."

"Yeah, he should have told you. I think he's regretting that now. He sounds pretty stressed out. He left one long message saying he felt helpless because he's across the country and can't be with you right now. I was afraid the two of you had broken up or something."

"No, but I did practically hang up on him yesterday."

She smiles. "I love it when you get sassy."

The next time Ian calls, I answer, and we talk through it. He's so sorry he didn't tell me what he'd done. I forgive him, but also let him know that I don't want to hear any other secrets about my fiancé from anyone other than my fiancé. If we can't have honesty between us, then we're doomed.

- 23 -

BREATHE

2 months later

"Just think, the next time you're home will be for your wedding," my mom says as we work on party favors for my bridal shower. "Just a few months now."

"December will be here before you can blink," Tessa says. "Are you sure you wanna do this? Marriage is so *permanent*."

We all laugh and keep tying tiny ribbons around each candy jar. Thirty-five women will be coming to my shower this weekend. We've had so much fun getting everything ready for it. It's tedious work, but actually more relaxing than the rest of the wedding planning.

Ian came the second week into my trip. We had one of the best visits yet. It completely wiped away any worries I was having. We talked everything to death and put all the Asher drama to rest. He vowed to be upfront about everything from here on out. I reassured him, too, that I am ready for this. It felt like a timely discussion, to put it all on the table and move forward with our future.

I cannot wait to be his wife. I was excited when he asked me, but I am ecstatic now. The more I know about Ian, the more in love with him I am. It just gets better and better. Ian seems more excited now, too. The first few months of our engagement, I wasn't always confident that he didn't have second thoughts, but I know without a doubt that he's sure now.

I don't get to see him for another two weeks, and it's torture! I will be so happy when we're in the same place at the same time. Ian's career is going well—he's really happy with the direction it has taken. His songs are being recorded right and left by various artists, and the royalties are pouring in. I did a flying leap the other night when I heard one of his songs on the radio. He's playing a show in Vegas right now, but come January, it's been finalized for him to begin his solo project in New York. His tour will start in April and as soon as I graduate in May, I'll be joining him on the tour. Penguin has pushed my release date back, which was disappointing at first, but now I know it's for the best. I would have been working on edits while planning a wedding and that would have been way too much. Now, I'll be working on edits while I'm on tour with Ian.

When all the wedding stuff seems really stressful, I imagine us traveling: me with my laptop, Ian with his guitar. That's what I'm looking forward to—not the wedding so much as starting my life with him.

When Tessa leaves that night, I text Ian to let him know I'm going to bed early. He has a late show tonight, and I don't think I can stay awake for him.

He texts back: **Sleep, Little Bird. I'll talk to you tomorrow. I love you.**

I crash pretty hard. Early in the morning, I feel a little chilled and I pull an extra blanket onto my bed. When I fall back to sleep, I dream.

I see the doors. They're the same as always, except this time I feel like a tiny child in front of them. They're bigger than they've ever been. I'm scared to open the right side but I do. Asher is the first one I see. He points at me, laughing. He has a drink in his hand and he passes it to Laila. She looks at me as she takes the drink and then she starts laughing at me. Michael sits, sunken into a big oversized chair, but when he sees me, he adjusts his posture and lets out a loud laugh at my perplexity. I look around. Where are my parents? Where is Tessa? I need Ian. I can't breathe. And then I see him. He's by Laila now, in that weird skip that dreams do. He leans over and takes a drink out of her glass, his eyes on me the whole time. I start crying for him to get me out of this room and he just watches me, never blinking once. I turn around and try to open the doors, but neither will open. I'm locked in.

I sit up in a cold sweat. My heart is pounding and I push the covers off, hoping to calm down. Instead of trying to go back to sleep, I take a shower. Are these wedding jitters?

All morning, I try to shake the funk, but I just can't seem to get it off of me.

Ian calls a few hours later, and he hears it in my voice right away.

After trying to change the subject, I finally tell him about my dream. When I'm done, he's completely quiet. Nothing, not a word.

Then something comes out of my mouth, and I'll never know why or where it came from or why not sooner, but I say: "When do you think you'll be over Laila?"

My own words rattle me, like the wind is being knocked right out of me by my own mindless doing.

Ian's voice sounds strangled and very far away. "What do you mean?"

"I-mean-when-do-you-think-you'll-be-over-*Laila?*" An island of single words strewn together that are going to ruin my entire life. I already know, without him saying a thing, that this will change everything.

"What do you want to know?" he whispers.

"I want to know everything. Start from the beginning." I don't even know this person who's using my voice to speak. The words and the calm are surely not my own. "Are you having an affair with her?"

"No," he says.

"Have you had an affair with her?"

He pauses and his voice cracks as he says, "Yes."

"When?"

"Baby, I don't—"

"Was it while we were together?"

Silence.

"WAS IT WHILE WE WERE TOGETHER?" I yell, my heart coming out of my throat like a ravaged animal.

"Yes," he says, broken.

My whole body begins to tremble, starting at the crown of my head and rushing over every pore like blood when it oozes after a deep cut.

He's saying in a rush of words, "Listen to me, I love you. I can't lose you, Sparrow. Do you hear me? I made a mistake, but I cannot lose you. I'm coming to you. Are you listening?"

I throw the phone across the room and watch as the

screen shatters.

I go in my closet and shut the door, leaving the light off. I don't know how long I sit in there, crying and raging, but when I stand up and walk out, I wipe the tears and go pretend like nothing has happened.

If I have to talk about it with a single person, I will lose my mind.

During supper my mom and dad are chatty about the reception. I push food around on my plate and when they ask if I'm not feeling well, I tell them I'm not and go to bed.

The next morning, Charlie comes in my room early and wakes me up, "Sparrow? Honey? Wake up."

I open my eyes and feel so angry that I'm awake. I was hoping the death I feel hanging over me would claim me, but it's only my insides that are dead. The rest of me apparently has to keep on living.

"Sparrow, why is Ian parked in front of the house? He's been out there since early this morning, and I just realized it's him."

"There's some trouble," I say, as if I'm discussing a new nail polish color.

"What sort of trouble? Should I let him in?" Charlie looks completely confused.

"I guess when he comes to the door, you can let him in," I tell her.

She gives me an odd look, but when she realizes that's all I'm gonna say, she doesn't push it for once. I pull the covers back up to my chin and turn over. So very tired.

I get up a few hours later and freshen up before going out to the kitchen. When I walk in, Ian is sitting at the bar, talking to my parents. They all look rough. My mom's face is splotchy, like she's been crying. My dad looks sad and angry. Ian has circles around his eyes and looks like he hasn't slept all night. He rushes over when he sees me.

He starts to hug me but stops when he sees the expression in my eyes. He holds out his hand to touch my face and thinks better of it. "Baby, will you please talk to me?"

"I don't have anything to say to you right now." I move out of his reach.

Ian looks at my parents and then back to me. "I told your parents, and I've asked their forgiveness."

I glance at them and they look heartbroken. My mom comes and hugs me. I feel like I'm the one comforting her as I pat her back while she cries. When she steps back, Ian puts his hand on my arm. I flinch.

"Please let me talk to you," he pleads.

I turn around and walk out of the kitchen and back to my bedroom. He follows me and nearly trips when I stop suddenly at my door. I'm afraid the room will close in on me if I go inside the small space with him. When we walk inside, I sit on my bed and he sits next to me. Staring at me. I look straight ahead.

"Look at me, please. You'll know how I feel about you if you look at me."

I keep looking straight ahead.

"I have never loved anyone but you. I never will."

"I guess love isn't enough," I say.

"Love is everything to me, Sparrow. You changed my life by loving me. I'm not gonna let you go. I can't give you up."

"I guess you should have considered that before you

fucked Laila." And with that I look at him. Empty. Hollow.

He visibly cringes and holds his head in his hands. When he lifts his head, tears are streaming from his face. "My life didn't begin until you breathed into it. I know what I have in you, Sparrow. I do. I will never fuck it up again. I promise you."

"I don't want to hear your promises," I yell. "Just tell me about Laila!"

Ian wipes his face and the tears keep pouring out. He's always said he stopped being able to cry when he was a kid, but the floodgates have opened. "It started a long time ago. We were friends—we'd actually been friends long before Jeff ever met her…"

"I kinda caught that from what she said that night at your show."

Ian looks up at me, relieved that I'm talking back.

"Jeff was always gone and Laila started showing up wherever I was. If I was in L.A., she ended up there. If I was at the San Francisco house, she'd come there. I knew she was lonely, and I felt bad for her. She was fun then, not this gross person she's become."

"I guess watching the man you're in love with get engaged to someone else will do that to you," I reply.

He makes the gasping sound that you make when you're trying not to cry, but it's still coming. "That's not the way it is."

I stand up and whirl around to face him. "If you really believe that then you're more "idealistic" than I've ever been."

His face falls. "I love how idealistic you are."

"Was," I say. "Was."

That hits him hard, and he can't speak for a few minutes. Finally, he stands and paces the room. He sees my cell phone, picks it up and lays it on the nightstand. "We'll get that fixed," he says.

"So, tell me, what does Laila have that makes her so irresistible?" The sarcasm drips off my voice. "She's beautiful, I'll give you that. But you told me *I* was the most beautiful woman you've ever seen, so ... it must be all her ... experience. Is that it?"

"It wasn't like that."

"Well, that's what I'm wanting to know, Ian. Do I have to ask the exact question for you to tell me the answer? You'd probably say this hasn't all been a lie—you and me—because I never ASKED you until now if you'd slept with Laila. The truth is, withholding information like this IS lying. Our whole relationship is a lie!"

"No. Don't say that. It isn't. Please don't say that." He grabs my hand and holds it even though I'm trying to pull it away from him. "Sparrow, please, listen to me." He leans his head on mine and something in me breaks from deeper still, and it takes my breath away. I choke on it. The tears start falling and I can't breathe. I begin to panic, and he looks me in the eye and whispers, "Breathe, baby. I'm here. I'm so sorry. I love you. Breathe."

Gradually, I calm down and my heart rate returns to a fast pace, instead of the out-of-control sprint it was just doing.

When I can speak, I say, "Just tell me when it began and when it ended."

"You have to know that I've been on a vicious cycle my whole life of sabotaging myself when anything good comes along. I knew I didn't deserve you and Laila played on that. I'm not blaming her, I take responsibility for my actions in this, but it's just the truth. I never felt anything for Laila; in fact, I *hate her*," he says quietly. "I despise everything about her."

"So you risked everything for someone you *hate*. I don't know if that should make me feel better or not. When did it start, Ian?"

His eyes cloud over. "After our day in San Francisco."

There goes the wind again, being knocked right out of me. When I get a grip, I say, "And when did it end?"

"There was one time after we got engaged … that was the last time anything happened."

If I could just go to sleep right now and never have to open my eyes again. I close my eyes and will it to happen. I can't bear this kind of pain. It's too much. He was my life and now he is nothing.

"We didn't have sex, we stopped before it got to that. I knew I couldn't continue destroying my life. I knew I wanted you more than I want anything in this world. You are everything to me. I stopped and I haven't touched her since."

"Am I'm supposed to be proud of you for that?" I give him a look of disgust.

"No, I just … I needed to know I was capable of being the kind of husband you need, the kind of husband I want to be, and I know now that I am." His eyes search mine, looking for any hint of hope.

I shake my head. "No."

He puts his hand on my arm and I brush it off.

"Who else?" I ask. "Reagan?"

"We kissed once, but never anything more than that.

She wanted to be more and was persistent for a while, but realized I meant it when I said I didn't."

"When?"

"Before you met her."

"Who else? Who do I not know about?"

"No one. No one, I promise."

"Don't. Say that to me." I close my eyes. My whole body aches. This is what grief feels like. Agony. Torture. Anguish. Torment.

"Sparrow, if I stood in front of witnesses today, I would promise to love you and honor you and only you for the rest of my life, and I would mean every single word. Please—I know it will take time for you to believe me, but if you will only give me a chance, I will spend *every* day for as long as I live, proving my love for you."

"I wish I'd never given you my heart." I twist the ring on my finger, the ring that has become second nature since he put it on me, and I take it off. I hold it up to him and put it in his hand.

"No." He shakes his head. "No. I won't take it. I don't want it back." He tries to hand it back to me, and I don't let him. He lays it on my chest of drawers and says, "It's yours."

I walk into my closet and shut the door. He tries talking to me through the door for a couple of hours, but I fall asleep so I don't know when he stopped, if he did.

- 24 -

Sept 21

Sparrow—

I miss you.

I love you.

Please forgive me.

Ian

Sept. 22

I love you, Sparrow.

You've got me by the heart.

Sept 23

Sparrow.

I know there are billions of people in the world.

In my 31 years, I have found one who made me believe that I could love, and be loved, forever.

I can't let you go.

Ian

Sept 25

Sparrow—

My prayer has been that God would somehow let you feel the true scope and depth of the love I have for you. I would sacrifice every earthly thing to make you know that my heart is truly yours.

Please try and find a way to forgive me for hurting you.

Lost without you—

Ian

Sept 26

Oh, Sparrow—

If you could know my heart. If you could know my motives. The noble and the vile. The selfish and the pure. If you could truly know me...

If you could feel my sorrow and my shame. Know how I hate the things I have done—my sins, my failures, my weaknesses. How I despise them. How I loathe the memory of them and how I wish they could be wiped away.

Know the frustration of a man who has been so close to living out his highest ideals and yet fallen so far short...

Know the fear of a boy who could never quite trust another human being with his life. Hiding behind the living room curtain from unreasonable dangers.

If you could know my deepest desires. My dreams. My prayers. My innermost longings. To love without prejudice or greed. To be real...

287

To be known. To be loved. If I could somehow just open my chest, or my brains, or wherever it is that my soul is kept, and reveal myself to you in an instant. That you could see me completely. The truth. Not just the facts but the whole truth. The person.

This is the one hope that I have never dared to hope for. Yet, in the heart of my heart, I know I have always yearned for it more than anything on earth— to be known. Truly. Completely. Intimately. As God knows. And still, to be loved.

Oh, Sparrow. If only you could know my whole heart. How much love is there for you. Love that you haven't seen yet. Love that no one has ever seen. A lifetime of love withheld. Concealed.

Love that could heal and hold. And endure.

Sparrow, you have seen me. And you do know me. More than anyone ever has. The evil and the ugly that you have seen, as well as the good, are me.

But there is still a heart. A soul. A person who

aches to be yours.

To be released.

To wrap himself inside you and know that he is safe.

From deep—

Ian

P.S. I beg you for your forgiveness, my freedom...

Sept 27

Missing you.

Every day.

I love you, Sparrow.

Ian

Sept 30

Sparrow, Sparrow, Sparrow—

Thinking of you...

Missing you...

I arrived in St. Paul yesterday afternoon. The drive was long and beautiful. I'll have to tell you about it.

For now, some highlights:

I slept on a mountain east of Salt Lake City. It was awe-inspiring. A lake far below, reflecting a sky full of stars. I had a feeling of being blanketed in God's creation (an illusion, I woke up freezing).

Just west of Des Moines, a deer ran in front of the car. Awful. I was fine (not the deer, I'm afraid).

St. Paul was a welcome sight. Everything is so green and the temp was about 80-90 (above 0). Rain yesterday and today.

Wish you were here.

Writing is strange and difficult for me right now. I write these few sentences while my mind thinks a thousand thoughts—draws a thousand pictures. My heart beats with a thousand emotions.

This is why I have finally begun to pray. Maybe

your dad was onto something with that whole thing. Because I know I just can't adequately express what's inside of me on my own.

I'm sorry for all the messages. I wish you'd let me fix your phone. My number is the same. I carry my phone everywhere I go and fall asleep holding it ... just in case. I will always wait for you.

Ian

Oct 4

Sparrow—

Am spending a couple days with Mom in Lutsen, MN, a ski resort on Lake Superior.

Beautiful.

Waves, rocks, cliffs, birches, pines, wildflowers, vast blue horizon.

Thinking of you

Missing you

Loving you

Ian

Oct 5

Loons are the state bird of Minnesota.

There is a pair living outside our room.

They are known to mate for life.

My mom and I watched "On Golden Pond" last night.

Oct 6

The Lady Slipper is the Minnesota state flower, also called moccasins.

Song of Songs 2:2

(This book on wildflowers reminds me of us. We can survive anything too.)

Oct 7

Every day and every night, I'm loving you. Steadfast love in my heart for you.

Nothing can ever take it away.

All my love—

Ian

Oct 12

Sparrow—

I love you. With every deep, sighing breath I take, with every heavy beat of my heart. Every time I lay my head on my lonely pillow. Every morning when the sun first breaks through my dreams. I remember. I feel you. I love you.

You are in me. In the deepest part of me. Deeper than my memories, my unconscious thoughts. Deeper than my ever-changing emotions. You are in the place right next to where I keep my faith in God (a faith that I won't let go of now, in spite of it being shaken many times, from without and within). You're deep in me.

It was not this way the first time we met. But something in me knew that someday it would be this way. Deep was calling to Deep. I was hearing hopes and feeling longings that were impossible for me to fully understand.

I said, "I'm in love."

Hopefully. Skeptically.

I had never experienced true love. I didn't believe in true love. I had learned about infatuation and disappointment. I had tried on romantic "love" and failed. I was sure that I had never seen an example of true love in real life.

I loved you then. But only as much as I could.

I look back now and I see love growing. Maturing. Gradually. By days. By moments. Firelight hugs. Mountain drives. Teary face kisses. Awful, angry, frustrated silences. Erased with one forgiving smile. Barefoot walks on slippery rocks. Holding on. Breaking down. Opening up. Hurting. Healing.

Slowly peeling the callus from one scarred, scared heart.

If I could go rushing back and whisper in the ear of that poor fool in the restaurant. If I could tell him what was ahead. Tell him about the joy and hardship and pleasure and agony of finding true love. If I could somehow convince him that the inkling he was feeling was just exactly what he wanted to believe it was, he might have been changed instantly.

But, I can't go back.

He'll just have to learn about love for himself. Again and again in my memory.

And make the same mistakes over and over until they are forgiven.

Little Bird, our love has been hard-earned from the very beginning. It is more precious to me than anything on earth. I can't just let go of it. And I won't stop fighting for it.

It's only over if you want it to be.

My hope is that what has gone before is only the introductory chapter of our love story. There are more memories to be made.

For us—

Ian

Oct 14

It's a half-moon tonight and it's shinin' half-bright

As if the sky could understand the way I feel inside—

Half of me is livin' half a world from here

Half of me is dyin', cryin' one lonely tear

Silently

In the half-moon light

Sparrow.

Nothing will be completely right until you're with me.

Ian

Oct 16

If you ever think of me, I'm thinking of you at that very moment.

All my love

Ian

Oct 17

I believe in you and me.

Ian

Oct 21

We Belong Together.

Well, Baby—

Think. Words Beginning Thus Would Be Tender Words—But True.

Wonderful, Beautiful, Thoughtful Words, But They Would Be Truthful Words.

Believe Them.

Wishes Become True.

Wisdom Brings Trust.

We're Being Tested.

We're Both Tough.

Who Buys That?

Waiting By Telephone.

Wake Before Twelve.

Work Before Television.

Wiggle Big Toe.

Well ... Be Thinking

Warm-Blooded Teddy

World's Biggest Turkey

Way Back Then

Warm Bellies Touched

We Began Trembling
Weeping Boy Thinks,
"Where's Baby's Touch?"
What Big Tears.
We Belong Together.

Oct 25

Dear Sparrow—

I was awakened at 5:30 this morning by the sound of your voice on the phone. I hate dreams that end in the middle. I didn't have time to hear you say anything but, "Hi, it's Sparrow." I didn't have time to tell you that I love you.

But, I did get an early start on the day. And several hours to think and write you this letter.

I think I'm gonna stay here a while. I can't seem to function without you. No pressure, but ... I can't live without you.

You probably think that when I tell you how much I hurt, and describe the pain of missing you, I'm trying to gain your sympathy or pity. I'm not. What I am trying to do is help you know the truth of how deeply I love you. How much you really mean to me. How much you are a part of me.

No pain, no rejection, no separation, no depression, no opposition, no fiery hell can drive you out of my heart.

This is proven fact.

I have been brought as low as I can possibly go. I have tasted the bitter core. I have been abandoned, forsaken. I've been to the edge of despair. I've had every reason for hope ripped away.

And I know it is all my fault. I am the one who ruined us.

But I have not lost my faith.

And I haven't lost my love for you. It's stronger than ever.

I suppose I might never have known or believed that love could be so strong if I hadn't seen it dragged through this hell. Now I know that love can truly endure anything.

My old fears are gone.

I used to fear that I had never had the ability to really love someone. To be vulnerable to someone. To trust someone with my heart.

I feared that I wouldn't have the strength to persevere through the hard times.

I feared rejection.

I feared that love wouldn't last.

I feared that love would be used against me. To hurt me.

I feared that no one could really love me.

Real fears.

These fears go way back. And I realize now that they played a huge part in how I have formed my relationships ever since I was a kid.

Trying to feel loved without becoming vulnerable.

Trying to find affection and closeness without the danger of commitment.

Always keeping a way to escape.

Never trusting anyone. Ever.

Never giving anyone reason to rely on me completely.

Never believing in true love.

This was how I protected myself. This was how a tenderhearted little boy decided to survive.

Was I like this when we met? Did I bring this into our relationship? Yes.

Those fears and those patterns and those defenses were as much a part of me as the calluses on my fingertips.

Then came love.

Unexpected.

Seemingly out of nowhere.

Gradually taking root and growing.

Breaking through.

Fighting against everything that I had come to believe about it.

Invading my safe, lonely place.

Softening my heart.

I was afraid.

I'm sorry.

I don't think I can finish this letter. But I still want you to read it. It's full of truth.

I don't expect for you to understand. But I hope you will.

I want to talk to you. Please. Call. Tell me how and when I can call you. Write. Let me come to you. Let me bring you to me.

Anything.

It's right for us to talk.

You are my first

And last

And only

True Love—

Ian

Oct 29

I love you, Sparrow.

W.B.T.

Nov 1

I love you more than anyone knows.

It would take a lifetime to show you.

Ian

Nov 3

I love you today and for always.

It's a love that didn't grow up overnight.

Ian

Nov 4

Your smile makes the sun shine.

I live to see that smile on me again.

Nov 5

My nights are a constant reaching for you ....

Nov 8

Dear Sparrow—

Don't know where you are or who you're with or what you're doing. How you're feeling, what you're thinking. When you're smiling, when you're crying. If you miss me like I miss you. If you've got someone to talk to.

I know I'm still here and I still love you.

And I always will.

Ian

Nov 12

SparrowSparrowSparrowSparrow—

Another fabulous day.

I heard your voice last night.

Slept in 'til 9. Ate.

Hope I've heard from you before you get this letter. What did we talk about?

I'm so glad we talked.

I love you.

Ian

Nov 13

There is a miracle in the way love keeps enduring ... across a million miles.

Nov 14

Sparrow—

I want to write I want to talk I want to

communicate somehow

Words are not coming easy.

I hurt to my very soul.

I feel your pain and I'm not allowed to comfort you.

I know the certainty of my love for you and I have no way to give it to you.

I'll stop here. I know I can't express myself in this letter.

But please know that I love you.

I'm doing everything I know to do.

I want what's right and what's best for you.

I don't believe that us being apart for life is necessary or best. Do you?

So much more I want to say.

For us

Ian

Nov 15

Do you get tired of people trying to help you "get over it"?

Forever Love.

Ian

Nov 16

Sparrow.

I miss you so much.

Ian

Nov 18

I mourn for the time we've lost. There's a lot of life ahead. I don't want us to miss out on any more of it. I'm so lonely without you. I love you, sweet Sparrow. My love.

I'm so ready to be with you.

Nov 19

Still barkin' up your tree...

Nov 20

Yesterday I went into the library and just sat down, imagining you there.

Nov 22

Little Bird

It's been about a half-hour now since I wrote the two words preceding this sentence. It's so hard to have a one-sided conversation. I can't address any of your thoughts or feelings and I want to so much.

We're not strangers, Sparrow. I keep appealing to you because I know that no one else can really understand what is between us. These well-meaning people who say, "Life must go on," have no idea. I can no more "go on" without you than I could if half of my body was cut away.

My soul is knit to yours. My life is hinged to yours. I move, I breathe, but I don't really live without you. All that keeps my heart beating is the hope that it will someday beat next to yours again.

I love you, Sparrow.

Nov 24

It's cold. You're far. I'm saving your place.

Nov 25

I love you.

Give me a chance to show you how much.

Give yourself a chance to know it.

For us. Forever.

W.B.T.

—

Dec 1

You may have to break this heart

Before you can use it.

You may have to take it apart and start all over
with me.

I know it hurts to change, but I don't want to
stay the same

Take me. Break me.

Do whatever it takes to make me what you need
me to be.

Happy Birthday, my Little Bird.

I love you. I will always love you.

These are not adequate words. I write them, and
a stream of half-fulfilled desires, snapshot memories,
soul-deep emotions, nameless feelings rushes through
me.

I think of everything I have ever loved,
possessed, wanted, worked for, hoped for, treasured

in my life.

I love you more.

More than my music. More than my career. More than my reputation. More than my independence. More than my life.

I would give up any or every one of them for your sake.

I would never be so bold as to make such statements, except that every word has been tested and proven true to me beyond any doubt. In the past couple of long months, I have, in some measure, felt the loss of all of these things. It has been painful— but nothing at all, compared to the loss of you.

My love for you is pure.

In September, something began in me that, I believe, I may spend the rest of my life trying to fully comprehend and describe.

I loved you before then—deeply.

But that night, in your room, after you finally

came out of your closet, something changed.

I saw so many things that night. I saw myself. My unworthiness. My faithlessness. I saw the bitterness that had been in me, holding me for so many years. And I felt the full weight of my sins.

You were there, Sparrow, you know.

I broke my heart open. I pleaded with you and God and anyone else who would listen to search me and cleanse me and release me from all of that. To change me and forgive me.

And God heard me.

I saw something else. As I looked into the tearful, red face of the one person I loved more and had hurt more than anyone else in my life, I saw mercy and compassion. And I saw the pain it cost to give them.

I will never forget that moment. I have memorized that face. I have not let go of the hope it gave me.

Since that night, I have never stopped hoping to be reconciled with you.

I have forsaken my old ways completely.

I have been faithful to you.

I have been broken, again and again. Purged, tested, refined. I have new desires, new priorities, a new heart. It embarrasses me to say these things about myself. I just hope you'll understand.

One thing I'm not afraid or ashamed to say is, I love you, Sparrow Kate Fisher.

I can withstand anything because I am sure about our love and I have determined to fight for it to the death. If you are afraid, if you are doubtful, I can make up the difference. You did that for me when I was fearful, and now I want to do that for you.

I love you.

Ian

P.S. Please use this calling card. :)

P.S.S. If you don't want to talk to me, you could

call and talk to my voicemail.

- 25 -

Roses AND Time

Our wedding date comes and goes.

Fed Ex brings an express letter to Sparrow Kate Fisher from Ian Orville Sterling. So official. I read the letter from Ian and spend the rest of the day holed away in my room.

It kills me, just like all the rest.

Sparrow—

These days and these nights. They're endless. Merciless.

The time just seems to crawl. I would pray for it to pass quickly, but I know that every moment that slips by is one more moment I'll never be able to share with the one I love. That's you.

This is the day we were supposed to get married. I can't stop seeing your face and wishing *that you were saying yes to me today. Forever.*

I've got a hundred kisses for every tear I've caused. A hug for every heartache.

Oh, I miss you. My body aches. My heart groans. I call your name and hope that somewhere deep in your spirit, you'll hear...

I love you.

Ian

My wedding dress hangs in a heavy garment bag in the guest bedroom. I probably wouldn't be able to wear it now anyway; it would just hang on me. Food is not cooperating with me right now. I try to eat, but besides having absolutely no appetite for the first time in my entire life, it makes me physically sick in one way or another every time I do eat. My parents think I have an ulcer, and they're trying to force me to go to the doctor, but so far, I've managed to avoid going.

I've barely functioned in school the last few months and now that I'm home for Christmas break, I'm not so sure it was a good idea for me to come here either. I see Ian everywhere. There's no escaping him.

My room is covered with roses of every shade. Red, various pinks, and my favorite, the Sterling roses. Since I sent Ian away, he has bombarded me with flowers and love letters and books and candy and whatever else he says reminds him of me. It's funny—he never once gave me flowers or a love letter when we were together.

Jeff and Laila's marriage is in tatters, but I guess it always was and we just didn't know it. Jeff is devastated. I think it hurts him more that it was Ian having an affair with Laila than the fact that she had an affair at all. Laila called me once. If I had been able to see that it was her, I never would have answered it, but my parents have an antiquated house phone. She's scared of losing Jeff. She said it *really had ended* with Ian long ago, and she tried to make nice. But then she said something about me really being "so naive" and that one comment wiped out any chance of making peace.

One minute I feel like I did the right thing by ending it with Ian, and the next, I am desperate for him. I weep. A lot. I long for that brief interval I had before the tears took over. I read his letters over and over again, and they make me angry and hopeful and afraid and lost and bitter and loved.

I do believe he loves me.

I just don't believe it's enough.

I wasn't enough for him for the last couple of years, why would I think I could be enough now?

When I'm in New York, he writes or emails obsessively. When I'm *home*, he knows he has a chance of reaching me on the house phone, so he calls and calls until one of us picks up. One of my Christmas presents to my parents is a new box of house phones to stagger all over the house, with a huge caller-id display. It's already wrapped, and I'm tempted to give it to them early.

A few days ago, he caught me in a vulnerable moment vs. a bitter moment. When he begged to please let him come see me, I finally caved and said he could. He'll be here soon. My parents are still furious with him too, so he's taking his chances with coming back into this house. They've made themselves scarce for a few hours, to give us a chance to talk.

I get ready and sit in the living room, waiting for him. When the doorbell rings, it feels alien to be answering the door for Ian. He used to come and go from this house as if it was his own.

I slowly open the door and a garbled sound comes out of Ian's throat. He rushes toward me and stops just as he reaches me, unsure of what to do.

"Baby," he whispers. He looks at me questioningly and my eyes must tell him it's okay because he gently wraps his arms around me and pulls me close.

Despite everything, being in his arms is the only time I've felt whole since all of this happened. I close my eyes and inhale him, feeling the shift in the air around me … that deep breath that I've been struggling to get since he left finally making its way into my lungs and giving me relief. He runs his hands through my hair, whispering his love for me, caressing me with his words and making me weak with the momentary reprieve from grief.

And then I open my eyes and the fog lifts and I see him and what he did to me. I back up and step inside the house. Windows closed, shutters drawn. I can't afford to let my guard down. "You can't call me that."

Ian stands in the doorway and openly gawks at me. "Little Bird," he says in a choked voice.

"Or that," I whisper.

He winces. "I'm sorry. Sparrow. You don't look—" He shakes his head and doesn't finish the thought.

I study him for the first time and feel a twinge of horror at how awful he looks. His color is all wrong. His eyes look dull and there are dark circles around them. He's lost a lot of weight and his lean, muscular frame now looks gaunt. His hair is longer than I've ever seen it, soft waves falling over his collar. The hair is actually nice, but with the rest of him in such bad shape, it just adds to his almost frail look.

He clears his throat and says, "What if we go to the park? Maybe bundle up and sit by the water?"

"Okay."

It's chilly for California. I pull my coat up higher as we walk to the car. Ian is quiet and watchful. He keeps starting to say something and then stops. I don't bother trying to talk.

We go to a park that we used to always visit and sit on our bench that overlooks the lake.

"There's so much I want to say, Sparrow. So much. But first—is there anything you want to say to me?" He turns to face me, and I look at him briefly before turning back to the water.

"I don't really know what to say to you anymore, Ian. I used to be able to tell you everything, and now—I just feel really *stupid* for all the times I did."

He nods, his eyes hurt. "I have never, *ever* thought you were anything but brilliant. I love your thoughts. To have the luxury of your thoughts suddenly gone from my life is like death. All the light is gone."

"I'm not so light anymore," I tell him.

"Are you taking care of yourself, Sparrow? You look—I'm worried about you." He strokes my cheek with his fingers and when I shiver, he puts his arms around me, warming me up.

I don't say anything.

"I've wanted to say that you can't imagine how much I miss you, love you—how empty I am without you. But now that I see you, I wonder. Maybe you can imagine? It's like a constant sense that part of me is missing and that things will never be right without that part. It gnaws at me all day and night. Do you feel any of that?"

Tears roll down my face, and I angrily swipe them away. "Of course I do. I put all my hopes and desires and love … into you. You think I don't feel it? Imagine how you feel and then *add* the pain of knowing that I was never enough for you, that you didn't value what I gave you, that you were with someone else the entire time you were with me … put that all together and then you'll know how *I* feel."

"I know you're the one who was hurt, Sparrow, I know that. All that I tell you in my letters is not to diminish your hurt, but to let you know how sorry I am and how *deeply* I ache for you, every single minute of every damn day. It's excruciating. I guess your silence has made me wonder if you've found a way to move past it somehow."

"I haven't."

"Please come back to me," he says, softly touching my cheek. I push his hand away and stand up.

"I want to go home."

Ian runs his hands through his hair. It doesn't stick straight out anymore. "Okay. Okay, I'll take you home. Can I still be with you?"

I nod.

The next few days are more of the same. I don't know

why I keep seeing him. I just can't *not* see him. He's my air. Even if it's a nightmare, I can *breathe* when he's in my proximity.

It's tense with Ian and my parents. He tries to talk to them and they listen, but not much progress is made. They've given him a piece of their minds more than once, and yet, they've also been kind to him. For the most part, they are trying to give us our space. Charlie asks for details every night when Ian leaves, but I think she knows I'm just not up for hashing it out right now, so she doesn't push very hard.

Christmas comes and Ian is still here. He hasn't said how long he's staying in town and I haven't asked. I know it's not healthy for either of us to carry on like this—it gives him hope, and I really don't have any to give.

When he comes over Christmas afternoon, holding a pretty package wrapped with a bright silver bow, I place two gifts beside him.

"You didn't need to get me anything," he whispers. He seems more exhausted today, like these days are taking their toll on him.

"I was going to give you these presents the night before our wedding."

"Oh." He tries to muster up a grin, but it looks more like a grimace. "Thank you." He tries to coax a smile out of me, but I've got nothing.

"Go ahead and open them."

"Should I open the big one or the little one first?"

"How about the big one…"

He slowly unwraps the box, that way he does where it seems he is cherishing every scrap of paper. He doesn't rip a single piece and when it's off the box, he carefully folds it and sets it aside. He opens the shoebox and sees the black combat boots. He smiles then, and I can't help it, I smile back.

"I wanted you to wear them at the wedding."

He nods. He's never been one for dress shoes. "I love them, Sparrow," he says softly. "You know me, I'll probably wear them until they're falling apart. Here, open this."

I take the box from him and once I have the bow off, I quickly tear it open. Inside the box is a gorgeous watch in white gold; tiny diamonds are on the face in place of numbers. "I wanted to give you this before the wedding too," he admits. "Look right there." He points to the back.

I turn it over and read: Time is on our side.

"It would have said something different if we'd gotten married, but we … didn't, so … I'm glad I didn't put the date on it," he tries to sound lighthearted.

"It's beautiful. Thank you." I put it on my arm and it fits perfectly. "Wow, usually watches don't fit my wrist on the first try."

"I know your wrist is about this big." He holds up his thumb and forefinger and makes my wrist size.

"You were right."

I'm suddenly overwhelmed with heaviness. I point at his present to keep the tears from starting. "Open your other one."

He picks it up and when he opens it, he lets out a small laugh. "Same page…" He pulls his watch out of the box and gives it a long look. "It's really nice. I've never owned anything so nice." He turns it over and his breath hitches. "My heart will always beat your name." The 'heart' is the symbol so it will all fit. There wasn't room for the date on his either.

"Do you mean it?" he asks, his voice brighter than it has been, hopeful. "Is this true?"

"I'm afraid it might be," I say.

All the light goes from his eyes when he realizes that I don't want it to be true. The thought really does make me afraid. He clutches the watch and looks at me, his whole body anguished. "I will never give up hoping that you mean what this says." He waves the watch around and slaps it on his wrist, holding his arm up when it's clasped. He comes up to me and grasps both my shoulders with his hands. "What will it take, Sparrow? I'll do whatever it takes, please, just be with me. Let me show you that I mean everything I've said. We'll work it out, we will … I'm coming to New York and I'll stay. My record deal didn't work out, but—"

"Wait? What do you mean? You already signed, what—?" I shake my head. "I don't understand!"

"They wanted me to be in LA in October and November and I told them I needed—" He drops my shoulders and walks to the window. He looks out the window a long time before continuing. "I just needed time. I haven't been able to do anything. Except write you pathetic letters." He turns around and gives me a forced smile. "And I've been writing songs. Songs that would make people want to jump off a bridge, but songs, nonetheless." He shrugs. "They had gigs lined up every night. I told them I needed time, and they wouldn't give it to me. I walked away. I'm telling you: I can't do anything, Sparrow, not without you."

For some reason, this is harder for me to take than the whole gift exchange was. "I can't believe you gave that up. Ian! You're going to regret it once you're—feeling better. Your recording! And the tour—you've worked so hard for this! You can't just walk away from it all."

"It doesn't mean anything to me, Sparrow. Maybe I'll regret it like you say, but right now, I can't see past *this*. I have to see this through with you. We have to work it out. I'm not gonna 'feel better' without *you*!"

I walk over to him and stand beside him. "Ian. You need to do whatever you can to make it right with the label." I touch his arm and he looks at me. His eyes are hungry; he leans into my hand. "Ian, you have to let me go."

His chest deflates and he backs away from me. "No. Don't. Don't say that."

"I can't … I can't be with you. I don't know how I'm gonna live without you. But I don't think I can live with you either. You have broken me," my voice gives out. "I don't see how I can ever trust you again."

"You could, you just don't want to," he cries.

"You're right. I don't."

With that, he leans over and crushes me with a kiss, and then walks across the room, picks up his boots and the wrapping paper and walks out the door. "I still believe in us, Sparrow. I'll never stop," he says before the door shuts behind him.

- 26 -

9 months later

Fall in New York is exceptional this year. The trees are brighter and more colorful than I ever remember. I walk home, shuffling my feet through the fallen leaves while running through the to-do list in my head.

Tonight Tessa is throwing a small party for me to celebrate the release of my book. It comes out next week and the relief of being completely done with the project is immense. I'm happy with the way it turned out, and with the way my brain is always working, I wasn't sure I could ever say that.

I pick up my dress from the dry cleaners and mentally check that off the list.

When I get to the apartment, there are flowers from Ian sitting outside my door. The delivery guy is on a first name basis with me now and usually shakes his head sadly when I open the door. I'm glad I missed his pity today.

My Little Bird—

I'm so proud of you. I heard about your book. I will

be the first in line to buy it.

I love you.

Ian

It's been a year since Ian and I broke up. Exactly a year. And he still hasn't given up. I still get letters, although they have gradually become less frequent. Around graduation, he sent a CD of songs he's written for me over the year. They were heartbreaking, excruciating songs about love and loss and longing. I cried for days and then put the CD in a box, high up on my closet shelf and haven't revisited it.

I've been working on a letter for the last two months. A letter that I work on every night before bed, saying all the things I've wanted to say to him since everything fell apart. I pick up the notebook that I've been writing it all in and read where I've left off:

I can't do this anymore. I need you to stop. The letters, the gifts, the flowers, all of it. I can't take it anymore. It's killing me. Each time you send something, another piece of me whittles down further. I can't be with you. I wish I could, but I'm just not able to get past it. All these letters from you feel like a way to appease your guilt and I'm hereby releasing you.

I forgive you, but I can't forget.

I will love you forever, but I can't be with you.

I rifle through the pages of the notebook that details all the thoughts of love and loss and longing *I've* felt and realize I can't say any more than this. It's all been said. I put it in an 8 1/2 x 11 envelope and before I can think it to death, I seal it and address it to Ian Sterling. I will mail it on the way to my party. Check.

Andy calls to make sure I don't need a ride to the restaurant. I assure him I don't and that I'll see him there. I've been going out with Andy for a few weeks now. The first time he kissed me, I cried. We were outside, so I was able to blame it on the wind, but since then I've been putting distance between us. He knew I was on an I-hate-men tangent when we met and somehow weaseled his way into being my friend. I tell him I'm not ready for a relationship, but he keeps doggedly pursuing. I know a big talk is due because I have no desire whatsoever to kiss him again. Or touch him. Or really even look at him. I know I should have never gone out with him to begin with, but Tessa keeps telling me I have to start getting out.

Everyone is worried about me.

Maybe this letter/book to Ian is what it will take for me to move on ... be okay. I don't know. I don't really think I will ever be okay, but I'm exhausted with peering at the world through this negative, cloudy, hateful veil.

I despise the distrust I have for everyone. I guess it was time I developed a more cynical skin, instead of being so gullible or 'idealistic'. If I've learned anything from Ian—and Asher, too, for that matter—it's that the world isn't this beautiful, happy place that I always imagined.

It's full of gross ugliness on every side. No one can be trusted. Everyone will disappoint. And it's up to me to watch out for myself. No one else is going to do it for me.

Well, except for Tessa. She doesn't count in my harsh new worldview. She is an entity all her own, and I don't know what I would do without her.

Jared and Tessa are waiting for me in front of the restaurant. I hug them both, and then they lead the way. Jared would have to count as an exception to my All Men Are Evil campaign. For at least six months after Ian and I broke up, I watched Jared like a hawk, just waiting for him to make a wrong move. He hasn't. He genuinely loves Tessa and treats her so well. I can't help but love him for it.

The party is nice. I'm grateful for the school friends I've made from NYU. A couple of friendships I know will last forever. My editor, Louise, is great too. Everyone wishes me well, and it's a fun night.

I've become used to that hollowed-out feeling in my chest that's present even when everything is good.

I duck out after telling Andy that I don't need a ride home. Before I tell him goodnight though, I pull him aside.

"Andy, I know this isn't the right time to talk, but I—I can't go out with you anymore. If you're not okay with us just being friends, let me know. If you are, great. I'm sorry if I've hurt you in any way."

He nods and says, "I saw this coming."

And with that, I walk outside and breathe in the brisk night air.

"Hey, beautiful."

I turn around quickly at the sound of his voice. The

rasp that I hear in my dreams.

Ian is standing just outside the door. He points to the window of the restaurant. "I saw you in there with your friends … I was torn about what to do. Should I go inside and ruin your night just by my presence?" He laughs a harsh laugh. "Or do I disappear and pretend you're not within 100 yards of me? What to do? I've just been standing here in a conundrum. You caught me."

I stare at him. He looks better than the last time I saw him. His hair is back to its short, haphazard chaos and his face is a little bit fuller, almost back to how it was when we were happy.

Finally, I speak. "What are you doing here?"

"Jagged flew me in for their new recording … I'm laying guitar tracks tomorrow. I'm supposed to meet them here in a few—"

Andy walks out of the restaurant and comes to a screeching halt in front of us. He looks back and forth from Ian to me and back to Ian. He recognizes Ian and moves in closer to me.

"Sparrow? How 'bout that ride?"

"I'm fine, Andy. Thank you, though. Really," I add when it seems he doesn't believe me.

"Okay, if you're sure. I'll call you later." He nods to Ian and walks away.

"Is that your boyfriend?" Ian asks, his face expressionless.

"No."

"He wants to be," Ian says emphatically.

"Yeah."

Ian nods and releases a long sigh. "Can we go somewhere, Sparrow? Anywhere? Did you eat dessert?"

"You said you're meeting the band here."

"Screw the band. I'm seeing you. I can't miss a chance to be with you. I would have called to tell you I was coming, but the whole phone number issue…damn, I wish you'd give me your number. I did write to tell you. Maybe you haven't gotten that one yet?"

I shake my head no.

"Ahhh. Well, what do you say? Come with me? Let's catch up? Celebrate? You have a lot of celebrating to do…"

Out of all the people in the world that I would want to celebrate with, way down deep, Ian is still the one. But I say, "I should get home. It's … been a long day."

His face falls. "I understand," he says thickly. "I'll be here until Monday … I'll make time for whatever works for you, Sparrow, if we can get together."

I do a number on the inside of my mouth, biting hard to keep from falling into his arms and going off with him into the night.

"I hope it goes well," I say softly. "It's good to see you, Ian."

"So good to see you, Sparrow." He reaches out and touches my arm. "I still love you."

"I still love you, too, Ian. It just doesn't mean anything anymore."

I walk away before I can fully digest the sucker-punch look in his eyes that my words just caused.

I'm dragging into the grocery store the next morning. It was a long, sleepless night. Someone says, "Sparrow Fisher?"

I turn around and don't recognize the guy who's

walking in with me.

"Are you Sparrow Fisher?"

"Who are you?" I ask.

"I'm Leo Naik. Bass player for Jagged."

I nod. "Oh yeah, sorry, I didn't recognize you. Have we met before?"

"No." He laughs. "Sorry, I just realized we haven't ever met. I feel like I know you, though. Ian talks about you all the time. I've seen a ton of pictures. That guy is crazy over you."

I look away uncomfortably.

"He was fucked up last night, man. What did you do to him? He was piss drunk by the time we got to the restaurant—we had to drag him home. He talked about you all night long."

"Is he okay?" I ask. "He never gets drunk. Ever. He barely even drinks."

Leo leans in close and says quietly, "I'm worried about him. Dude's messed up—he was on the floor all night, huddled in a ball, talking nonsense about you."

I shut my eyes and put my hand over my lips. When I open my eyes, I edge toward Leo and get in his face. "Don't talk about it, okay? Ian's private, and he wouldn't want anyone to know this."

Leo holds up his hands. "The guy's my friend. I'm only telling you because—well, how crazy is it that I ran into you here, today, after the night I've had with your ex? I'm getting some Advil and taking it back to him. If there's any part of you that wants to give him another chance, get your ass back to him and give the poor guy a break."

I back away from him, anger taking over. "Mind your

own business. You don't know me," I snap.

"Oh, I know plenty. I've had to hear about you for a long time now. Don't get me wrong, I'm sure you're great and all, but you've fucked him up royally. He walked away from his career and everything over you."

"I never asked him to do that. And the next time you're chatting about me, why don't you ask *him* how we got to this point?"

"All I know, is Ian Sterling will *never* get over you."

With that, he walks away and leaves me staring after him, wondering how in the world my life ever became so complicated.

Every time I leave the apartment, I halfway expect to see Ian around every corner. I'm on guard and jumpy. Saturday morning, I open the door to get my mail, and there's a note taped to my door.

~~Sparrow~~ Kate—

I was hoping I'd see you again. I've decided to leave today. I know if I stay any longer, I'll try to twist your arm into seeing me. I finished my work early and have the opportunity to play on Cape Cod tonight. I'll be staying there a few extra days. If you'd like to get together before I head home, I can stop back through here. I'd like that very much. I promise I would behave.

Ian

I shrug off the disappointment that runs through me. My fickle will is loathsome.

I sent him away.

I'm mad that he went.

I can't love him.

I can't hate him either.

Ian Sterling has ruined me. And he's ruined me for anyone else.

- 27 -

New Year, NEW LIFE

4 months later

I don't make any New Year's resolutions this year. I've sworn off of them. Anything that makes me feel guilty or requires much thought or is too responsible—I'm giving my responsible brain the year off. I resolutely resolve to not resolute to anything, period. We'll see if I'm onto something.

The letter taped to my door four months ago was the last time I heard from Ian.

I've played it over in my head a thousand times:

He left that note with high hopes that I would see him again while he was in town.

He didn't hear from me and went home even more discouraged.

When he got home, my huge letter to him was waiting.

He's finally given up.

I know I asked for this, but a part of my heart breaks all over again with the realization. In some ways, though, it *has* helped to have the quiet. I feel better for getting all of my thoughts out and finally closing the door for good.

But, oh, I miss him so much. I realize now that I don't have it, how much every little morsel of information from him was still causing me to hang on for dear life. Now it's a dull ache rather than the biting one that used to come with each letter. It's for the best that I completely ended it, but it doesn't stop the torment I feel every single day.

I'm dating someone new. His name is Carl. He's cute and fun and doesn't expect too much from me. He's a writer, too, and we met at a luncheon for up-and-coming authors. We were seated at the same table and had a nice conversation. We went out to dinner and a movie tonight and had a really nice time. His kisses are even nice. They almost help me forget. For just a few moments at a time, I can almost forget.

Tessa is over at Jared's, but she picked up the mail before she left and I thumb through it. My heart starts pounding when I see a letter from Ian.

Sparrow,

It's Ian.

I started writing this letter a while ago. In the meantime I got your letter. That set me back a bit. Thanks for sharing some of your feelings—I understand most of them perfectly. I sure know how hard it is to put a true, complete expression of your thoughts and emotions on a piece (or a hundred pieces) of paper. Here's one more attempt.

I know your intention in writing was not to open up a dialogue (too bad). You want it to just be over and done with. Finished. Ended. No more. Nada. Kaput. Fini. Amscray. The End. Quit. Stop. Go away. Take a hike. Bye-bye. Period. Exclamation point! (Am I getting your drift?)

So anyway, I'm not really writing to respond, though I would love to. There are so many things I wish I could make you understand—me, my heart, my motives, my true intentions toward you (what they were, what they are now, what they could be), what I mean when I say, "I love you"—but I can't.

I can't make you do anything against your will.

I'm not sure when I first started to understand that fact. Maybe I always have. But I know when I saw you in New York last, it became vividly clear to me. I felt as if I was looking right through you and

337

yet not seeing you at all. As if every part of you had turned away.

And I knew then that I was powerless to do anything about it.

God knows I would have done absolutely anything to make our relationship work.

I've spent the last year (plus some months) hoping and praying for the miracle that would reunite us and give me the chance to love you and share my life with you again.

Now I've come to believe that it may never happen.

There's nothing I can do.

If you don't want to be with me, you won't.

I'm trying to let you go.

I've decided to start seeing someone else. I don't know how to fall out of love, but apparently, it's possible. We'll see.

It's taken me months to write this. It doesn't say

a fraction of what I want to say, but I guess some things will just have to go unsaid. Maybe we'll talk again someday. It'll be up to you.

With shaking hands, I hold the letter and slide my back down the wall until I'm on the floor. My tears drop on what he's written, leaving blurred ink in its place. I cry for everything that's lost. I cry that he gave up. I cry for the anger in his words. I cry that he's found someone that has made him consider letting me go. I cry for the day I ever met him and thought I could handle someone like him. I cry that the girl he met that day in the restaurant is long gone.

And I cry because I don't know what to do with this person that's left.

- 28 -

Home

6 months later

Tessa tapes the last of her boxes and stands up, brushing the cardboard residue off her hands. "I think that's the last of it." She wipes her forehead and looks at me with a grin. "I think we should go out on the town tonight. Eh? What do you think?"

I know she's trying to cheer me up and I'm determined to show her that I'm going to be all right. Tessa, Jared, and our fabulous red couch are moving to New Orleans tomorrow. Jared got a job with an excellent law firm there. They're engaged, but no wedding date any time soon. Tessa wants all the bells and whistles for her wedding, or as she says, 'all the balls and whistles'.

I am going to miss her desperately, but I'm so happy for her. She's excited for a new start. We've agreed to call and text all the time, visit each other lots, and Skype whenever possible. Still, it won't be the same. I've had her by my side since fifth grade.

"Yes. Yes, I definitely think we should. And we should stay up all night and watch movies. Jared can do all the driving tomorrow. That's what he gets for taking you so far away."

"Yeah! That's right!" She yells back. "Okay, let's get

340

cleaned up and go!"

We are into our second drink when she brings up the topic of me moving back home. "Have you given it any more thought?"

"A lot of thought, actually. I think it's time. With you leaving, there's really nothing else keeping me here. I miss my parents and California. And with book sales going well, I think I could finally afford to live in California on my own. I've mentioned it to Louise, and she doesn't see why we can't handle everything through email and video chats, so … I'm going for it."

Tessa looks relieved. "I think it will be a good move, Ro. You need a change. I know home might not seem like much of a 'change', but maybe it's just what you need."

I nod.

"There's one other thing I want to talk to you about. Please don't get mad at me."

My brows crinkle up and I laugh. "You know it's impossible for me to be mad at you, Tess."

"Well, just hear me out and know I'm saying this because I love you."

"You're scaring me."

"I just want you to be careful," she says.

"Okay … what do you mean?"

"Well, I know that you've gone through hell over everything with Ian and you seem better than you were—which I'm SO glad about—but I'm just worried about the way you're going about getting better *lately*."

My skin flushes and I look down at my glass and wipe off some of the condensation with my napkin.

"Ro," she says softly, "I don't think you've done

anything wrong. God knows, I would have done far worse in your situation. I've done far worse NOT being in your situation…" She giggles and reaches for my hand. "It's just not *you*, Ro. It's not you and it won't ever be. Some of these guys you're bringing home—I don't trust them. At all. And I won't be around to kick their ass if they hurt you—not that you would need me to at this point, I've *seen* you in Taekwondo class. I'm just worried about you. Don't let what he did to you turn you into someone you're not."

A single tear falls. It's been a long time since I've cried. The last letter day was the last time.

I look up at Tessa and grasp our hands with my free hand. "I love you, Tess. I hear ya. I need to stop this downward spiral I'm in. I've been looking for anything that will get him out of my head. It's not working, nothing is."

"Maybe it's time to stop running *from* him and time to start running *to* him," she says.

I shake my head and smile weakly. "When did you become so … inspirational?"

She laughs. "That did sound pretty good, didn't it?"

"You know he's dating someone else now. He's moved on."

"I think he's only doing the same thing you've been doing—trying to survive."

I think about that conversation with Tessa often. The apartment feels lonely, and I'm tempted to slide back into my bad habits. Instead, I begin making preparations to move back to California. Everything falls into place, almost as if it's meant to be.

A few nights before I'm scheduled to leave, I've just had one last dinner with Louise and I'm in a cab going home. We stop outside The Living Room, a cool, eclectic music venue. Striding by with his guitar on his back, I see him. He walks with purpose. He has a little bit of his swagger back, which makes me smile. He looks healthier. Maybe letting me go was the best thing for him.

Of course it wrecks me, but I mark it down in my journal as a significant day. I think Ian is going to be okay and now I have to be too.

My parents try to talk me into moving back into my old bedroom. Besides the fact that I'm 24 and hoping to avoid going backwards with my life, being in my room gives me claustrophobia. I have to stay a week before I can move into my new place, and I want to climb the walls.

I've found a guesthouse in Los Gatos, a pretty suburb of San Jose. The cottage in the back is so charming. I absolutely love it. Jenny, the owner of the main house, is wonderful. She used to be a model back in the day. She's beautiful and practically floats with every step. We hit it off within minutes of meeting and she said the place is mine.

Moving day is a gorgeous, sunny day. I'm glad to be back in the mild temperatures and sunshine. And this place—it feels really good. As I'm unpacking, Jenny comes over with a plate of cookies. I could get used to this.

"You've got it looking so cute in here!" Jenny sings her words.

"Thank you. I'm thinking of painting that…" I point to the desk sitting in the middle of the floor. Everything else is in its place, except the desk. "I think it has to be painted blue," I tell her.

She nods like she completely agrees and I feel relief—and it's not about the desk. This is where I'm supposed to be.

The days fade in and out without much excitement, but more peace than I've had in a long time. Until I begin dating Reggie. Who names their kid Reggie anyway? Reginald, Sr., that's who. I should have steered clear when I heard the name, but I give him a try. He's funny and that counts for a lot with me. He's cute in a nerdish way— wavy hair, blue eyes and glasses. He's the kind of guy that will probably be good-looking when he's a lot older. Right now, he still just seems gawky. But, for whatever reason, I go out with him and then can't seem to get rid of him.

We argue. A lot. I've never fought with anyone, much less a boyfriend, and it's kind of therapeutic. I say exactly what I think and scoff when I don't agree with him. Maybe it's the way I should have been in every other relationship, I'm not sure, but the fact is, after months of getting a charge out of spouting whatever I want to spout out, I realize that I really don't like Reggie. As a person. At all. In fact, everything he does bothers me.

He seems heartbroken when I break up with him.

"You don't even like me! You don't agree with anything I say!"

"I love not agreeing with you!" he yells.

Please.

A few months later, I go out with Art, short for Arthur. I know. It's not much better than Reggie, but he's dark and brooding and I kinda dig him. Catch this—he's an artist—how perfect is that? Of course, I have to give him grief over that, but he handles it in stride. Nothing ruffles Art, nothing … except when I tell him after two months that I don't want to exclusively date him. He suddenly goes into a rage and throws a chair across the room. It was a light folding chair, but still, I get out of there fast.

He calls every now and then, but I don't see him again until I'm stopped at an intersection, waiting for the light to change. He's facing me, waiting for the light on the other side. I lift my hand to wave, when a car slams into my car … on my side.

The airbags puff up and nearly break my nose. Glass is everywhere. My knee is killing me. My neck, too. The impact pushes the car across the road and I sit in shock indefinitely. Art talks to me through the window and then opens the door.

"Don't move," he says, grabbing my hand. "Hold still. I've called the ambulance." And then he looks down with tenderness and a touch of malice and says, "I remember when you used to hold my hand like this…"

Bastard.

Totaled car and back problems for life later, I meet Cam, the hunky construction worker who comes to work on Jenny's house. He's wonderful—so down to earth, hilarious, really cute and all about me. He thinks I hung the moon, he seriously does. I go out with him and have the best time. He can make me laugh SO hard, and he thinks I'm hysterical. He takes me on all kinds of fun, unique dates—like a hot air balloon ride and go-kart racing! I like him so much that I break up with him before we can even officially start dating. He doesn't need my baggage.

Tessa calls early one morning.

"Hello?" I say groggily.

"I'm SO SORRY, I couldn't wait to call you!"

"What's going on?" I prop up on both elbows.

"We have a date!"

This wakes me up. "Tessa! When?"

"September 21st!"

"Like 6 months from now, September 21st? What? How did you do it? Where?"

"You're not gonna believe it, Ro. There was a cancellation at—wait for it—the RITZ CARLTON!"

I pull the phone away while she screams. I'm screaming too.

"The Ritz?" I yell. "HOW did you manage *that*?"

"It's all too crazy. The wife of one of the lawyers at Jared's firm is a wedding advisor there. How crazy is that? We hit it off when I came to one of Jared's work thingies, you know, when we first moved—" she takes a huge breath and continues "—she put me on the waiting list then and said she'd call me the minute there was a cancellation … that I'd be at the top of the list. She thinks Jared and I have waited long enough." Tessa giggles. "Anyway, she called at 7 this morning and told me the good news. Well, good news for me; bad news for the poor bride who was *supposed* to get married that day…" Her voice trails off.

"Tessa, let's not think about her right now. Let's just be happy for you, okay?"

"Okay!" she says happily. "I'll be coming home to go dress shopping—I'll let you know when I have some definite dates."

"Can't wait."

"And you'll come early before the wedding too, right?"

"YES! Of course! If you'd said it was this weekend, I would be hopping on a plane right now to get there."

"Love you, Ro."

"I love you, too."

And then Michael comes for a visit. My parents inform me that he's coming when I'm over for Sunday dinner the week before. When Michael went back to Seattle, he got his degree and went on to medical school. He decided the ministry wasn't really for him. My dad has stayed in touch with him, but this will be the first time they've seen him since he left.

"He's just staying with us for the weekend. He wanted to see everyone before he starts his residency," my mom says.

"He's staying here?" My eyes narrow at her, trying to decipher if she's setting this up to try to get us back together or if she's as surprised as me. I can't be sure.

She nods and gets very busy scrubbing a pan.

I'm looking forward to seeing him … as long as he doesn't try anything with me.

As I get ready to have dinner with Michael and my parents, I think back to our time together and how much has changed. I wonder if we'll still recognize each other, if the people we used to be even show through anymore. I pack an overnight bag. I'll be staying at home while he's there, so we can get the most time out of this visit.

I pull up to the house and help my mom with the last-minute preparations. When Michael arrives, we all go to the door and yell excitedly when we see each other. Michael hugs my parents first and then his eyes settle on me. He wraps me up in a big hug and grins his huge grin.

"Hey, Ro. It sure is great to see you."

"I'm so happy to see you!" I tell him and I mean it. "You look great!"

"You look more beautiful than ever. I can't believe how long it's been since I've seen you."

"I know, I can't either," I say as I take his arm and walk with him inside.

Conversation flows easily as we all catch up. Michael always had a way of telling a story and his laugh is infectious. My heart is full as I think about all he's accomplished and how well he's turned out. I knew he would be a wonderful man and he is.

Later, after my parents have gone to bed, I stay up talking to Michael.

"I've heard bits and pieces about what happened with you and Ian," he says after we've exhausted a few topics.

"Yeah, it was … hard." I feel horrible even talking about it with him after I broke his heart … over *Ian*.

"I won't lie, I wanted that guy to suffer for a long time … after I lost you. But I never wanted you to go through anything like this." Michael looks at me, and I see the sincerity in his eyes. "Are you okay, Ro? Are you really okay?"

"I haven't been," I admit. "It's been long enough now that I should be snapping out of it sometime soon here." I laugh awkwardly. "But I just can't seem to…"

"Well, he was an idiot for wrecking his chances with you. I know that no one is perfect, but you come pretty close." He reaches over and touches my cheek softly. "And I want to kill him for hurting you."

"You're a good man, you know that, Michael?" I smile. "I've missed you. There are times when I'm going through something and I wish we could talk … just to have someone who knows the old me, you know? The fun, lighthearted me. Do you know what I mean? I don't recognize myself anymore. I'm moody and dark and cynical. I don't like it."

"You're still in there. I still see you. Only now, you wear better clothes, are even hotter, and have an edge to you that's not all bad!" He dodges as I throw a pillow at him.

The rest of my time with Michael is more of the same: fun, easy, sweet. After we all hug him goodbye, and he's getting in his car, I yell one more time for him to drive carefully. He laughs over his shoulder, waves one more time and that's the last time I see him. He goes home and decides to finally commit to his girlfriend.

- 29 -

I DON'T *Think* SO

There's a little coffee shop table that I've taken over to write when my cottage is caving in on me. It's by the window, has an outlet just under the table and is, simply put, the best spot. I come about four times a week and it's always open, just waiting for me to get to work.

Running a little later than usual, I impatiently wait in line to get my morning blend with cream. When I turn around, I notice him. He's hard not to notice—he's at least 6'5" and hot. *Really* hot.

I get all set up at my table and am getting ready to dive into a new book idea that I can't stop thinking about, when I feel someone standing over me. I look up, and he's standing there, looming over my table, scowling.

"I usually sit here," he says.

I raise an eyebrow. "Nice choice."

"Yeah, it's the best table in the place."

"I agree, which is why *I* always sit here."

"Well, you haven't been here any other time…"

"Look," I interrupt, smiling sweetly, "if you wanted an excuse to talk to me, you could have just said so. Really, I don't bite."

His mouth drops open and the corners of his lips begin to quirk up.

I roll my eyes. "Get lost. I was here first."

He quickly clamps his mouth shut, but the grin stays … grows, even. "I tell you what, I have a great idea. How about we share this table? Yeah, I like it."

I look him over. Crisply pressed shirt, filled out with his broad chest and defined shoulders, polished cuff links, brown hair combed with not a single strand out of place. *Maybe this is perfection. Sure fits the bill.*

I let out a long sigh. "No."

"C'mon, it'll be fun. I'll be quiet. There's plenty of room." He lifts his eyebrows and puts both hands together in a comical pleading pose.

"Oh, all right," I snap.

He laughs and holds out a hand. "I'm Shane. Sorry I was such a grump. I need to drink some of this before I can be nice." He holds up his coffee mug.

"I'm Sparrow. Have a seat."

We don't get any work done, but do set up a date for Friday.

"Unless, I see you before then at 'our' table," Shane says as he leaves.

One date leads to two and before I know it, I've been dating Shane for three or four months. My stance on All Men are Evil ended a while ago, but I still don't fully trust them. I don't think I ever will. Shane is intelligent, fun, witty, so sexy, and he stirs up some lustful thoughts that I haven't had since ———.

He plays golf, though. Obsessed with it. Any guy I've met who is a golfer doesn't just play it for fun every now and then. They play it every single time the weather is

351

above 55, if the skies aren't unleashing hail, and if they happen to have a day off work. In California, that's pretty much every day, unless you're a workaholic. Shane isn't. And since I don't have a "real job"—Shane's words—he thinks I should be able to play golf with him *every day*. Maybe if he were an old retired man, but he's 25!

I don't *think* so.

It's a good thing he knows how to use his hands.

Tessa meets Shane when she comes. After shopping for a couple days straight, we meet Shane for drinks.

"God, he's gorgeous," she whispers when he walks up to the bar. "Do you do nothing but stare at him all day? I would."

"I do enjoy looking at him." I grin at her, watching him tap his fingers against the wood while he waits. "I think it's what I like most about him."

"Uh-oh," she says. "I thought this one was…" she stops when Shane turns around and sets our drinks on the table.

We make small talk for the first fifteen minutes, until Shane gets going on a self-help book he's been reading. The fact that he reads is a plus, but his reading material annoys me. He talks for a solid twenty minutes about it, singing its praises for helping him in his sales job.

Tessa's eyes cloud over. She looks at me and raises both eyebrows.

So he's somewhat dull, too.

When I drop Tessa off at the airport, she says, "You're welcome to bring Shane to the wedding—that is, if you're still dating him by then."

I roll my eyes. "We'll see."

Shane has stayed over the last few nights. My place feels like it's a mouse hole when he's here any longer than a day. The walls are closing in on me.

"Why don't we get out for a while? Movie? Beach?" I suggest everything that comes to mind while he stands there and tosses a golf ball. Up, down, catch. Up, down, catch. Uuuuppp, down, catch.

"STOP!"

He turns to me with a frown. "What?"

"Stop with the ball for a second. Wanna go to Santa Cruz?"

"I thought maybe we could go for at least 9 holes … come on. It'll be fun."

Every part of me cringes. I have to fix my stare to avoid rolling my eyes. "I'm not spending the day driving your cart around. No."

"We could walk … good exercise?" He moves in front of me and leans down to kiss my neck.

I brush him off. "You go ahead. I need to go see my parents today, anyway. I need to borrow one of my mom's suitcases for the wedding. We're trading—she'll bring one of my smaller ones when she comes." I shake my head. I don't know why I'm explaining all this to him. He tuned out when I said 'no'.

"Okay, well maybe I'll meet up with you later? Dinner tonight?"

"I think I'll hang out with them tonight. It's been a while since I've been over there."

"Will I see you before your trip?" he asks as he ties his shoelaces.

"You know what? Probably not. I have a conference call with Louise tomorrow to discuss my new manuscript. And then I have some errands to do before I leave the next day. This is probably it."

"Okay." He leans down and kisses me. "Have fun. Tell Tessa she still has some time to back out." He laughs at his own joke, grabs his duffle bag, and waves as he walks out the door.

I'm so glad I didn't invite him to the wedding.

Instead of hanging out at my parents' house, I pick up the suitcase and come home to pack. Normally, I like to plan an outfit for each day and night—no extra. But since I'm packing for almost a week and Tessa has been a little scattered on details lately, I throw in a couple extra dresses and an extra yoga outfit, just in case. Tessa wanted to make my dress, but we found a beautiful gown while we were shopping for her dress. I convinced her that she didn't need the added pressure of making the bridesmaid dresses.

All of the dresses are a muted red. Mine has extra detail since I'm the maid of honor, with a plunging halter neckline, cinching in the waist, and a low cutout in the back. It's exquisite. I leave it hanging so it doesn't get smashed in my suitcase yet.

Louise and I accomplish a lot the next day. We talk for a few hours, first discussing upcoming signings and then covering the timeline for my new book. I love every bit of this work. It's the only time I am fulfilled.

After I'm done with all the errands, I go to my parents' and spend the night. They will take me to the airport in the morning. We have a fun night, but I crawl into bed early, feeling worn out. I think about Shane and inwardly groan. It's not going to last with him. In fact, I need to just be done with men altogether. It won't do any good. I can't forget *him*.

I stare at the ceiling, and as always, it settles on me. The grief. It's been two years, ten months, and four days and it still cuts just as deep. I turn over and open my nightstand drawer. I haven't done this in a long time. It's not smart, but I pull out the small photo album of Ian and me. It's got about 100 4x6s of us, from the very beginning to the end. I flip through the pictures and see the way he looked at me, the love in his eyes. The light in my face that went away the day I knew what he'd done.

I will never love anyone the way I love him. Ever.

All this searching for something, someone, ANY-THING to dull the ache that he left … I know it will never be filled. He's the only one I'll ever love.

I wipe the tears from my face and shake my head in frustration. I thought I was past crying over him. I set the album back in the drawer, and when I do, my fingers brush against the box. I pick it up and open it. My engagement ring sparkles back at me.

I put it on my finger and fall asleep wearing it.

I stand facing them for an eternity, the intricacy of the woodwork blurring together as I stare at the doors too long. Finally, I take a step and go inside. The room is a peaceful blue. I take a deep breath. It feels warm in here, safe. I turn and see Ian standing by the window. He smiles, holding out his hand to me, and I'm not afraid.

- 30 -

4A & 4B

Two years, ten months, and five days since he broke my heart

"How's Laila?"

A long, painful silence stretches out into minutes.

When Ian finally speaks, it's with a quiet, even tone. "I haven't seen Laila in over three years. I talk to Jeff often—we've managed to put together a relationship of sorts. He's still trying to work things out with Laila. I don't know how he ever forgave me, but he…" his voice trails off.

I nod and pull on my skirt, wishing I could be off of this plane *now*.

"I heard you're dating someone," Ian says, looking straight ahead.

"I've dated a few someones," I say softly.

"Last I heard, you were *serious* about someone." Ian turns to me now, and the pain in his eyes is threatening to undo me.

"No, not really," I tell him. "I heard that about you too, though."

"We broke up. I dated her for 9 months, but we've been broken up for a while now."

The captain begins to give the final instructions before we land. Ian takes my cup and throws it into the bag when the steward walks past.

My brain is still attached to the 'we broke up', and I want to hear more about that.

"Did you cheat on her?" It comes out of my mouth before I can stop it.

Ian takes a breath before speaking. "Well, if you consider being in love with someone else the entire time we dated, then yes. But no, I didn't—she knew about you all along. We were friends first, and she thought she could 'cure' me."

He gives me a weak smile, and my heart does that turn over plunge.

Just then, the wheels make contact with the pavement and we go bouncing along to a stop.

We sit and wait until the seatbelt sign goes off, Ian staring at me the whole time. It's a bit disconcerting. I can't stop looking at him, either. His face—his eyes, his lips, that sexy slow grin, his full eyebrows that can show so much expression. I love this man. I can't stop loving him.

Finally, we're filing off the plane and now that I've gotten my wish, I just want to redo the past hour with him.

Ian is silent on the way to baggage claim. When we stop in front of the carousel to wait for our luggage, Ian touches my arm with his hand. I look up at him and he smiles.

"When I said you changed me, it was the truth." He grasps my hand and puts it on his heart. "Time has only solidified it for me. And today has simply been icing on the cupcake." His eyes twinkle with the memory. He puts my hand back on my purse and gives it a pat before letting go.

I don't know what to say, so I pretend to watch for my luggage. I'm looking but not really seeing.

Ian scoops up his suitcase and asks what mine looks like. I give him the description, and it's already rolling past us on the conveyor belt. He chases it down and brings it back to me.

"Need a ride?" he asks.

"No, Tessa will be here for me. She's probably already been texting." I've been oblivious to my phone.

"Do you mind if I ask where you're staying?"

I blush. "The Ritz Carlton."

"No!" He rears his head back and his laugh echoes. "Me too." He grins from ear to ear.

"Nuh-uh! You're just saying that."

"I kid you not," he vows.

"What's going on here?" My eyebrows have developed a mind of their own—this frown will probably give me wrinkles for life.

He holds up both hands before taking the handles of both our suitcases and leading the way outside. "If you were looking for a sign from heaven, baby, I'd say they're all around you. Take note."

There's the cocky man I once knew.

I keep scowling and follow him out the door.

Tessa is waiting outside. I see her just a few cars back

and begin waving wildly. She pulls up slowly and hops out of the car, eyes bugging out.

"Sparrow! *Ian…*" She comes to a screeching halt in front of us, not knowing what to do with herself.

I step up and hug her. "Hey! Ian and I were on the same flight!" I say in an obnoxiously chipper voice.

Ian laughs. "Hi, Tessa. Great to see you. I hear you and Jared are sealing the deal." He leans down and hugs her. "Congratulations."

She smiles up at him, momentarily struck by his beauty. I know that look on her face. "Hi," she whispers.

I give her arm a little nudge to shake her out of her stupor. She snaps out of it and gives him a glare. I didn't mean for her to go that far with it, just to close her mouth a little bit.

"Yes. Yes, we are doing it," Tessa says and then she blushes, which might be a first for her.

My eyes meet Ian's and we laugh softly.

"Do you need a ride?" Tessa asks Ian and then hurriedly looks at me like she's kicking herself.

"I was, uh—well, I'll be going back in to rent a car. I just wanted to walk Sparrow out," he looks at me sheepishly. "I know you have things to do for the wedding, but if you want to get together, even for a few minutes, please … call me." He holds up his cell phone and waves it. "Or I'll be checked in under *Ian Sterling*," he says mischievously.

"Maybe we'll run into each other then—you know—sign from heaven and all," I say with a slight bite.

He takes my hand and kisses it. "I will be looking around every corner, nook, and crevice, then," he promises. "Sparrow," he takes a breath before continuing,

359

"4A and 4B … think about how crazy that is. Just … think about it. Maybe the heavens really did stop and orchestrate this whole thing, just maybe."

He watches as I get in the car and when we turn the corner, I look back and he's still standing there, watching as we drive away.

"What the hell?" Tessa jumps right in. "Start from the beginning."

"I think I'm still in shock. I've just spent the last hour with Ian—it was like no time had passed. He told me he still loves me. Oh, and he's broken up with his girlfriend." The snark creeps up in my voice with that statement.

"Are you gonna see him this week?"

"He's staying at our hotel, Tessa!"

She turns to look at me quickly and then tones down her expression when she sees my face. "It's a big place. It's possible you won't even run into him."

"Yeah … not really going to count on that with the way this day has gone."

"Do you think—um, what if this really is, you know, a sign or something?" she asks.

"I gave up believing in signs a long time ago, Tess." I look out the window. To hear myself say it, I almost believe it.

"You know I wanted to kill him when it all came out. I still do. But, all those letters, all that time … I really do believe he loved you, Sparrow. And if he's saying he still does, even though so much time has passed since you've even seen him—I just think you might need to think about it. Hear him out. I *know* you still love him. I knew it before I saw the two of you looking all mushy-eyed at each other, but that did make it even clearer!" She laughs and then sobers up quickly when she sees me staring at her. "Ro, don't take this the wrong way … I know you're the one who was hurt and you've suffered and I am SO angry at him for that! What if, though—what if maybe he's suffered enough now?" She says it so softly and with a guilty expression. She's biting her lip, waiting for my reaction.

I don't say anything. I need to think. My head is too foggy.

Finally, I say, "It's never been about making him suffer or even about my pride, although that certainly took a nosedive a long time ago."

"What does it come down to then? Now, after all this time, what *does* it come down to?"

I think about it for a while. "It's about trust. I don't think I could ever trust him."

"Do you believe he's changed?"

When I've thought about it over the weeks and months and years, I've hated to admit to myself that I do— I do believe he changed. I don't know if it was once he decided to end it for good with Laila. Or if it was when I found out the truth. Either way, I have believed for a long time now that he really did change. Part of me figured I made him healthy for someone else.

I heave a huge sigh. "Enough with the heavy talk. Yes, I do think he's changed. I still don't know what to do with that. This is your week, Tessa. I want it to be all about you, not my insane life."

"It's been about me for a long time," Tessa says. "You have been with me through my whole relationship with Jared, helped me plan the most spectacular wedding ever, even though you live across the country, you've listened to me ramble on the phone about how great my life is when you're miserable. I think it's your turn now."

I reach over and squeeze her arm. "I love you, Tessa. And I love all your rambles." We both laugh then and the air feels lighter.

When we get checked into our room, Tessa bounces on the bed and says, "You know what? We really don't have to do anything the next few days but have fun! Everything has already been done or has been handed over to someone else."

"I thought we had all kinds of work to do!" I playfully toss the pillow at her. "So what are we gonna do with ourselves?"

"Well, I have a spa day scheduled for us tomorrow," she says proudly.

"Yay!" I plop down on the bed.

"A few special dinners here and there and COCK-tails." She's always loved to emphasize the 'cock' for the sheer purpose of tormenting me.

"I like a little cock with my tail," I say, giggling. "Or a lot of cock, I should say."

Tessa goes red. "SPARROW!"

"What? I'm not allowed to say that?"

"*No!* No, you're not!" She looks mortified.

I laugh until I hurt. "I give up! I guess I can't say 'fuck it all' either then, right?"

Tessa pulls me back on the bed, covering my mouth and tickling my side. "Give me my Ro back! What have you done with her?" she shouts.

"Fuckshitassdamnhellfuckcrapcrapcrap!" I yell at her.

"I think I'm not the one you need to be saying that to!" she yells back.

We laugh until we cry and then hug until we're laughing again.

We get ready for a late supper and go down to the lobby when Jared arrives. When we get off the elevator, I shouldn't be surprised to see Ian and Jared in conversation, but I am. I feel like I did the time I fell out of a tree and got the wind knocked out of me. Ian turns just as we get near him and his eyes are shining so bright they're like two lit sparklers. I hadn't exactly forgotten how beautiful he was, but I really think he might be even more so now.

His eyes slowly scorch over me, taking in every curve, every inch of my body, like he's remembering all the ways he used to love it. Heat rushes through me, and I curse my splotchy, traitorous self for ever being born.

"Sparrow," his voice comes out in a husky rasp, "you couldn't possibly be any more gorgeous. You ..." he shakes his head and pulls on his lips in that nervous gesture that always gave him away. "God, you make my insides shake." He laughs and then he realizes he has an audience. "Sorry, that was probably way more than any of you needed to know." He looks at Jared and Tessa who are staring at him with slack jaws. "Sparrow here turned me into a "feely man" when she exposed my dark side. I used to be so stoic and mysterious, and now I spew things like 'God, you make my insides shake.'" Ian looks around and laughs awkwardly and now *my* jaw is hanging open too.

Jared, bless him, takes that opportunity to hug me and says, "Well, she'd make anyone's insides shake in this dress!" He looks at Tessa apologetically as he says it, and she beams at him. She knows he's only trying to diffuse the situation.

"You're so perfect for Tessa," I whisper in his ear.

He looks at me gratefully and smiles.

"So uh, I guess you're all leaving for dinner?" Ian asks and my heart goes out to him. I don't know why, but I just can't leave him standing here looking so alone.

"Yes?" Jared and Tessa both look at me, unsure of what to do next.

Ian smiles sadly. "Have a great night." He does a mini bow and wave and begins to back up.

"You're welcome to join us, if you'd like," I say. And then I clamp my mouth shut in disbelief. I can't take this mouth anywhere, it seems.

He stops immediately. "Yes! Yes, I would love to. Are you sure, Little Bird?"

"Yes." I divert my eyes because he's staring me down like he wants to devour me. I can't take the intensity.

Over supper we have a surprisingly calm, enjoyable time. Sprinkled throughout all the other topics we cover, I find out that Ian has started a center for troubled teens and spends a lot of time with them. As if I needed to hear something that heartwarming about him. He doesn't drop it into conversation for my benefit either; in fact, throughout the night, he evades being the center of attention at all costs. When Tessa finally gets pushy to find out where Ian Sterling has been spending so much of his time, we get a couple reluctant answers out of him. The teen center is one; the fact that he's still writing songs like a madman is another.

He wants to know all about how things have gone with my book. He read it, even though he isn't really a big reader, and thought it was brilliant. I don't let it go to my head since he doesn't really read much, but I must say that the fact that he's a writer does make it flattering.

All evening, he devours everything I say. I don't say much because I have become a nervous stuttering mess, but even when I'm listening, he's watching for my reaction and gauging my thoughts. He knows me so well. I just know that he does.

When we reach the hotel, Jared walks Tessa up to the room, and I linger with Ian to give them a minute alone. At least, that's what I tell myself.

"Can I see you tomorrow?" he asks.

"Tessa has a spa day planned for us." I twist my fingers together as I say it. My hands itch to touch him, so I have to keep them busy.

"Tomorrow night? I will be with Elliot tomorrow, but can work around whatever your plans are," he says.

"We'll see. I don't know yet what's happening tomorrow night."

"Okay," he says with a smile. "Thank you for tonight. It meant … everything to me." He reaches out to touch my cheek, and I don't pull away.

One facial, massage, pedicure, manicure, a blowout, and three glasses of champagne later, I feel like a new woman. After a whole day of pampering, I was concerned that all I'd want to do is go to bed afterwards, but I feel *good*.

"We need to go dancing while we're looking this hot," Tessa says. "Jared said we should just have girl time, but I told him he didn't need to miss seeing me like this. Even if he only dances for a few minutes, he needs to see my HAIR!" She laughs and gives her head a toss. She's feeling a little champagne happy herself.

I do a snort laugh at her—she always brings them out of me—and zip up the back of my dress.

Tessa goes still when she sees me. "Oh no. No, no, no. You better *hope* we don't run into Sterling tonight. He will be *on you*," she sings the last two words and then giggles at herself. She shakes her head, still laughing as we walk out of the door.

We sit in the lounge as we wait for Jared, and of course, there he is. This time he's with another man—I think it might be J. Elliot, but I'm not positive. Ian sees me right away, and I see him gesture to the man to follow him. They're in front of us within moments.

"Sparrow Fisher, it's sinful to have a body like that," Ian says with a smirk. "You sure know how to fill out a dress."

"Is that supposed to be a compliment?" I ask, tilting my head to the side.

"Hell, yes." He laughs. "You know it is. Sparrow, meet J. Elliot. J, I'd like you to meet Sparrow Fisher, the love of my life."

My eyes go wide as I shake J. Elliot's hand. "I can't believe you just said that," I say to Ian, even though I'm looking at Mr. Elliot. *Focus, Fisher.*

They both laugh and Elliot says, "Miss Fisher, I've wanted to meet you for a long time. I needed to see the girl who turned Ian Sterling around." I study Mr. Elliot then and try to read how much he knows.

"Hello, Mr. Elliot," I reply.

"No 'Mister', please. Call me J … or Elliot. You know what? I'll answer to anything you say," he says smoothly.

Ian introduces Tessa, and she quickly takes the pressure off of me.

"We're going dancing!" she says with excitement.

"Is that right? Well, let us take you—no need to get a cab, right, Ian? We were about to head out on the town ourselves."

I wonder what mischief they were about to get up to … on second thought, no, I don't want to know.

Jared walks in just then, saving us once again.

With the three of them chatting around us, Ian touches my elbow. "Sparrow? I'd love to be wherever you are, but I don't want to make you uncomfortable. Will I? Can we be together tonight?" Ian asks it innocently enough, but my mind goes to all the nights we've had and it's far from innocent.

When I go purple, Ian smiles a wicked grin and leans down by my ear, his breath tickling my neck and sending chill bumps all over my skin. "I'll behave," he whispers.

"You don't know the meaning of being 'have'," I whisper back. It's amazing how easily we fall back into our lusty banter.

The Maison 508 is going strong when we get there. Tessa and Jared start dancing immediately. J sees a musician he knows and gets engrossed in a conversation.

Ian stays by my side, not touching me, but no more than an inch away at all times.

"Dance?" he asks.

"I'm not sure that's a good idea."

"Okay." He nods, as if I've said something very intelligent.

"You know what? I do want to. It's been a long time since I've danced."

He lights up and holds his hand out for me to take.

It's a strange feeling after you've known someone so intimately, to maintain any sort of distance or to pretend that you don't know their body better than you know your own. When Ian pulls me in and his body makes contact with mine, the currents pulse through us both. I know what he feels without looking at him. I know if I touch the small of his back like this or slightly rub my chest against his just so, it will drive him wild. He knows that my neck is sensitive and that I love it when he pulls my back against him. We try for about ten minutes to avoid these triggers, but the rhythm picks up in the room and the impulse is too strong. He swipes my hair off my neck first to say something in my ear, I rub my chest against his, lightly touch his back, he whips me around and presses me against the front of him.

Like dominoes falling one by one, our pretenses fall away and we dance.

My hands say what my mouth cannot. I look in his eyes and see the love I feel gazing back at me.

He touches my face, my hair, my shoulders, my heart, my back, my thighs. I get lost in it. I move into him, matching him touch for touch. It's intoxicating. His hands on me feel like finding water after years in the desert. It fills me up, as only he can do.

- 31 -

It All Comes DOWN

Jared and Tessa are long gone. Elliot left before them. Ian promised to take me to the hotel as soon as I said the word, but his look also pleaded with me to not stop this—whatever this is that's happening.

We close down the club and get a cab to the hotel. Ian is awkward with his hands now that we're not dancing. He keeps touching me somehow, but stopping when he realizes what he's doing. He is full of nervous energy. In the elevator, he studies me.

"Talk to me?" He reaches out and grasps my hand in both of his and holds it up to his chest as he waits for my answer.

I nod.

Air whooshes out of his lips when I agree.

It's silent as we climb up, up, up. When we get off the elevator and wind around the floor, the only sound is our feet padding on the carpet. It's when he shuts the door behind us—I lean my back against the door and he stretches both arms on either side of me—that I realize I won't be able to talk at all. I look at him and all I see are his lips, so close that if I move even slightly, I will bump into them. I rest my head against the door to get some space, but then I can see the desire in his eyes.

369

"Tell me you don't still love me, Sparrow, and I won't touch you. Tell me you don't still need me, that your body doesn't still ache for mine. Tell me," he whispers urgently.

I close my eyes and turn my head away. He draws me back by taking my chin and straightening it again. "Look at me, Sparrow, *please.*"

I open my eyes and a tear rolls down my face. I'm weary of fighting it.

He kisses each tear that falls.

"Aren't you worn out from running?" His lips follow a tear down my neck, and then he brushes my face with his hand. "I don't want to live without you *another day.* I'm begging you for another chance. *Please.*"

He's holding his hands on my cheeks now, his eyes searching. He waits for me to say something, but for now, I'm unable to speak. I don't want to talk. I just want to be with him—without having it all figured out or knowing the future—I need to be with him one more time.

He sees the shift in my eyes. That's how well he knows me.

"Are you sure?" he asks.

I give a faint nod.

"Little Bird," he says softly as he comes in for a kiss. It begins as gentle as a sunrise, but quickly gains ground as the urgency of all the feelings and heartache and pain and years of anguish collide. I open my mouth to him and he groans as his tongue meets mine. I clutch his hair, pulling his head harder into me. There is not a breath of space between us, and still, I cannot get close enough. Ian feels the same because as he's kissing me, he's also picking me up and carrying me to the bed.

He lays me back carefully and touches my face softly before crushing my mouth again. I want to feel skin. He's being so cautious with me. I unbutton a few buttons of his shirt and then pull it over his head, taking the opportunity to look at him. His chest looks even more defined than it did before. Maybe he's upped his weights routine. I approve.

He grins. I sit up and trace my tongue along his skin, his neck, his pecs, his tiny nipples that are puckered from my touch. He moans and unzips my dress and pulls it over my head.

He reaches out and cups my breasts with reverence and then with a slow and deliberate touch, he rubs my nipples through my blue lacy bra before reaching around to undo it altogether. When it drops, his pupils dilate with lust and he pushes me back and follows with his head. His tongue flicks around and around my nipple, and then he grabs it in his mouth and sucks until I can't think straight. Now that my bra is off, his hands are everywhere. His fingers push aside my panties and he strokes me there, teasing: in an out, in and out, until I'm gasping.

"I've missed you," he whispers.

And then he's ripping my panties off, and I'm undoing his pants and pulling them off as fast as my hands will let me. His briefs and pants come down at the same time and he leans over me, holding himself up with his arms, staring at me.

"I love you, Sparrow Kate," he says. I pull his mouth down to mine, and show him how much I love *him*. He kisses me back hard and then leans back. "I haven't done this—with anyone—since you," he says and then he slowly eases inside of me. I'm so ready for him. I'm processing what he just said, but I can't focus on that right now. I'm so ready that I don't wait for him, I wrap my feet around and push him the rest of the way in, until he's in so deep, my eyes blur and roll back in my head.

We begin to move, unable to go slow or take our time or wait one second longer.

I start to moan first and then, when I can't take it anymore, "IAN!" rushes out of my throat in a ravaged wail.

The tears pour out of me while my body shudders. Ian slows, but as my body comes down from the high, our pace picks up again. He drives in me deep, all the way out, in deep, slowly out, deep, DRAGGING out, IN, out. And just when I can't take anymore, he drives in again. Hard. It sends me over the edge. Ian lets out a hoarse groan and the pulses overtake us both. And then he's kissing my face. He searches my eyes when he realizes my face is wet. He slowly pulls out of me and holds me tight, wrapping his arms around me and bringing the blanket up to my face.

"Baby?" His hands wipe the tears and they just keep coming. "Are you okay?"

I'm not.

I feel as if my whole chest has been cut open and laid bare. My body feels content and sated, but my mind has just woken up after a long sleep. I start shaking uncontrollably.

Ian lets out a choked cry. "Sparrow, baby..." He kisses my hair and pulls my face back to look at me. His eyes are terrified, and I wish I could stop, but the floodgates have opened and there's no stopping it now. His tears drip onto my face and he tries to wipe them off. He leans his forehead to mine. "Talk to me, please, Sparrow. Anything, please say something."

"Why?" It gushes out, sounding foreign through all the tears. "*Why*, Ian? What did she have that I didn't? Why wasn't I enough? How could you take my feelings and just toss them aside like trash? I *lived* for you." I'm choking now and making horrific, gasping sounds, but I can't stop. "I believed you loved me. I trusted you. I thought what we had was beyond any love I'd ever seen. Why did you throw it away? Again and again?" I sit up and the blanket falls around my waist, I yank it up quickly, uncomfortable now with my nakedness. I rock back and forth and try to shake off the tremors.

The moon streaks lines of light through the room, casting strange shadows. Ian and I are in the middle of one, our skin highlighted by the moon. Ian sits up beside me and crushes me to his chest.

"I'm so sorry, Sparrow. I know it will never be enough, but I am. You were more than enough for me. I didn't think I could ever deserve you. With every *ounce* of breath in me, I wish I could go back and make it right. I would run from Laila. I would tell you every single self-doubt and insecurity and fear. I would break all my bad habits and never be far from you again. When we were together, I could almost dare to hope that I could have you, but when we were apart, I was tormented, knowing I would never be good enough. For a long time, I tried to prove that theory right. But I did stop. You know when it was? Not long before that week I came to you—you were so worried about me that week, saying I wasn't myself. But we were engaged and it had hit me that I might really be able to be happy. I never believed that before. I thought I was stuck…" He leans back and looks at me, pushing back the hair that's sticking to my face.

"Tell me again, how did it all … start?" I ask. "I know we've hashed and rehashed, but I just need to hear one more time."

"Not long after our day in San Francisco, I flew to L.A. and stayed in their house. I was sleeping one night and Laila came in. I thought I was dreaming about you, to be honest. I was still high on our date, but she'd told me how young you were. She knew I didn't think I had a real, lasting chance with you and played on that, and on all my craziness. I woke up and she had me in her mo—" He shakes his head. "I'm sorry. You don't need to hear this again."

"I do need to hear. I know you've tried to tell me many times, and I haven't been able to fully hear it all."

"I could have stopped it. I can't blame her for all of it. I can't. I should have cut off all ties with her…"

We talk until the sun comes up, and our stomachs are growling. Neither of us move from the bed. I listen—it's all things he told me from the moment I found out, but the details are finally clicking into place, and I'm finally able to register all of it. The ache doesn't go away; it still hurts like hell. There are some pieces I will never understand, ever. And a lot that I do understand.

I take deep breaths and slowly start to feel calmer. "What made you believe in us finally? And would it have lasted? It was seven months that you weren't with her, but if I hadn't found out, would it have happened again? And if not her, with someone else?"

"No, I really don't think I ever would have again, Sparrow, even if you had never known. What I do know without a doubt, though, is that after the truth came out and I realized what I'd risked and the agony of knowing the hurt I caused you—" a ragged sigh comes out of him and he angrily swipes the tears off his face, "—I changed. For good. You did that. I know it was too late, but I vowed to be the man you thought I was. I have never been the same, thanks to you. Even though I should have already been that man when we met, you're the one who made me finally grow up." He shrugs. "None of it sounds significant enough when I say it, but it's still the truth."

I look at him and really see, maybe for the first time in all these years, the truth in his words. I run my hand along his cheek. "I believe you," I whisper.

His breath hitches and he rubs his eyes before looking at me, his expression haunted. "Thank you," he whispers back.

We sit there longer still, our limbs tangled under the sheets, not saying anything else, but feeling as if a lot is being said.

Finally I speak up. "You haven't had sex since you were with me? What about your 9-month relationship? I find that hard to believe."

"It's true. Tara would be glad to confirm," he laughs softly. "I feel bad for hurting her. We were friends, but she had feelings. She knew I wasn't over you, but she wanted to try to help me forget. And at that point, I knew I was losing my mind, so I agreed to try to have a relationship with her. I just couldn't get past you."

I can relate to that. I also feel guilt for the guys who wanted to help me forget. Why did I put them through that?

"We kissed, but every time it got to a certain point, I stopped. I felt like I was betraying you. I was such a mess. One night, Tara was watching her niece and Beauty and the Beast was playing. I saw Belle in the library with all those books—she even *looked* like you—and I fuckin' lost it." He leans down and kisses my hair. "All the crying is also thanks to you. I'm kind of ready for the tears to go back inside now," he confesses. "A few degrees back from wussdom would be appreciated." His mouth quirks up slightly at the corners.

"We went to a movie another time, and the actress had hair similar to yours. I started in again with the crying jag," he shakes his head, "so fucked up. Tara got me out of the theater and we fought about it. She said you were never coming back. I told her I knew that even if you weren't, I'd never stop waiting and hoping for you. We broke up then and actually stayed friends. She's dating someone else now and is a lot happier."

I think this through and realize my shakes are long gone. I look over at Ian and he's watching me tentatively, looking almost scared to breathe.

"I've never gotten over you either, Ian. I've gone from one relationship to the next, trying to fill the void you left. The night before I left to come here, I was still crying over you, looking at old pictures and missing you..." I look at him and bite my lip. "I *have* had a lot of sex—" I feel his body cringe next to mine. "I'm sorry." I scrunch up my nose and keep going. "I have. And none of it has made me feel loved or cherished like I did last night ... even though I had the breakdown after..." I end awkwardly and take a gulping breath. "After everything, I still know that you're the only one for me..."

Ian kisses my hand and rubs it along his cheek. "Every day that I wake up, I think about you," he says. "When I go to sleep at night ... you. The other day when I got ready to leave for the airport, I wondered what you would think of my shirt, if you would still like to look at me," he says shyly. "I think about what you're doing and who you're laughing with—it has *killed* me that you might be happy without me, and yet, I've wanted you to be happy more than I've wanted to *live*." He turns to face me, lightly running his fingers across my shoulders. "To have this time to talk to you and hear what you're thinking—it's all I've ever hoped for. I'm sorry I didn't know how to go about it the right way. That first year, I just—I lost it. I apparently have some stalkerish tendencies when it comes to you. I just couldn't NOT try to tell you everything that was in my heart and mind. Maybe if I had just let you think it through for a while and quietly proven myself … I don't know … I just didn't know what to do."

"We can't go back. To be honest, I don't know *what* I even want right at this moment, but I'm so glad we've had this time." I lean over and kiss him.

This time when we make love, we take our time. And when he whispers that he loves me, I whisper it back.

"Sparrow?" he says softly when we're catching our breath. "If you give me another chance, I'll spend the rest of my life showing you how much I love you. There will never be a doubt, I promise you."

When I leave his room to go to mine, it's early afternoon. I have some explaining to do with Tessa. I've texted her a few times, but she will want details. I lightly rap on the door, and she opens it immediately, pulling me inside. She can't stop smiling and I can't stop smiling back at her.

"Tell me everything."

So I do.

That night, Tessa and I have dinner with her parents, Jared, and his parents. We discuss a few details of what needs to be done for the rehearsal dinner the next night, but other than that, we simply catch up with one another. It's a lovely night. I feel like a huge weight has lifted off of me. I've been dragging a big boulder around, trying to live with the heaviness for so long, that I don't even know what to do with this airy feeling. My emotions are all over the place, but in the best of ways.

I finally gave Ian my phone number, and he calls as we're riding back to the hotel.

"Hi, Sparrow," he says tentatively.

"Hello," I say softly.

"I'm just finishing up with J and thought I'd give you a call. Have you had a good time?"

"It's been great." Tessa's dad is driving, and Tessa and I are in the backseat. I smile over at her. She's watching me like a hawk and smiles back with relief.

"Well, I won't keep you. Just wanted to say—if you feel like seeing me later—I hear there are really good desserts in the lounge…"

"Hmm, well, I'll give it some thought," I say slyly. "We'll see if fate allows…"

Ian groans and laughs. "Okay…"

Tessa motions to the phone and mouths, 'Can I?' I nod and tell Ian to hold on while I hand the phone to her.

"Hi, Ian, it's Tess. Sorry to interrupt your phone call. I just wanted to invite you to the rehearsal dinner tomorrow night and also the wedding on Saturday." She looks at me and smiles. "Yes, I've already discussed it with Ro, and she is fine with it. Okay, I understand. Yes,

I'll leave it up to the two of you; just know you're welcome to come. Jared and I would love to have you there."

We pull up to the hotel and say goodnight to Tessa's parents. Our arms are entwined and we're laughing about something Jared's dad said over dinner.

We're about to open the door, when it's opened for us. "Ladies, wow, what perfect timing. I'm just getting here myself. It's almost as if *fate* designed it," Ian says with a smile.

Tessa laughs and kisses me on the cheek and goes up to the room. Ian and I sit on a luxurious couch and a waiter comes and asks if we'd care for anything.

"I'm always up for crème brûlée," I speak up.

"I'll have the bananas foster," Ian says.

After a sweet, brief time together, I chastely kiss him on the cheek and tell him I need sleep. He kisses both of my cheeks and walks me to my door.

The next two days are a flurry of bustling activity. The wedding is spectacular. Every detail—from the bridesmaids' black calla lily and feather bouquets to the archways draped with rich, colorful material—is unique and completely Tessa. She looks stunning in her dress. Her hair is up, with loose curls. She has a peaceful glow about her that makes me happier than I can say.

As I listen to Tessa and Jared recite their vows, holding onto Tessa's bouquet and mine, I glance out and find Ian. His eyes mesmerize me from across the room. And I know. I know I am ready to take the risk. I know we've already survived our worst. And I know we're coming out of it like gold after it's been through the refiner's fire.

- Epilogue -

One year later

I haven't regretted marrying Ian for a single second. When I said 'I do' seven months ago, I made heads spin with my decision.

The naysayers:

"You're crazy!
"How can you be so stupid?
"You're just asking to be hurt…"
"He doesn't deserve you."
"Once a cheater; always a cheater!"
"You'll regret this!"

But there were also a few believers:

"I've never seen two people love each other more."
"You were made for each other."
"You've survived this; you'll survive anything."
"If you're sure, I trust you…"
"I do believe he's changed."

And the middle-of-the-roaders:

"Ohhhkay … but if he hurts you, I will shove his freakin' dick down his freakin' throat. (Maybe this doesn't really belong in the middle-of-the road category)

"I guess we'll wait and see what happens."

"I hope you know what you're doing."

"We'll be here for you either way."

Believe me, I thought long and hard about it. Anyone who knows me knows that I can't make a decision without over-thinking it to death. And then some. It really came down to love.

Love *is* enough.

Love *does* conquer all.

Love really does always protect, trust, hope, persevere...

I'd even go as far as saying that love never fails. I finally believe that.

And once Ian and I made our vows before God and our friends and family on a beautiful beach in Maui, we certainly had a better understanding of true love. We both boohooed throughout the entire ceremony and haven't cried since.

Until last night on our tour bus, when I did my hair up with pencils and gave Ian a present.

"Oh, baby, we get to play Librarian AND you're giving me a present? What have I done to get such treatment?" He grabs my bum and presses against me.

I point at the present. "Open that first and then me..."

With that incentive, he takes the wrapping paper off a teensy bit faster than usual, but he still folds it so neatly.

"Hurry!" I lean against him and nuzzle his neck.

"You're just messing with me now," he mutters.

He lifts the top of the box and stares. Nestled in pretty tissue paper, so he doesn't have to touch it, I have the pregnancy test laying face up. That plus sign might as well be blinking for how vivid it looks against the tissue.

Ian sets the box down and I look up to see his reaction. He looks stunned, and then he's laughing and has tears running down his face at the same time. He grasps my face in both hands, kissing me hard. Then he kisses his way down to my stomach.

"Ianow Orvillate Sterling," he whispers, grinning up at me, "you were made with love."

Acknowledgments

Thank you, Tarryn Fisher, for putting my chapter at the end of your book. That was beyond generous and has meant so much to me.

Thank you, Elena Cermaria, for painting the gorgeous "Saffo o dell'Amore" and allowing me to use it for my cover. I am so grateful!

Thank you, Ken, for finding the painting and working your magic with it. And for reading this book so many times...

Thank you, Sarah Hansen from Okay Creations (http://okaycreations.net), for putting your special touch on the cover. You're a cover rockstar.

Thank you, JT Formatting, for making everything look so pretty.

Thank you to all the wonderful book bloggers out there who have spread the word about this book! Your help is invaluable and so appreciated.

Thank you to my family and dear friends for getting me through this—even if you didn't realize you were! Thank you to those of you who have been pushing me to publish my books for so long, especially my three loves who I first told over coffee. You know who you are. Thank you to my fairy angel—your constant encouragement gets me through each day. Thank you to all of my dear betas. You saved me, especially during the last month before publishing. I feel like I made lifelong friends throughout this entire process!

I love each and every one of you.

A huge thank you to The Two. My best friends. The ones I don't want to do life without. Ever. I certainly couldn't be doing THIS without either one of you. You have my heart.

A lifetime of thanks goes to my husband and kids, without whom I could not function and wouldn't even want to—I love you! Thank you for putting up with me while I wrote this book. I promise to listen without a dazed expression from here on out! Or at least until I begin the next book...

For information about Willow Aster and her books visit:

http://www.willowaster.com/

Facebook
https://www.facebook.com/willowasterauthor

Goodreads
http://www.goodreads.com/author/show/6863360.Willow_Aster